A Taste *fur* Murder

A Taste *fur* Murder

DIXIE LYLE

St. Martin's Paperbacks

This is a work of fiction. All of the characters, organizations, and events portrayed in this novel are either products of the author's imagination or are used fictitiously.

A TASTE FUR MURDER

For information address St. Martin's Press, 175 Fifth Avenue, New York, NY 10010.

ISBN: 978-1-250-03107-5

Printed in the United States of America

St. Martin's Paperbacks edition / March 2014

St. Martin's Paperbacks are published by St. Martin's Press, 175 Fifth Avenue, New York, NY 10010.

10 9 8 7 6 5 4 3 2 1

For my son Dez, who will read this someday and realize just how weird the author really is.

Chapter One

Ever had a job that threatened to drive you straight into a loony bin?

I'm an extremely capable, modern woman, but sometimes I feel like the mother of a dozen deranged children on a trip to the zoo, just after giving each one an espresso sundae and a megaphone. Screeching, pleading, yelling, crying; I have to deal with all of that at full volume while juggling a hundred different—and sometimes bizarre—tasks.

"No, the tiger cage goes over *there*. Yes, I'll sign for that. Hello? Let me put you on hold. No, no, we don't get that in until Tuesday. I'm sorry if the crab is fresh today, you'll just have to wait for the asparagus. Hello? I'm sorry, Mr. Gates, the pool is being cleaned that week. I can schedule you for the seventeenth—Bishop Tutu's going to make a soufflé. Excuse me, I told you *not* to put that there. Let me put you on hold—Hello? Yes, that's not a mistake, that's how much dry ice we need delivered. Make two trips."

And so it goes. When you're the Gal Friday to a crazy old lady—sorry, "eccentric senior"—with too much time on her hands, too much money, and poor impulse control, you either learn to deal with the plural of the word *crisis* or become one yourself.

I have learned to deal.

My name is Deidre F. Lancaster. The *F* stands for "Foxtrot," which started as a little joke between my parents and eventually became what everyone called me. I'm five foot six, a hundred and cough cough pounds, my best physical feature is my dazzling smile, and my worst is my obstinate, currently brown hair. I work for a woman named Zelda Zoransky—whom everyone calls ZZ—and while my proper title is administrative assistant, I think *chaos wrangler* would be a better description. I keep that to myself, though.

Today was no different from any other day. I made phone calls, answered emails, delegated whenever I could—which wasn't often—and took deliveries while sucking back my umpteenth mug of Irish breakfast tea.

ZZ lived in a big old mansion on a big old estate, with two wings, large grounds, and her own private zoo. The zoo took up a lot of space, too, because ZZ believed in giving her animals room to roam; they also had their own private live-in vet to keep them healthy and happy, and ZZ gave priority to animals who needed a place to stay. Then there were the tennis courts, the Olympic-sized swimming pool, the gardens—all that old money could buy and then some.

ZZ was a dear and I loved her to pieces, but working for her was a little like trying to ride a tornado that kept changing direction. About the only real constant were her salons—regular gatherings of interesting and eclectic people ZZ read about online or in magazines. Scientists, authors, activists, movie stars, celebrities of every stripe; she'd invite them all for a week of fine dining, lounging around the pool, and stimulating conversation. The only rule was that everybody had to attend the nightly dinners, which lasted for hours and always had an open bar. I had a standing invitation to attend anytime I wanted to. Sometimes I couldn't resist—I mean, who wouldn't want to be present for a debate on ethics between Stephen Hawking and Mick Jagger?

Crunch time for a salon was always just before all the guests arrived, and I had finally gotten over that hump. Or at least that's what I thought before my boss showed up.

ZZ swept through my open door, wearing a bright, tropical caftan, sandals, and a chunky necklace of highly polished, square wooden beads. Her curly orange hair was piled on top of her head and held in place with a matching barrette. "Foxtrot! There you are, dear. How's everything going?"

"Let's see. Everybody's here, nobody's luggage is missing, the kitchen and bar are properly stocked, and the pool is clean."

"Excellent. I just have a few last-minute details for you to take care of."

"Shoot."

"I want to raise that donation to the African girls' school—make it an even fifty thousand. Spielberg is messengering me a hard-to-find film from Korea he highly recommends and I'd like to show it next week in the theater. I just finished this *amazing* book on the nutritional value of organic kale and I'd like to serve some this week—have Ben get some locally and do something interesting with it. Oh, and get the UPS guy something nice for his birthday, will you? It's on Tuesday and he's *such* a sweetheart."

"How did you know it was Bernie's birthday?"

"We're Facebook friends."

I smiled and made some notes. "I'll get right on it. Anything else?"

"Yes. Has Caroline managed to find that dog yet?"

"Not yet." For the last two days, a stray dog had been prowling around the grounds. ZZ was worried he might get hit by a car—we're not that far from the highway—or find his way into the zoo and get into worse trouble there. We have large animals on hand, and some of them would consider a dog a tasty snack.

"He's wily, I'll give him that," ZZ said. "But I'm starting to think—no, it's ridiculous."

"What?"

"Well, I saw him when I was out for a walk this morning. He was in the gardens, sort of crouched under a bush. Just staring at me."

That worried me a little. ZZ described the dog as looking like a pit bull but larger and completely white; that made me nervous. Pit bulls could be aggressive. "It wasn't threatening you, was it?"

"No, that wasn't it at all. It seemed very alert, but not menacing. I decided I'd try to approach it, but when I got closer it darted away. It ran toward a corner of the garden where there's a high wall—"

"ZZ. Tell me you didn't corner a strange and possibly dangerous animal."

"But that's just it—I didn't. When I got to the corner it was gone. Now, there's a little vegetation in the way so I couldn't see it all the time, but there's no way it could have gotten past me. It just *vanished.*"

I frowned. "So what's the explanation?"

"Depends on who you ask. I told Shondra what happened and she went to take a look." Shondra was ZZ's head of security. "She thinks someone could have helped the dog over the wall before I got there, though I don't see how. And when I asked Shondra why someone would do that, she started talking about trained attack dogs and the kind of crazies that use them. She seems to think it's a professional assassin sent here by some white supremacist meth-lab biker gang."

"I see. You tick off any white supremacist, meth-lab biker gangs lately?"

ZZ got a thoughtful look on her face. "I don't *think* so . . . but you know what the Internet's like, dear. It's so hard to tell these days."

"Well, I kind of doubt you're being stalked by a deranged Nazi drug dealer with a killer pit bull, but I'll keep my eyes open."

"Thank you, Foxtrot." And she swept back out of the room.

It didn't take me long to polish off ZZ's chores. When they were out of the way, I considered what to do next: I could actually take a break, get a little fresh air, and hope my mobile didn't start buzzing.

My office was on the second floor, in a corner parapet with big windows. I looked out over the gently rolling sweep of the perfectly mowed grass below, taking comfort in its sprawling green lawnosity—and then an ostrich tore through my placid field of vision.

A second later Caroline Durrell, the estate vet, tore after it. Oswald was loose again—he was something of an avian Houdini. I sighed, and realized there was only one place I could go if I really wanted to relax.

I made it down the grand staircase, through the atrium, and out the front doors without anyone buttonholing me. It would've been shorter to cut through the house, but that practically guaranteed I'd get sidetracked by a guest, a staff member, or my own slightly obsessive behavior. Instead, I skirted around the main house, ducked through the corridor that led from the front yard to the pool in back, around that, and through the gate in the hedge.

Into the graveyard.

The Zoransky family had owned this land since before

the turn of last century, back when most people still got around in horse-and-buggies instead of cars. This part of the estate was undeveloped then, filled with scrubby trees and big stumps, the area logged for its timber and then unoccupied. A local from the nearby town asked Obadiah Zoransky if he could bury his dog on the land, and Obadiah said yes. Somehow, the practice spread, and after a decade or so there were hundreds of ex-pets interred among the trees.

The trees were mostly gone now—along with the stumps—though a few tall oaks and maples still stood. The family had to clear them out to make space, because over the last century the graves multiplied until they reached into five digits; over fifty thousand at last count, ranging from the smallest goldfish to full-grown horses. It wasn't just animals here, either. More than a few human beings had elected to be laid to rest with their companions, though local regulations prevented actual burial—instead, more than five hundred sealed urns containing human ashes could be seen atop headstones throughout the cemetery.

It was an overcast day, but the spring air was warm and full of the fresh smell of plant life eager to explode pollen straight up the nostrils of allergy sufferers everywhere. I headed down my usual route, past the life-sized statue of Piotr, the Russian circus bear, then right at the grave of a parrot inexplicably named Fish Jumping. This led to a small stand of trees nicknamed the Cathedral, six big oaks that surrounded Davy's Grave. Davy was the very first animal to be buried here, a golden retriever who loved to hunt with his owner. There were four marble benches around the plot, and it was a nice place to just sit and collect my thoughts.

I wasn't there for long before I was interrupted, though; I heard the roar of an industrial riding mower getting closer, then saw it crest the rise of a hill with Cooper, the groundskeeper, at the wheel. When he saw me he waved and shut the mower off, then dismounted and ambled over.

"Hey, Cooper."

"Hey, Foxtrot." Cooper dressed like an old hippie, which was exactly what he was. Droopy gray mustache in a long but friendly face, long gray ponytail poking out from under a beat-up straw hat. Fringed buckskin vest over an ancient GRATEFUL DEAD T-shirt. Blue jeans belted around bony hips, buckled with a chrome peace symbol. Scuffed and dusty cowboy boots. "How's things up to the house?"

"Same as always, Coop. Crazy casserole with a side of mayhem. How about you?"

A rare frown crossed his face. "Can't complain, I guess. But something ain't right."

"How so?"

He shook his head. "Can't rightly say. The boneyard's been talking to me, though, and it don't sound happy." Cooper had a tendency to put things in quasi-mystical terms, even when he was talking about the most mundane subjects; he once told me that the plumbing in his caretaker's cottage was undergoing a nasty Mercury retrograde. Took me a while to realize that he was referencing astrology and not a toxic chemical spill.

"What's it been saying?"

"Nothing real specific. Just giving off weird vibes, you know? Had a dream last night that a catfish in a tuxedo tried to turn the place into an amusement park for crawdads. All the admission prices were in tadpoles."

"You have to stop reading Dr. Seuss before you go to sleep, Coop."

He grinned at me, but I could see he was still worried. "Maybe so. Hell, with everything I've poured into my skull, I'm lucky my dreams make any sense at all." He paused. "Still . . . be careful out here, huh? Just 'cause I'm paranoid don't mean I ain't right."

"No problem, Coop. I'll keep my eyes open."

He tipped me a nod and a smile, then ambled on back to his mower, fired it up, and rode off over the hill.

I sat on the bench and inhaled deeply through my nose, enjoying the smell of fresh-cut grass. I closed my eyes. Nice, peaceful, quiet.

And then, in the dark behind my eyelids, I saw something.

A little flash of light, somewhere in the distance. I know it doesn't make sense, to talk about distance when you can't see any farther than your own shut eyes, but that's what it was like: as if I were looking out over a vast, pitch-black field, and something a hundred yards away had just lit up for the briefest second.

Random neuron firing in my brain, I told myself, and tried to ignore it.

It happened again.

This time it was as if the flash went off behind something, silhouetting it. Even though it was quite far away and there was nothing to provide scale, I had the strong impression it was something big.

I opened my eyes. Still sitting on the bench, marble cool and hard beneath my seat. Still quiet, still peaceful. "Well, that was weird," I muttered.

I'm the curious sort. I closed my eyes again.

Another flash, this one different. It wasn't so much a flash as a crackle, like a bolt of lightning that hung in the air for a second. It was brighter than before, and bigger. So was the shape it outlined, a kind of rounded hump.

No, not bigger. Closer.

My heart jumped and my eyes snapped open. Suddenly the graveyard didn't seem so peaceful—or so empty. The quiet was the held breath of someone lurking just out of sight.

"Sure," I said to myself. "Lurking in your *imagination,* you idiot." I shook my head and forced a laugh.

But I didn't close my eyes.

Coop's managed to spook you, I thought. *You're stressed out, that's all. Probably drank too much tea and not enough H_2O today. Shake it off, lady—time to go back to work.*

I got to my feet, glanced around nervously, then marched out of the Cathedral, wondering how long I'd been in there; it seemed a lot darker than when I'd entered.

Normally I kept my eyes straight ahead when I walked, but now I couldn't stop looking side-to-side, scanning the grave sites next to the path. They weren't always arranged in neat rows, and there were quite a few large structures: tombs, statuary, obelisks. I wouldn't admit to myself what I was watching for—

There.

A flicker of light, the harsh kind given off by a flashbulb, behind that marble doghouse. *Somebody taking a picture, has to be.*

Except that for an instant I'd seen something else, and it definitely wasn't someone with a camera. Something behind the doghouse but bigger than it—three times its size, actually, almost as big as a real house. Something massive and rounded, but not like a hill; an organic shape. The shape of something alive—or something that used to be.

I started to hurry. I hated myself for doing so, but I couldn't wait to get out of the graveyard. It didn't seem peaceful or relaxing or even safe, not anymore.

I didn't close my eyes.

I got all the way back to the gate in the hedge, yanked

it open—then stopped. Took a deep breath, turned around. Nothing behind me, of course, nothing except tombstones and grass and a few trees.

I closed my eyes.

For a second there was nothing, just empty blankness. Then another flash lit up that darkness, illuminating a huge, rounded mass shambling right at me. A tentacle that seemed to be made of pure shadow peeled itself away from the main bulk, reaching for me—

I shrieked and stumbled backward, tripping over my own feet and landing on my butt. My eyes flew open.

I was alone. Just me and the dead.

I got shakily to my feet, closed the gate, and walked toward the house. Backward, with my eyes wide open. I managed to make it without falling in the pool.

Then I got in my car and drove home. I'm not sure I blinked the entire way there.

I lived in a small bedroom community named Hartville, about three miles away from the Zoransky estate and a little over thirty from New York City. Despite its proximity to NYC, it was quiet and unassuming and mostly forgettable. I liked living there, I guess, though I couldn't tell you why. It was ordinary and stable in a way ZZ's estate never was, a little refuge where I could just take my time with a Lee Child novel in the local Denny's while eating breakfast on my day off, or lounge around the house in my pajamas and shop for old mystery novels online. I was a bit of a collector when it came to books—nothing too compulsive, though, nowhere close to being a hoarder. Okay, I had a separate room for my library, but I was choosy about what I bought and choosier about what I kept.

It got dark quickly as I drove—night didn't so much fall as dive headlong. I kept seeing shapes at the side of the road, glowing outlines that vanished if I looked directly at them. *Tricks of the fading light,* I told myself. *Reflections of the setting sun off scraps of litter.*

Sure. Except those scraps kept taking the form of animals—the humped back of a raccoon, the sharp-eared outline of a fox. A deer with a full head of antlers. By the time I pulled into my driveway, I was starting to think I was experiencing some sort of breakdown. I was having a hard time catching my breath, my heart was racing, and my eyes stung like I'd been crying. I shut off the car and just sat there, trying to get myself under control.

And I did. My breathing slowed and so did my pulse. My eyes still felt sore, but I could go in the house and rinse them with some cold water. *I'm fine,* I said to myself. *I'm going to be okay.* I got out of the car and walked to the front door, fishing my keys out of my purse.

I almost tripped over the cat.

I stopped myself just in time, teetering on my heels on the top step while the cat gazed up at me calmly from the step's edge. It was a long-haired black-and-white, an elegant visitor in a fur tuxedo.

"Oh! Geez, kitty, you startled me. But at least you're not glowing." I bent down and offered my hand for her to sniff, which she did before butting her head against it and starting to purr.

"Well, aren't you friendly?" I forgot how freaked out I'd been just a minute ago—cats had a naturally soothing effect on most people, and I was definitely one of them.

But this cat was more than friendly—it was *familiar.* Tuxedo cats are pretty common, but each one tends to be a little different; this one was virtually identical to a cat I had as a child, right down to the little white almost-question-mark on her forehead. Of, course, my cat was a bit odd, with six toes on both her hind feet—

I moved my hand from her back to her hind legs, first one, then the other. She didn't try to stop me.

Yep. Six toes. Twice.

"That's—impossible," I whispered. "Tango's been dead for ten years. You can't be—"

And then I heard the raspy, weary voice inside my head.

<*But I am, Toots. I'm exactly who you think I am. Now let's go inside and maybe open a can of tuna, huh? I've come a long way, and I'm* starving.>

So that's what we did.

I didn't scream, or faint, or run away. I'm a practical girl, and I do well under pressure. Okay, so my whole worldview was just turned upside down; what that meant to me was that now that everything was all jumbled up it was going to take a lot of work to get it straightened out, so I better get moving. You can't get anything accomplished in a state of panic.

I unlocked the door and Tango zipped inside, down the hall and straight to the kitchen, where she waited patiently while I got a can of tuna, opened it, and dumped it in a bowl. I got her some water, too, then watched as she wolfed the food down. On closer inspection, she did seem a little worse for wear: Her coat was dusty, with a few mats and tangles in it that she never would have tolerated when I knew her.

When she was done, she glanced at me and licked her lips clean. <*Damn. That beats the hell out of field mice and rest stop trash, I'm tellin' you.*>

You might be wondering why, after seeing and talking to a long-dead pet, I wasn't reacting a little more . . . emotionally. Didn't I care? Didn't I wonder if I was losing my mind? Well, yes. To both. I'd loved Tango very much, and losing her hurt like nothing else I'd ever felt. But at the moment, I was in full-on crisis mode, where I went into this almost Zen-like state of super-efficiency and nothing could make me lose my cool. I'd had three-hundred-pound roadies high on amphetamines scream into my face from six inches away and never stopped smiling—it's what I did, it's what I was good at. I just mentally scheduled a breakdown for later, and added five minutes of sobbing or breaking things for every thirty seconds of hell I happened to be currently enduring.

"So. Tango. Been a while. How's that whole dead thing working out for you?"

She cleaned a little grit from her front paw with her teeth. *<Ugh. My claws are disgusting . . . tell you what, why don't we go sit down on the couch and I'll tell you all about it? I could use a good lap.>*

"Sure. Super. Let's go."

So she padded out of the kitchen and down the hall and into the living room, me following right along behind. Part of me wondered if this was a dream or an extremely vivid hallucination, but I didn't feel like I was asleep or under the influence of a drug. Maybe late-onset schizophrenia?

Tango jumped up on my leather sofa, but—struck by the sudden realization that I wasn't quite ready for my dead cat to curl up in my lap—I detoured to the high-backed chair across from it.

And almost sat on the dog.

[Ahem,] rumbled a deep voice.

I froze, halfway to sitting down, straightened up, and slowly turned around. Lying on the chair was a tiny, big-eyed, very cute dog—I wasn't sure of the breed, but it looked like a dirty dust mop with floppy ears and an underbite.

"Uh-huh," I said.

<*Oh, terrific.*> I could practically hear Tango rolling her eyes.

"Hi," I continued. "And you are?"

[Just as reluctant to be here as you two. But let's try to make the best of it, shall we?]

I heard the voice in my head, just as I did Tango's—but where her feline rasp sounded like a chain-smoking ex-chorus-girl, the dog's voice was that of a barrel-chested but refined gentleman, a butler who used to box in the heavyweight division.

<*I was wondering who'd show up. You're it?*> Tango eyed him with obvious skepticism. <*Kinda puny, aren'tcha? Or do you just work the puppy angle, with the licking and the eyes and the piddling on everything?*>

The dog drew himself up and directed what was obviously supposed to be a withering glare in Tango's direction. [I assure you, madam, that looks can be deceiving. And I do not—under *any* circumstances—piddle.]

"I'm glad we've cleared that up. So what do I call you?"

The dog sighed. [My *given* name is Mr. Tiny. But I—]

It was a day for firsts, and another one suddenly arrived: I heard a cat laugh.

<*Ha! Are you* kiddin' *me? Mr. Tiny? What, Mr. Cutesy-Wutesy Widdlekins was already taken?*>

[It wasn't up to me.]

<*What is? A grasshopper's knee? A hunchbacked mouse? Bacteria on stilts?*>

[It surprises me that someone of your persuasion would harbor such an attitude toward size.] Tiny didn't sound offended; if anything, his voice was drily amused.

<*What's that supposed to mean?*>

[That even if I were the size of a moose, you'd still be trying to get my goat. Unsuccessfully.]

There was a pause. Tango gave her head an annoyed little shake, just like she used to when I was ten and that butterfly she was chasing had gotten away, again.

Back when she was alive.

Ten years ago.

I blinked. I turned around. I walked to the bathroom. I could feel both animals watching me as I left.

<You got here too soon. I was supposed to show up first, ease her into this.>

[Don't blame me, I just go where I'm told.]

<Right. Typical dog. Just following orders.>

[Oh, and I suppose you don't have superiors? Nobody tells a cat what to do?]

<Knock it off, willya? She can still hear us.>

No I can't, I thought to myself. *Nope. No magic talking animal voices in* my *head, nosirree.* I opened the medicine cabinet, found the tranquilizers, and took three of them. *Appetizer, main course, and dessert. Check, please.*

I left the bathroom and went upstairs. Tango followed me, but I studiously ignored her.

<Hey, Toots—you okay? I know this is a lot to take in all at once, but—>

I opened my bedroom door just wide enough to step through, and quickly closed it before she could follow me. Unless, of course, she could walk through walls—hey, that seemed to be a skill most regular cats had, so why not dead ones?

I waited, but she didn't appear. She did, however, keep talking—and weirdly enough, even though I still heard her voice in my head, now it sounded like she was talking from the other side of a closed door. *<All right, I understand. You need some time to think about all this. Get a good night's sleep and I'll explain everything in the morning.>*

I didn't answer. I undressed and got into bed, instead.

Then I lay there, eyes wide open, trying very hard to not think about anything. After a minute or so, I sighed, then said loudly, "Attention, four-legged possibly imaginary guests! If you need to go to the bathroom, do not whine or yowl outside my door at three AM! If you can learn how to speak English, you can figure out how to use a flush toilet!"

I paused. "Non-piddling entities can ignore the preceding announcement!"

Then the tranquilizers hit my empty-stomached, overloaded nervous system, and I passed out.

Chapter Two

The tranquilizers did their job, well and truly knocking me out for a good ten hours. I woke up muzzy-headed and disoriented, with the ghosts of dreams chasing their own tails around my head. Something about my deceased childhood pet and a talking dog—

[Ahem.]

<Geez, jump down her throat before she's even awake, why don'tcha?>

I sat bolt upright, blinking groggily. *They're still here.*

I had a brief moment of panic as I tried to figure out what I should do next. Sneak out the window? Ignore them and hope they fade away? Neither was my style—I preferred to meet my challenges head-on, though I was usually a little better prepared.

The panic passed, replaced by the realization that I was so hungry I was a little nauseous. Okay, first things first.

"I'm going to shower and get dressed," I announced. "Then all three of us will discuss this like civilized . . . beings . . . over breakfast. All right?"

[Certainly.]

<Go right ahead, sweetie. Me and the dust mop will wait.>

I *have* heard a dog sigh before—but not with a British accent.

Jumped in shower. Did my best to furiously scrub my brain into some kind of working order. Got dressed in a hurry, took a deep breath, and opened the door.

Two pairs of eyes looked up at me. Tango sat regally upright, tail curled around her front paws. Mr. Tiny was on his feet, little pink tongue protruding over his underbite, tiny brown eyes peering at me through a tangle of fur.

I gave them a quick, formal nod, marched past them and down the stairs to the kitchen. They followed, of course.

I made eggs and poured myself a glass of orange juice. Tango accepted some more tuna, but Mr. Tiny said all he wanted was a bowl of water.

I sat down and attacked my breakfast. Apparently not needing her mouth for speech, Tango talked while she ate her own.

<Okay. First of all, I'm no ghost. I'm the same cat you knew, reincarnated; this is my seventh life, out of a total of—surprise!—nine. Why am I here? Because of the graveyard.>

I made an inquisitive noise around my eggs.

<Yeah. See, the Zoransky graveyard is kind of a big deal. It's what they call a mystical nexus, which is to say it's where a whole bunch of things come together—those things being the afterlives of different animals.>

Right. Cats have more than one life, check. So animal afterlife—sorry, afterlives, plural—equals all dogs go to Heaven? I swallowed and said, "So what are you, Mr. Tiny? A canine angel?"

Tango snorted. Tiny said, [Not precisely. A better description would be animal spirit—]

<*Ghost, you mean.*>

[—or astral manifestation, perhaps—]

<*Spook.*>

[—even an ectoplasmic—]

<*Casper the butt-sniffing ghoul.*>

[—being, if you like.]

"Ghost and kitty 7.0, got it. What's the deal with the graveyard?"

<*We don't know, exactly,*> Tango admitted. <*What we do know is that someone—a human someone—is gonna die, and that the graveyard's gonna be in big trouble as a result.*>

"How do you know? Who sent you? And what do I have to do with all this?"

[I'm afraid we can't disclose too many details about our superiors.] Tiny's deep voice was apologetic. [And our information is mystic in nature, which means it's neither precise nor detailed. That's just how things work.]

<*But what you've got to do with the situation is simple. You have to stop it.*>

I got up from the table and put the kettle on for some tea. "Simple. Sure. I have to stop something without knowing what it is or who's responsible, you can't tell me who I'm doing this for, and I'm supposed to take everything you're telling me at face value. The faces, I might add, of two species that I never expected to have a conversation with in the first place."

<*Aw, c'mon, Toots—we used to talk all the time, remember? I'd stretch out on your lap and you'd tell me about that cute boy that lived three streets over—*>

"I meant have a conversation where I could ask a question and expect a response." I pulled a mug from the cupboard and stuck a tea bag in it. "I'm sorry, but this just isn't holding up. There's no independent way to verify any of what you're telling me, which means it could all just be a product of my own brain. You might not even be here, let alone talking—"

Tango jumped up on the table. *Hey, Toots—I'm* here, *okay? I'm* real. *What do you want me to do, sing?* She broke into an earsplitting yowl.

[I have a better idea. Go find a dictionary, drag it in here, and turn to the definition of *caterwaul*. You've not only woken the dead, you've given them a headache.]

The water began boiling, and I filled my mug gratefully. "No, sorry, that's not going to cut it. The more I think about it, the less I believe this is actually happening. What I need to do is book the day off from work, call a shrink, and Google antipsychotic medication—"

[That won't be necessary. I can provide you with the proof you require.]

"Oh? How?"

[As an ectoplasmic being, I have certain paranormal abilities. I haven't displayed them until now because I didn't want to alarm you—you must already be feeling overwhelmed by what we've revealed thus far.]

I felt a little prickle of annoyance at that. *Overwhelmed* was not a word I was friends with, and the fact that it seemed to have snuck into my house when I wasn't looking was all the more irritating. "Look, whatever magic powers you're about dazzle me with, it doesn't matter. It's still me and my malfunctioning brain, alone in my kitchen."

[Then, by all means, let's go out.]

I paused halfway through adding sugar to my tea. "Out? But—you mean other people can see you?"

[Indeed they can.]

I finished adding the sugar and took a sip. "So what are you going to do? Demonstrate to people that I now have a small dog? That's not exactly the kind of indisputable supernatural evidence I was thinking of."

[Find me something that approximates a leash, and I'll prove you wrong.]

I used a length of rope, tied loosely on Tiny's instructions. He felt and smelled just like a real dog, which made me worry all the more: If my hallucinations were this detailed, how could I trust any of my senses?

<I can't believe you let people drag you around by the neck.> Tango watched the whole process with something approaching pity. *<Dogs—lowering the dignity of the whole animal kingdom for the last ten thousand years.>*

[Cats—abandoning the very concept of dignity since the discovery of catnip. Shall we go?]

"I guess." I paused with one hand on the doorknob. "Tango? Are you—"

She was studiously licking one paw. *<I'll hang out here for now. Easier to explain one new animal in your life than two, right?>*

"Uh—yeah, I suppose." I hadn't even thought of that, which for me was way out of character. I was all about the ramifications and consequences, and I suddenly realized just how many had been dumped in my lap. What was I going to do with them while I was at work, for instance?

I opened the door, and we stepped out into early-morning sunshine. I still had half an hour before I had to be at the estate, which meant no more than fifteen minutes walking my new dog.

[Deidre?]

"Call me Foxtrot," I answered automatically. "Everyone does. What?"

[Observe, but try to keep your reaction to a minimum.]

"Observe what?"

We had left my yard and turned right onto the sidewalk. There was no one else in sight.

Mr. Tiny *changed.*

One second he was a little, tousled wig of a dog, and the next he was a dalmatian. Taller, sleeker, much spottier. He glanced back at me and cocked a canine eyebrow. [Ectoplasm is much more malleable than flesh and blood. I can take on the appearance of any breed, with an accompanying change in size and weight. However, to ensure discretion, I can't transform if anyone—other than you—is watching.]

"So how are you going to prove—"

[Like this.]

An elderly woman in a worn purple sweater and long gray skirt was shuffling toward us. Tiny trotted up to her, wagging his tail, and gave her a friendly, panting look. She stopped, smiled, and patted him on the head. "Well, hello," she said. "Aren't you friendly?"

[Ask her what breed I am.]

"Uh—yes, he's very friendly. I'm walking him for a friend. He's one of those, you know, what are they called again . . ."

"A dalmatian?"

"Yes. Yes, that's it. Thank you."

We continued on our way. Once she was no longer in sight, Tiny changed again—this time into a short, waddling English bulldog. The next people we ran into were a young girl and her mother, heading off to day care or kindergarten. The girl ran up, knelt down, and let Mr. Tiny sniff her fingers. "Oh, he's so *ugly,*" she said, grinning.

"Now, Madison," her mother said. "That's not nice."

"No, I mean he's so ugly he's cute," the girl said. Mr. Tiny licked her fingers and she giggled. "What's his name?"

"Um. What do you think his name is?"

"Grumpy McBurger," she said immediately, in that utterly self-assured way small children have.

"That's a great name," I answered. "Do you know what kind of dog he is?"

"No. What kind?"

"Ask your mommy."

Her mother smiled. "That's called a bulldog, sweetie. Now, come on, we're going to be late."

"Okay. Bye, Grumpy McBurger!"

Mr. Tiny turned to me, his tongue lolling out. [Are you convinced, yet?]

"Can we do a few more?"

So we did. We talked to a guy in a suit heading off to work, a boy delivering newspapers, and a woman in her front yard watering her plants. Tiny became a sheepdog, a Great Dane, and a Chihuahua even smaller than his original form—which, I realized, probably wasn't original at all. "Okay, I'm convinced," I admitted after he'd demonstrated his impression of a wiener dog. "Unless I'm so far gone that I'm imagining everyone's responses, too, you're no ordinary dog. And I just realized something else: *You're* the stray that's been hanging around the estate, aren't you?"

[Yes, that was me. I arrived before Tango and thought I would do some advance scouting before contacting you.]

"So is that big white pit bull your true form?"

[No.]

"What is?"

[All in good time, dear lady. Suffice it to say that in my former life, I was often employed by the military.]

We'd circled the block and now were almost back at my house. "Of course. Your attitude is extremely . . . professional."

He'd shifted back into dust mop mode, and now he sat down on the sidewalk just outside my front gate. [As opposed to Tango, you mean? I hope you won't hold that against me.]

"What? No, not at all. Actually, that kind of matter-of-fact approach is helping me keep my grip on my self-control. Because, well, you know . . ."

[This all seems insane? Yes, I understand. But I know you have the strength of character and wit to not only adapt to your new circumstances, but also accomplish what needs to be done.]

"Uh-huh. And you know this how?"

[Because you were the one who was chosen to do so.]

I glanced down at my watch. "Uh-oh. Going to have to hurry if I'm not going to be late for work. We'll talk about this later, okay?"

[I'm afraid not.]

"Excuse me?"

[We've already delayed one night. We can't wait any longer; Tango and I will accompany you to the Zoransky estate.]

"But—how am I supposed to explain you two?"

[Pet-sitting. You're an intelligent woman; I'm sure you can add enough details to make it convincing.]

I sighed. "And if I say no, you'll just follow me out there anyway. Won't you?"

Tiny tilted his head ever so slightly to one side. [We have a job to do, Foxtrot. Let's get on with it, shall we?]

I resisted the urge to snap off a salute. "Yes, sir," I muttered, and fumbled in my purse for my keys.

You know what's funny? I was driving in to work with two talking animals in my car—one of whom was technically among the nonliving—and I kept worrying about seat belts. My obsessive-compulsive side gets stronger when I'm under stress.

Tiny sat upright in the back, now wearing the form of a golden retriever. Tango lay curled up on the passenger seat, her front paws hanging over the side.

I'd told them about what I'd seen in the graveyard, and they'd both nodded knowingly. [You have certain abilities of your own now,] Tiny told me. [You're able to perceive animal spirits, such as myself.]

"And talk to them?"

<If they're dead, yeah. You can't talk to living animals—not unless you speak fluent Hamster or Canary or Siamese or whatever you're talking to.>

Different species, different languages—I should have seen that coming. "But I can understand you two."

[We're speaking English. Well, one of us is, anyway—I don't know what you'd call the mangled carcass of linguistics Tango chews up and spits out.]

Tango responded with a series of odd grunts and coughs that sounded like they might precede a hairball. "Are you okay?"

<Fine, Toots. I was just telling Mr. Chameleon back there what I thought of his remark. In Chameleon; it's one of over three hundred languages I speak. Fluently.>

[And how many of those are feline dialects?]

Tango didn't answer.

[That's what I thought. Very impressive, if the murder we're trying to prevent takes place at a cat fanciers' ball.]

"Murder," I said out loud. It didn't sound real to me, so I decided I'd just treat it as another problem I had to solve in my long and complicated day—that made it manageable. Whose death would put the graveyard at risk?

Once I thought about it, it was obvious. "It has to be ZZ," I said. "My boss. Her family owns the graveyard, but she only has one heir, Oscar. He's been after her to get rid of the land for years—if she dies, he'll sell it to a developer before ZZ's in the ground."

[Which means he's also our prime suspect.]

"I guess—but I doubt it. Oscar's a schemer, not a

killer. He'd gladly take advantage of the situation, but I don't think he has the backbone to cause it."

<That's a little naive, Toots. A killer can look as innocent as a baby.> She stretched a paw out and showed her claws, then retracted them and gave me a sleepy, cuddly look. *<Believe me, I know.>* It was exactly the kind of thing she used to do, and I experienced a sudden urge to reach over and stroke her fur. I didn't give in.

It's not a long drive from where I live to where I work, and I usually use the time to go over the day's itinerary in my head. Not today, though; when I rolled through the front gates, my mind was firmly on how to keep ZZ safe.

I parked in my usual spot in front, got out, and opened the door for my passengers. "This is going to be a little tricky, all right?" I told them, looking around. "Do you think the two of you can stay out of sight and out of trouble while I talk to someone? I'll meet you back here in fifteen minutes."

<Good idea. It'll give me a chance to eyeball the place, check everything out.>

[Absolutely. You can expect one of us to be late, however; cats are notoriously lax about being punctual.]

Tango glared at him. *<Oh, I know all about punctuation, toilet-breath. Keep giving me lip and I'll punctuate that flea-bitten thing you call a coat.>*

She went one way, Mr. Tiny the other. In a second they were both gone, Tango into some bushes, Tiny around the corner of the house. I took a deep breath, firmed up my resolve, and went off to find ZZ's head of security.

Shondra Destry had converted one of the mansion's many bedrooms into an office. It was on the second floor of the house and had a great view of the sprawling grounds, though she was seldom there to enjoy it. Shondra spent most of her time prowling the estate like a restless cheetah. With the way she acted you'd think we were under imminent threat of attack: From security cameras to triple locks on the front and back doors, she was prepared to fend off anything from overzealous paparazzi to a horde of invading zombies.

I was lucky, though—I caught her at her desk, drinking an extra-large coffee and scanning the security feeds on the bank of monitors mounted on the opposite wall. Destry was short but lithe, with the build of a runner and hair shaved down to military-grade stubble, dressed in dark pants and a light blue long-sleeved shirt that on her looked like a uniform. She sized me up when I entered and said, "Morning, Trot. Problem?"

I sat down on the chair across from her. "Maybe. I'm not sure."

"Tell me."

Sure. Tell her what, exactly? I needed her on high alert, but I had zero evidence, a crazy story, and nothing to point her at. Destry was as dangerous as a loaded gun, but I had to be careful I didn't shoot myself in the foot. "Well. I think we need to be extra careful about ZZ's safety for the next little while."

I swear, the woman's ears grew points. "Why?"

"I think she might be in danger."

"That's twice you said 'I think.' *Why* do you think it, and what sort of danger?" Destry was staring at me now with a focus she must have learned in the military, and it was more than a little unnerving.

"I—well—" I reached desperately for something that wouldn't sound half-baked. "The salon that's starting today. I've got a feeling about some of the guests."

"Which ones?"

"I can't really pin it down. I just feel as if . . ."

"ZZ's in danger."

"Yes."

She nodded, never taking her eyes off me. "Anything else?"

Okay, that went well . . . "Not really," I said, and gave her a lame attempt at a smile.

"Foxtrot, I think you need to slow down for a minute. Maybe take a day off. You're overworked, overstressed, and just plain frazzled. I've checked out each and every guest—like I always do—and none of them is a threat. Really, everything's fine." She gave me back a smile of her own, which was cool and professional and made my smile seem like it needed a straitjacket. "I'm always here, though. If you have any legitimate concerns."

"Okay," I said. "Thank you." I got up and left, trying not to tuck my tail between my legs as I went.

Stupid. I should have had a plan. Not like me to go in without a plan. I could have told her I got a threatening email or something, or saw someone lurking outside. I realized I was a little panicked, that the idea that ZZ could be hurt or even killed had shaken me up more than I was willing to admit.

I liked ZZ a whole lot. She was smart and funny and completely fearless, always taking life in big bites and chewing with gusto. I hoped I'd enjoy myself half as much as she did when I got to be her age—but right now I had to focus on making sure her age didn't come to an abrupt stop.

Even if Shondra didn't seem worried, she did respect me—that, plus her own professional paranoia, meant she was now just that little bit more alert than she'd been ten minutes ago. That was something, anyway. And maybe T and T would find the killer hiding in the bushes and this whole mess would no longer be my responsibility.

I sighed and marched myself down the hall. Responsibility always seemed to land on my shoulders, and this time probably wouldn't be any different. Well, at least I had plenty of practice—maybe that was why I'd been picked for the job.

The next step, I supposed, was telling ZZ herself. That would be tricky; while ZZ believed in intuition, she tended to act as if she were bulletproof, immortal, and immune to bad luck. She relied on me for hard information, and this was one time I just couldn't give it to her. I wasn't sure what the solution was, and at this point I couldn't embellish the story I'd given Shondra without looking suspicious myself.

I went looking for my boss, starting in her bedroom. It was a suite on the third floor, an enormous room with a gigantic four-poster bed, an eclectic mix of furniture ranging from antique divans to beanbags strewn about, and a hot tub. The door to her walk-in closet was open, and I could hear someone moving around inside.

"ZZ?" I said, walking into the room. "Got something I need to talk to you about—"

The occupant of the closet, however, wasn't ZZ—it was Maria Wong, the head maid. She was a short, stout woman, in a black dress with a white apron. Her usual smile had been replaced by a scowl.

"Oh. Hi, Maria. Have you seen—"

"The crazy lady? She not here. She off doing more crazy things, I bet. Leave all the hard work to me."

I raised my eyebrows. Maria was generally the cheerful sort, but ZZ could infuriate just about anyone. "Uh-oh. What's she got you doing this time?"

"All this!" Maria waved a hand at the clothes, shoes, and hats that lined both walls twenty feet deep; the back wall was one large mirror. "She want all her clothing rearranged. Look!" She dug a piece of paper out of her apron pocket and thrust it at me. "All like this. Crazy!"

I scanned the paper, which was all about a new theory of color harmonization and how it affected the moods of people around you. If I was interpreting it right, pretty soon ZZ would be wearing yellow sneakers, a purple dress, and a green hat. I doubted anyone would notice.

I handed the paper back. "My condolences, Maria. I'll schedule one of the girls for an extra shift to make up the time, okay?"

She gave me a grudging nod. "Okay. Top-floor bathroom in east wing need new showerhead, too. Leaking."

"I'll tell maintenance." I waved good-bye and left her there, muttering as she surveyed the Everest of outfits she was about to scale.

I was on my way to the sitting room when I saw the helicopter.

I don't mean I saw it through a window, either; it was right in front of me in the hall, hovering around six feet off the floor. It looked kind of like one of those radio-controlled kids' toys, the kind with four rotors arranged in a square—except a little more industrial, almost military. It was painted a flat black instead of bright primary colors, and made less noise than an electric fan.

Before I could do much more than stare, it darted back the way it came, through the doorway to the sitting room. That's what ZZ insists on calling it, though it's more like a brightly lit cocktail lounge than anything from the Victorian era. I followed it in, where I found two of ZZ's guests and ZZ herself sitting on a tubular, overstuffed couch that snaked around the room like a fat white anaconda.

ZZ perched to the right. She smiled when she saw me and waved me over. "Foxtrot! Good morning, dear. Mr. Estevez was just showing me his *fascinating* device."

Juan Estevez, a skinny young man in a polo shirt and jeans, sat next to ZZ, his eyes flickering from the small device he held in one hand to the machine now hovering over the coffee table in front of him. He tapped the device's screen a few times, and the helicopter settled onto the table gently.

Before I had a chance to reply, there was a deafening screech from the other side of the couch. It came not from the bearded, portly man in the Hawaiian shirt and white Panama hat sitting beside Juan, but from the monkey perched on his shoulder; the poor creature seemed more than a little frightened by the giant, flying bug that had just landed mere feet away.

"There, there, Amos," the bearded man said softly. I'd met him before, at a previous salon; his name was Kenny Gant, a businessman who'd turned his eco-friendly pet food into a household name through a clever advertising campaign using a variety of exotic animals. "It won't harm you, I promise."

"I'm not so sure," ZZ said, with an all-too-familiar steely smile on her face. I knew that look well; it meant she was about to do the verbal equivalent of slapping someone in the face. "After all, it was designed to kill people—isn't that right, Mr. Estevez?"

Chapter Three

Juan Estevez looked more like he'd been kneed in the groin than slapped in the face. His eyes widened, his face flushed, and his jaw dropped an inch or so. "That—that's not true!" he managed after a second. "The GEQ is for gathering information—in a covert setting, yes, but it's hardly meant to be some sort of, of *assassination* tool."

ZZ mock-frowned. "Oh? Then what's this?" She pointed to the open metal case beside the machine. "Looks like a weapon to me." I moved over beside ZZ so I could see better.

"I was about to demonstrate that," Estevez said. He reached into the case and pulled out what looked like a toy handgun: It had a thin, rectangular grip below a long, tubular barrel. There was no trigger, and the whole thing was painted the same flat black as the copter.

"GEQ?" I asked.

"Gecko Enabled Quadracopter," Estevez said. He picked up the GEQ and clipped the gun to the underside, then took four floppy black ovals from the case and attached them to the GEQ's landing struts. "The projector is made from plastic and powered by compressed air; it's far too light and flimsy to fire a bullet."

"Then what does it fire?" asked Kenny Gant.

"Bugs," said Estevez. "That is, electronic listening devices designed to adhere to nonstandard surfaces. We're still fine-tuning different glues—but it's how the GEQ itself can cling to smooth surfaces that's really revolutionary."

He put the quadracopter down, picked up the controller, and tapped the screen a few times. The GEQ whirred to life, lifting off the table in a rush of displaced air. It was eerie just how little noise it made.

The machine darted to the far side of the room, where a large, oval mirror hung on the wall. For a second I thought it would crash right into it—but at the very last moment it flipped in midair, planting its new oval feet against the glass with a soft *smack*.

The whir of the rotors died. The GEQ stayed right where it was, clinging to the mirror like—well, a gecko.

"Suction cups?" said Kenny Gant, in a voice more amused than impressed.

"Oh, no," said Estevez. "Those are highly unreliable. The pads on the GEQ's feet work exactly like the toes of a real gecko do—they're covered in tiny microscopic extrusions that are so small they interact with the surface at an atomic level. They use what are called van der Waals forces—basically, an attraction between particles of very small size."

"Animal magnetism?" said Gant.

"No, van der Waals forces are present in all matter—it's just that geckos seem to be the only animals that take advantage of them. It's very useful for a machine like the GEQ, because it can cling to almost any surface—even upside down."

I looked down at the device in Estevez's hands, but it took me a second to understand what I was seeing. "It's got an onboard camera, too?"

"Oh, yes," said Estevez, beaming proudly. "It wouldn't be much good as a surveillance device without one, would it?"

"A surveillance device for the military," said ZZ.

"Well, I couldn't really say what its end use will be—"

"But your *funding* comes from the military."

"I—I can't disclose that kind of information—"

"It occurs to me," ZZ continued, "that you wouldn't need a firearm to make your little toy lethal. You could use it to deliver something other than a bullet—poison, maybe."

Estevez's face had gotten very still. He said nothing, but his eyes looked panicked.

"Of course, I'm only speculating," said ZZ with a smile. "We can talk more about your plans for this marvelous invention at dinner. And now, if you'll excuse me—Foxtrot?"

"Yes?"

"I need to have a word with you. Can you meet me in my office in five minutes?"

"Uh—sure."

I took the opportunity to duck outside and talk with my new partners. Tiny lay patiently in the shade of a large bush, while Tango crouched inside the foliage.

I looked around, then knelt down. "You two find anything?"

<Nothing obviously homicidal, other than a six-foot chicken with a bad haircut. I tried asking it a few questions, but my Poultry's a little rusty.>

[That's an *ostrich,* Tango. Apparently there's a menagerie on the premises—I cataloged quite the inventory of scents. Nothing I couldn't identify, of course. But I'm afraid I saw nothing overly suspicious, either.]

"My luck wasn't much better—though I did see ZZ unnerve one of our guests." I told them about the quadracopter and Juan Estevez's reaction to ZZ's questions. "I have to go meet with her right now. I'll be back as soon as I'm done—"

[I should go with you.]

I thought about that for a second. I couldn't hide them forever—and the sooner everyone got used to having them around, the sooner they could come and go without causing problems. "All right. I'll say an old friend dumped you two on me without warning and left the country for an undisclosed length of time. You were raised together so you're inseparable, but you can't be left on your own because—no, wait, that's contradictory. If you're always together you're never on your own, are you?"

<Don't sweat it, Toots. We figured this out already. Tiny'll be the inside man, I'll be the outside. Nobody pays a stray cat much attention, beyond maybe leaving a bowl of food out now and then. I'll play it skittish, except around you—you'll be the one human I trust, right? Though I don't know how you'll explain my being able to stand the ugly mutt always hanging around.>

[Oh, that's easy. Brain damage. You think I'm a giant bowl of milk.]

Tango's eyes narrowed. *<Okay, honey. I can go that route. Just be careful around us brain-damaged types—we can be kinda volatile, you know? In an unpredictably violent way.>*

[I'll keep that in mind.]

Tango turned and darted deeper into the bushes, vanishing in a second. I started to tell her to wait, then stopped myself. Tango would act the way she always did: She'd leave when she felt like it, and show up when it suited her.

That's what I told myself, anyway. The truth was, I felt more uncomfortable around her than I did Tiny. I straightened and looked down at him, still in golden retriever form. "You going to stick with that one?"

[It seems the most prudent choice for now. Golden retrievers are largely regarded as utterly loyal, extremely friendly, and just a little dim. It makes, as they say, for a good cover.]

I grinned. "All right, then, Blondie—let's go meet the woman whose life you're here to save."

ZZ's "office" was on the very top floor of the house, a little corner parapet she had added that jutted up from the rest of the house like an off-center conning tower on a submarine. The exterior surfaces were made entirely of glass, with internal shutters that rose from slots in the floor and let her conjure walls at will. As I ascended the spiral staircase into the room, I saw that today all the shutters but one were up, which indicated a darker mood than I was hoping for. ZZ was at her desk in front of the single pane of glass, studying the monitor of her computer intently.

I needn't have worried. As soon as Tiny's shaggy head popped above floor level, ZZ's serious look brightened to a brilliant smile. "Well, hello!" she said. "Who's your new friend, Foxtrot?"

"This is, uh, Tiny. I'm looking after him for a friend. He's a good dog, but a little neurotic—apparently he can't be left alone or he'll eat all my furniture, set my car on fire, and write bad checks in my name. I hope you don't mind that I brought him to work—"

ZZ was already kneeling beside Tiny, scritching behind his ears while he panted at her with a big, doggy grin on his face. [You see?]

"He seems like a very *good* dog, to me," said ZZ. "Aren't you, Tiny?"

Tiny licked her hand enthusiastically, which made her giggle like a schoolgirl. "How is he around other animals? He's not going to go crazy and start barking if he sees Oswald strutting around, is he?"

"No, I don't think that'll be a problem. He's very . . . *civilized* toward other animals." Tiny cocked an eyebrow at me, a look that ZZ thankfully missed.

"Well, then, I think it's perfectly delightful that you'll have a sidekick for a while. Now—the reason I called you in here." She stood up and crossed her arms. "It's about Oscar."

Uh-oh. "What's he done now?"

"He's run up a *massive* bill on an online gambling site. I've paid it off and canceled that particular credit card, but he needs to be taught a lesson. I want you to reduce his monthly allowance by twenty—no, twenty-five—percent. We'll see if *that* smartens him up."

I did my best not to sigh. Oscar's problem wasn't smarts; he had plenty of those. Ethics, on the other hand . . . "Have you told him already, or do you want me to swing the ax?"

ZZ blinked in surprise. "Oh, *no,* dear, I'd never do that to you. You're here to bring a little order to my life, not handle unpleasant family duties. I told him last night—we had *quite* the shouting match."

That was unusual—Oscar was usually too wily to actually lose his temper, and though ZZ could be a real firebrand in service to a worthy cause, she was normally terrible at disciplining her own offspring.

"You must have really laid down the law," I said.

She nodded, her eyes unhappy. "I did. It's been a long time coming, but I don't know who was more surprised when it finally arrived—him or me. He stormed out and hasn't been back since."

"I'll take care of it." I paused. "ZZ, will you do me a favor? Will you be . . . *careful* for the next few days?"

She studied me for a second before replying. "What do you mean, dear? Careful about what?"

"Your—" I swallowed, then forced myself to say it. "—your personal safety."

She raised her eyebrows in astonishment, then burst out laughing. "What? My goodness, you're not suggesting that Oscar might try to *harm* me, are you? That's absurd!"

"Not Oscar himself, no. But—" I reached desperately for a plausible explanation, and actually managed to come up with one. "He hangs around with some seedy characters, and he drinks too much. What if one of *them* gets the wrong idea?"

She frowned. "It's true, he has awful taste in friends. But I don't think—"

"Just promise me, all right? Humor your gal Friday?"

Her frown dissolved into a smile. "All right, Foxtrot. I'll stay alert for villains skulking in dark corners. But I'm sure I have nothing to worry about—not with your new friend around, right?" She leaned down and stroked Tiny's head.

"Well, I hope not . . ."

"Will we be seeing you for dinner tonight? The first night of a salon is always entertaining."

I hesitated, then said, "Yes, I think you will. As long as I can bring Tiny along."

"If he's as well behaved as he is right now, I don't see why not."

[Well done, Foxtrot.]

"Thanks," I said. "I'm sure it'll be interesting."

I spent the day doing what I usually did, which was a flurry of everything. I checked on deliveries, did some online ordering, talked to a plumber, three contractors, and two antiques dealers. The morning went by in a blur. I had a quick lunch at my desk, then scheduled a meeting with the household staff for the afternoon. Through it all, Tiny stayed by my side, rarely talking, going out of his way to make friends with everyone he met. I've always taken the sociability of dogs—well, most dogs—for granted, just part of who they are, but I was starting to view that trait in a different light: Tiny wasn't just being nice, he was evaluating potential suspects.

I asked him if he wanted anything for lunch, and he politely declined. [I don't require sustenance, as such.]

I talked around my mouthful of roast beef on rye. "So you don't eat or drink?"

He gave my sandwich a longing glance. [I don't *need* to. But I can . . . if the situation calls for it.]

I grinned and tossed him some roast beef. He snatched it out of the air and wolfed it down. [Thank you.]

"You're welcome. Does this mean you'll have to . . . you know . . . later?"

[Most definitely not. Ectoplasmic digestion is one hundred percent efficient.]

I held the staff meeting in the main kitchen, which was big and modern and wouldn't have looked out of place in an upscale restaurant. It was pretty informal, with me filling in the maids on the guests' personal quirks (Mr. Gant's monkey should never be fed by anyone by him; Mr. Kwok requires solitude in the morning to perform tai chi in his room) and discussing a few dietary restrictions and preferences with the kitchen staff. I had Tiny wait outside—I knew he wasn't a health risk, but there was no way to explain that.

When the meeting was over, the head chef approached me. Ben Montain was tall, with sandy-blond hair, dark eyes, and the sort of rugged, broody look that seemed more suited to jeans and a denim shirt than a chef's whites. Which made sense, if you knew where ZZ found him: One minute she was eating breakfast at this tiny diner in the wilds of New Jersey and the next she was marching into the kitchen and demanding to know who'd made her omelet. When Ben asked her if there was a problem, she said, "Yes. This is the best omelet I have ever eaten, and if I were to abandon its creator in this godforsaken place then mine would surely punish me in whatever afterlife exists." Then she offered him a job as her personal cook for three times his salary and four weeks' paid vacation every year. Ben's worked for her ever since.

"Hey, Ben. Everything all right?"

"Sure, Foxtrot. I was just, uh—well, I was wondering . . ."

"What?"

He had that wretched look on his face that men get when they're about to put their ego on the line. "I was wondering if maybe you'd like to have lunch with me."

"Um—thanks, but I just ate. A really spectacular roast beef sandwich, which I believe you made."

"Thanks. But I meant—some other lunch. Some other day. I mean, I'd still make you lunch, but I'd like to eat it, too. Not your lunch, I mean." He started to look a little panicked. "I'd *make* your lunch, I just wouldn't *eat* your lunch. That would be yours. I'd eat *mine*. Lunch, that is."

I blinked. "Together?"

He nodded, obviously avoiding opening his mouth again for fear of what might jump out.

"Sure," I said. "How about tomorrow?"

The panicked look subsided, replaced by relief. "Yeah, that's good. I eat a little later than most—say one o'clock?"

"Sounds good." I smiled. "See you then." And I turned around and walked out the door.

Wow. Ben Montain just asked me out.

I really wasn't sure what to think about that. My default response to being asked for a favor was usually to say yes—not because I was a pushover, but because it made people easier to deal with in the moment. I could always say no later, when I'd thought of a plausible excuse and could let them down easy. That might seem dishonest, but you needed to strategize when you had as many balls in the air as I usually did—and it was funny how often people remembered your initial "yes" more than your follow-up "sorry, we're going to have to reschedule."

But did I *want* to reschedule?

I really should. Dating in the workplace was tricky at best, disastrous at worst. I hadn't been on a date in ages, mostly because I just didn't have the time. And now, with this whole crazy supernatural craziness? A romance that could get me fired was the last thing I needed. No, better if I just called him later and told him I couldn't make it; the poor guy looked flustered enough that he probably wouldn't try his luck a second time.

But still . . . that jawline. Those shoulders. That easy-going, country-boy grin of his . . .

I shook my head and put those thoughts firmly out of my mind. *Focus, girl. You've got enough on your plate already without staring longingly at the dessert cart.*

No matter how *yummy it looks.*

Chapter Four

The day went by faster than I expected. Tango didn't make an appearance until shortly before dinner; she suddenly popped up at poolside, where I was tapping away at my laptop.

<*Hey, Toots.*> She sauntered over, sat down in front of me, and started to groom herself.

"Hi. And how was your day?"

<*Exhausting. I need a nap.*> She gave her paw one final lick and then curled up and closed her eyes.

Tiny lifted his head from where he lay at my feet. [Ah, yes. The rigorous demands of the feline lifestyle. How do you manage on only sixteen hours of sleep per day?]

"Did you find anything out?"

<*What, you mean like mysterious strangers in purple ski masks skulking around with duffel bags that clank and trying to get into the house through locked basement windows?*>

"What? Yes! Is that what you saw?"

<*Nah. I did spot a few squirrels that looked kinda sketchy, though. Beady little eyes.*>

[Agreed. Never trust anything that's fifty percent tail.]

"I'll keep that in mind if anyone is killed by acorns." I filled her in on the fight between ZZ and Oscar. "That's motive, I guess, but I still don't see him as a murderer. He's not here right now, anyway. Tiny and I are going to attend tonight's dinner—he might show up for that."

<'Kay. Gonna grab some shut-eye now.>

I tried to get some more work done, but it was impossible to concentrate. Who knew that reincarnated telepathic cats snored?

She dozed for almost an hour, then sprang to her feet and darted into the bushes with no warning. I looked up from my laptop to see ZZ, now dressed in a stunning floor-length gown made of equal parts iridescent blue fabric and delicate cream-colored lace. She had a string of black pearls around her neck and high-heeled shoes that seemed to be made of feathers. "Foxtrot? Time for dinner, dear—you're off the clock." She paused. "Did I see a cat just now?"

"Uh, yes. Not sure where she came from. She seemed friendly, but you know how cats are."

ZZ smiled, a little incredulously. "First a dog, now a cat? I thought Caroline was our resident animal magnet."

I smiled and shrugged. "I've always loved animals—I just don't have the time for pets."

"I'm a little surprised at how your new friend took it. He must be used to cats."

[One never gets *used* to cats.]

"Oh, he grew up around them. He's doesn't mind them at all."

[The best you can do is build up a tolerance. It's akin to smashing your head into a rock until your skull starts to go numb.]

"He's quite fond of them, actually."

[Of course, having your head caved in holds the promise of death's sweet release, whereas the mere knowledge of the *existence* of cats is an unending torment—]

"Dinner," I said, getting to my feet. "Yes. A good meal, that's exactly what we need. Tiny, you stay out here, all right?"

[Where else would I go?]

The dining room was about what you'd expect in a mansion: big, tastefully decorated, with a highly polished wooden table huge enough to put a sail on and take for a cruise and an immense crystal chandelier overhead. But ZZ had added a few modern touches for her salons, including replacing all the antique chairs with high-backed, plush ones so comfortable you could fall asleep in them, an automated drinks trolley that rolled around delivering whatever alcoholic refreshment might be required, and three massive, high-resolution flat-screen monitors mounted on the walls. They were currently in default mode, showing a steadily changing montage of art, and were controlled by the tablet ZZ placed in a filigreed silver stand next to her wineglass as she sat down. "Hello, everyone!" she said in a loud voice.

People paused in their conversation and called hello back. There were eight of us that evening: ZZ and me; Juan Estevez, the roboticist; Kenny Gant, the pet-food magnate; Hana Kim, a teenage Olympic gymnast, and her trainer, Mr. Kwok; a British rock star named Keene, who'd been there before and always flirted with me; and Oscar, ZZ's son.

ZZ didn't bother with formal introductions, as she liked to keep things loose. I found myself seated beside Keene, and across from Kenny Gant and his monkey, perched on his shoulder. It was a tiny thing with a pink face, the fur on its upper body and head white but black everywhere else.

Gant smiled at me. He'd changed out of his Hawaiian shirt and into long-sleeved linen of a pale green. "Nice to see you again, Foxtrot."

"You, too, Kenny." Gant had stayed here before, and made a favorable enough impression to be invited back. "No cockatoo this time?"

He chuckled. "No, I try not to repeat myself. Amos here is a little spooked tonight—I'm not sure why."

I thought about the graveyard next door, and the impending doom I was supposed to avert; I'd bet every animal within twenty miles was spooked right now, and with good reason. Poor Caroline—she'd have her hands full tonight.

"I'm *so* glad you brought a monkey," said Keene. His accent was a little thicker tonight, which was what happened when he'd had a few drinks. "Far as I'm concerned, it's just not a party until a monkey shows up. Wouldn't you say, Foxtrot?"

Well, at least he wasn't calling me "Foxy" anymore. "I *would* say, Mr. Keene. Fun, barrel of, right?"

He flashed me a dazzling, rock-star smile. Keene was tall and slim, with curly black hair down to his shoulders and eyelashes that were far too long for his DNA. In the right clothes, from behind, you could mistake him for a supermodel. Right now he had on the kind of puffy-sleeved, deep purple silk shirt only pirates and lead singers could get away with, and he was probably wearing leather pants tight enough to qualify as paint. I asked him once how he was able to move in those things; he grinned and said, "Lots of yoga, plenty of lubrication, and a willingness to suffer. It's much like my dating life, really."

"That's what I like about you, Foxtrot," he said, then paused. He had features just this side of pretty, with a wide mouth, killer cheekbones, and dark, gypsy eyes. I waited, but he just met my gaze and said nothing.

I finally gave in. "And what would that be, exactly?"

"That thing you do which I am currently failing to."

"Stay sober?"

He laughed. He had a good laugh, full and throaty and totally uninhibited. "Guilty! But no—I'm referring to the way you effortlessly *sum up* things. I may, on occasion, smell like a distillery, but you never fail to function as one. Even when it comes to a concept as inherently subjective and indefinable as 'fun.' "

That stung a little bit, though I wasn't sure why; I hid my frown behind a quick swallow of wine. "You make me sound almost mechanical."

He shook his head. "No. Absolutely not. One cannot comprehend the *nature* of fun without, on some level, *relating* to fun. Scratch a mathematician and you'll find a child who loved counting games. You're good, *bloody* good, at your job, Foxtrot—and you wouldn't be, you *couldn't* be, unless you enjoyed not only doing it but the end result." He spread his hands expansively, spilling a little of his drink in the process. "This. You like making people happy. You *do* make people happy. And it is appreciated."

I couldn't help but smile. "Thank you. I get paid for it, you know."

"You do?" He boggled at me, almost convincingly. "Well, then, bollocks to all that. You mean this isn't a clever ploy to win my heart and steal my virginity?"

"Not so much."

He emitted a theatrical sigh. "Then I shall be forced to drown my unending sorrow in the dubious pleasures of the grape. And possibly that worm that lives at the bottom of tequila bottles."

He turned to his other side and said, "What do you think, Oscar? You know her better than I do—what's the proper beverage to sluice her out of my shattered hopes?"

Oscar Zoransky finished his own drink—two fingers

of extremely expensive whiskey, neat—and hit the button on the underside of the table that summoned the booze trolley for a refresher. He was a short, round, balding man, with a wide friendly face and the kind of tan you got from lying around at poolside seven days a week. I had a running bet with myself as to where Oscar would wind up: the skin cancer ward or a prison cell. It usually ran about even, but tonight the Big House was definitely ahead. "I wouldn't know," Oscar said, pronouncing his words with the care of the mostly drunk. "I drink constantly, but she won't go away."

I ignored the jab—Oscar was no doubt still smarting from the decrease in his allowance, and I wasn't going to let myself to get sidetracked by a pointless argument. I focused my attention on another guest, instead: Hana Kim, the Olympic gymnast from South Korea. She sat across the table from me, sipping from a glass of water and looking a little intimidated.

"How are you settling in, Hana?" I asked her. "Is the makeshift gymnasium we set up for you in the dance studio okay?"

She gave me a quick nod and smile. "It's fine, Ms. Lancaster. I used it this morning."

"Well, if you need anything else, just let me know. Our cook here is very good; he's following the diet specifications Mr. Kwok gave him exactly."

Was that the briefest flash of disappointment I saw on her face? "Oh. That's good. Really good."

I snuck a glance at her trainer, who was talking animatedly with ZZ. She stared intently into his eyes as they talked—ZZ took the art of conversation very seriously.

"Well," I said, "that's not to say that you can't enjoy a little cheating on your regimen. The French pastries Ben makes are enough to tempt an archangel."

Now Hana was the one to glance at Kwok. She leaned forward and whispered, "Only if the Warden isn't looking."

I nodded and whispered back. "I'm sure we can work something out. I know a guard."

The smile on her face got a lot less tentative. Keene was right about one thing—I did enjoy making other people happy. And I was good at it.

But that wasn't the question. The question was, how good was I at preventing a murder . . .

That was the thought running through my head when things got crazy.

Gant's monkey leapt off his shoulder and bounded down the center of the table at high speed, scattering silverware and napkins as he went, straight at ZZ. Was that a knife in his hand?

But Amos never made it there. The simian veered at the last moment, launching himself like a furry missile at Keene, landing on top of his head. Both of them screeched as the monkey grabbed a fistful of curly black hair and yanked.

"AAH! *Bugger!*" yelled Keene. He flailed at the monkey with the hand that wasn't holding his drink. The monkey flailed back with the silverware it clutched in one tiny paw—a fork, not a knife—then threw it across the table. Mr. Kwok caught the fork nimbly.

"Amos!" Gant yelled. "Get back here!"

Amos had other plans. He scampered down Keene's arm to the elbow, grabbed his wrist, and wrenched the hand holding the wineglass upward. The table watched in astonishment as the monkey guzzled the drink, still in Keene's hand.

"That's no way to treat a nice Cabernet," said Keene.

Amos took the criticism poorly, letting out another loud screech and bounding away. His trajectory took him to the top of the automated drinks trolley, which looked a little like a vacuum cleaner mounted on a rolling cart. Oscar had just used it to refill his drink, which Amos now eyed greedily. Oscar studied the beast, then offered him the glass. "Chin chin," he said. "Welcome to the party."

"Oscar!" ZZ snapped.

The monkey gulped half the drink in one swallow, then dropped the glass and leapt for the chandelier. He hung there, chattering and screeching, swinging back and forth. I already had my cell phone out. "Caroline? Get down to the dining room, stat—we've got a situation with a monkey. We'll need containment—"

I heard a sharp *pffft!* A crimson-plumed dart appeared in the center of the monkey's chest; he screeched and yanked it out, throwing it in my direction. I ducked.

"Don't worry," Kenny Gant said. He holstered the air pistol he'd just shot Amos with. "He'll be down for the count in a minute or so."

Amos was already slowing down. He hung from one arm, then dropped down onto the table. He staggered a few steps, then pointed at Gant in a very human and accusing manner.

"It's okay, little fella," Gant said. "Nap time."

Amos swayed on his feet, then decided that curling up and closing his eyes was a good idea. In another few seconds he was unconscious.

"Was—was that really necessary?" ZZ asked.

"Afraid it was," said Gant. He looked sad. "Poor Amos—he's been real upset ever since we got here. I thought he'd calm down once he got used to the environment, but after he had that drink—well, the last time he got hold of some alcohol he bit someone pretty bad. Couldn't risk it."

"So," said Keene, who'd recovered his composure and now appeared to be enjoying himself immensely, "your monkey's a mean drunk?"

Hana Kim shook her head. "I can't believe you let him drink at all!"

Gant chuckled. "I don't, I don't—but monkeys are sneaky, smart, and pick up bad habits real fast. Knew a chimp once that liked to steal cigarettes and smoke them; good enough at it that he acquired one helluva nicotine addiction, too."

"So," said Keene, "I had a monkey on my back with a monkey on his back?"

Gant got up from the table and retrieved the dart from where it had landed. "He's not that far gone—just likes the taste, I think."

Oscar nodded. "Don't we all . . ."

I told Caroline the crisis had passed, but I still needed her; I was worried what the anesthetic mixed with booze would do to the poor creature. She showed up a few minutes later, a little breathless, carrying her medical kit in one hand. Caroline was short, plump, and blond, and preferred jeans and T-shirts to scrubs or white coats. She checked Amos's breathing, quizzed Gant about the dosage and brand of tranquilizer, and asked how much the monkey had imbibed. When she was done, she frowned and said, "He should be fine, but I'm a little worried about the combination of drugs and alcohol. I'd like to keep him for observation overnight."

Gant shrugged. "Fine by me."

"Soup's on," said Oscar, who had never stirred from his seat. We all returned to the table, and the dinner itself commenced.

That was the most eventful part of the evening. The food was delicious, but I was too preoccupied to pay much attention to what I was actually eating. I spent the meal scrutinizing everyone without being obvious about it, doing more listening than talking. Keene was his usual witty self, Oscar sank into a sullen, alcoholic haze, Hana

Kim told a funny story about Olympic drug testing. Juan Estevez, while initially seeming nervous, gradually relaxed and opened up a little, talking about his research. ZZ held court, listening intently, asking relevant questions, occasionally telling a short anecdote of her own or using her tablet to call up some relevant information on the wall screens. Mr. Kwok didn't say much at all. He spent a lot of time staring at ZZ, though, and she didn't seem to mind.

When dinner was over, I heard a familiar voice in my head. *<Hey, Toots—learn anything interesting?>*

I glanced around, then saw a pair of yellow eyes shining at me through the window. I opened my mouth to answer, then shut it again and concentrated. *Um. Monkeys shouldn't drink.*

<There's a news flash. Anything else?>

Not so much.

ZZ rose from the table. "Well, this has been most delightful. Feel free to enjoy the pool as late as you like, or any of our other amenities. Don't let Oscar hustle you at snooker, though; even inebriated, he's quite capable of running the table. I believe he counts both Prince William and Mr. Springsteen among his victims."

"Willy still owes me a horse," Oscar said. "Never take a royal IOU."

"I'll see you all tomorrow," ZZ said.

"Uh—are you turning in already?" I blurted. "I mean, it's still early."

ZZ gave me an odd look. "Yes, it is. In fact, Mr. Kwok and I are going into town; a lovely little blues bar just opened up, and there's a local musician I want him to hear. I expect we'll be quite late."

Uh-oh. I couldn't exactly invite myself along, and there was no way either Tiny or Tango could keep tabs on them there. "Well . . . have fun," I said weakly.

"Oh, I'm sure we shall."

Everybody dispersed, though Keene tried to convince me to have a drink with him by the pool. "No thanks," I said. "I remember last time. You're a little too fond of skinny-dipping for my tastes."

He took my rebuff gracefully, and wandered off with Oscar in the direction of the billiards room. I went outside to let Tiny know what had transpired, and Tango joined us.

"I guess we go home," I told them. "I know ZZ. She likes cappuccino with her blues, and that means she'll keep Kwok up all night. In more ways than one."

[Your assessment is correct. While not in heat, her hormonal level was elevated.]

"You—you can *smell* that?"

[Of course.]

For some reason, I found that more disturbing than the telepathy, the shape-shifting, or the reincarnation. "Okay. Well, we can't hang around here all night, and we can't follow her. I say we go home, get a good night's sleep, and tackle this again tomorrow."

[I could stay and patrol.]

<No, you can't. How are you going to explain that responsible, trustworthy Foxtrot left you here overnight?>

[I'll stay hidden.]

Tango snorted. *<Right. Dogs don't do stealthy—they think the height of strategy is to charge forward in a pack, barking at the top of their lungs. If anyone should stay, it's me.>*

[Oh? And what are you going to do if there's an attempt on ZZ's life? Meow loudly? Scratch at a window?]

I sighed. "Guys. You're both right. Leaving either of you here makes no sense. If we're going to do this, we're gonna have to work as a team. And as the member of that team with a driver's license and house keys, I say we retreat for the night."

There was some more grumbling, but they couldn't argue with my logic. In the end, we all piled into the car, went home, and went to sleep.

It wasn't the alarm that woke me in the morning, however. It was the phone.

I was the second person Shondra Destry called.

The first had been 911.

Chapter Five

We drove right over, not even stopping for breakfast. I slammed to a halt in the front drive, right next to the police car and the ambulance that were already there. Tango leapt out of the car and sprinted for the bushes, while Tiny stuck close to my heels. I ran inside, almost knocking over Shondra.

"What—what happened?" I blurted out.

Shondra studied me gravely. "Paramedics are saying heart attack or possibly a stroke. Happened sometime in the night."

I swallowed. "I just—I just talked to her yesterday. She seemed fine."

Shondra nodded. "I know. But these things happen, sometimes out of the blue."

I shook my head. "Where is she?"

"ZZ's bedroom. She was working late, reorganizing the closet. Must have felt dizzy or tired and lay down on the bed—that's where she was found, by one of the other maids."

Maria Wong. I'd known her for years, and now she was

dead. I was sad and shocked, but also a little relieved it wasn't ZZ and more than a little guilty for the relief. I was confused, too; how could I have gotten the victim so wrong? And how on earth could Maria's death affect the graveyard?

But despite my conflicted feelings, I was still a professional—and I've always dealt with overpowering emotion by concentrating on the practical. Change what you can, accept the changes you can't. "Does ZZ know?"

"Nobody knows where she is. Victor brought her home last night, but nobody's seen her since." Victor Hausen was ZZ's driver. "She's not answering her cell."

"Check Kwok's room," I said. I sprinted up the stairs, Tiny right behind me. We passed the paramedics going the other way, their faces composed in the careful way of those who lost to death on a regular basis.

Sheriff Brower stood in the hall outside, the door to the bedroom open. He was in his sixties, with a pork-barrel belly and sparse white hair. He held up a hand when he saw me. "Sorry, Miss Lancaster. Can't allow you in there." Tiny stopped beside me, sniffing the air.

"Why not?"

"Someone died. That makes this a crime scene until the coroner signs off on it."

I'd only met Brower a few times before, but we'd never gotten along. He had the officious attitude of a small-town official who thought he should receive more respect than he got, and probably deserved less. We'd locked horns on zoning ordinances, noise complaints, and even traffic regulations, with most contests going to me. He may have been sheriff, but ZZ had a lot of pull with the town council.

"I thought it was natural causes."

Brower stuck out his chin. "Most likely. But that's for the coroner to decide."

I sighed. "All right. I'll be downstairs, letting the staff know. If you need to talk to anyone, we'll be in the kitchen."

I turned around and headed back the way I'd come, Tiny beside me. [Foxtrot? There's something you should know, concerning my abilities.]

"Hmmm? What's that?"

[Most canines have very sensitive noses, and can remember a wide array of scents. As a spirit, I have access to . . . well, a sort of canine library of aromas. The accumulated olfactory knowledge of all the dogs who have lived and died before me.]

I stopped on the second-floor landing. "That's amazing. But why are you bringing it up now?"

[Because—though I wasn't actually in the room, and both were very faint—there were traces of two very distinctive scents in that doorway. One I've smelled before. The other I know only from the library.]

He paused, and looked up at me seriously. [The stored scent is that of a powerful anesthetic. The other is that of a capuchin monkey.]

Tiny's revelation stunned me, but I didn't have the luxury of sitting down to process it; it was my job to handle crisis situations, and that's definitely what this was. The first thing I did was to call a meeting of the household staff, so everyone knew what was going on. Word had already spread, of course—we're a small, tightly knit community, more family than employees. There were a lot of tears, though I managed to keep mine in check for the moment. I told Consuela, the maid who'd found her, she could take the day off once she'd talked to the sheriff, but she refused.

"I don't know, I don't know," Consuela whispered, wiping her eyes. "So sad. I knocked and knocked, but no answer. I try the door, but it was locked. I try my key, but door locked from inside. Didn't make sense."

I frowned. "Why didn't it make sense?"

Consuela sniffed and looked away. "Because—because I know Ms. Zoransky not in there. Victor told me."

Victor Hausen was ZZ's driver. If anybody knew ZZ wasn't in her own bed, it was probably him; he would have driven her and Kwok to the club and then home again. Staff gossip being what it was, news of ZZ's latest fling—something not exactly uncommon—had disseminated quickly.

"Where is Victor, anyway?" I asked.

"I am here," said a gruff voice. I turned to see Victor striding in through the kitchen's back door, looking grim and Germanic—but that was generally what he looked like, anyway. Vic was tall, with a bony face and a severe haircut. He was wearing a gray coverall and wiping his hands with a greasy rag; he must have been working on one of ZZ's cars. "I was in the middle of changing the oil on the Porsche. I am sorry."

"That's okay," I said. "Consuela, is ZZ in Mr. Kwok's room?" Consuela hesitated, then nodded.

"If the door to ZZ's bedroom was locked," I asked, "how'd you get in?"

"I did it." Carl Jeffrey, our maintenance man, held up his hand. He was a potbellied man in his fifties, with a bristly gray crew cut. "Knew there had to be something wrong. Only one way in or out of that room, and Maria didn't wear no headphones while she was working." Carl shook his head. "Didn't put up with it from anyone else. Wouldn't do it herself. Knew something had to be wrong." He shook his head again, staring down at his feet. Carl and Maria hadn't always gotten along, but right now he looked like he was sorry for every harsh word he'd ever spoken to her.

"You did the right thing," I said gently. I knew Maria didn't carry her cell phone while she was working, either; she hated being interrupted, especially by one of ZZ's whims.

I rearranged the maids' schedules and called Maria's family. That was hard. Her husband sounded more disbelieving and angry than grief-stricken, as if I'd made a terrible mistake and now he had to fix things. That was just how some people reacted to news of a death; it was such a massive disruption that the mind refused to accept the facts at first, looking for any kind of alternative explanation that would allow things to go back to normal. When that proved impossible, the next step was usually searching for someone to blame. Maria's husband wouldn't have to look very hard, though—I was already blaming myself.

Then ZZ showed up.

She was devastated, of course. She was still dressed in last night's clubbing clothes—she couldn't exactly go into her room to change. Kwok wasn't with her. I gave her a big hug, and then she and I sat down at the dining room table with Shondra and Sheriff Brower. Tiny lay down at my feet. The table looked big and empty with only the four of us huddled at one end, its glossy expanse of polished wood reminding me of a casket; the flower arrangement in the middle only made it more funereal.

Though distraught, ZZ had a core of steel; she could make hard choices even while tears streamed down her face. She was already asking me about Maria's family, and telling me that she would pay for the burial and service.

"That's fine," said Brower, a hint of impatience in his voice. "Ms. Zoransky, I need you to answer a few questions."

"Ask," ZZ said, turning the full force of her stare at

Brower. A few flowers at the edge of the event wilted and died, but Brower was undaunted.

"I'd like to know why Mrs. Wong was in your room last night instead of you."

"She was reorganizing my closet."

"All night?"

"She was working late at my request. I was paying her overtime. And no, she shouldn't have been there all night—I didn't expect her to stay much past ten."

"And why weren't you in your own bed last night?"

ZZ gave him a cold smile. "I was. I own every bed in this house."

Brower frowned. "So you were in the house, but in another room?"

"Yes. How is this relevant to what happened to Maria?"

"Which room? And can you verify that you were there?"

"Oh. I see." ZZ's smile grew fangs—you could barely see them, but I knew they were there. "I was in the guest bedroom currently occupied by Jun Kwok. He can definitely verify I was there, since we didn't get much sleep."

Brower blinked. "You were—all night?"

"Having sex, yes. All night. Mr. Kwok has committed the entire Kama Sutra to memory; in fact, once you establish the time of death, I should be able to pinpoint exactly which sexual position we happened to be enjoying. Is that enough detail for you, or would you like me to take you by the hand and lead you there right now so you can sniff the sheets?"

She smiled again. The guy who operated the guillotine during the French Revolution would have worn that smile after an especially satisfying decapitation.

"Just calm down," Brower said. "I'm only doing my job."

"Oh? You get paid to harass people in the immediate aftermath of tragedy? What a *fine* occupation. Any children you have—well, those willing to admit they're related to you—must be *very* proud."

"That's uncalled for—"

"I can't believe I ever slept with you."

Okay, I admit it: My eyes bugged out a little. Shondra sighed and looked away.

"That's neither here nor there," Brower snapped. "It was a long time ago, and I doubt it's much occupied either of our minds since then. Fact is, Zelda, someone died. I have to make sure everything that led up to that death is recorded, because someone other than you or me might want to know. Maybe her husband, or her kids, or maybe just your insurance company. I know it's a damn nuisance and you're upset, but taking it out on me won't help *those* people, will it?"

ZZ narrowed her eyes, then nodded slowly. "You're right. I apologize. Let's start over."

Which they did. The details were pretty much what I'd already gathered: ZZ and Kwok left around eight PM, came back around three AM, had been together until then. Shondra reported nothing suspicious around the estate while she was working, and she'd been in her office until nine PM. The maid knocked on the door of ZZ's bedroom at seven this morning.

"Going to have to talk to the other guests, too," said Brower.

"They haven't been told yet," I said. "I'll go do that now, and send them down to you one by one, all right?" Brower told me that would be fine.

Juan Estevez answered his door fully dressed, his hair still wet from a shower. I had to pound on Keene's door while he muttered "G'way," in fluent hangover-speak. I finally opened the door, marched in, and told him the police were here—that at least got him to open his eyes.

"D'they have an arrest warrant?" he asked sleepily. His tousled, curly hair looked annoyingly adorable. "Hope not. Didn't pack my getting-arrested clothes."

"They're not here for you." I gave him a quick overview, told him he had twenty minutes to make himself presentable, and left before he could wake up enough to start peppering me with questions.

Kenny Gant wasn't in his room.

The last guest I woke was Hana Kim. I knocked on her door, got no answer, and tried the knob. Locked. I have a master key, so I pulled it out and used it. Maybe I should have tried knocking again, but after dealing with Keene I was feeling impatient.

I immediately saw why Hana hadn't heard me: She was wearing earbuds and hunched over an open laptop. I guess she caught some movement out of the corner of her eye, though, because the second I stepped in the room she slammed the laptop shut and whirled around in her chair. The expression on her face was pure panic—and was quickly replaced by a feigned calm when she realized who I was.

She reached up and pulled out the earbuds. "Foxtrot! Hi! Uh—I thought the door was locked."

Before she could switch gears and go from pretending to be glad to see me to pretending to be angry, I told her about the situation. She seemed genuinely shocked, but I wasn't sure that emotion was any more authentic than the others.

"That's awful," she said. "Is there going to be an investigation?"

That seemed like an odd thing to ask, but she was an Olympic athlete—paranoid levels of security were something she'd encountered before. "I don't know. The sheriff thinks it's probably natural causes." I wasn't so sure, myself. "Anyway, things might be a little chaotic today, but nothing you have to worry about. Come down for breakfast when you feel like it."

"Okay, thanks."

As I closed her door, I wondered what it was she was doing on her computer she was so determined to keep a secret. "Tiny?" I said softly. "Did you get a look at her laptop's screen before she slammed it shut?"

[Not really. A blur of colors, moving quickly—that was about it. She smelled of surprise, though.]

"That I got on my own. Let's go find Tango."

"Tango!" I called, hoping no one other than her was in earshot. Luckily, most of the staff were inside, either talking to Brower or waiting to.

<Over here, Toots.>

Tiny darted around the side of the house, and I followed. The grass was wet with more than dew; it had rained sometime last night, and pretty hard from the puddles I could see.

Tango sat at the base of a slender birch tree next to the house, staring up the trunk.

[Ah. Have we interrupted you in the process of obtaining breakfast, or are you studying the tree's feasibility as a scratching post?]

<Neither, genius. See that little open window up there, sitting on top of the big window? That's ZZ's bedroom, and the only window that opens.>

I don't know why I was surprised, but I was. "Good work, Tango. How do you know that?"

<I climbed up and looked, of course. Not hard for me, but almost impossible for a full-grown human—the tree barely reaches, and it's really skinny at the top.>

I looked up and studied the layout. "You're right. That window's awfully small, too; ZZ keeps it open for ventilation, but it would be a tight fit for just about anybody. Almost impossible to get up that high in the tree, too."

I paused. "But not impossible. Not for someone small, strong, and acrobatic . . ."

We examined the tree with Tango, but the rain had washed away any scents and there were no tracks visible in the wet grass. There was a concrete walkway that ran beside the house, though, and it wouldn't have been difficult to step from it to the tree.

Tiny let out a doggy sigh. [This is a waste of time. The killer is clearly the monkey.]

<What, the one they carried out on a pillow? He seemed pretty out of it, to me.>

[True. But I smelled monkey in ZZ's bedroom—as well as something else.]

Tiny didn't know the name of the chemical he'd caught a whiff of, just that it was a powerful anesthetic sometimes used by veterinarians. I thought he was just smelling whatever Gant had doped Amos with, but Tiny insisted it was something different. [The olfactory repository has two entries for that particular scent—the other one comes from a Russian military source.]

I didn't know what to make of that—but then, I didn't know what to make of the whole situation. "Guys? Did we totally mess up, here? Does Maria's death mean the graveyard is . . . well, dead? Or doomed, or whatever horrible thing is supposed to happen to it?"

[I don't know,] Tiny admitted. [I need to talk to my superiors.]

<I don't. No way the maid was the target. This is a case of wrong person, wrong place, wrong time. ZZ's still the one we need to protect—and the best way to do that is

to find out who tried to kill her and got a Wong number instead.>

I winced.

<*Too soon?*>

[It'd be painful no matter when you said it.]

<*Dogs. No appreciation for wordplay.*>

[Cats. No appreciation for decorum.]

"Human beings," I said. "No time for screwing around."

Our next stop was Caroline Durrell's office. She wasn't there, but we found her right next door in the medical clinic, along with Kenny Gant. They were both peering into a cage that held a small, sleeping monkey lying on a pillow.

"Foxtrot!" Caroline said as I came in. I'd left Tango and Tiny outside, beside the door. "I just heard about Maria. How are you doing?"

"I'm all right. A little shaken up, but not as bad as ZZ. How's your patient?"

"Still sawing logs," said Gant. He didn't seem concerned. "Told you he'd be fine. It's a damn shame about your maid, though."

"Thank you. Uh, Kenny—were you and Amos in ZZ's bedroom earlier?"

"Well, yes—we popped in on her yesterday when we first showed up, just to say hello. The little rascal didn't steal anything, did he?"

"No, no. I just—never mind, it's not important."

I turned back to Caroline before Gant could ask any other questions I couldn't answer. "So Amos was here all night, then?"

Caroline looked puzzled. "Of course. Where else would he be? I slept right there, on that cot." Caroline pointed to the corner of the room, where a small folding bed was set up. Caroline was used to being up all night with a sick animal, and wouldn't dream of leaving one alone.

"Okay, then," I said. "Just thought I'd drop by and make sure the little guy was all right." I ducked out with a smile and a wave.

<*I need to talk to that monkey,*> Tango announced.

"No, you don't. Amos was passed out all night—in fact, he's still snoozing."

<*Ha! You don't know monkeys like I do—they're conniving little SOBs. And you don't exactly need acting lessons to pretend to be asleep.*>

[How would you know? You've never *pretended* to be asleep in your life.]

"He was shot with a tranquilizer dart!"

<*Yeah? Loaded with what?*>

"Okay, I don't know exactly what was in the dart. But Caroline examined him *and* slept in the same room all night. So unless you're suggesting Caroline—*and* a trained monkey—are part of a plot to murder our head maid, your line of reasoning doesn't really go anywhere."

Cats are stubborn. I knew this. It just never occurred to me the trait might crop up as a problem while trying to solve a murder. <*You ever been to the circus? Monkeys can be trained. And maybe* you *trust this Caroline, but I never met a vet that didn't try to do horrible, horrible things to me the second after she gained my trust.*>

[She's got a point.]

"Okay, okay. You want to talk to Amos, fine—Caroline usually leaves a window open, so you can probably get in without my help. But the most you're going to find is a groggy capuchin who doesn't understand why a strange cat is interrogating him."

[And I believe "strange cat" is unnecessarily repetitive.]

<Yeah, and if dogs were cattle you'd be an oxymoron. Later.>

We left Tango there, while Tiny and I went back to the house. "So if ZZ confirms Gant and Amos were in her room earlier, it explains what you smelled."

[Not all of it. We have yet to identify the source of that second smell.]

"And you're sure it wasn't from the dart?"

Tiny snorted. [Positive. It would be like me asking if you'd confused a piece of classical music with a pop song.]

"Well, then—I guess we have to identify that particular aroma."

So I did what everyone does these days, when they have a vague question they need an answer for: I sat down at my desk and Googled it. Oddly enough, the terms *Russian military, anesthetic,* and *veterinary,* when combined and fired into the ether, produced a result almost instantly: carfentanil, one of the most powerful opiates in existence. Ten thousand times stronger than morphine, it was used almost exclusively as an animal tranquilizer for extremely large creatures like tigers and bears—or even elephants. During the 2002 hostage crisis in a Moscow theater, the Russian army supposedly used an aerosol version of the chemical to knock out both the terrorists and their captives; unfortunately, the gas was so potent that it killed at least 127 people.

"That has to be it," I said. "You're right, there's no way that could have been in the dart gun."

[Thank you for stating the obvious. Assuming we're looking at the murder weapon, what sort of physical symptoms does this chemical produce?]

"Respiratory distress. The person just stops breathing."

[Would that resemble a heart attack or stroke?]

"Beats me. I don't know what the victim of a fatal heart

attack or stroke looks like. Probably just a dead body—unless they actually clutch their chest as they die, like in the movies."

[So Maria Wong could have been poisoned by this drug.]

I looked away from the monitor and down at Tiny. "It's possible, I suppose. But only the medical examiner can find out for sure, and they have to run tests for that. I'm not sure they do those sorts of tests unless they're looking for something specific."

[Then we need to ensure those tests are done.]

I thought about that. Anonymous call to the coroner? Sure, but not from my own cell or even on the estate. Best to do it from a pay phone in town, which meant arranging a plausible excursion. I was probably overthinking things, but I had to be careful about covering my tracks—there was no way I could explain this in any rational fashion if I got caught.

I ran into town on a fairly regular basis, sometimes for personal errands, sometimes for business. A trip to the local florist to pick out some nice flowers for Maria's family was already on my to-do list; I could make a quick call while I was there.

Before I left, though, I thought I'd check in on Tango. While I didn't think her questioning of a semiconscious monkey would produce much in the way of results, I was a little worried about her. Gant seemed pretty quick to draw and fire that dart gun of his, and the last thing I wanted was a comatose kitty on my hands.

Turned out to not be a problem. When I walked out to my car, Tango was crouched underneath it. <*Hey, Toots. We should talk.*>

I glanced around, then opened the car door. "Get in."

She jumped up and made herself comfortable in the passenger seat. I put Tiny in the back, then got in and started the engine. "I'm headed into town—we'll talk on the way."

[Yes, we can't wait to hear what invaluable information you uncovered. I'm guessing it has something to do with the edibility of bananas.]

Tango was cleaning her front paw with an air of satisfaction. <*Oh, it was enlightening, all right. Not so much with the bananas, though. Kinda cliché, don't you think?*>

[I do think. Often. Sometimes I even have to think for two, when one of my associates seems intent on chasing phantoms down blind alleys—]

Tango rolled her eyes. <*Just shut up and listen, okay? The monkey was pretty out of it, but I got him talking. Nothing like a friendly ear when you're locked up, right? Anyway, I asked him about last night. He told me it was all kind of blurry, but it seemed like a pretty good shindig right up until the part where he got shot.*>

[Now, *there's* an earth-shattering observation.]

<*Oh, it gets better. See, the longer I talked to him, the more convinced I was that he was telling the truth. Capuchin's an interesting lingo; there's a certain kind of phrasing they use when they're making stuff up that's obvious to a non-native speaker, but they seem oblivious to it. Linguistic blind spot, you could call it.*>

I glanced at her. "Wow. That's impressive—but what does it tell us?"

[That she's wasted time talking to a hung-over primate.]

<*That wasn't the interesting part. See, I started asking Amos about the guy who shot him. Seems Gant likes to get the little guy drunk—thinks it's funny. In fact, the more he cuts up the more Gant seems to like it. And he's never, ever shot him with a tranq dart before.*>

I frowned, thinking back on what Gant had said at dinner. "Well, that doesn't contradict what he told us. He said

Amos likes the taste of booze and that he gets sort of wild once he's had it. That's pretty much the truth."

[But a very slanted version of it. A man who derives enjoyment from giving animals alcohol is ignorant at best, abusive at worst.]

I couldn't argue with that, but it didn't really fit with my image of the man. He was pleasant, charming, intelligent, and quite knowledgeable about the animals he used in his TV spots. Even the pet food he sold was ecologically friendly. ZZ usually had pretty good people radar, which was why he'd been invited back.

"Look, bottom line is that you got your information from a groggy monkey. He's not necessarily the most reliable or objective of witnesses. And . . ." I stopped myself, but it was too late.

<And what?>

"And . . . Capuchin isn't your first language. Maybe you misinterpreted something he said."

Boy, was that the wrong choice of words. I could almost feel Tango's icy glare on my face. When she finally spoke, it was with great formality. *<I believe you misspoke. Or, to put it another way, you made a mistake. You could even be said to be laboring under a misapprehension. These are all proper uses of the prefix* mis, *unlike your previous statement. I do not 'misinterpret.' I* interpret. *You see the difference?>*

"Yes," I said meekly.

<Good.>

We rode the rest of the way in silence.

Tiny, oddly enough, had nothing to add.

Chapter Six

I made the call from a pay phone outside the drugstore, leaving a message with the coroner's office and making sure the woman who answered the phone wrote down exactly what I said. I hung up as soon as she asked who I was, then quickly got back in the car and drove to the florist's shop. They knew me there, and were shocked to hear about Maria's death.

I picked up some cat food while I was in town, and a bagful of doggy treats. Tiny might not have to eat, but he certainly seemed to enjoy it. Tango didn't seem impressed by the brand I picked, but I got the impression she wouldn't have been impressed by an entire salmon served on a bed of catnip in her current mood.

"Okay," I said when we were back on the road. "New game plan. If Tango's right and ZZ is still the target, we have to keep her under constant surveillance. If Maria was the one who was supposed to die, we need new instructions."

[Agreed. In fact, we shouldn't have left ZZ alone.]

"I don't think the killer would strike again so soon, not while the police are there. If it was a mistake, he or she will bide their time and wait until things settle down before trying again. That'll give us an opportunity to catch or stop them—and once the police learn Maria was poisoned, they'll be doing the same thing."

[Perhaps. Brower didn't seem terribly competent to me.]

"You're not wrong. Tango and I will do a little more investigating, while you get in touch with your superiors. Uh, how exactly do you do that?"

[I'll have to visit the graveyard.]

I nodded. I knew that sooner or later I'd have to do the same, but I was in no hurry. "Something I've been meaning to ask you guys. The last time I was in the graveyard, I had an . . . unusual experience. Right after that, I started seeing things—ghosts, I guess. Animal ghosts.

"It's just that, well—I saw something in the graveyard, that first time, that kind of freaked me out." I hesitated. "It was big—like, SUV big. And made of out shadows. And sort of . . . crackling."

[It was on fire?]

"Not that kind of crackling. More like it was plugged in and short-circuiting."

<Sure. Giant, shadowy, electrical. We get those all the time.>

"You do? What is it?"

<Black-pelted Sasquatch Robot. Nasty piece of business.>

[Oh, that's mature.]

It was my turn to glare. "Guys, I'm serious. It was huge, I could only see it when I closed my eyes, and every time I did it was closer. Are you trying to tell me you have no idea what it was?"

[I'm sorry, Foxtrot. There are many entities on the spiritual planes; some of them are harmless, some are not. Whatever that was, it doesn't sound like anything I've ever heard of, other than—] He stopped abruptly.

"What?"

[Never mind. They haven't been seen in centuries, and they were rare before that.]

<Look, it was probably just a side effect of having your brainwaves suddenly tuned in to the supernatural channel. Hard on the old noggin. I remember the first time I recalled a past life—man, what a trip! Thought someone had slipped me some heavy-duty 'nip.>

"Come on, Tiny—finish your thought. What did you think it could be?" I glanced in the rearview mirror and saw him shake his head, which made it look a little like he was trying to dislodge a flea.

[My apologies again. We're simply not allowed to tell you certain things—there are rules.]

Rules. Sure, there were always rules, especially when it came to the supernatural—vampires couldn't go out in daylight, a leprechaun had to grant you three wishes if you caught him, ghost dogs couldn't reveal the secrets of the afterlife. "Okay, but—who makes these rules? The same ones that gave me the ability to see spectral wildlife?"

Tiny didn't reply, which was an answer anyway. Just not a very helpful one.

"All right, fine. When we get back, here's what we're going to do: I'll find ZZ, try to get her outside where Tango can watch her. Then Tiny and I will slip away to the graveyard, where I'll let him in and wait for him by the gate until he's done. Then we'll rejoin ZZ, and Tango can do a little spying."

<On who?>

"Whoever looks suspicious. The killer has to be nervous at this point, having tried and failed. He or she might tip their hand. Use your instincts—I'm guessing yours are a lot sharper than mine."

<*Well, yeah—but you're only human.*>

[Don't be a specieist, Tango.]

I sighed. "Work with me, guys. You don't want anything bad to happen to your graveyard, I don't want anybody else getting killed. We can do this."

I wished I were as confident as I sounded. But I was used to facing disaster with a easygoing smile and an optimistic approach—that was what I did for a living.

For now, anyway.

If there was a single mantra I had for my professional life, it was that things never went as planned. Planning was good, planning was essential, but so was the ability to improvise; whenever possible, you wanted a Plan B, C, and even D ready to pull out when events decided to suddenly veer away from your carefully laid-out itinerary and into oncoming traffic. Sometimes, those alternative plans were nothing more than the words TAP DANCE AND SMILE! scribbled on a napkin.

So I really wasn't surprised when, on our return, I couldn't find ZZ anywhere. She wasn't answering her phone, she wasn't in the house, no one seemed to know where she'd gone. Brower was still talking to the staff, but the body had been taken away by the coroner.

I didn't panic. "Tiny? Can you track her by scent?"

[If she's on foot, yes. If she drove, probably not.]

ZZ rarely drove, preferring to leave that to Victor. I checked the garage anyway, and none of her vehicles was missing. "Okay. Tango, you keep an eye on the house in case she comes back. Tiny, you and I are going to the graveyard—it's about the only place we haven't checked."

So we did. Tiny stopped at the threshold, sniffing the air, then abruptly shifted his shape to that of a sad-faced, droopy-eared hound—a bloodhound, I realized. [Better sense of smell.] He sniffed again. [Yes. She came this way, and recently. Shall we follow?]

I hesitated. I wasn't inside yet—in fact, I couldn't even *see* inside, because I was standing next to the open gate, behind the hedge. This was not an accident. "I—I don't know if I'm ready for that, yet. I mean, you and Tango are one thing, but a whole graveyard full of ghosts? Not to mention whatever that gigantic black shape was."

[I understand. But this is where ZZ went—]

Tiny abruptly leapt to one side, changing back into a golden retriever at the same time. [Never mind. The question has just become academic—here she comes now.]

I breathed a sigh of relief—but I still didn't get any closer to the entrance.

ZZ walked through a minute later, looking around. "Foxtrot! I didn't expect to find you here—I thought I saw a dog run through the gate a second ago, but it wasn't Tiny."

"Must have been. We're the only ones here."

She looked troubled. "I could have sworn it was—never mind. I didn't get a good look and it was only for a second, anyway. Hello, Tiny." She leaned down and petted him. Tiny wagged his tail and panted at her idiotically. "Going for one of your daily constitutionals? I've always thought they were a splendid idea, but I never seem to have time to do so myself. So I made the time, just now." She was smiling, but her eyes were sad.

"Thinking about Maria?"

"Yes. She was with me a long time—fifteen years, I believe. She used to be a meek little thing, until she figured out that I didn't want someone to push around; after that, she wasn't shy about expressing her opinion. She was smart and tough and hardworking, and I feel like I failed her."

"You didn't," I said quietly. "She told me once you were the biggest pain she'd ever worked for. When I asked why she didn't quit, she looked at me like I was crazy and said it was the best job she'd ever had."

"Oh, fantastic. So I was a slave driver, but she couldn't do any better?"

I shook my head. "No, no. I sort of implied the same thing to her, and Maria interrupted me and told me I didn't understand. 'Job is so good *because* of ZZ,' she said. 'Big pain in the ass, yes—also best boss I ever have. Pays me with more than money. Pays me with *respect*, too.' "

I saw ZZ's eyes fill with tears. "Thank you, Foxtrot. I needed to hear that. And I'm very, very glad to know she understood how I felt about her. She used to swear at me in Cantonese, did you know that? Surprised the hell out of her when I looked up what she'd been saying and taught myself a few choice phrases of my own. Well, surprised her for all of a second—then she replied with something else, just as vehement but more obscure. Took me a while to figure that one out, but I did. It became a little game between us. How many employer–employee relationships are based on cursing at each other?"

"All of them. Just not face-to-face."

She raised an eyebrow at me. "Except the one between you and me," I said with a grin. "Of course."

"Of course."

"Uh—I was wondering something. Did Kenny Gant take his monkey to see you when he first arrived?"

"Why, yes, he did. He introduced us—Amos seemed much calmer then. Why do you ask?"

This time I was prepared with an answer. "I was looking for that pair of earrings you said you'd lend me, but I couldn't find them. Gant mentioned Amos could be a bit of a thief, and I had this crazy idea maybe he took them."

"Oh, the little silver things? They should still be there. I'll check when—" Her face clouded up. "—well, when Brower's finished playing authority figure. I'm sure they're still there; Amos didn't get anywhere near my jewelry box."

Tiny whined at me in an impatient tone, and glanced from the open gate to me and back again. I wondered why he didn't just say whatever was on his mind—and then I understood. "I was just taking Tiny to—do his business," I said. "I thought the graveyard would be okay for that. And I'll clean up after him, obviously."

"Oh, yes, I'm sure that would be fine. It might be considered disrespectful in a human graveyard, but animals are more practical about such matters. I'll see you back at the house."

When she was gone, I said. "Good thinking. You don't actually have to go, do you?"

[I told you before—ectoplasmic beings don't require that sort of thing. I'll be back as soon as I can.] He dashed through the open gate, leaving me alone.

I stood there, shifting from foot to foot, consciously avoiding staring at the opening in the hedge. Then I started glancing in that direction, convinced that while I wasn't looking something would sneak through. I realized that I had no idea what the rules were; who said animal spirits couldn't just stroll right out of the graveyard? All the roadside ghosts I'd spotted the first night seemed pretty unrestricted. For all I knew, there were a dozen dead mice unliving under my bed.

I had just about worked myself up past nervousness and into actual dread when I felt a hand upon my shoulder.

And yes, I made a loud shrieking noise.

And spun around.

And punched someone in the face.

"I am *so* sorry," I said again.

Ben Montain did his best to smile. He had a handkerchief held to his face to stem the flow of blood from his nose. "S'ogay. Really. Shouldna snug up on you like dat."

I was about to launch into my third apology when, out of nowhere, it began to rain.

I looked around, thinking maybe a sprinkler in the graveyard was spraying us from the other side of the hedge, but no—it was a sun shower, one of those weird weather events when rain falls from a clear blue sky. Well, not completely clear, of course; I could see some dark clouds off to one side of the sun, though I hadn't noticed them before.

"I'm fine," Ben said, and took the cloth away from his nose. "It's stopped bleeding already, see?"

"Oh, good. Now all we have to worry about is getting wet—oh, and it's stopped, too."

"Yeah. Listen, I came by to ask you if you still wanted to do lunch. I mean, with Maria's death and everything, I understand if you're too busy—not that I *want* you to cancel, I just don't want to, you know—make things more complicated. Not that lunch is complicated, I got that all planned, but you might be, you know—"

"Ben. It's all right. I'll still have lunch with you. Are we doing this on the grounds, or going out?"

"I thought we'd have a picnic, actually."

"Sounds great, as long as the rain doesn't come back."

"Oh, don't worry about that. I have a real lucky streak when it comes to nice weather—I get invited to the weddings of people I barely know, just to guarantee a sunny day."

"Really? That's a useful skill to have. I'll keep it in mind if I ever get married."

He grinned and nodded, started to say something, then thought better of it and just waved as he walked away. I did my best not to laugh.

Tiny came trotting through the gate a moment later, looking worried.

"What's the word?" I asked.

[Maria's death was not the event we're here to prevent.]

"Good news and bad news, I guess. The graveyard's not doomed, but ZZ's still in danger. She is who we're supposed to be protecting, right?"

[I'm afraid I have no new information on that front.]

"Of course not." I forced a smile and added, "Well, let's go find ZZ before a piano falls on her or something."

The dark clouds that spritzed us earlier had disappeared, and it was shaping up to be a hot day. The air had that lovely summery smell to it that always makes me think of trees lying on the beach getting a tan, wearing sunglasses and dangling their roots in the surf, turning their leaves over every twenty minutes so they don't burn.

"All right, so we confirmed Gant's story," I said as we walked. "He and Amos were in ZZ's room. But we still don't know where the carfentanil came from, or who brought it."

[We should do a thorough search of the house, both of guest rooms and staff quarters. If there's any left, I can find it.]

"Okay, but that'll be tricky. I have a passkey to the guest rooms and I can think of a plausible excuse, but staff quarters will be harder."

[I'm sure you'll come up with something.]

But before I could, I heard Tango's familiar, raspy voice inside my head. <*Hey. How'd it go?*>

I told her. "Where are you, anyway? I can't see you."

<*I know. It's a cat thing—nobody sees us unless we want them to. It's almost like being invisible—*>

[You're over by the rhododendrons.]

<*—except for smart-ass dogs with noses bigger than their brains. Luckily for us, none of the guests seems to have brought one of those, which lets me watch them without them watching me.*>

"Anything to report?"

<*Not much. But I did find a handy tree outside Hana Kim's window—ideal for snooping. Not that she did anything interesting—she's staring at one of those little pizza-boxes-with-buttons you humans find so fascinating.*>

"A laptop. I don't suppose you could tell me what she was doing with it?"

<*Same thing all humans do. Tapping. Frankly, I don't see the attraction—though they are nice and warm to lie on.*>

[Tango—could you see the screen?]

<*There wasn't one. If the window was open, I could have jumped right in.*>

It took me a second to realize she was talking about an entirely different kind of screen. "No, Tiny meant the laptop's screen."

<*Oh, the shiny-colored part?*>

"That would be it, yes."

<*Squarish? Next to the part that gets tapped on?*>

"That's the one."

<*Then, no.*>

I was beginning to think Tango's occasional cluelessness had less to do with ignorance and more to do with baiting me—but she'd provided some useful information nonetheless. "That branch you were on—would it support the weight of a person the size of Hana Kim? And is her window big enough for her to climb through?"

Tango considered the questions. <*Yes to both, Toots.*>

"Then I think that—after we locate ZZ—our first stop on the guest list is Hana Kim."

I found ZZ talking to Shondra Destry in the foyer of the main entrance. Shondra gave me a cool but unreadable look when she saw me. "Foxtrot," she said. "I was just talking to ZZ about what happened to Maria."

Her voice had that careful quality people use when they're trying not to give away how they really feel. I'm used to it from harried wait staff or frustrated salespeople, but not from ZZ's security chief; it looked like she'd reevaluated our earlier conversation in light of Maria's death, and she didn't like the conclusions she was coming to.

"It's terrible," I said. "But we'll get through it. We're a family, right? We'll just have to stick together." I met her eyes as I said it, hoping she'd get the message.

After a moment, her expressionless gaze slid from me to ZZ. "Absolutely. I was just telling ZZ we need to update a few of our security procedures for safety's sake. Emergency protocols, evacuation routes, disaster preparation."

Normally, ZZ would brush off anything like that—but now she looked troubled. "I suppose. Will it take long?"

"Don't worry about that," said Shondra. "I'll walk you and the staff through them personally. We can all use a little togetherness today, right?"

I nodded, relieved. "Yes. Safety in numbers, and all that."

ZZ frowned. "What an odd thing to say, Foxtrot. We've

lost someone close to us, yes—but we're not under *siege,* dear."

"Sorry. Bad choice of words. But that's my point—numbers safe, words tricky. What with the sentence-making and the grammar and the proper mixing of the metaphors."

ZZ's frown softened. "Yes, dear. Do you want to take the rest of the day off?"

"What? No! I mean, no, I'm fine. And I think Shondra's right—I've been meaning to talk to you about exactly that thing. Shondra, you stick with ZZ until you've got everything updated, okay?"

"Oh, I'll stay closer than her own shadow."

"Great, great. Well, I've got to go—"

"Trot?" Shondra said, raising one eyebrow. "When you've got a minute, come see me, okay? We need to discuss a few details."

"Uh, yes, sure. Soon as I've got a minute, I promise."

I could feel Shondra's eyes on my back as Tiny and I climbed the stairs.

[She's going to be trouble.]

"Tell me something I don't know," I muttered. But with Shondra keeping an eye on ZZ, I had less to worry about.

Unless, of course, Shondra herself was the killer.

All right, so it wasn't the perfect solution. But it was the best I could do on short notice, and sometimes an all-or-nothing gamble was the only option you had. If Shondra was safe, so was ZZ; if not, then I'd just made a huge mistake. But I didn't think I had—Shondra, like all of us, was too devoted to her employer. And frankly, if Shondra had wanted to off her, she wouldn't have screwed it up. She's ex-military, trained to kill in a hundred different ways.

I found myself wondering, though, if she had any connections with the Russian army.

Standing outside Hana's door, I debated with myself whether or not I should just use my passkey without knocking. I might be able to catch a glimpse of whatever Hana was doing on her laptop that held so much of her time and attention. Ultimately, though, I couldn't justify it to myself; it was a gross violation of privacy that would be hard to explain away. I decided that knocking first, the same way I had previously, was still the best option.

But this time she called out, "Just a second!" and then opened the door. Behind her, the laptop was now closed. "Hey, Foxtrot. What's up?" There was no trace of guilt on her face or in her voice—either she hadn't been doing anything suspicious, or she was just a better actress when not caught unawares.

"It's about Maria—the woman who died?"

"Oh." Her eyes got a little wider.

"We're trying to figure out exactly when she—well, you know. So I'm going around and asking all the guests if maybe somebody heard something—a loud thump from upstairs, something like that."

"No . . . but I turn in pretty early. Asleep by nine, keeps me feeling fine." She said the last part almost in singsong, the way you'd repeat a slogan—or something drilled into you by a coach.

"So you didn't go downstairs for a drink of water, anything like that?"

"Nope. In my room, all night." She met my eyes squarely, which was something I found people did when they were trying hard to impress you with how honest they were.

I was searching for an excuse to invite myself into the room when Tiny shoved past my legs and through the doorway. Hana was wearing shorts, and Tiny began to lick her kneecap enthusiastically.

"Ha! That tickles!" She giggled and took a step backward. Tiny lunged into the room and jumped up on the bed, then sprawled on his back and started to do that ecstatic, rolling-around-and-writhing thing dogs usually reserved for places where something died and rotted.

"Tiny!" I said, trying to sound irritated. "That's no way to behave! Get down from there!"

[I shall, momentarily. Then I will make a circuit of the room and try to detect any traces of carfentanil.]

He leapt down on the far side of the bed. I stalked into the room, saying, "Bad dog! Come back here!"

[Please don't say that. I know you don't mean it, but it still hurts. Words have teeth, you know.]

I stopped as he began to nose his way around the room, an apology halfway to my lips. "I don't mean to step all over your feelings, Mr. Tiny, but you really need to come with me, okay? Or I'll have to put you on a leash."

[You don't own a leash. Almost done.]

"Aw, it's okay," said Hana. "He just wants to check things out. That's what dogs do, right? Come here, boy." She bent down and offered her hand. Tiny, after one last sniff at her luggage, came over and butted his head against it. She scratched him behind the ears, a big smile on her face.

[Ahh. Very pleasant. And no, I didn't find anything.]

"Okay, Tiny. That's enough. Let's go."

[Just a moment, please. This is most soothing.]

Well, he was still a dog, after all.

After a brief, blissed-out interlude, Tiny gave his head a reluctant shake and trotted out the door. "Bye," said Hana. "Come back and visit anytime!" I could tell she was talking to Tiny, and not me. I tried not to take it personally.

We continued on down the hall. "Nothing, huh?"

[No. But that simply means the chemical was not in her room. Even if she handled it, she could have worn gloves and disposed of them later.]

The next room on my list was Keene's. He wasn't in it, which made things much simpler—I just used my passkey. We were in there for a while; Tiny discovered traces of a wide variety of substances, most of which were illegal—but no carfentanil.

"Well, it seems Mr. Keene certainly has access to exotic forms of chemical recreation," I said. "And my research indicated that carfentanil, being an opiate, is sometimes used that way."

[That seems unlikely. Considering the drug's potency, wouldn't the chance of an overdose be rather high?]

"Oh, yeah, definitely. But that would increase the attraction for some, not reduce it. The risk factor is a big part of the thrill for certain kinds of people, and Keene's lifestyle is all about extremes. He's been in rehab more than once."

Tiny's ears suddenly perked up. [Foxtrot. Someone's coming!]

I froze, not sure what to do.

And then I heard the key slide into the lock.

Chapter Seven

My first impulse—crazy though it sounded—was to jump on the bed. Not under, on. I was pretty sure that image would cause whatever functioning brain cells Keene still possessed to seize up—long enough for me to talk my way out of there, anyway.

But I didn't do that, because it would be unprofessional, and give him the wrong idea. It wasn't that I didn't trust myself, or that I was afraid I might do something stupid, or anything like that. Really.

So instead, I just stood my ground and smiled when he walked in. He smiled back. He was wearing a bathing suit, his tangled black curls were wet, and he had a damp towel slung around his neck. "Hello, Trots. Is it my birthday? Give me half a mo and I'll change into something appropriate."

It took me a second to realize what he was talking about. "No, no. I'm just filling in for Maria. We're one maid short today, so . . ."

I hated to play the dead-body card, but it had the desired result: He nodded, the smile vanished, and he said, "Yeah. Sorry to hear about that. You two close?"

"I'm . . . not sure, actually. We worked together every day. We liked each other. We were work friends, I guess. Now I wish I'd known her better."

"Isn't that always the way? Too many friends of mine that I can say the same about. Don't know what you've got 'til it's gone, and all that."

"I suppose we've all lost people."

He gave his head a rueful shake. "Oh, I haven't lost 'em. Know exactly where they are, in most cases. Various plots or urns, usually—though I know one bloke had his ashes scattered from a plane. He could be a little hard to locate, if I needed to find him in a hurry."

"You don't think there's an afterlife, then?" I really shouldn't have asked that—his personal beliefs were just that, personal—but recent circumstances had altered my own views on the subject in ways I hadn't even had time to consider.

"How the hell should I know?" He grinned. "I'm sorry, that was rude. I just get tired, sometimes, of people asking me important questions as if my answers actually mattered. I sing songs and make an idiot of myself on stage—I don't have any deep insights on philosophy or economics or politics. I had one journo inquire as to whether I thought capitalism was still a viable model in a post-kleptocracy world-state. I told her sure, as long I didn't have to pay taxes on my private army of robot ninjas."

"I hear they're expensive to maintain."

"It's the dry-cleaning costs, really. You'd think black would be good at hiding stains, but all the really posh models of android bleed white. Bad design, that."

"I can see why it annoys you when people take you seriously."

He laughed. "Yeah, well. It's a bit of a reflex, now, innit? So, to answer your question seriously: I believe in

Mystery. Capital *M*. Things that are unknown, but powerful. Things that affect us, always have and always will, but can't be defined."

"Some things man is not meant to know?"

"That's not it, really. I don't think there's some cosmic list of facts we aren't allowed to read; more like there are some things that are—by their nature—unknowable. Quantum physics, right? You can know the velocity of a particle or its position, but you can't know both at the same time."

I raised my eyebrows at him. "Careful. That sounded awfully close to a serious statement. You'll ruin your reputation."

He shrugged. "You try to quote me, I'll sic my lawyers on you. I have them specially bred and fed a regular diet of paparazzi."

"They must have strong stomachs." I paused, wondering how to phrase the question I wanted to ask. "Sorry about waking you up this morning. I know you're a bit of a night owl."

"No worries. I turned in around three—early for me, really."

"Not much to do around here at three AM, I guess."

"No, but it's a lovely time to take a stroll in a graveyard. Which my gracious host has located right next door."

I stared at him. "You were in the graveyard? Last night?"

"Yeah. That a problem? ZZ told me it was open to the public."

"No, no, it's fine. I just wondered . . . I mean, why?"

"You kidding me? Inspiration, darling—rock and roll is all about sex and death. Not much sex in cemeteries, granted, but lots of Grim Reapery."

"But—they're all animals."

"Even better! Some of the epitaphs I read were brilliant: HERE LIES GERALD, MY HAMSTER. HE ATE MUM'S COOKING. Not sure how Mum feels about that, but Gerald's probably having regrets."

I had to admit I'd done the same, many times. "Yeah, there are some good ones. You out there long?"

"A few hours. Left when it started to get wet. Rain adds to the atmosphere, but I prefer my water in a pool or hot tub, not falling from the sky."

"Which reminds me." I held out my hand for his towel. "Let me take that. I'll go get you some fresh ones."

"Cheers."

I tried not to stare as he slipped it from around his neck and gave it to me. His body was long and lean and muscular, with Celtic knotwork tattoos around his upper arms and some sort of mythic beast on his chest. I resisted the urge to ask him about it; Tiny and I needed to make a graceful exit, the sooner the better.

"Hello, pup," Keene said, looking down. He got down on his haunches and regarded Tiny quizzically. "Enjoying your new digs? Quite the place, eh?"

To my surprise, Tiny answered. [It's an interesting and stimulating environment, that I can't deny.]

"Is that so?" said Keene. He nodded thoughtfully. "Well, then, I won't keep you. Off you go."

Tiny got up and trotted toward the still-open door. Keene straightened and said, "Ta."

I followed. When I'd closed the door behind me, I said, "He didn't—you didn't—I mean, that wasn't—"

[Don't worry, Foxtrot. You're the only one who can hear me talk. But some humans are quite attuned to other species; Keene seems to be one of them.]

Huh. Interesting. I'd never really thought of him as an animal person, but I guess it made sense; rock and roll was all about primal emotion, after all, not to mention animalistic behavior. Which was a very cerebral way of saying rock stars liked to party naked, wreck hotel rooms, and generally overdo everything that could be overdone. His room, though, while a little messy, was still in one piece. He'd worn a bathing suit in the pool. And so far, he'd limited his substance abuse mainly to alcohol, and even then hadn't approached Oscar's usual level of intoxication.

I didn't know what to make of his being in the graveyard. It fit with his personality, but it also meant he didn't have an alibi. Unless someone—or something—in the graveyard could verify his story. Which meant that, sooner or later, I needed to set foot in there myself.

I chose later, and continued on to Kenny Gant's room.

We got lucky once again, as he wasn't there. Tiny reported a definite aroma of capuchin, but no carfentanil. We quickly moved on to Juan Estevez's quarters, where we also had no luck.

"Well, that leaves Mr. Kwok," I said. "But he was with ZZ, so it makes no sense for him to be the killer."

[Could someone have slipped past Destry's safeguards?]

"I don't think so. She served in Iraq—she's knows how to maintain perimeter security. I guess someone could have been smuggled in, in a vehicle or something, but then they'd have to get out again without being detected."

[Which leaves someone who lives here.]

"Yeah." I sighed. "We'll check Kwok's room, and then we'll go talk to Oscar." I glanced at my watch. "He might be awake by then."

Kwok's room was another negative, so Tiny and I headed over to the guesthouse, on the other side of the estate. It was called the guesthouse, but Oscar had lived there long before ZZ ever hired me, and would probably still be there long after I was gone—unless, of course, he wound up in prison or fleeing extradition first.

There was a car I didn't recognize in the parking area beside the house, a bright yellow convertible with the top down. It had seen better days: It was at least a decade old, with a nasty dent in one door and a broken taillight that had been badly fixed with red plastic and duct tape. The interior upholstery was torn and faded, with a drift of fast-food wrappers in the backseat. A thick cushion lay on the driver's seat.

[Intriguing. This vehicle smells strongly of horses.]

"Tango?" I said aloud. "You around?"

No answer. I shrugged and knocked on the front door of the house.

Oscar answered it a moment later. Not only was he up, he was dressed and had company, the driver of the convertible visible behind him. I realized he had to be the driver at the same instant I understood what the cushion was for: The gentleman in question was extremely short. It was hard to tell exactly how short while he was seated, but I guessed his height at four feet or less.

"Good morning, Foxtrot," Oscar said. His eyes were a little bleary, but other than that he was his usual well-groomed self. Oscar's ethics might have been slippery, but his attention to appearance was quite strict. "How can I assist you today?"

"I was wondering if I might come in. I wanted to talk to you about Maria's death."

"I don't know if now is the right time to—"

"What was that?" the man at the table said. He had a high, nervous-sounding voice. "Somebody died? *Who* died?"

"A maid," Oscar said, turning his head. "Heart attack, I believe."

"You said the police were out here for a zoning violation!" the man said. He sounded even more agitated. "You didn't tell me someone died!"

"Can I come in?" I asked again.

Before Oscar had a chance to reply, Tiny pulled the same trick he had last time, slipping past me and then squeezing through the open doorway. In a second he was inside.

Oscar gave me a long-suffering look. "Oh, very well," he said. "Your canine companion seems to have made himself at home, you may as well do the same." He opened the door all the way and ushered me in with a resigned wave.

The guesthouse was only a single story, a large central living room with an adjoining dining area and small kitchen. The kitchen was all spotless stainless steel, the stove never used, the fridge mostly for wine and a few snacks. Oscar had never cooked a meal in his life—he probably couldn't even identify a can opener, let alone use one.

The room was neat and clean, of course, courtesy of the housecleaning staff, and decorated in designer furniture that looked both elegant and timeless; Oscar had picked it out himself, though ZZ was the one who'd paid for it. If he ever got really hard up for cash, he could always hock one of the chairs for a couple grand.

Oscar's guest, currently perched on a titanium stool that probably cost more than my last vacation, viewed me with suspicion and a touch of hostility. "Francis, this is Ms. Lancaster, ZZ's executive assistant, known to all and sundry as Foxtrot, for reasons that escape me. Foxtrot, this is Francis. He is rather excitable, as I'm sure you've noticed."

"Hey!" said Francis.

"No need to demonstrate, Foxtrot has a keen mind for details. Now, as I said before—how can I help you?"

This was going to be harder than questioning the guests; Oscar wasn't as smart as he thought he was, but he was still smarter than most. I'd given the matter some thought, and decided the best approach was to play on the fact that he'd just been busted for something else. "Oscar, where were you last night?" I kept my voice firm, my attitude stern.

"After dinner, you mean? Here, for the most part. Why?"

"What do you mean, for the most part?"

Normally Oscar wouldn't put up with this kind of questioning from me, but I had him on the defensive due to his recent gambling debacle. "I went out, briefly. Francis was kind enough to pick me up, as Mother's driver was occupied."

Well, at least he didn't try to drive drunk. "When did you get back?"

"Before ten, I'm sure. Francis dropped me off and I retired early."

I could check with Shondra on that—she had motion detectors and things that kept track of comings and goings. Now, if my partner did his part—

Right on cue, Tiny darted across the room, heading for the hallway that led to the bedroom. Unfortunately, that's where our luck ran out; the bedroom door was closed.

"Oh, good Lord," Oscar muttered. "Foxtrot, will you please control your companion? I don't understand why he's here in the first place—our zoo is already overstocked."

"I'll get him," Francis said. He bolted from his chair and down the hall ahead of me. Tiny was already there, sitting patiently. I was debating with myself how to get the door open without seeming obvious when Francis stepped between Tiny and the door.

Tiny growled.

Which didn't faze Francis at all. He just smiled and said, "You're gonna have to do better than that, pooch. I boss around bigger critters than you every day."

"Tiny, cut it out. C'mon, let's go." I thought he was probably bluffing—all that biting someone would do was screw up our investigation. After a second, Tiny reluctantly got to his feet and followed me back out into the main room.

"He needs a collar," Francis said. "And tags, for that matter."

[And you need a bath. You smell like a horse barn.]

"Bigger critters, huh?" I said to Francis. "You work with animals?"

Francis glanced at Oscar, who was currently adding vodka to a glass of tomato juice. "Yeah. I'm a jockey."

A jockey. Small, athletic, was on the grounds at around the right time—and worked with the kind of large animals that might occasionally require a powerful anesthetic.

"Is this your new role, Deidre?" Oscar said, stirring his drink with a small silver spoon. He only called me Deidre when he wanted to annoy me; it didn't, but I pretended it did. If he was going to be vindictive, I preferred it be verbal and face-to-face. "Are you my parole officer as well as my accountant? Am I going to be required to void my bladder into a cup for your inspection, too?"

"I suggested that to your mother," I said. "But she vetoed the idea—said any samples I collected would be a fire hazard."

He saluted me with his drink, then took a sip.

I glanced at Francis. He looked nervous again; something about the conversation was making him uneasy. "Have you talked to Sheriff Brower, yet?" I asked Oscar.

"No. Why should I?"

"Because he'll probably ask you the same questions I

just did. I don't care if you lie, but he might. That's why I came down here—to give you a heads up."

He studied me for a second, then gave me a grudging nod. "In that case, thank you. Not that I have anything to hide."

"Of course not. Come on, Tiny." I headed for the door. "Nice to meet you, Francis."

"Yeah, likewise."

I let myself out, Tiny in tow. "That could've gone better," I said quietly once the door was shut.

[We can always come back later. For now, he remains a viable suspect.]

"Along with everyone else. About the only two people we've ruled out are ZZ herself and Mr. Kwok."

[We haven't talked to Juan Estevez or Kenny Gant yet.]

"Or the staff."

The sun was high and hot enough now that I was glad the path back to the main house was shaded. The green of the lawn seemed too bright, like it was being illuminated from underneath.

[Oscar's companion seemed ill at ease.]

"Yeah, he did. Oscar didn't, but he's slippery; he could, with great sincerity, warn you about the dangers of pickpockets while lifting your wallet."

[Deception is a universal trait. Most species eventually discover its usefulness in mating, hunting, or evading predators—but yours is the only one that practices self-deception.]

"Oh, we excel at that. For instance, right now I'm trying to convince myself that I don't really need to question every single member of the staff and search the entire estate."

[You don't. You just need to find out which staff members were actually on the grounds last night, which I'm sure Shondra can help you with. I can conduct a thorough outdoor search without you, and your passkey should get us into any staff quarters. It's still a large job, but—]

"But I don't need to set actual foot in the graveyard."

He gave me a doggy look, one of those quick, sideways glances complete with raised doggy eyebrow. [Well. Perhaps not immediately.]

I waved my hand. "No, no. I'm good at a lot of things, but lying to myself isn't one of them. If nothing else, maybe I can clear Keene—that'll drop our suspect pool by one."

[Interesting that you would choose him to eliminate as a suspect.]

"What's that mean?"

[Nothing.]

"Choice has nothing to do with it. It's just the logical way to proceed."

[Of course. Very sensible.]

"Scentsible? Great. Not only do I have a partner who can use his nose to check my hormone levels, he makes bad puns about it."

Tiny stopped and looked up at me seriously. [Foxtrot. Let's get two things straight, shall we? First, I regard any information I might acquire via my sense of smell concerning your emotional state to be private, and therefore not to be commented on. Second, dogs do not pun.]

"Really?"

[Really. Most of us are quite literal. You don't know how many times I've had to explain the concept of "irony" when another dog learns my name. It's quite tiresome.]

"I'll bet. If you hate it so much, why do you keep it? Or is that one of the rules you can't explain?"

He didn't say anything for a moment, just walked alongside me, panting in the heat. When he did speak, he sounded thoughtful. [No, it's not that. I can choose to be called something different, if I wish. I keep it to honor the one who gave it to me.]

"You must miss them."

We were close to the house now, and Tiny stopped again. This time he sat down and studied me intently. [No, Foxtrot. I don't miss her at all.]

I stared down at him and frowned. "I'm sorry, did I say something wrong? I'm sorry if did—"

[That's not it. When I talked to my superiors, I was given clearance to share additional information with you. But you can't tell anyone else; that's very important. Do you promise to keep what I'm about to tell you confidential?]

I didn't hesitate. "Yes, of course. What is it?"

[I don't miss my former owner because I just saw her.]

"I'm not following."

[She's dead, Foxtrot. Just like me.]

It took me a second to understand the implications. "So you're saying . . . oh. *Oh.*"

I'm not stupid, all right? But I hadn't had a moment to really sit down and think about all this supernatural stuff, or what it ultimately meant. Maybe a religious person wouldn't think any of this was unusual, and the fact that animals have their own little afterlives wouldn't be much of a shock.

But Tiny was talking about *people*.

I was an agnostic. I was pretty sure there was something else going on in the universe that mankind hadn't quite figured out yet—I just didn't know what it *was*.

Now I did. Sort of.

There was an afterlife. People went on. My grandparents, my aunt Gillian, all the people who ever lived and breathed and died before I was ever born—they were still *somewhere*. Weren't they?

Maybe this all sounded obvious, but it wasn't to me.

My whole view of the world—of everything—had just changed. I felt a little dizzy, and put a hand against a nearby tree to steady myself.

[Are you all right? Do you need to sit down?]

"I'm fine," I managed. "Wow. I feel really stupid and incredibly enlightened, all at the same time."

[It's a lot to take in, I know.]

"Can—can I ask you a few questions?"

[It's best if you don't. I'll tell you what I can, how about that?]

"Sure. Go ahead." I braced myself, both physically and mentally. The tree felt real and solid under my palm.

[Try to imagine the graveyard like a train station—]

<*Okay, that's enough of that.*> Tango's voice sounded vaguely irritated.

"Where are you?" I said, glancing around.

<*Wrong direction, Toots.*>

I looked up. A black-and-white face looked back at me from a branch ten feet above. <*I was just going to listen, but I can't let this go on.*>

[I assure you, I have the proper approval—]

<*Yeah, yeah. I got no doubt you've dotted all the* t*'s and crossed all the* i*'s. It's your explanation that needs work. A train station? Please. Don't listen to him, Toots—it's all about* love.>

"Love?"

<*That's right, love. It's a universal force, binds everything together. Especially souls.*>

[I was getting to that. I just wanted to her to envision the physical structure first—]

Tango snorted. <*Physical structure, my litter box. Look, here's the thing: If you loved an animal, and that animal loved you, then death won't keep you apart. Death loses, love wins. It's that simple.*>

I was expecting a snarky retort from Tiny, but he said

nothing for a moment. When he did reply, it was simply to say, [Well put. Continue.]

<*Gee, thanks ever so. This is why the graveyard's so important, Toots; it's . . .* >

[Yes?]

<*A transfer point. Where animal souls can leave their afterlife, and enter the human one.*>

[Heading from one place to another. Travelers crossing paths in a large central area.]

<*Okay, okay, it's sort of like a train station. Only there are no trains, just doorways. That's what the graves are.*>

I was beginning to see how it worked. "So if, say, the spirit of a hamster wanted to visit her previous owner, she could scamper out of one grave, across the graveyard, and dive into another?"

[Not just any graves. The grave of a hamster, and the grave of a human being.]

"The cremains," I murmured. Plenty of pet owners wanted to be interred with their pets, but state regulations wouldn't allow anything but cremated remains—so while Fido got an actual burial, his owner would be perched on the headstone in a brass urn. "Does it work the other way around, too? Can human spirits visit the animal afterlives?"

<*'Fraid not.*>

"That doesn't seem fair."

[It's not a question of fairness, Foxtrot; it's a matter of respect. In life, pets are forced to live in the human world. In death, don't they deserve their own?]

I had to admit he had a point. "I suppose they do. But what happens if the owner isn't dead yet? Or gets buried someplace else?"

Tango jumped down from her perch, then stretched and yawned. <*Well, if one is alive and the other is dead, guess which one has to hang around and wait? But it doesn't matter where either one is buried—well, except maybe for human ghosts. They seem to have a real obsession with sticking to one place—*>

[Tango,] Tiny said warningly.

<*Yeah, yeah. All I'm saying is that animal spirits don't tie themselves down like that. We don't haunt places, Toots.*> She started cleaning one claw with her teeth. <*We haunt people.*>

It was starting to sink in. "So the graveyard—it doesn't just hold the ghosts of the animals that are buried there, any more than Grand Central Station houses all the people that pass through it. Ghosts come there from other places."

[Exactly so.]

"Are there . . . a lot of them?"

Tiny looked at Tango. Tango stared off into the distance and didn't say anything.

[You'll see,] said Tiny.

But I didn't, not right away. First I had to track down Juan Estevez and Kenny Gant and quiz them about where they were, talk to the rest of the household staff and find an excuse to have Tiny roam through their quarters—while remembering to periodically check in on ZZ and make sure she was still breathing—and do my regular job. But before she slipped away, Tango asked to speak with me privately for a moment, which is to say she told Tiny to get lost while she and I talked. He told me he would see me in a few minutes and lay down to wait.

Tango and I wandered over to the gardens. Just me and my dead cat . . .

We stopped by a bench and I sat down. Tango studied me without saying anything. That was something I'd seen her do many times over many years, but her keeping quiet was suddenly in the abnormal column.

"What?" I said.

<*You don't trust me anymore.*> She sounded sad.

"What? That's not true. I *do* trust you—both of you. Honestly, you seem to have a better grasp of the situation than I do—"

<*I don't mean you think I'm incompetent. I mean you don't* trust *me, Foxtrot.*>

"I don't know why you'd say—"

<*You haven't touched me since that first time, on your stoop. Not one scritch or stroke, let alone a cuddle. Are you that afraid of me?*>

I stared at her and didn't reply.

<*Maybe you don't believe I am who I say? Or are you still having trouble believing I'm real?*>

"That's not it. Not exactly." I hesitated, trying to put into words what I barely understood myself. "I don't think this is all in my head. But you . . ."

<*I what?*>

"You *died*," I said quietly. "I loved you so much. I knew you my whole life and then you left. I know it wasn't your choice but it *hurt*, more than anything else *ever*. I guess I'm still a little angry about that. And then to find out that not only are you *not* really gone but that you had whole other *lives* I don't know anything about? I feel more than just angry about that—I feel *betrayed*." I realized that tears were running down my face and tried to cover them by turning my head and making a joke. "What, you couldn't pick up a phone?"

Tango jumped up beside me. <*Toots, listen to me. You know that there are certain things I'm not allowed to talk about. So listen carefully, because I'm about to tell you something no cat is ever supposed to say.*>

I turned back to face her. Very carefully, she put one soft paw very gently on the back of my hand, the first physical contact we'd had since I found her on my doorstep. She looked, unblinking, into my eyes.

<*I'm sorry.*>

And then something broke inside me and I was laughing and crying and she didn't say anything else, just leapt into my arms and my *cat* was back, she *wasn't* dead, she was alive and warm and furry and oh God, I'd missed her *so much*. And she let me hold her tight and cry and tell her that I loved her, and she didn't need to use words to answer me. Her purr did that, just like it always had, a strong, steady vibration straight from her heart to my own.

And when we were done she said, <That's *better,*> and told me she was off to prowl around and generally watch for any suspicious behavior. And I let her go without complaining, because I knew—really, truly knew for the first time—that she would come back.

Always.

Shondra was as good as her word: Every time I saw ZZ, her security chief was right there by her side. Staff quarters turned out to be easier than I figured—only ZZ's cook and driver lived on site, the driver in an apartment over the garage and Ben Montain in three rooms behind the kitchen. Ben was in town picking up some groceries, so that took care of one problem. I felt more than a little guilty snooping through Ben's stuff, though, so all I did was let Tiny in and then out again. He didn't find anything.

Victor lived over the garage, but that didn't mean his place was small; ZZ had quite a few cars, and the building that housed them was spacious. Tiny and I checked the garage itself first, and found Victor waxing the red Rolls-Royce that was ZZ's favorite ride.

"Hello, Victor," I said.

"Ms. Lancaster," he said. He was one of the few people who didn't call me Foxtrot; there was a certain stiffness to Victor's personality that wouldn't relax if you dunked it in a hot tub full of white wine and Valium. He was extremely good at his job, though, ferociously punctual, and as loyal to ZZ as a cult member to a messiah. I found him just a touch scary, but I got the feeling most people did.

"Sorry to interrupt," I said, "but I was wondering if I could talk to you for a minute about what happened to Maria."

Victor stopped his waxing, dropped the rag on the hood, and straightened up. He didn't quite snap to attention, but the effect was the same. "Yes. What do you want to know?'

"You drove ZZ and Mr. Kwok into town last night, right?"

"Yes. They stayed until very late—quarter to three."

I nodded. Official operating times didn't mean much to ZZ—she was perfectly willing to wave a thousand dollars under someone's nose to convince them to stay open longer, and add a few hundred more at the end if she'd enjoyed herself. Her tipping habits had become the stuff of legend in local restaurants. "Then you drove them home?"

"Yes." He hesitated, then added, "We made one stop."

"At?"

"The all-night drugstore."

I grinned. ZZ kept her own supplies well stocked, but she was gracious enough to inquire about her partner's preference when it came to brand. "I see. So you got back here shortly after three AM?"

"Yes."

"Did you see anyone when you got here? Notice any lights on, hear anyone?"

He frowned. "No, ma'am. I let Ms. Zoransky and Mr.

Kwok off at the front door, then drove into the garage and parked. I went straight upstairs and to bed."

"What time were you up and around this morning?"

"I rose at eight o'clock."

"Anyone else up at that hour?"

"I did notice Ms. Kim going for a jog through the gardens."

Part of her workout routine, no doubt. "Okay, thanks. Oh, and I was wondering if you could do me a favor? ZZ was going to donate a few books to the local library, and asked me if you could drop them off. There's a box in the foyer."

"Certainly. I'll put them in the trunk and do it this afternoon."

"Would you mind going now? The library's expecting them before noon."

"Of course. I'll take one of the other cars." He sealed the jar of wax and put it on a shelf, then turned and strode off.

[I think you may have offended him,] Tiny observed.

"Don't worry about it. As far as Victor is concerned, *brusque* is just another word for 'efficient.' "

I waited until Victor came back with the box I'd set out, put it in the trunk, and drove off. Once he was out of sight, Tiny and I went up the exterior stairs to the door of his apartment and I used my key to let us in.

The place was just as neat and orderly as Victor himself: modern, streamlined Ikea furniture, a metal bookshelf holding volumes on history, aircraft, and architecture—Victor wasn't much for fiction, it seemed—and a gleaming, mostly stainless-steel kitchen.

"Go to it," I said.

Tiny nosed his way around the room. While he worked, I took a closer look at the bookshelf. Down at one end, on the very bottom, there were three books that looked out of place: Not only were they thinner and smaller than the reference material, they were considerably more worn—and very familiar looking.

"No *way,*" I said. I pulled all three out and stared at the covers, one by one. "Tiny! You won't believe this!"

[What is it?] He trotted up to me eagerly.

"Look! *The Mystery of the Stuttering Parrot*! *The Mystery of the Singing Serpent*! And *The Mystery of the Headless Horse*!"

He sniffed at them. [All I smell is old paper and ancient ink.]

"Then your nose isn't as sharp as you think. What you're smelling is my childhood—you're smelling adventure and teamwork and mysterious beggars with scars on their faces. These are Three Investigators books!"

He gave the barest puzzled whine. [I fail to see the significance. Enlighten me, please.]

"With pleasure. The Three Investigators are Jupiter Jones, Pete Crenshaw, and Bob Andrews. They're adolescent boys who live in Hollywood, have the coolest headquarters ever, and solve mysteries with the help of Alfred Hitchcock."

[Oddly, I don't feel enlightened at all.]

I brandished the books at him excitedly. "I've been looking for these three titles forever! I *collect* them!"

[Ah. It all becomes clear to me now.]

"Really? Well, I'm still confused. I mean, I guess I could have mentioned it to Victor—wait, I think I remember talking to him about it a few weeks ago. I mentioned that the books were really popular in Germany, and asked if he was familiar with them. He said he wasn't. So why would he lie?"

[I think perhaps I can clear this up. On what day were you born?]

"Day of the week, you mean? A Monday, I think."

[No, I mean the date.]

"June fifth. Why?"

[Because it means you have a birthday coming up.]

I blinked in surprise. Really? Cold, precise Victor went to the trouble of finding me three books I didn't own based on a single conversation I barely remembered? "Okay, but—how did he know I don't have these?"

[He strikes me as being the straightforward type. He probably asked someone.]

ZZ, of course. She knew how much I liked the series, and she was very resourceful when it came to planning surprises. Of course, I was usually the first resource she turned to . . . but she was entirely capable of enlisting others. Shondra, maybe, or Avery. For all I knew, a crack team of elite ninjas broke into my house while I was at work and cataloged my entire library.

"This is thoughtful," I said. "Maybe a little *too* thoughtful. I mean, Victor's okay, but I don't find him attractive. I hope this isn't some kind of romantic gesture."

[I hate to interrupt your musings on a potential future mate, but do you think we could get back to looking for the murder weapon?]

I carefully replaced all three books. "Sorry. Back to work, right."

Tiny finished his circuit of the living room, then went through the kitchen, the bathroom, and two neatly organized closets. We left the bedroom for last.

It was just as clean and tidy as the rest of the house, but he'd left some magazines on the floor next to the bed. When I got a better look at them, I realized my fears about a possible infatuation were groundless. Victor's tastes seemed to run more to large hairy men than medium-sized, mostly hairless women. Tiny didn't comment on the magazines, and neither did I, though I now felt both embarrassed and ashamed at invading Victor's privacy. Sure, I was trying to catch a killer, but I wasn't a big fan of the ends justifying the means. Next time I'd let Tiny do the snooping and keep my nosiness to a minimum.

Mental note: Make sure Victor gets a BIG bonus this Christmas. And maybe the biggest, glossiest coffee-table book on the history of aircraft architecture I can find.

When we'd subjected the entire place to Tiny's olfactory glands, he pronounced it carfentanil-free. I made sure everything was exactly where we'd found it—Victor, I thought, would notice the slightest deviation—and then left, locking the door behind us.

[Who's next?] Tiny asked.

"Juan Estevez."

We found him in the library, reading a novel. "Shouldn't you be out by the pool?" I said. "I can get someone to bring you some refreshments."

"I don't like the sun. Too much risk of melanoma." He kept his eyes on his book.

"We've got plenty of shade, too. And sunscreen, if you forgot to bring any. We can even supply swimming trunks."

He finally put his book down and looked up at me from the divan he was perched on. "Thank you, but I prefer it in here. The air-conditioning is nice, and it's quiet. Mostly."

I deliberately misinterpreted his statement. "Yes, that was quite an uproar earlier, wasn't it? I'm so sorry about all the disruption."

His expression softened. "Not a problem. I was sorry to hear about your maid."

"Thank you."

"These things happen, I guess."

"You didn't—hear anything, did you? Your room is directly below ZZ's bedroom, and the sheriff is trying to establish a time of death."

"Hear anything? Like what?"

"Well—a loud thump, maybe?"

He winced as he realized what I was talking about. "Oh. No, nothing like that. But I was exhausted last night—I turned in around eleven and slept straight through. If it was any later than that, I wouldn't have heard a thing."

"Okay, then. Sorry to have bothered you." I left him to his book.

Only Kenny Gant was left to talk to, and we'd already searched his room. "Tiny, I think you should get started searching the grounds—it's a big job, and the sooner we begin the better. I'm going to have a little chat with Mr. Gant and then we'll reconvene. Meet me under that tree Tango was perched in earlier, okay?"

[I shall.]

He trotted off, and I went in search of Kenny Gant.

Which, it turned out, was harder to do than I'd thought. Being an animal person, he'd been quite intrigued by our collection the last time he was here, so I checked there first. No sign of him, or of Caroline. He wasn't out by the pool, or on the tennis courts or in the gardens. I could have simply called him, but I wanted to talk to him face-to-face.

I checked the house last. I'd just been there, but it was a large place and I could easily have missed him. I decided to start with his room.

The door was ajar. I knocked gently and then pushed it open. "Kenny? I was wondering if you had a minute—"

The door swung out of the way. Kenny Gant wasn't there, but someone else was.

Caroline Durell. And she had a gun in her hands.

Chapter Eight

I froze.

Caroline and I stared at each other for a second.

Then she grinned and said, "Foxtrot, hi! I'm just returning Kenny's monkey, but he's not here. I was about to call you and see if you could track him down for me."

I glanced down at her feet. Amos screeched at me from the carrier he was locked in, apparently fully recovered. "Oh. How'd you get in? And what's with the firearm?"

"The door was unlocked. And I was returning the pistol, too—Kenny forgot it at the clinic."

I realized it was the same dart gun Kenny had shot Amos with last night. "I'm sorry, but I don't know where he is, either. I guess I'd better give him a shout."

I pulled out my phone and looked up his number, then called. "Hi, Kenny? Foxtrot. Caroline's brought your monkey back and he's all bright-eyed and bushy-tailed."

"Oh, that's wonderful," he replied. I could hear traffic noise in the background; apparently he was no longer on the grounds. "I'm in town, at a garage. Came in to get a little something to cheer Amos up and ran into some engine trouble."

"Nothing serious, I hope?"

"Well, I hope not. They did ask to weigh my wallet before giving me an estimate, though. Is that bad?"

I laughed. "Not if your wallet was planning on going on a diet. Do you need a ride back?"

"No, they're giving me a loaner. I'll be back in around twenty minutes or so. Do you mind keeping an eye on Amos until I return?"

"No, not at all. I'll see you then." I hung up.

Tiny had edged forward and sniffed in the direction of the gun. [Negative,] he reported. [A commonly used animal tranquilizer, much less potent than what we're looking for.]

So close, and yet so far. I hesitated, then said, "That pistol seems a lot smaller than what I've seen on TV—aren't rifles usually used to fire tranquilizer darts?"

"Yes, the pistol's a little unusual. But tranqs are generally only needed to put big animals to sleep, and you want to do that from a safe distance. Rifles are much more accurate at range."

"And they probably need more sleepy juice, too—I mean, it must take a pretty big dart for a buffalo."

"It's not really a question of the dart's size, more one of the drug's potency. Large animals get a super-concentrated opiate, knocks them right out."

"A super-concentrated opiate? That sounds dangerous—do you keep any of it around? You know, for our larger animals?"

She studied me for a second, and pushed her glasses up with one finger before answering. "Yes, I do. It's under lock and key, of course, and I don't advertise the fact that we have it. But any veterinarian dealing with large exotics like ours needs it on hand."

So the carfentanil could have come from the estate's own supply—but according to Caroline, only she had access. I leaned down and peered at Amos. He looked back at me with wide, intelligent eyes. "I wonder what monkey Heaven is like," I murmured. "Lots of bananas, I guess."

"Not necessarily," said Caroline. "Capuchins are omnivores, like humans—they'll eat just about anything. Fruit, yes, but also seeds, nuts, buds, frogs—even crabs."

"Crabs?"

"Sure. They use rocks to smash open the shells."

"That sounds pretty violent. I mean, aren't capuchins used as helper monkeys?"

Caroline tossed the gun down on the bed. "Oh, absolutely—they're the smartest of the New World monkeys, they're adaptable, they're easy to feed and train. But I wouldn't really characterize them as violent—from a species point of view, they're lovers, not fighters. Polyamorous and polygamous. Frankly, a rambunctious monkey is more likely to attempt mating with something than wrecking it."

"Or in Amos's case, guzzling it."

"There's a reason for the saying *Monkey see, monkey do.* As fellow primates, they're very good at imitating our behavior—good and bad. Stealing the occasional gulp of booze is hardly the worst animal habit I've come across."

"Actually it's two—theft and substance abuse. No wonder Oscar and him seemed to hit it off."

She sighed. "Well, I don't know about the theft, but Oscar's pretty good at hitting the bottle and spending money. Which, by the way, is another behavior it turns out capuchins have an affinity for."

"What, spending money? You're kidding."

"Exaggerating, maybe. They did a study where they taught capuchins they could choose between getting food directly, or get a token instead—a token they could then trade in for larger amounts of food. Money, in other words. They picked it up surprisingly quickly."

"Money handling, drinking, stealing . . . so *that's* how stockbrokers evolved."

"Afraid so. Along with the rest of us . . ."

I didn't feel comfortable waiting for Kenny Gant in his own room, so Caroline and I went downstairs with Amos. She asked me how Tiny and I were getting along and I told her the truth, which was just fine.

"Where is he, anyway?" she asked. "I thought you two were inseparable."

"He's—being taken for a walk," I said. "I'm trying to get him used to other people."

"Oh? Well, you can leave him with me anytime you want. He seems like a real sweetheart."

"Deal. I'm sure he'd love to hang out at your digs for a while."

Caroline left me and the monkey in the living room while she returned to her animals. I hoped Tiny was keeping out of sight . . . and then I remembered that he could alter his appearance. Caroline might see him, but she wouldn't recognize him.

I sat there and collected my thoughts. I'd done just about all the searching I could, and turned up nothing. I'd talked to all the guests. What I needed to do now was look at Shondra's video logs so I could see if anyone had arrived or left the estate last night.

The last time anyone had seen or talked to Maria had been a little after seven PM when she'd taken a break for a quick meal in the kitchen. Consuela had knocked on ZZ's bedroom door at seven AM. Sometime in those twelve hours Maria had died, and I wouldn't be able to narrow that window down any more until—

I dug out my phone, looked up the number of the county coroner's office, and punched it in. I had to deal with an assistant first—a different one from the first time I'd called—but I was good at that; it was what I did on a regular basis. Whether you called them receptionists, executive assistants, secretaries, or even interns, it was these people—people just like me—who actually ran things. I understood how this system worked, and in fact had invented a martial art I called chat-fu to deal with it.

It broke down something like this: We began with the greeting ritual. I established a friendly but professional tone. First strike: I gave her my name. It got inside her professional detachment and she responded with her own. Point to me.

We circled, warily. I feinted with a harmless question and she answered automatically, lowering her guard further. I segued effortlessly into small talk, a whirl of movements meant to occupy her attention and shift her stance from combative to receptive.

I made her laugh. I offered sympathy for how hard her job was and apologized for taking up her time. Her impatience for getting me off the phone was tempered by the fact that she now liked me. When I finally got around to what I wanted, I phrased it in such a way that it was me and her against our respective bosses, neither of whom understood or appreciated how much we did for them. In this particular case I made it all about the insurance, which was always a convenient catchall to obtain all sorts of esoteric information. She consulted a file and told me that the initial estimate of the time of death, according to the state of rigor mortis the body was found in, was between 10 PM and 5 AM.

I thanked her and hung up. Down to seven hours—not ideal, but better.

Kenny Gant strolled in a few minutes later. "Ah, there

he is," he said, bending down to peer into Amos's crate. "Naughty monkey. From now on you need to wear your collar." He produced a short leash and collar from his pocket, and when he opened the crate's door Amos meekly let him put it on. "Good boy."

The monkey scampered out of the crate and onto Kenny's shoulder. "I think I should keep him in my room until we leave. Excuse me."

"All right. Take it easy, little guy."

When they'd left, I got up myself and went upstairs. I found Shondra and ZZ in Shondra's office, ZZ looking a little impatient. She brightened when I came in, and said, "Foxtrot! Be a dear and take over, will you? Shondra should really be going over these changes with you."

Shondra looked annoyed. "But I still need your approval before I implement—"

"Just clear it with Foxtrot, all right? She can bring me up to speed later. Right now I'm going downstairs and getting Ben to make me a snack—I'm famished."

With that, she practically leapt out of her chair and through the door. I stared at the ZZ-shaped afterimage she'd left behind and chuckled. "I wondered how long that would last."

Shondra grunted. "You want to take a turn guarding her, or do I have to bring in outside help?"

"Guarding? So you *do* think we have something to worry about?"

"I'm always worried. But you've given something specific to worry *about,* which notches things up." Her voice was as hard and flat as a sidewalk. "And that means I require facts, Foxtrot. Not vague warnings followed by a visit from the coroner's office."

"I swear, Shondra, I just had a bad feeling. Intuition. Or don't you believe in that sort of thing?"

"Oh, I believe in it. You see combat, you learn to trust

your gut or you don't survive. But what my gut is telling me right now is that you know more than you're letting on."

I swallowed. "I can see how it might look that way. But it wasn't Maria I had a bad feeling about—it was ZZ. And I still do."

"Okay. Let's say you do. Let's say that feeling is accurate, and something bad is going to happen to our mutual employer. In that case, how do you explain what happened to Maria?" Her face was grim. "Coincidence? Or are you suggesting this house is under some kind of curse? Because I'm going to have a hard time believing either of those explanations."

"You're right." I met her eyes calmly. "Neither of those explanations makes any sense. What does make sense is that someone tried to hurt ZZ, and got Maria instead."

"Really."

"Really."

Shondra shook her head. "The authorities are saying it was natural causes."

"No, Brower was saying that, and he's hardly an authority on anything. Maybe I'm wrong, but—what if wasn't a heart attack?"

"The door was locked, Trot. From the inside."

"There was a window. Not locked. Someone could have gotten in and out that way."

She looked skeptical. "Those windows are tiny. Who's your suspect, a ten-year-old kid?"

"I'm just saying it's possible, all right? Think about it."

Her eyes narrowed. "The Kim girl?"

"I'm not accusing anyone. But I think the smart move is to treat this like Maria *was* attacked—and then try to eliminate as many potential suspects as we can."

She gave me a grudging nod. "No harm in that, I suppose, as long as you're not talking about interrogating ZZ's guests. She wouldn't stand for that, and neither would they."

"Interrogating? Of course not . . ."

I told her about my call to the coroner's office and the possible time of death. "We need to find out if any of the guests left the grounds between seven PM and five AM."

"I'll check the video logs."

She tapped away at her keyboard, and the bank of monitors on the far wall blinked and began to scroll through footage of the previous evening. Shondra had all the entrances and exits to the grounds covered, as well as concealed cameras that kept an eye on virtually every inch of the high walls around the estate.

"Here's ZZ and Kwok leaving at eight seventeen PM," Shondra said. One of the monitors showed ZZ's red Rolls-Royce driving through the main gate. "And here's them coming back at three oh four AM."

"They left together after dinner," I said. "Maria would still have been alive when the meal started."

"The only other person was this guy." She tapped a key and one of the screens froze on the image of a yellow convertible. "He showed up around eight thirty and picked up Oscar. They came back around ten, he dropped Oscar off, then left."

"His name's Francis." I told her about the conversation I had with Oscar.

"So he's a possibility." Shondra studied the screen, her eyes narrowed. "You think he could fit through that window?"

"I do. But the time between him arriving and he and Oscar leaving is even shorter than he is—I'm not sure it's enough time to climb a tree, clamber through a window, commit a murder, and then return."

"If he didn't do it, that leaves Oscar himself, one of the

guests, or one of the live-in staff. Can you think of any reason Ben or Victor would want to harm Maria?"

"No."

Shondra nodded. "How about Oscar? Or any of the guests?"

"No," I said again. "But like I said—what if Maria was an accident? What if ZZ was supposed to be the target?"

"Well, that would at least give us a motive—Oscar has a few million reasons to hope his mother stumbles into an early grave. But I don't see him as a killer, do you?"

"Not really," I admitted. "But ZZ's made other enemies. You know how outspoken she is, especially online."

Shondra leaned back in her chair. "Yeah, her and everybody else. If you could find a way to turn all the rage that pours through the Internet into an energy source, you could power the whole damn world."

"One of those people might be Juan Estevez," I said. "ZZ seems to think he's developing weapons for the military." I told her about the quadracopter and ZZ's accusation. "Estevez seemed rattled, but ZZ backed off over dinner and he relaxed."

"That doesn't sound like her."

"Oh, I've seen her do it before—softening him up for the kill. She'll save the coup de grâce for later, when his guard is down. More entertaining. Remember that senator from last year?"

Shondra grinned. "How could I forget? He stormed out of here in the middle of dinner."

"Closer to the beginning, actually—halfway through the soup. Real shame, too."

"You didn't think he deserved what she did to him?"

"Oh, he deserved it, all right. But I figured he'd last until the main course; I lost five bucks betting on the pool. She peaked early."

"Happens to the best of us." Shondra drummed her fingers on her desk. "Okay, one of Oscar's sketchy friends, one limber guest, and one nervous one. Is that it?"

I didn't see how I could mention the carfentanil, at least not until the coroner confirmed it. "Uh, I think so. For now."

"I'll do some checking. And we'll both keep an eye on ZZ."

I stood up. "Agreed. I'll take the next shift, and then you can spell me, all right?"

"Sure. Just give me a call or text me."

I left Shondra's office and went downstairs, intending to catch up with ZZ in the dining room—but I didn't make it there.

I was halfway down the main staircase when I saw the turtle.

It was big—its shell maybe three feet across—glowing a luminescent blue-green, and floating in midair. It had flippers instead of feet, and was doing slow, patient laps around the chandelier. It glided past level with my eyes, dignified yet graceful, and met my astonished gaze with a calm and knowing stare. Behind it, the sparkle of high-end cut crystal seemed cheap and gaudy.

I was supposed to follow it. I knew that the second our eyes met, just as I knew it wasn't a demand but an invitation. It swooped lazily toward the front door and passed right through it.

I managed to stumble down the rest of the steps without breaking my neck. When I got outside it was waiting for me, still in motion, describing slow circles over the driveway. Even though the sun overhead was bright in a cloudless sky, the light emanating from the creature seemed just as deep, just as vivid. It was the aquamarine of a tropical ocean, the rippling, mysterious light that filters through the warm waters of a South Seas lagoon. I couldn't take my eyes off it, and I didn't want to; it was one of the most beautiful things I'd ever seen.

Then the arc of its flight gently curved. Toward the graveyard.

I followed.

I'm all about the planning. But as I've said before, sometimes plans fall apart. And sometimes they go so far off the rails that Plans B, C, and D are no longer an option, either. When that happens you have to jettison all your expectations, roll with the punches, and keep your eyes wide open; information is the only weapon you have, and the more you know the faster you can implement damage control when there's a lull in the battle.

None of which prepared me for tagging along behind a flying, spectral sea turtle in a state of semiconscious bliss.

It wasn't hypnosis, exactly. I didn't feel like I was being forced to do anything. It was more like chasing the world's shiniest, most delicious carrot, something made of chocolate imported from Heaven and wrapped in foil of purest gold. It led me around the house, into a narrow passage between the beach cabana and the hedge, and down to the gate.

It executed a careful loop at the entrance, came back around and met my eyes once more. I didn't know what it was trying to communicate this time, though; maybe it was giving me a chance to change my mind and turn back. Then it disappeared, over the gate.

I stepped forward, put my hand on the latch. The gate was an old wooden thing, high enough that I couldn't look over it. More like a door than a gate, really.

I steeled myself, and pulled it open.

The graveyard looked the same as it always did. Gravestones scattered in uneven rows, statuary and marble roofs jutting up here and there. The turtle was nowhere in sight.

I took a deep breath, and stepped over the threshold.

I don't know what I expected. Lines of animals patiently waiting their turn, like commuters at a bus stop? The crazy bustling chaos of Grand Central Station, with animal ghosts milling around like extras in a remake of Noah's Ark? I honestly had no clue.

What I saw—at least at first—was nothing. Nothing but the graveyard itself, under the hot sun. Maybe all the action happened at night—

Then one of the graves opened.

I don't mean literally—there was no actual door or gate involved. It was more like a camouflaged eye opening in the ground itself, a hidden eyelid pulling back to reveal an oval of white beneath. A sleek head poked out of that oval and peered around; I thought it was a gopher at first, but then recognized it as a ferret. It had the same sort of phantasmal glow to it the turtle had, but golden-hued instead of blue-green.

The ghost ferret scurried out of the grave, looked around curiously, then humped its way toward the nearest grave with an urn mounted on it. When it got there, another eye opened in the ground, and the ferret bounded through. The eye closed. I wondered who was there to meet it on the other side.

I walked up to the first grave and peered at it. It had a small headstone with the name SNARKY inscribed on it, and an elegantly carved picture of a ferret above that. Snarky had lived and died over thirty years ago, but his grave was apparently now a portal to wherever ferrets went when they passed on.

I was examining the grave with the urn on it when I heard someone cough.

I looked behind me. A large white bird with dark eyes was perched about ten feet away, on the arm of a stone cross. I realized after a second that, despite the color, it was a crow.

"Uh—hi," I said.

"Uh-huh," the crow replied. It didn't sound impressed. It stared at me in that intent, speculative way crows have, as if they're trying to decide which bits of you they'd eat first if they found you dead in a ditch. "So you're her."

"I'm . . . me, yes." I hesitated, not sure how to proceed. I hadn't expected to be doing this without Tango or Tiny around. "And who are you, exactly?"

"Name's Eli." The crow's voice was a raspy croak. "You gonna tell me your name, or do I have to make one up?"

"Foxtrot. Everyone calls me Foxtrot."

"Hmmm. You don't look much like a fox."

"That's because I'm not."

"Good. I don't like foxes."

"Did you see a turtle fly by a minute ago? I was sort of following him." The second the words left my mouth, I felt both ridiculous and a sense of déjà vu. At least I wasn't chasing a white rabbit with a pocketwatch.

"Yeah, that was Ambrose. He enjoys the occasional outing, which is why I sent him."

"*You* sent him?"

"That's right. I thought we should meet."

"Um—why?"

Eli cocked his head to the side. "Because I'm your opposite number. Well, technically old Coop is my opposite number, but seeing as how he's an acid casualty who likes to smoke a big doobie before hopping on his riding mower and pretending he's doing laps at the Indianapolis Five Hundred, and you're the newly appointed human liaison to the most important mystic nexus in a thousand-mile radius, I thought you were the higher priority."

I'm pretty quick on the uptake. "You're the caretaker for this place."

"In a manner of speaking. I keep an eye on things."

"For?"

"The ones in charge. And no, I can't talk about them."

"What a surprise." I glanced around and smiled casually, but I was also thinking furiously.

I've had a lot of jobs. I've worked for large corporations and celebrities and small, family-run businesses. I've gotten coffee, cut deals, hired people and fired people. And no matter what the position was called or what I was actually supposed to be doing, one thing never changed: office politics. I learned strategies long ago for dealing with such things, and I understood exactly what Eli was doing and why. He was establishing the pecking order.

Rule the First: When meeting a new co-worker, never let the conversation turn into a job interview. Information is power, and if you let them grill you, you not only gave them too much ammunition to use later, you put them in a position of power right off the bat.

But you also didn't want to make enemies—well, not right away, anyway. So you didn't counterattack, or get too defensive. You took control early, and deflected rather than meeting any questions head-on.

"What an awesome responsibility you have," I said. "Have you been doing it a long time?"

"Compared with what? How long you've been on the job?"

Aha. A worthy opponent.

"No kidding. Whoever's in charge, I have to wonder what they were thinking picking me." Rule the Second: Everybody—whether they'd admit it or not—resented the boss. Get your co-worker to admit that and it was you and them against the Powers That Be.

"So you don't think you're up to it?" he said.

"Well, I just don't know. You're the expert—what *does* it take to do this job?"

Rule the Third: A little subtle acknowledgment of their power was okay—it mollified them and prompted them to respond with an acknowledgment of yours. And asking for someone's advice was always a good strategy—suddenly they were invested in you succeeding.

"*Your* job?" Eli said. He took two short hops, from the end of the stone cross to the center. "Hmmm. I was hoping you'd know."

"What?"

"Yeah. See, my job is pretty simple—I watch, and I report. Nothing to it. But you—you're supposed to protect this place from some unknown threat? I gotta tell you, I have no idea how you're going to manage *that*."

"It's not completely unknown. I've already figured out that it probably involves a murder—"

"Probably?"

"Well, yeah—"

"A murder of who?"

Of crows, I thought darkly. This was rapidly spinning out of control. "Of the graveyard's owner."

"Ah. And who, exactly, do you think *owns* a mystical nexus?"

"I misspoke," I said carefully. "The person who legally owns the land the graveyard is on. Strictly in human terms, of course."

"By the way, we call this place the Great Crossroads, not the graveyard. So you're going to murder this person?"

"No! I'm going to *prevent* her death."

"Really? Well, good for you. Now I understand why you were chosen."

I shouldn't ask this, I really shouldn't. "Which is?"

"If you want to protect a place full of dead things, just

send someone who can *prevent* death. Makes the whole life–death process irrelevant, doesn't it?"

"That's not—"

"Try to stay humble, though. I mean, sure, beating death is impressive, but you wouldn't want to give the impression that everyone who *didn't* is some kind of failure." He looked from side to side, his gaze taking in all the graves that surrounded us. "Just sayin'."

I sighed. A worthy opponent? He just kicked my ass. "*Terrific* advice," I managed. "Anything else?"

"A few things come to mind, but I'd like to stay focused. You mind me asking *how* you're going to prevent this death?"

"My colleagues and I are keeping her under guard. And we're doing our best to figure out who the killer is."

"Wait. You don't even know *who* the killer is?"

"Not . . . yet."

"Well, that could be a problem."

"You think?"

"It's just my opinion."

Okay, this guy was used to being finessed. Time to switch tactics. "Look, we both want the same thing—to protect this place. I'm doing what I can with what I've been given. Do you have anything to offer *besides* your opinion?"

"I just might. Follow me." He launched himself off the cross with another hop, extending his wings so he could glide to the next headstone. I walked briskly after him, head up, back straight. If you're going to follow someone, always do your best to look like you've chosen to do so, not like you're being led.

We made our way up a rise, then stopped at the top, Eli perching on a small statue of a horse.

What I saw below astonished me.

Chapter Nine

On the other side of the rise, the graves were denser, closer together. And very, very busy.

Animal spirits of every kind bounded, flew, scampered, galloped, and scurried from grave to grave. There were ghosts continually popping out of those eye-like portals and just as continually jumping into other ones. The ones they were coming in by were all over the place, while the ones they were using to leave were fewer and always had a sealed cremains urn on them.

We just stood and watched for a while. The ghosts all had that internal glow Ambrose and the ferret had, but in a huge variety of colors: From the deep, burnished red-gold of an Irish setter's fur to the silvery glitter of scales, it was like an animated, luminescent rainbow. Even animals that were mainly black seemed to be illuminated, somehow. While all sorts of pets were represented, four groups dominated: cats, dogs, birds, and fish. The fish swam through the air as if it were water, darting this way and that, glinting in the sun, the bright markings on many of them now glowing like actual neon. Tropically plumed parrots, budgies, and songbirds swooped and dove through the air, and below them a tangle of dogs and cats darted among the gray headstones and white marble monuments.

But *tangle* wasn't the right word. It looked like a mass of confusion at first, but my eyes adjusted after a moment and started to identify patterns. The dogs seemed to move in packs of their own breed, like clusters of tourists all dressed the same; I followed some bulldogs as each one stumped out of a portal, then waited patiently at graveside for the rest of his fellows to join him. When they were all gathered, they moved in a waddling bunch to an urn-mounted grave and vanished into it.

The cats were another matter entirely. Their movements were much more chaotic, some of them jumping from headstone to headstone, others dashing between the graves.

"As you can see," Eli said, "I have a few responsibilities of my own."

"It's *amazing,*" I breathed.

"Yes, it is. Your people have a name for it: They call it the Rainbow Bridge. Notice anything strange about how the animals are acting?"

I studied the tableau below me. "No fights," I said after a moment. None of the animals was paying any particular attention to any species other than their own; there was no aggression, no displays of dominance, not even any butt-sniffing. The dogs were ignoring the cats, the cats were ignoring the birds, the birds were ignoring the fish. "They're all behaving—"

"Civilized? Nope, that ain't it. They all lived domesticated lives, true, but they're still animals at heart. No, there's another, simpler reason they're all getting along. See, even though each of them now lives in their own special Paradise, they all—every one of them—are rushing to go somewhere else. Someplace better than Paradise. You know what makes it better?"

"Love," I said. I could feel tears stinging my eyes, trying to get out.

"Yeah. They're going to be reunited with someone they love, with someone who loves them. In the face of that, who's got time to pick a fight or stop for a snack? Who would even want to?"

Not me, I wanted to say, but didn't. I was afraid I'd start crying if I tried to talk.

"What's driving them is the most powerful force in the universe; it's the force that created this place. It's worth protecting, don'tcha think?"

I understood why Eli had brought me here. It's one thing to get drafted; it's another thing to know—really know, deep inside yourself—what you're fighting for.

And now I did.

"All right," I said. "I understand. I do."

"Good," he rasped. "Now—what can I do for you?"

"There's a few questions I need to ask—mundane ones, I promise. Will you answer them?"

"If I can."

"There's a person who claims he was here, in the—the Crossroads, last night. Can you confirm that?"

"Would if I could. But I don't really take that much notice of the still-breathing, two-legged types—no offense."

"How about the . . . commuters? Any chance one of them might have seen something?"

Eli chuckled. It sounded like gravel rattling inside an old tin can. "Nah, they're pretty focused on other things. But one of the prowlers might have."

"Prowlers? What are those?"

"Restless spirits. Animal souls caught between the worlds, not ready to move on. A lot of them are drawn to this place—they're kinda like vagrants that hang out at bus stations, you know? Never actually get on a bus, but they like to use the facilities."

"Facilities? I thought spirits didn't have those kinds of needs."

He gave his head a single shake, his white beak whipping back and forth. "They don't. I'm talking about deeper needs—that feeling of being connected to others of your own kind. Even if all you do is watch them."

"So they're lonely."

"Lonely ain't exactly right. Some animals are loners by nature; they don't need much in the way of companionship. Sometimes they come here because they're confused. They don't know they're dead, or they know but refuse to admit it."

Great. Mentally confused vagrants—or, put another way, crazy street people. "What kind of animals are we talking about, here? Stray dogs and feral cats?"

"Sometimes. But mostly you get the in-betweeners—creatures that weren't quite wild, but didn't have anyone really love them in life, either. Animals raised in captivity, mostly."

I was trying to figure out who might fit that description, and got an image of a huge herd of pigs and cows. They were being ridden by chickens. "Livestock, you mean?"

"No, they get routed through a different place entirely. What we get here is a little more rarefied—animals from zoos, circuses, aquariums."

"That doesn't say much for those places."

"It's not as bad as it sounds. These days, only a small percentage of exotic animal owners mistreat them—but it used to be much higher. And souls have been gathering here for over a hundred years . . ."

I thought about that. "Any chance one of them might talk to me?"

"Maybe. But I'd be careful—not all of them are friendly. Normally that wouldn't be a problem for someone who still has a pulse, but you're different now; your new abilities come at a price. You can be affected by spirits, even attacked."

That, of course, immediately reminded me of the shadowy bulk I'd encountered before. "Anything really big? Like *T. rex* size, made out of solid blackness?"

Eli cocked his head skeptically. "Not a lot of *T. rexes* in zoos, Foxtrot. And none of the big dinos were black, anyway. In fact, some of them had plumage that was downright showy."

I didn't know if he was pulling my leg or not. "I don't know what it was. But it was the first thing I saw here that I couldn't explain, and it was big and dark and giving off flashes of light."

It was hard to read the expression on a crow's face, but I could have sworn Eli frowned. "It might just have been your eyesight adjusting to its new range, trying to focus on things it couldn't see before. Flickering lights, dark spots."

"Maybe." I never had vision problems that seemed to be chasing me, but Eli was right: It could just have been a trick of my new vision, a temporary side effect. In any case, it didn't seem to be affecting me now. "One last thing. Any tips on who I start with, and where I can find them?"

Eli considered this, then gestured with one white wing. "Try Two-Notch. She does a regular circuit of the entire Crossroads, and this time of day she's probably near the outer edge. She might talk to you."

"Thanks. How will I know her?"

"I don't think you'll have any problem with that."

I knew a competency test when I heard one. I shrugged, thanked him again, and set off down the slope, keeping parallel to all the activity. In a minute I'd reached the bottom of the rise, where a path curved around another gentle hill. I followed it, and in another minute all the rushing ghosts were out of sight again.

This part of the graveyard was newer, the graves more orderly, the paths forming a grid. I saw a lone skunk scurry out of a grave site, eye me benignly, then totter off across the grass. I wrinkled my nose; seems my eyes weren't the only sense that had been spiritually amplified.

The perimeter fence was made of sturdy, chest-high iron. When I reached it I debated whether to go left or right. I decided the best choice was neither—if Two-Notch did a regular patrol, then it was smarter to let her come to me rather than risk going in the wrong direction.

So I waited. I sat down on the grass with my back to the fence and kept my eyes open. Every now and then one of the plots would spit out a rabbit or a hamster, and it would bound away over the hill. I even saw a snake that must have been six feet long slither out of a grave, which sounds creepy but wasn't; its scales gleamed with an amazing aurora of color, startling reds and vivid greens and unearthly blues, all so deep and rich that the pattern seemed three-dimensional, not two. It was like watching a fluid neon sign come to life.

And then I saw something approaching me, from the left. It was ten feet off the ground, moving about as fast as Ambrose had but in a different way. Ambrose had reminded me of a spaceship gliding serenely through interstellar space; the newcomer was more like a cruise missile looking for somewhere to detonate. It was at least eight feet long from head to tail, and in life must have weighed several hundred pounds.

It was a shark.

It passed right over my head without stopping, its underbelly a gleaming white. I couldn't see its dorsal fin, but I was willing to bet it had two gashes on it. "Hey!" I called out. "Two-Notch!"

It kept on going. I stood up and tried again, this time thinking the name as hard as I could. *Two-Notch! Shark! I'm talking to you!*

It banked sharply to the left. Circled and came back around at me. I suddenly wondered just how good an idea this actually was—I swear I could hear the *Jaws* theme playing in the background as the shark got closer and closer.

But it veered away at the last second, settling into an orbit twenty or so feet in diameter and four feet over my head. It—no, *she*—tilted to one side so she could get a good look at me, studying me dispassionately with one large, black eye.

what does food want

The voice I heard in my head was a little unnerving, like a woman with an accent I couldn't identify speaking in a very loud whisper. And it took me a second to realize that Two-Notch wasn't posing a riddle—she was referring to me as a potential snack.

"I'm not food," I said firmly. Sometimes you need to clarify things right up front. "And what I want is to ask you a few questions. That okay with you?"

Two-Notch continued to circle and stare. *i will answer*

It was taking an act of will not to spin around as we talked, but that would just make me dizzy. I forced myself to stay in one spot and tracked her with my eyes when I could. "My name is Foxtrot. I was wondering if you saw another human here, in this graveyard, last night."

Notch kept moving. Was she a little lower this time? *i am waiting for question*

I thought back and realized I hadn't actually asked one. "Did you see another human being in the graveyard last night?"

don't know what graveyard is

"This place. Everything inside the boundary of this

fence." I gestured with my hand at the fence, which was about six feet away.

not fence~~glass~~wall of aquarium

Oh. For the first time, I noticed that Notch's orbit took her right up to the fence but not beyond it. She believed that—just like when she was alive—there was an invisible barrier there.

Because she didn't know she was dead.

"All right," I said carefully. "Let me rephrase that. Did you see any other human beings last night in the aquarium?"

yes

"What did they look like?"

not female~~black kelp on head~~lower half like seal

A man with curly black hair, wearing leather pants. Keene. I smiled, wishing I could tell him he'd just been alibied by the ghost of a confused shark, then realized that maybe I was putting a little too much faith in the word of said confused ghost. "What was he doing?'

playing with shell

Okay, Notch was definitely getting lower with each pass. She and I were almost eye-to-eye now, and every time she circled behind me my shoulder blades started to itch. I needed to wrap this up quickly. "What kind of shell?"

shiny on top~~many colors

That sounded like—what? A phone, maybe? "Was he holding the shell up to the side of his head?"

no~~watching colors~~pinching with claws

Pinching? Oh, that probably meant using his thumbs or fingers—which sounded like he was texting, or maybe surfing the 'Net. Keene claimed he came out to the graveyard for inspiration, so maybe he was even writing a song.

"Thank you, Two-Notch." Now that she was lower, I

could see that the fin on her back did indeed have two triangular notches in it. "I appreciate your help."

don't know word appreciate

Except for maybe the *ate* part. "It means . . ."

What *did* it mean, exactly? That I now owed a favor to a non-corporeal entity? Or that I was mouthing meaningless social niceties to a creature that in other circumstances would view me as food?

Neither.

What it meant was that Two-Notch had never been appreciated. That she'd been displayed, but not loved. That she—

Was trying to eat me.

It happened so fast I barely had time to react. One second she was arcing behind me—and then I caught a blur of motion out of the corner of my eye. I spun, panic exploding through my brain, and got a close-up glimpse of that dead black eye as it shot past only inches away.

I knew a few things about sharks, mostly due to Shark Week on the Discovery Channel. I knew, for instance, that most victims never saw the attack coming; sharks liked to attack from below or behind, often doing massive damage with the initial bite and then leaving their prey to bleed to death before chowing down. But some used what was called the bump-and-bite method, where they slammed against their target first. Luckily for me, that's what Two-Notch did; I could see that her mouth was closed as she zoomed past.

Except it wasn't so much *past* as *through*.

She was obviously trying to ram my shoulder—and while her accuracy was good, her solidity wasn't. It had a definite effect, too, though not the one she was aiming for: Her ghostly body intersecting mine felt like an icy gust of wind blowing through my upper body. I gasped, off balance and terrified, and almost lost my footing.

She was already coming around for another pass. This time, her mouth was open.

I ran.

Straight at the fence. It wasn't that high, but at that moment I think I could have cleared something taller than I was. I dove over the top railing headfirst, did a shoulder-roll I learned in fourth-grade gymnastics, and wound up back on my feet. I was pretty sure I sprained something along the way.

Two-Notch eyed me as she glided along parallel to the fence, exactly like a fish in an aquarium. I wondered what those jaws would have done to me if she'd tried for a bite instead of a bump; somehow, I didn't think all I'd feel would be a cold breeze.

"You tried to *eat* me!"

i answered questions

"And you think that's a *fair trade*?"

yes

I took a second to compose myself and get my breathing under control. Okay, sure, why not? From a shark's point of view, it almost seemed reasonable. Get in a little polite conversation, then devour your dinner companion. "Look, here's the thing. I'm *not* food. We can talk, but you can't try to eat me."

why

I thought for a moment before I replied. This was like negotiating with a toddler; you had to use logic, but you couldn't let yourself get bogged down by long explanations they weren't equipped to understand. "Because it won't work. You passed right through me, didn't you? If you tried to bite me, the same thing would happen."

i try and see

"No. I don't like that. Try that again and all that will happen is I'll leave. Then we can't talk anymore."

I held my breath. This was the crux of the matter—if

Two-Notch didn't care about talking to me, then she wouldn't care about driving me away, either. I was gambling that she was probably more bored than hungry, and that her attempt to turn me into lunch was more habit than need.

i will talk~~not feed~~yes

I let out my breath in a sigh of relief. "Yes. Good."

And then I walked forward, and climbed back over the fence.

Was it stupid? Maybe—but it was also necessary. Standing up to someone bigger and scarier than you are was all about confidence, and in a situation where you'd just faced someone down, you needed to reinforce their impression of you as quickly and forcefully as you could. Winning once wasn't enough; you had to make them believe that you'd win next time, too, so that there *wasn't* a next time. And while sprinting for my life and leaping over a fence wasn't exactly a grand victory, I did get Two-Notch to agree to my rules. Acting like I wasn't worried about her anymore not only made me look stronger, it implied that I trusted her.

None of which explained why she abruptly turned around and zoomed away at high speed.

"Was it something I said?" I asked pointlessly. I hate it when people just leave without acknowledging you in any way; to me, that's the height of rudeness. I think it has something to do with abandonment issues—

Flash.

I think, right at that instant, that my idea of what was scary changed forever. I had always associated fear with darkness; the dark was where monsters hid, the dark represented the unknown and unknowable. *Anything* could be lurking there, and your imagination held more terrors than reality ever could.

But it wasn't dark now. It was a bright, hot morning,

the sun holding the shadows at bay. What difference could a little more light make?

Ask the ghosts of Hiroshima or Nagasaki.

It was unearthly, that light. It wasn't so much its brightness as the way it *overpowered* the sunshine, like a harsh noise drowning out a softer one. That light had edges; it was hard, sharp, and unforgiving. It didn't illuminate, it exposed.

And what it exposed was death.

The graveyard didn't change, yet everything was different. The shadows of the tombstones were black, bottomless pits, while the tombstones themselves were granite hammers poised to smash down at any second. The freshly mowed grass was a sea of slaughtered, rotting life, a thin layer of decomposing scum over dirt made from finely ground corpses. The sky was the white-blue of frozen flesh.

I saw—I felt—all this in an instant, and I knew why Two-Notch had bolted.

The thing that emitted that flash was here.

The light had come from behind me.

Chapter Ten

I had turned to the right to watch Two-Notch dart away. To my left was another hill, one with a large tomb on its top—one of a horse, I think. The shadow-thing must have been behind it, and stepped out when my back was turned. I had no idea how far away it was.

Maybe I should have run. But some animals would chase you if you did that, because that action automatically classified you in their brains as prey. And some animals—even large predators—would back down if you confronted them. I had no idea if any of these rules applied to dead animals, or even what kind of animal I'd be facing—but fleeing in blind terror just wasn't my style. It's not that I'm brave; I'm just too damn curious.

So I turned around to see exactly what my bogeyman looked like.

It was halfway down the hill and as large as I remembered, a huge black bulk at least ten feet high. But this time, I got more than a glimpse; I could see the whole thing, though the intermittent flashes it was giving off made focusing on details difficult.

It was an elephant.

But like no elephant I'd ever seen. It was made of pure blackness, its trunk an inky tentacle that lashed from side to side like an enraged python. The flashes were electrical, miniature lightning bolts arcing between the chains that it wore like some kind of riding harness over its head. Chains trailed from its neck, too, one on either side. It had two long tusks, each of them a curving black slash, one shorter than the other. Neither the lightning nor the chains made any sound at all as the black shape lumbered down the hill straight at me.

Okay. *Now* I could run.

I sprinted for the fence, figuring what worked once would work again. That was my first mistake. My second was that I hadn't put on my jumping-over-graveyard-fences shoes that morning, and doing one impressive, spontaneous leap was really all this pair was good for. I cleared the fence okay, but totally blew the landing—my heel skidded on some leaves, I went sideways and slammed into the ground with my shoulder. Ow.

Getting back to my first mistake . . .

Two-Notch had apparently resided inside an aquarium when she was alive. How she got to the graveyard I didn't know—from what Eli told me, it seemed prowlers weren't actually buried here—but once she arrived, she simply fell into old habits. She hadn't stayed inside the grounds because she had to, she did so because it fit how she saw the world. Other animals clearly didn't have that restriction, as Ambrose the Orbiting Sea Turtle had demonstrated.

The shadow elephant hadn't lived in an aquarium.

That was good news for fish trying to avoid electrocution, but bad news for Foxtrots that were trying to avoid high-voltage elephants. It stomped right through the fence like it wasn't there, tendrils of lightning snaking to either side down the iron railings as it passed through them and came to an abrupt halt in front of me. I thought for a second I had misjudged its intentions.

And then it reared up on its hind legs.

I knew what was coming. It was going to smash down on me with the full weight of all that blackness, and stomp my soul flat. My body might not be crushed, but it would kill me dead all the same.

That didn't happen.

What did happen was that a streamlined gray blur arced over the fence in the frozen instant the elephant stood upright, and skidded to a stop in front of me. I had an instant to realize it was a greyhound, and then it changed.

I don't know what to call the thing it changed into.

Calling it a dog was like calling a tiger a tabby. It was the size of a bear, massing at least three hundred pounds. Its head was huge, broad and flat like a pit bull's but much larger, its snout long and heavy, its face jet black. It had pointed ears and a bushy tail like a wolf's. Its fur was gray-black on top, fading to a tan underneath, and it stood almost four feet high.

Next to the elephant, it looked puny. It crouched in the shadow of that immense black weight about to fall like a pile driver, and *snarled.*

The snarl scared me more than the elephant had. I may have shrieked—just a bit—but I honestly believe that the biggest, meanest, badass on the planet might have done the same. That snarl was . . . well, let's just say that if I ever had trouble going to the bathroom, all I had to do has remember that snarl and peeing would get a whole lot easier.

The elephant paused.

The dog-thing snarled again. I managed to retain control of my bladder, but movement seemed impossible.

The elephant lowered itself to the ground. There should have been an earthshaking thump, but there wasn't. The canine and the pachyderm stared at each other, the elephant's trunk twitching like a cat's tail. The elephant seemed more irritated than afraid.

[Foxtrot,] Tiny's voice said in my head. [Now would be a good time to run.]

I scrambled to my feet. "I—I can't leave you here with—"

[RUN!]

I ran.

I'm not proud of it. I spent a lot of time thinking about it afterward, and even though I knew he was right—I was out of my depth, while he was doing a job he was good at and prepared for—I still felt bad. Whenever I replayed that scene in my head later, it always turned into a fantasy where I whipped a little shadow mouse out of my pocket and said, "Ha! Deal with *this,* Monster Elephant Lightning Ghost!" And then the mouse went all kung-fu on his giant, wrinkly ass while I laughed evilly.

But that was just a fantasy. In reality, I ran.

The graveyard was bordered by a wooded area, a small stand of trees that abruptly ended at a shallow ditch beside a paved road. I cut to the right and kept going, splashing through puddles left by last night's rain. I hoped nobody on the road noticed the crazy lady running through the ditch.

I veered back after a few hundred feet, because I could spot the outer wall of the Zoransky estate and knew I was about to come into range of one of Shondra's cameras. No way was I going to explain this to her. The trees thinned out near the junction where the high stone wall of the estate met the iron fence of the graveyard, and I ducked in there where I couldn't be seen from the road. I paused when I came to the fence, then steeled myself and climbed over it again.

I was back in the graveyard.

<*Foxtrot!*>

"AAH! Don't *do* that!"

I looked around wildly. Tango was nowhere in sight. "Where are you?"

<*Next to some statue of a parrot named Fish Jumping. Where are* you*?*>

I told her which corner of the graveyard I was in. "Listen, Tiny's in trouble! He was facing off against—"

<*I know, I know. Don't sweat it, kid, he can take care of himself. Right now we have to get you someplace safe. Stay close to the hedge and go straight for the gate, okay? I'll let you know if big, black, and Dumbo is headed your way.*>

"But it isn't restricted to the graveyard! It attacked me on the other side of the fence!"

<*It's not being outside the graveyard it's afraid of, it's large groups of people. Get back to the house and you'll be fine. Now move, okay?*>

So I did. I kept close to the hedge, and moved deeper into the graveyard, my heart hammering. I hoped Tiny would be okay. "Hey, how come I can hear you when you're so far away?"

<*I'll tell you if you'll calm down. Your thoughts taste like adrenaline and fear-sweat.*>

I realized my hands were shaking. "Breathe, dammit, breathe," I muttered to myself, and then made myself do it. "I'm . . . under control, now. I am."

<*You're doing fine. The reason you can hear me is that the graveyard is a natural psychic amplifier; it's one of the things that draws restless animal spirits here. As a side effect, it also increases the range we can communicate with one another.*>

"Sure, yeah, got it. Keep talking, okay?"

<*I'm right here, sweetie. No way that critter gets past me. And it's too busy relearning a few things about the*

difference between carnivores and herbivores at the moment to even think about coming after you. You're safe.>

I didn't feel safe, though. I wondered if I ever would again, or if I'd wake up screaming from nightmares about huge black thunderclouds chasing me. "What *was* that thing?"

<*An elephant. Or something that used to be an elephant, anyway.*>

"That much I figured out. An elephantom, huh? But it was *electric*!"

<*Yeah, that's pretty weird. Okay, I can see you now—keep going, don't stop.*>

I glanced over my shoulder. I could see the main path now ahead of me, and the statue of Piotr, the Russian circus bear. Tango had moved away from the parrot's grave—she'd climbed on top of the bear's head. I almost expected her to wave, but that's not really a cat thing.

A moment later I was at the gate. I hesitated with it open and looked back. Tango was gone. "Hey, where'd you go?"

<*To check on Rin Tin Tiny. We'll meet you back at the house, okay? Go!*>

I swallowed, then did as I was told.

I was halfway to the mansion when I realized that—despite what Tango had told me about the graveyard amplifying our thoughts—I hadn't heard anything from Tiny since I left him.

Thank God there was no one at poolside. I didn't know if I could face another human being just then, and definitely not one that was flirting with me. I just wanted to find a corner to have quiet breakdown in—no more than three minutes of hysterical crying, tops—and then go back and rescue my friend.

But since I had absolutely no idea how to do that, I

settled for just the quiet-corner part—a bench in the gardens that was mostly hidden from casual view by an enormous rhododendron bush.

To my own surprise, it turned out I didn't need the crying after all. My little breakdowns were generally a chance to wallow in self-pity for a bit before throwing myself back into the fray, but it wasn't self-pity I was feeling. It was worry and guilt and fear.

And the beginnings of anger.

At myself, yes. But also at whoever or whatever had thrown me into this mess with no preparation or warning. Okay, a little warning and two qualified helpers, but still—*electric elephants?* How in the name of Oprah's Pap Smear was I supposed to deal with things like *that*?

I didn't know. And if I didn't figure it out soon, somebody else was going to die. Maybe even me.

That was about as far as I got in my stew of self-recrimination, anxiety, and anger. Tango came trotting around the corner, looking entirely unconcerned, with no sign of Tiny.

"Tango! Where's—"

<Dial it down, Toots. He's right behind me, just moving a little slow.>

And sure enough, a second later Tiny limped into sight. He was wearing his golden retriever form again, but he looked . . . odd. A little lopsided somehow, like a drawing where the artist hadn't gotten the perspective quite right. I squinted at him, but couldn't put my finger on exactly what was wrong. "Tiny! Are you okay?"

His mental voice sounded exhausted, like a man panting after a long run. [I'm fine, Foxtrot. Just . . . a little drained. Excuse me.] He flopped down at my feet and put his chin on the ground.

I jumped off my seat and knelt down beside him. "What happened? Are you hurt? What *was* that thing?"

<Whoa, Toots, back off a little. He's gonna be all right, just don't crowd him—>

[Let me answer your questions. First: We fought. Second: I am wounded, but not seriously. Third: It was an elephant.]

I did my best not to roll my eyes. "I *know* it was an elephant! But that's like saying King Kong was an ape! *This* elephant was spitting lightning and made out of blackness so black it was like—like something really, really black!"

[Was she always this eloquent when she got upset?]

<Worse. She used to stammer, too. And stomp her feet.>

"I haven't done that since I was six. And don't change the subject."

[You know as much as I do. It's a hostile spirit, obviously. The darkness is a manifestation of its rage. The lightning . . . I don't know. Perhaps that's how it died.]

"You said you were injured. How badly? What can I do to help?"

[You can't. I just need some time to rest, that's all.]

It had never even occurred to me that Tiny could be hurt; he was already dead, after all. I put my hand down to give him a comforting stroke on the head—

And felt my fingers sink into his skull like it was made of soft mud.

"AAH!" I yanked my hand away, horrified. Tiny stared up at me with reproachful dog eyes, and Tango sighed. *<Oh, boy. Now you've done it.>*

"I'm sorry I'm sorry I'm *sorry*—"

[Hush. You didn't hurt me. This is what happens when an ectoplasmic entity like myself is injured: It becomes harder to hold ourselves together. I require time to meditate, which will allow me to regain my former cohesion. A smaller form will make this easier; therefore, I am going to shift into one now.]

He shrank, his shape condensing, his shaggy fur getting shorter while his floppy ears got longer and pointier. His color changed from a burnished orange to white. Within a minute I was looking at a tiny, pale Chihuahua with enormous brown eyes and whiskers like a mouse. He stared up at me solemnly, and those tears I thought were gone threatened to come back. "Oh. You're so . . ."

[Don't say it, please. Now—can you find a place to hide me? A drawer will do.]

"Yes, sure. Just a second."

I glanced around, then spotted a paper sack of potting soil the gardener had left out. I dumped it in the bushes, then put it on the ground and held the mouth open. Tiny ducked inside, and I picked it up and curled the lip over a few times to close it. "You okay in there?"

[Fine.]

<Y'know, I finally understand what they mean by a "doggie bag.">

I marched briskly into the house with the bag under my arm, up the staircase and straight to my office. I found a filing drawer that was mostly empty, and gently took Tiny out of his improvised carrier and put him inside. "I'll look in on you later, okay?"

[Thank you.] He put his head down and appeared to fall asleep.

I went back outside, where Tango was waiting for me by the rhododendron bush. I sat back down. She jumped up and sat beside me.

<I told you he'd be fine—>

And that was when I started to cry.

I felt Tango climb onto my lap. She lay there quietly, and I stroked her soft, warm fur. After a moment she began to purr.

It helped, but I still felt terrible. "I . . . I don't know if I can do this."

<Huh. Well, that's a first.>

"What?"

<Hearing you say that. Don't recall you ever saying it before, not the whole time you were growing up.>

"Don't be ridiculous," I sniffled. "I must have."

<Nope. Don't think so. Remember when those boys built that tree house and they wouldn't let you join their little gang? They even threw rocks at you. And what did you do then?>

"I don't remember."

<Yes, you do. You challenged them to a duel.>

I didn't say anything.

<You told the biggest one that he was a coward, and that you were better at throwing rocks anyway. Then you convinced him to stand twenty feet away with three rocks in his hand, while you had three rocks in yours. "First one to duck loses," you said. Then you let him have the first throw.>

"He missed."

<You didn't.>

"No. I knocked out two of his teeth. Man, did I get in trouble for that."

<But you weren't sorry. And you weren't scared.>

"I'd seen him play baseball. He had a lousy arm."

<He was bigger and older than you, and he wasn't alone. But you still stood up to him.>

I sighed. "This isn't a bully throwing rocks, Tango. This is big and scary and supernatural. I can't exactly challenge a ghost elephant to a duel."

<You don't have to. Look, ultimately that thing is just a distraction. It doesn't have anything to do with what we're trying to accomplish. Stay away from it and it'll probably stay away from you.>

I considered that. Maybe she was right; one bad encounter didn't make the thing my archnemesis. It was probably just lost and in pain and half wild—not evil. "You know, you're right. I guess I'm just a little shook up, is all. Too much going on, and all of it weird."

<You didn't mind weird when you were younger. You loved books and comics and movies, about everything from aliens to wizards.>

I pulled a tissue from my pocket and blew my nose. "I did, didn't I? I was a real geek girl. I didn't think you noticed, though."

<How could I not? My favorite time of day was to curl up on your lap while you read or watched TV. I miss that.>

I stroked her head, rubbing my thumb and forefinger in those two little spots in front of her ears; she responded like she always had, closing her eyes and ratcheting her purr up to a rumble. *<Mmmm. Thanks. You always knew just how to do that.>*

"I missed you, too, kitty. It broke my heart when you died, you know? I cried for *days*."

<No more tears, Toots. I'm here. And no matter what happens—even if I have to go away for a while—I'll always come back. It's kinda what we cats do. I promise—hey, what did I just say about no more tears?>

"Oh, shush, you silly cat," I sniffled. "Can't you tell the difference between good tears and bad ones?"

I thought it was about time Tango met the household—partly because I was tired of sneaking around like a guilty housewife having an affair, partly because I just wanted her with me. Tango and I discussed it and agreed that it would be more believable if someone else "discovered" her; once she'd been introduced to the house, she could latch onto me. Her plan was to hang around the kitchen door and meow a lot, then shower whoever appeared with affection. *<Guaranteed crowd-pleaser, unless we run into allergies.>*

"Or someone who doesn't like cats."

She snorted. *<Please. There are no cat-haters, just people who don't know any better. And they can usually be taught.>*

"Yeah? What about the ones that can't?"

<We call those dogs.>

I left her to it, intending to go by the kitchen a little later and let her "befriend" me. In the meantime, I went straight back to my office to check on Tiny. He was still fast asleep.

I shut the drawer gently, then sat down at my desk. Now that the whole incident with the elephant was over, I felt restless and on edge. I needed to *do* something, something constructive.

So I did research.

Maybe back in the bad old twentieth century I would have needed to hit the local antique-book store for a dusty tome of mystic pachyderm lore, but here in the bright and shiny future I had the Internet. I Googled "electric elephant"—hoping it wasn't the brand name of a marital aid—and was pleasantly surprised to find exactly what I was looking for right at the very top of the page. I started reading.

My surprise, it turned out, wasn't that pleasant at all.

My elephantom was rather famous. Her name was Topsy, and she'd been born around 1875. Though elephants have a fairly long life span, Topsy's had ended when she was only twenty-eight. She hadn't been hit by lightning, though.

She'd been executed.

Topsy had killed three men over a span of three years. The last killing had earned her a death sentence, though some might have called it justifiable homicide—her abusive trainer tried to feed her a lit cigarette.

But that was only the start of the bizarre story. Once they decided Topsy had to die, the first method they proposed was *hanging*. Sure. Because that's the natural way to execute a creature that weighs a couple of tons. Apparently they were all set to do it with a crane when the ASPCA stepped in and pointed out this was cruel, unusual, and extremely stupid.

Enter Thomas Edison.

Yes, *that* Thomas Edison. The year was 1902, and Edison was in the middle of something called the War of the Currents; electricity was just being introduced across the country, and he and an inventor named Nikola Tesla were competing to see which was going to become the standard for household usage, AC (alternating current) or DC (direct current). Ultimately, Tesla won—AC is what's used worldwide today—but Edison was willing to fight dirty.

In order to show how *dangerous* alternating current was, Edison suggested using it to kill Topsy. The electric chair had already been in use to execute criminals since 1890, so why not an elephant? If AC could bring down a creature as large as Topsy, people would see it for the threat it really was.

And to make *sure* people saw that, Edison filmed it.

The film was shown across the country; it survives to this day. In fact, there was a link to it right on the Wikipedia page, with the title "Electrocuting an Elephant." I stared down at the blurry, faint image frozen on my screen, then moved my cursor over the little white triangle and clicked.

The film was only a little over a minute in length. Topsy was led out by a handler who held a coiled whip in one hand, trailed by several other men. The handler reached out and touched her trunk at one point, clearly to reassure her. She seemed docile enough, considering the fact that they'd already given her almost five hundred grams of potassium cyanide. She was wearing a harness made of chains, one I immediately recognized. The links wrapped around her neck, went over the top of her skull, and continued across her trunk. The chains were held in place by thick metal bands, one at eye level, one about two feet lower, presumably to keep them from slipping.

The film jumped to a shot of her stationary, chains trailing from her neck to two spots off screen. The background looked industrial, maybe docks. She pawed the ground once, as if impatient.

Smoke started to billow from beneath one of her front feet. Then the others. Her rear legs extended and stiffened as the muscles spasmed and locked, and she toppled forward as a cloud of smoke billowed from beneath her.

The smoke slowly cleared. Someone came forward to examine her, and her mouth fell open and twitched. That was it.

I leaned back in my chair and shook my head. The film was sad, disturbing, and creepy, but it explained a lot. Topsy had been a working elephant, and she'd worked—as both an actual laborer and a tourist attraction—at a place called Luna Park, on Coney Island. Children had loved her. Luna Park had recently reopened after a long hiatus, too; it had been shut down after a serious fire in 1944.

People called the fire "Topsy's Revenge."

I thought about all that arcane electricity sparking off those chains, and wondered if people hadn't been right . . . and if maybe, after the park shut down, Topsy had gotten bored and wandered off. Coney Island was less than fifty miles away. How long would it take a ghost elephant to walk that? A couple of days? Topsy had died over a century ago.

After, you know, killing three people. And now, apparently, she'd taken a strong dislike to me . . .

Chapter Eleven

I checked on Tiny again—still zonked out—then went downstairs to "discover" Tango. Sure enough, she was in the kitchen, contentedly sitting on Ben's lap while he rubbed under her chin and told her what a good cat she was.

"Guess I'm not the only one making new friends," I commented from the doorway.

Ben glanced up at me and grinned. "Found her making a racket outside the back door. When I opened it, she strolled in like she owned the place."

Tango had her eyes closed in ecstasy. *<Hey, Toots. Toldja I had it under control.>*

"Oh, what a sweetheart," I said. I bent down and stroked her fur. "She looks so . . . *nice.*"

One eye opened just a slit, and glared at me. *<Watch it, Toots. Them's bitin' words.>*

"So—you ready?" Ben asked. He picked Tango up gently and put her down on the floor.

"Ready?" I said. For a moment I was confused and a little taken aback—was he asking about the elephant? Because, while I might have been adaptable, I didn't think anyone was *ever* ready for an AC-charged serial killer elephant—

Oh. Wait a minute. I'd completely forgotten about—

"For lunch," Ben said. "Hope you're hungry, 'cause I may have gone a little overboard."

"That's—I mean—" Hoo, boy. In all the excitement, my lunch date with Ben had completely slipped my mind. A mind that suddenly couldn't come up with a convenient excuse. Funny, that.

"—sure, I'm ready. Picnic, right? Weather seems to be cooperating. We can even take along your new pal."

"Okay, great." He trotted over to the walk-in cooler and opened the door. "I'll be right back."

<Date, huh? This should be interesting.>

Oh, no, I thought furiously. *First dates are awkward enough without you kibbutzing in the background. You're going to take off, right now, and keep an eye on Tiny. I left my office door open. Go!*

<Spoilsport.> She took off into the house while I walked over to the kitchen door. "Oh, darn!"

Ben reappeared with an enormous picnic basket in one hand and a folded blanket tucked under his arm. He'd taken off his white cook's apron, revealing a blue chambray shirt and jeans underneath. "What's wrong?"

"I opened the outside door for a second and Tango ran out. Looks like we're on our own."

He studied me for a second, an amused look on his face. "Tango?"

"Yeah. She reminds me of a cat I used to have as a kid—spitting image, actually. If she sticks around, I figure that's what I'll call her."

"Oh, so you get naming privileges? What if I had something else in mind? Like, say, Quest?"

"Quest?"

"Short for Question Mark. Didn't you notice the pattern of fur on her head?"

"Must have missed that. Anyway, she seems much more like a Tango to me."

"Tango and Foxtrot. Well, I do like the sound of that."

"Good. Then it's settled."

He put down the basket. "Well, then. Since I just demonstrated faith in your judgment, how about you demonstrate some in mine?" He pulled a bandanna out of his back pocket and held it up.

"Lovely. You have definite taste when it comes to mucus-catching swatches of fabric."

His grin got a little wider. The more of it I saw, the more I liked; I'm a sucker for big white teeth all nicely lined up in even rows. "This one's clean, I guarantee. The question is, do you trust me enough to let me put it on you?"

I took me a second to realize he was talking about a blindfold as opposed to a kerchief or a fetching dust mask. "Oh. Well . . ."

Did I?

It was odd how certain moments wind up defining relationships. You hardly ever recognized them when they happened, though; it was only afterward, sifting through memories, that those moments suddenly became blindingly obvious.

But right at that particular moment, the only thing that was obvious was the blinding itself. Which—for no reason I could fathom at the time—didn't seem to bother me in the slightest. "What the hell," I said, and closed my eyes.

I wasn't the kind of woman that generally liked surprises, and I wasn't the kind of woman who liked to give up control. Maybe that was why I let him do it; after all the insanity of the past few days, the idea of tossing someone the keys and saying, *You drive for a while,* was irresistible.

But I wouldn't have thrown those keys to just anyone.

"This better be worth it," I said as he took my hand and led me outside. His hand was big and warm, the skin slightly rough.

"Oh, I think the moment when you take off the blindfold and see you're inside the leopard enclosure should be a pretty big payoff."

"Liar. We rewilded that leopard two weeks ago."

"My mistake."

I was starting to regret sending Tango away; she could have kept me informed while I played dumb. *No,* I told myself, *that's not fair. You agreed to do this, now let him do it. He's trying to impress you, stupid.*

Sure. But . . . did I mention I had a hard time giving up control?

I knew the grounds pretty well. I was already charting our path and extrapolating possible sites when I noticed we were veering sharply to the left. Really sharply. And really left—left, left, and more left, until there wasn't any more left left, and even the word itself seemed meaningless.

"We're going in a circle!"

"You're very perceptive."

"Stop. I'm getting dizzy."

He stopped immediately. I wobbled a little, and hung on to his hand for balance as well as guidance. His grip was sure and strong and extremely steady.

"All right," I said. "I'm okay now."

"You're trying to figure out where you are by listening."

"That's an unfair accusation with no evidence to back it up."

"Except the way you just cocked your head to one side like a puppy. It's very cute."

"Quiet. Is that splashing?"

"Yes, we're picnicking at the end of the diving board. Do I have to sing? Don't make me sing."

"I'd love to hear you sing. Are you really awful?"

"I have a voice like a bird. More specifically, some sort of poultry."

"It can't be that bad. Come on."

My feet had been on grass for most of the journey, but now they were on something harder—concrete? Wood? No, too uneven—packed dirt, maybe. Could be one of the footpaths in the gardens, though most of them had wood chips laid down.

"All right, we're here," Ben said. "Just give me a moment to lay down the blanket, will you? No peeking."

I resisted the urge to rip the blindfold off. Where were we? I had it narrowed down to two possible spots, but from the warmth on my face it wasn't shady enough for that spot under the oak, and anywhere in or around the gardens would have been given away by the flowers that were in bloom—

He gently lifted the blindfold from my eyes. "Ta-da!"

Oh, no.

I was back in the graveyard.

In retrospect, it should have been obvious. But somehow, it never occurred to me that our first date might be a nice outdoor meal surrounded by dead things.

And he'd gone a little farther than that. The blanket, it turned out, was misdirection; he'd set up a table and two chairs, complete with white linen tablecloth and napkins, wineglasses and silverware. There was a bottle of something chilling in a silver ice bucket on a stand, and a sun umbrella on the other side to provide shade.

"I," I said. It seemed worth repeating, so I said it again. "I. I . . ."

"I think you've mastered that one. Would you like to

try another vowel, or are you ready to move on to consonants?"

"Ah. Oh." I swallowed, tried to compose myself, and managed, "Why?"

"No, only *sometimes* Y," he said. "But in this case, the why is because I know you come down here all the time when you need a break. This is a break—the kind that comes with food and drink and conversation. Please, take a seat."

He pulled out my chair. I stared at it like it held a dead kangaroo, which it did.

The kangaroo looked at me. I looked at it. I wondered what would happen if I sat on it. I decided I didn't want to find out.

"Ow!" I said, clutching my thigh. "Hold on a second. *Nasty* leg cramp. Have to keep my leg straight." I stiffened my leg, glared at the kangaroo, and thought desperate thoughts at it. *Shoo! Go away!* Bad *kangaroo!*

"If you need to take your weight off it, sit down." He put his hands gently on my shoulders. "I could massage it—"

"No! I mean, *no,* thank you." I hopped away from his touch, holding my leg out awkwardly. The kangaroo studied me intently, as if he found my hopping technique fascinating from a professional point of view. I hopped right onto a small, pointy rock, which threw my balance off enough to make me spin around.

"Whuff," said the bear. He was on his hind legs, his jaws level with my face and about six inches away.

"AAAAAH!" I said, stumbled backward, and fell on my butt. I just hoped I hadn't landed on anything else.

"That's one heckuva cramp," Ben said. He was looking at me with wary amusement, as if he knew there was a joke being told but the punch line eluded him. The bear stared at me with undisguised curiosity, then got on his unicycle and rode away. Ah, *there* the punch line was.

I looked from one side to another, trying to do it casually. Ben had set up the table in one of the little natural valleys formed by the gentle hills of the graveyard, and the little path that ran through it was in constant use by ghost animals. Cats and dogs and gerbils and lizards and fish and birds and Vietnamese potbellied pigs, oh my. Oh, and the occasional kangaroo or circus bear, too.

But none of those worried me.

"Are you all right?" Ben asked. He offered his hand, and I took it and let him pull me to my feet.

"Sorry. Uh, hornet. Right in front of my eyes. Scared me a little."

"How's the leg?"

"My leg?"

"The cramp?"

"Oh, right! Fine, fine. They come and go. It came, it went. How'd you get all this stuff out here?" Without Tiny, Tango, or me noticing, I meant.

"It wasn't that hard. Vic helped me—underneath that serious Germanic exterior beats the heart of a romantic. Or maybe just the liver of one, I don't know. I bribed him with a bottle of cognac."

I limped over to my chair, not faking this time—I'd hurt my rear when I landed on it. The kangaroo, having gleaned what it could of my hopping expertise, bounded out of my chair and down the path with the rest of the ghosts. Maybe it and the bear were going to meet up to compare notes.

I hesitated with my hand on the chair. A blanket, that I could convince him to move. This—not so much. And if I bailed now, I'd be paying back all this effort by slapping him in the face. He didn't deserve that, and that wasn't the kind of person I was or wanted to be.

And if did hightail it out of there, he'd never ask me out again.

I sat.

I'd been attacked in a deserted part of the graveyard, and this seemed fairly busy. From what Eli said, prowlers avoided busy places. And Tiny couldn't have been the only one who got hurt in that fight; I've seen Great Danes that were smaller than that canine Schwarzenegger he turned into. Topsy was probably doing exactly the same thing Tiny was right now, holing up and healing. If nothing else, she'd be moving slower and I had a better chance of outrunning her.

Sure. Because I was so agile on my feet and all.

Ben was busy unpacking the contents of the basket. "This isn't too weird, is it? I mean, I know you come here all the time, but—"

"It's fine. It's better than fine. Sorry I'm such a spaz today."

"Considering all you've had to deal with in the last few days, I'd say you're justified in a little spasm or two."

I gave him a look. He actually blushed, then looked a little panicked. "I mean—"

"Just put down the grenade and back slowly away. I won't pull the pin if you won't."

It was his turn to give me a look. I refused to blush, but I did grin. "Hmm. That sucker just wants to go off, doesn't it?"

"No habla inglis, señorita."

"Yeah, me either." I glanced around, trying to be casual about it. Not like, you know, I was on the lookout for a giant killer elephant. A stream of guinea pigs scurried past, their pelts gleaming white and orange and brown. The utter silence of their movement was just as eerie as the way they glowed as if lit from within.

I made a conscious effort to pay attention to the table instead of the wildlife. I mean tamelife. I mean tamedeath. Oh, screw it.

"Wow," I said. "This looks delicious."

"Smoked oysters, pickled artichokes, and asparagus in a truffle oil vinaigrette. Just to whet your appetite."

"Consider my appetite *extremely* . . . um. How about this large weather we're having?"

"Yes, how about it. What with the air and the sky and the sun and all."

This time we managed to avoid blushing, but gave each other a look. And then both of us burst out laughing.

"Can we start over?" he managed after a minute.

"What for? I'm having a *great* time. I think for an encore I'll just trip over my own tongue and see if I can't land with both feet in my mouth."

"Okay, but that's not gonna leave a whole lot of room for food."

"Good point." I grabbed a fork, speared some asparagus, and tried it. "Mmm. You know what? I think I'll just stick with making appreciative noises. Much better than doing the word-using thing."

"And not at all suggestive."

"Can't talk. Eating."

He kept pulling out food. Fried chicken with a crunchy breading that would have made Colonel Sanders weep. Cold pasta salad with little bits of apricot and bacon in it. Thinly sliced barbecued pork on buttermilk biscuits with chipotle mayo.

I shut up and ate.

"Afraid I can't really offer you a good wine to go with all this," he said, pulling a bottle out of the ice bucket. "Since we're both technically on the clock, I didn't think ZZ would appreciate me getting her personal assistant *and* her cook soused. So I whipped up this—a little something my mother used to make me when I was a kid." He poured some in my glass, then in his. It was purple and slightly bubbly.

I took a sniff, and smelled grape. "What is it?"

"Concord grape juice and ginger ale. It's got a nice light flavor, I think, but I may be prejudiced. You know how it is with stuff you ate when you were a kid."

I took a sip. It was good, not too sweet or too fizzy. "Nice. And yeah, I do know. Comfort foods, right? No matter how white-bread or low-rent, you always remember your childhood favorites. Smooth peanut butter on saltines."

"Sure."

"Or mac and cheese with wieners cut into it."

"A classic."

"Or fried baloney sandwiches on soft white bread. Feel free to jump in anytime, okay?"

It was a playful jab over an innocuous subject, but he reacted like I'd just started babbling in Klingon. "Uh—sure, yeah. Baloney sandwiches. That was one of my favorites, too."

"I say something wrong?"

He shook his head. "No, of course not. I guess my childhood's just not a subject I like to talk about."

But you brought it up, I almost said, then didn't. He hadn't, actually—just referred to it once then shut down when I tried to take the conversation farther. Sigh. Chalk up another verbal blunder for yours truly, the great communicator.

I squared my mental shoulders and told myself to shape up. *Dammit, I'm good at this—I deal with people all the time. I'm a people person. People like me.*

He likes me.

Change the subject, change the subject. "This food is amazing. Tell me about it."

"Oh, it's nothing special. Just a few things I've picked up here and there."

"You must have had an interesting career. Where'd you work before ZZ hired you from that diner?"

He blanked. His eyes were wide open and he was smiling, but I could practically see the gears in his head seize up. This was not a question he wanted to answer.

No. It was not a question he knew *how* to answer.

"Here and there," he said. "You know how it is—one greasy spoon pretty much looks like another."

Well, at least he was a rotten liar. That can be a good thing, in the long run—I preferred to know when I was being lied to, as opposed to finding out later—but only if what he was lying about wasn't a five-year stretch in a federal penitentiary.

A parrot swooped down and landed on the table, right beside the basket of French bread. Its incandescent blue, green, and yellow plumage made it look like a rainbow come to life. "Awk!" it said. That startled me; most of the animal spirits didn't seem to make any noise at all. "Not true! Not true!"

I reached down carefully and picked up a piece of bread. "Not true," I said. "I've been to plenty of little hole-in-the-wall places, and each one has its charm."

"Maybe so, but you wouldn't say that if you were behind the grill."

"Hiding something!" the parrot squawked, fixing me with one bright yellow eye. "Hiding something!"

"You're right," I said. "I guess it's just something you have to experience in order to really understand it." My tone was noticeably cooler, which wasn't really fair; I wasn't being exactly honest with him, either.

"Brilliant!" came a familiar voice to my left. Keene strolled over the crest of the hill, hands in the pockets of his baggy, brightly colored shorts—which, other than sandals, was all he wore. "What's for afters?"

Ben glanced over, then shook his head and smiled. I didn't have to be a mind reader to know exactly what was going through his head: *Terrific. This date couldn't be a bigger disaster if I planned it. Maybe if I'm lucky I'll just be struck dead by lightning.*

At that very moment, there was a rumble of distant thunder.

Both Keene and I glanced up at the sky, which was a clear and cloudless blue. "How about that," said Keene. "Heat lightning, you figure?"

"I don't know if heat lightning produces thunder," I answered. "Maybe it was just a plane."

"I'd invite you to sit down," Ben told Keene, "but I'm afraid we only have two chairs."

"Oh, I'm perfectly happy perching here," said Keene, sitting on a nearby headstone. "I'm part gargoyle, on me mum's side. Should have seen them at Christmas dinners—stony-faced buggers, the lot of them. Had to have their clothes specially tailored to hide the bat-wings."

The parrot was now considering Keene. "Awk! Rock and roll! Rock and roll!"

Well, if nothing else, the bird's instincts were good. Though I was starting to wonder why I could have an intelligible conversation with a shark while Polly here sounded much the same as any other pet-shop pirate accessory. I tried thinking at it, the way I had at Two-Notch. *Hello?*

Good day, madam. And how are you?

"I could do with a bit of that, if you don't mind," said Keene, hopping down off his perch. He grabbed the bottle of grape juice and ginger ale and took a long pull. "Hmmm," he said after swallowing. "I'd get me money back if I were you. Someone's nicked all the kick from this."

"It's nonalcoholic," said Ben.

"It's what? That sounded like English, but made no sense."

"Awk! Boozehound! Boozehound! Liver begone! Liver begone!"

I apologize for the outburst. It's an unfortunate verbal tic, quite beyond my control.

"I'm sure," said Ben, "there must be a liquor store open by now. Somewhere."

"Ha," I said. "You know, I could do with some dessert. Can't wait to see what you're going to surprise me with."

"Me too," said Keene. He grinned. "Hope it's better than the plonk, anyway."

And may I say, dear lady, that I just wanted to be among the first to welcome you to the Great Crossroads. We all have the utmost confidence in your abilities and know you'll do everything in your power to protect and preserve this sacred and beloved nexus.

"Awk! I'm a blowhard! I'm a blowhard!"

"Tarts!" said Keene gleefully. "My favorite!"

My phone chimed. "Excuse me," I said. I pulled it out, glanced at the screen. Shondra. "I should really take this. Hello?"

"Trot. I just got a heads-up from a friend at the coroner's office. Seems that Maria's death *wasn't* accidental—she was poisoned."

I did my best to sound shocked. "What?"

"Yeah. My source tells me it was some kind of powerful animal tranquilizer. They found a puncture wound in her abdomen—and that's not all. Apparently someone called and tipped them off—even told them what kind of drug to look for."

"That doesn't make a lot of sense."

"No, it doesn't. About all I can come up with is two people working together, and one of them turns on the other after the fact. Maybe someone who's having second thoughts and doesn't want to see anyone else get hurt."

I could tell from her tone she was talking about me. Fair enough, since I was the one who made the call to the police. "It's not me, Shondra. If I knew who—you know—I'd tell you, I *swear*." A half-truth was better than none.

"Uh-huh. Well, you should wrap things up with your little picnic and get back here as quick as you can—Sheriff Brower's on his way and things are about to get a whole lot more intense."

"How did you—never mind. I'll be right there."

I hung up. "Sorry, guys, dessert will have to wait. I need to get back to the house, and both of you should probably come, too."

"Why?" asked Ben. "What's going on?"

I stood up. "Let's just say the afternoon is going to be less fun than the morning."

"Awk! Busted! Busted!" *Once again, I apologize for my rude and entirely unintentional vocalizations. I have full faith in your abilities as our champion and wish you nothing but the best.* "Awk! Kiss-ass! Kiss-ass!" *Oh, good Lord.*

"Well," said Keene, swallowing the last of the tart he'd popped in his mouth when I answered the phone, "fun is what you make of a situation, I always say . . ."

Chapter Twelve

After talking to Sheriff Brower for an hour, I was beginning to think being attacked by a homicidal dead elephant wasn't so bad.

"Look, I appreciate your thoroughness," I said. "But we've gone over this twice now, and I've given you every scrap of information I have." Which, of course, was a bald-faced lie—but I had given him everything I knew about the guests, the staff, the grounds, and the events around the murder. Everything that wasn't supernatural-related.

Brower squinted at me from the other side of my desk. "Seems to me you know an awful lot. Almost like you've been doing a little investigating on your own."

I sighed. Something I'd been doing a lot lately, it seemed. "Of course I have. I'm involved in virtually every aspect of life here, and it's my job to make it all run smoothly. I can't think of a better example of me *failing* to do my job than for someone to die on my watch, so I'm more than a little invested in finding out exactly what happened and why."

"Mm-hmm. Well, I'm going to be talking to Shondra

Destry next, and then everyone else. You sure what you told me is going to line up with everything *they* say?"

I considered another sigh, and decided against it. "No. Most likely some details will vary, because people remember things differently—but all the verifiable facts will stay the same. That much I'm sure of, and so are you. Because, at the end of the day, both of us are professionals, both of us deal with hard information, and both of us want the same thing."

"That so?" He got up out of his chair, his hat in one hand. "One big difference between us that I can see."

More than one, I thought, but kept my voice polite. "Which is?"

"I deal with people who lie to me every day."

He closed the door behind him as he left.

[He doesn't like you much.]

"Tiny!" I hurried over and slid the drawer on the filing cabinet open carefully. A big-eyed Chihuahua that looked like it had just stepped out of a black velvet painting stared up at me soulfully. "You're awake!"

[Very astute. I can see my superiors made a wise choice in choosing you as an investigator.]

"Is sarcasm a good sign? Does it mean you're getting better, or just . . . bitter?"

[If you're planning on working *biter* into your next sentence, please throttle the impulse.]

"I'm going to go with better. Can I get you anything?"

[A nice thick steak would do wonders.]

"I thought you didn't have to eat."

[Not normally. My ectoplasmic form exists in a state between matter and energy; it's not really one or the other until I will it so. I expended a great of energy fighting that creature, so my mass is accordingly reduced. Consuming a meal will allow me to replenish that energy.]

"I'll run down to the kitchen and see what I can scrounge up."

[I'll wait.]

I managed to get into and out of the kitchen without being noticed. I didn't know where Ben was; he'd vanished quickly after our date, and seemed more than a little preoccupied. Keene had stuck pretty close, though—even the sight of Brower didn't scare him off. I almost expected to find him hanging around outside my office door.

Tiny wolfed down the steak—well, Chihuahuaed it down, I guess—then said, [I need some time to absorb this. Can you put me back in the drawer?]

I did. He put his head down and was asleep almost instantly. "Sweet dreams, little guy," I said.

I decided I needed a little fresh air to clear my head; normally I would have headed down to the graveyard to sit on a bench, but that option was definitely off the table for the moment. I went for a walk in the gardens, instead.

ZZ's gardens were just as eccentric and varied as she was; I didn't know the names of most of the plants, but they tended toward distinctive and brilliantly colored. I tried to discourage her from acquiring poisonous varieties, but sometimes she overruled me. "For God's sake, Foxtrot, *rhubarb* is poisonous. Are you going to ban *that,* too?"

That remembered exchange summed up ZZ's attitude toward life in general: Embrace beauty, even if it was dangerous. Take chances. Live your life the way you wanted to.

I was no longer alone; I turned a corner in the path and saw Kenny Gant standing under a monkey puzzle tree, smoking a cigarette. He smiled at me and held a hand up in greeting. "Foxtrot! You've uncovered my dark secret."

"Tobacco? Compared with what Keene shows up with, that practically makes you a saint."

He chuckled. "Well, we can't all be rock stars, right? Somebody needs to be in the audience."

"So, how's your car?"

"Oh, it's fine. Turned out to be relatively easy to fix. Not so easy on the pocketbook, but they say I'll have it back by tomorrow."

"Well, that's something."

He finished his cigarette, carefully ground out the cherry, and put the butt in his pocket. "Shame about your maid. Never can tell when your number's up, huh?"

"No, I suppose not."

He nodded his head. "Well. My condolences." He turned and walked away.

I went back to the house and upstairs, trying to distract myself with paperwork. It worked, too—my obsessive-compulsive side gets stronger when I'm upset, which means I can spend hours concentrating on little, fiddly tasks. I lost myself in invoices and lists for a while, squeezing as much satisfaction as I could out of turning a jumble of numbers into predictable, orderly patterns.

I wasn't sure how much time had passed when I heard a minuscule whine from Tiny's drawer, followed by [Foxtrot?]

I jumped to my feet. "I'm right here. You okay?"

[Much better, thank you.] He stood up, yawned, then hopped out of the drawer and onto the floor. He seemed a lot more robust already. [Let's get back to work.]

"You sure you're up to it?"

[Don't worry about me.] He morphed into his golden retriever form. [I'm ready.]

"Okay. I'm not sure what our next step is, though."

[I thought about that while I was convalescing. I believe we should return to the scene of the murder and examine it again.]

"That could be tricky. The first thing Brower did when he got here was tape the room off again as a crime scene."

[My goodness, tape. You humans have such clever and impenetrable barriers.]

"All right, all right, we'll go. Brower's too busy reinterrogating everyone to notice, and he doesn't have the manpower to post a guard."

Sure enough, the only thing preventing us from getting in was a strip of yellow plastic across the door frame, though I did have to use my key. I stopped in the middle of the room, eyeing the bed nervously. It felt wrong to be in here, and that wrongness had nothing to do with breaking the rules; it was because this was where Maria died.

No. This was where Maria was *killed*. And I was going to catch the killer.

Tiny circled the room, sniffing at everything. I relied on my eyes, studying every detail, trying to figure out what had happened. The body had been found on the bed. The puncture wound was in her stomach. Was she stabbed with a hypodermic, or was it a dart like the ones fired by Gant's gun?

I went over and examined the window. It was long and slender, with a small pane on the top that opened out. I was careful not to touch anything. It seemed highly unlikely the killer would have left any fingerprints—this was obviously a well-thought out crime. But it would have been impossible to climb through that opening without coming into contact with it; maybe the killer had left some other mark or trace.

I leaned in close, hoping for a loose thread or some dirt. Nope. I leaned in even closer, trying to will my eyes to focus on the microscopic. Still no luck. I was so close my breath was fogging the glass, but my latent CSI vision refused to kick in.

[Finding anything?]

I stepped back. "Not so much. You?"

[I'm afraid not. Traces of a bad cologne that I recognize as Brower's.]

I frowned. "Wait a minute." There was something on the glass, a vague outline highlighted by my foggy breath. It was already fading, so I carefully leaned forward and exhaled again. There. Not one mark, but two—I breathed a little more to bring the full shape out. Two marks, right next to each other, spaced a few inches apart. They looked like flowers—no, more like fronds. And oddly familiar.

[What have you found?] Tiny stood next to me, then shrank down to Maltese size. [Pick me up so I can get a better look.]

I did. He felt a lot more solid than he had the last time I'd lifted him. [Interesting. What are those?]

"I'm not sure. I know I've seen them before, though . . ."

And then it hit me.

Total lightbulb moment. I knew what the marks were, and how they were made, and who the killer had to be. "Oh," I said. "Wow."

[What is it?]

"Hang on a second." I pulled out my phone, called ZZ, and asked her a single question. Then I thanked her and hung up. "We need to talk to Brower. Now."

Sheriff Brower wasn't happy about being disturbed. He was in the midst of questioning Consuela in the study, which he'd appropriated as his interrogation room. The bright light streaming through the windows and the rows of bookshelves didn't do much for the setting as far as making it intimidating, so Brower was trying to compensate by peppering her with questions.

"—and what *was* the last thing you ate for lunch that day?"

Poor Consuela was almost in tears. Brower's scattershot approach seemed to be to assume everyone was guilty and all he had to do was bully each suspect until the right one confessed. Or maybe just until he got something he could arrest someone for.

"Sheriff," I announced, striding into the room. Brower shot me an irritated look, while Consuela's was one of relief. "There's something you have to see."

"Not now," he snapped. "Now get out of here before I cite you for obstruction of justice."

"Now," I said. "If, you know, you actually want to learn who killed Maria."

Consuela gasped. "Someone *killed* Maria?"

"That's confidential," Brower said, trying to regain control of the situation. "And you have no business disclosing information in an ongoing police investigation—"

It took an act of will not to tell him to just shut up. "Sheriff. I have vital information. I want to share it with you. It may not be as important as the sandwich Consuela ate yesterday, but it will let you solve a homicide." I locked eyes with him. Sometimes, the only way to get an alpha male's attention is to challenge him—it kick-starts the intelligent part of his brain as he's forced to evaluate the threat instead of just reacting.

After a second, Brower snapped off a hostile glance at Consuela, said, "I'm not done with you," then got to his feet. "All right, let's get this over with."

"You can go," I told Consuela. "If he needs to talk to you again, he'll let you know." That earned me another disapproving glower from the sheriff, but he didn't contradict me.

I led him out of the study and upstairs to ZZ's bedroom. He stopped me outside the door with a hand on my arm. "Whoa, there, Miss Lancaster. That's now an official crime scene. I can't let you in there."

"You can and you will," I said. "Because I've *already* been in there, and found a key piece of evidence."

He eyed me skeptically. "And how do I know you didn't just plant said evidence?"

That stopped me. I'd been in such a rush to get what I'd found into the right hands—well, into the hands of a representative of law enforcement, anyway—that I hadn't thought about that. "I don't know. Why don't you take a look and decide for yourself?"

He nodded slowly. "All right. You just stop at the doorway and point out whatever it is that's so important—don't cross the threshold."

"Yes, yes, fine."

He took down the tape, then had to have me unlock the door. When he was inside and I was in the doorway, I told him about the marks on the window and how I'd found them. He repeated the process, then studied the patterns on the glass. "What am I supposed to be looking at, Miss Lancaster? You don't think someone's hands made these, do you?"

"Not hands. Feet. And not someone, some*thing*. I think you'll find those prints are an exact match to the landing gear of a remote-controlled quadracopter belonging to one of our guests—Juan Estevez."

"A *what*?"

And then I had to explain what the GEQ was, and how it could use those feet to cling to surfaces, and the fact that it was rigged with a blowgun-like device that could hypothetically be used to fire a dart. Brower took all this in with a long-suffering expression, then let out a wheezy sigh when I was done. "That sounds pretty far-fetched to me, Miss Lancaster. But I'll humor you—we'll take a look at this flying robot-thing and see if you're right. Even if you are, though, it doesn't prove murder."

"We'll see."

Tiny had stayed by my side the entire time. [Foxtrot, are you sure about this?] he asked as we all headed for Estevez's room.

I am. There's no reason for those marks to be there—ZZ told me that neither Estevez or his machine had been anywhere near her room. The only thing that makes sense is that Estevez flew the thing inside, landed on the side of the window, then shot Maria with the dart gun.

[But why?]

Because of what ZZ was hinting at earlier—that the GEQ was funded by the military for use as an assassination tool. Estevez must have thought she was going to screw up his funding.

[So he killed her maid?]

Okay, it's not a perfect explanation. Maybe he just made a mistake—the camera on that thing wasn't the best. Or maybe he panicked.

Tiny didn't reply.

We got to Estevez's room. I knocked. A second later the door opened and a sleepy-looking Estevez said, "What is it? I was napping."

"You mind if we come in for a second?" I said, smiling brightly.

Estevez glanced at Brower, then gave us a grumpy shrug. "Yeah, sure, whatever. I'm up now."

The GEQ was sitting on a table, next to an open laptop. "Is that your quaddocopter?" Brower asked.

"Quadracopter," said Estevez.

"I'd like to examine it, if you don't mind—" Brower began, but that was as far as he got. Tiny suddenly shoved past me, running over to the bed. He began barking wildly.

"What's wrong with him?" Estevez said. He took a step backward, looking nervous. "Can you get him out of here? I'm not crazy about dogs—"

[Foxtrot! Between the mattresses!]

"He's trained to hunt rats," I said quickly. I ran over to the bed, but instead of restraining Tiny—who was trying to jam his nose between the bedspring and the mattress—I reached down, stuck my fingers in the crack, and lifted. "There's probably a rodent in here—"

But there wasn't.

What was lying there was a small glass vial with a plastic cap and a white label. I could make out the letters CARF quite easily.

"Well," said Brower. "How about *that* . . ."

"I don't know what that is," Estevez said. "It's not mine."

"Sure it isn't," said Brower. "Son, you're under arrest." He pulled a pair of handcuffs from his belt and took Estevez's wrist.

"What? What are you *talking* about? This is the room they gave me! That could have been here before!"

Brower secured Estevez's hands behind his back. "Looks like you were right," he told me. "But now I really need you to leave, and lock the door. I'll come back and collect the evidence once I've got Mr. Estevez in my patrol car. You have the right to remain silent—" He took Estevez by the arm and led him outside while reading him his rights. Tiny and I followed, and I closed and locked the door behind me.

[Something's not right.]

"I know," I muttered, watching Brower take Estevez away. "We searched that room before, and there wasn't any carfentanil there then. I guess he stashed it someplace else."

[Then moved it to such an obvious hiding place instead of getting rid of it?]

Tiny was right. Something smelled, and it wasn't of animal tranquilizer. We followed Brower and Estevez down the hall and then down the stairs.

"You have to at least tell me what I'm being charged with!"

"You're being charged with the murder of Maria Wong," Brower said. "Think you're pretty smart, huh? You used that flying gadget to stick her with a dart, but you forgot to get rid of the poison afterward. Not so smart after all."

"That's—that's ridiculous! Look, I can prove I didn't do that. The only way to pilot the GEQ is with the remote controller, and it logs all its flights. The data from the flight log will show the GEQ never went *near* Maria Wong."

"That kind of thing can be faked," said Brower tersely.

"You should at least take a look," I said. We'd reached the lobby, and I saw Shondra and ZZ hurrying over to intercept us.

"What's happening?" ZZ demanded. "Why is one of my guests in handcuffs?"

"This is all a misunderstanding," said Estevez.

"Where's the flight controller?" I asked.

"Upstairs, in my suitcase. Outside zippered pocket."

Shondra studied Estevez coolly, but said nothing. ZZ grabbed Brower by the arm. "Answer me, dammit!"

"This guest of yours," said Brower, "is being charged with homicide. I am going to put him in the back of my unit, and then I'll come back and explain things. That all right with you?"

ZZ let go of his arm and turned to me. "Foxtrot? Can you clear this up?"

"I can. Mostly." I ran through a terse explanation of what was happening. Shondra just listened and nodded; ZZ gasped and looked like she was going to either burst into tears or put her fist through a wall.

"This is my fault," she whispered. "This is all my fault."

"Don't jump to any conclusions just yet," I said. "Estevez claims the flight controller will clear him."

"And we're going to follow up on that." Sheriff Brower paused in the doorway, then stepped back inside and shut the door. "Now that my prisoner's secured, we can check out his story. But I wouldn't put too much faith in one of this guy's gizmos providing the alibi for another."

ZZ and Shondra moved toward the staircase, but Brower stopped them with an upraised hand. "Hold it. Chain of evidence is screwed up enough as it is—I don't want more bodies in that room. I'll go and see for myself."

"So will I," I said. "I've already been in there—and if needed, I could corroborate your testimony."

Brower didn't like it, but he knew I was right. "Okay, I guess I owe you that much. But don't touch anything—and leave the dog."

I nodded. "Tiny, stay here," I said.

Tiny whined, but sat down. [Stay alert. Brower could easily miss something.]

"Good dog," I said.

We went back up, Brower wheezing a little—I got the feeling that he and stairs weren't really best buds. I unlocked the door and stepped aside. "All yours, Sheriff."

Brower pulled on a pair of blue latex gloves before entering, me right behind him. He found the suitcase on an ottoman at the foot of the bed, and unzippered the outside pocket. "Nothing in here," he said.

I peered at the luggage. The pocket was empty. "Maybe it's somewhere else in the suitcase?"

He opened it up and rummaged as I watched. Nothing resembling a flight controller. "It's not in here, either. Does this thing actually exist?"

"I saw it myself." I had a sudden thought. "Could he

have it on him? He could have forgotten; I do that with my cell phone all the time—"

Brower snorted. "I patted him down before I put him in the car. Took a cell phone and a multitool from him, but nothing else." He pulled the phone from his pocket and showed me. "See?"

I looked at it, but it was just a cell phone. "Well, it's got to be here someplace."

Brower searched the room while I watched and offered helpful advice, which the sheriff seemed oddly unappreciative of. He didn't find it.

"It's not here, Foxtrot," he said finally. "Which probably means he got rid of it, for pretty much the opposite reason he gave us: It would verify he was the killer, not disprove it. Now, if you'll excuse me, I need to seal up this evidence." He took several folded plastic bags out of his pocket.

I went back downstairs, where Shondra, ZZ, and Tiny were waiting. I shook my head. "No go. It wasn't anywhere in the room."

"'Course not," said Shondra. "Device like that, you'd either wipe the memory or get rid of it as soon as you could. Disposing of it is the safer option."

"But not the smarter one," I pointed out. "Estevez built the thing. If anyone knows how to erase incriminating information from it, he does. Getting rid of it just looks suspicious."

"Not if you claim it's your alibi," Shondra countered. "That seems pretty smart, to me."

She might have been right—but I knew about the poison showing up out of nowhere, and she didn't. Not that I could tell her that. "He hasn't left the grounds since he got here, has he?"

"I'd have to check the footage for the last day—but up until the murder, no."

ZZ looked lost. "I can't believe he would—I mean, I knew what he was building that horrid little machine for, I just can't believe he actually *used* it . . ."

"You look like you need a cup of tea," I said. "Go sit down in the lounge. I'll make you one."

Shondra followed me into the kitchen, where I put the kettle on. Ben was nowhere in sight—I briefly wondered where he was, but didn't have the time or energy to spend on the question.

"ZZ told me a little about Estevez's project," Shondra said. "Took me all morning to pry it out of her. Turns out a whistle-blower got in contact with her via the Internet and leaked some of the classified details of the project. According to ZZ, it's not designed for surveillance at all—it's an assassination drone, plain and simple. She was going to denounce him at one of the salon dinners, make a big deal out of it. You know how she loves drama."

"I guess that's motive," I said, leaning up against the counter. "He tries to kill her to shut her up, and kills Maria instead. I wonder why we didn't find the dart?"

"Probably had a string attached to it so it could be retrieved. You come right down to it, the weapon itself isn't that high-tech—just the delivery platform."

"I suppose." I fell silent, thinking. Tiny had stayed behind with ZZ; he wasn't any more convinced than I was, and wasn't taking any chances.

We didn't know it then—but we were already too late.

I was jarred out of my reverie by a twin blast of frenzied barking and an urgent mental message: [Foxtrot! Come quickly—something's wrong with ZZ!]

I ran. ZZ was slumped on the couch, her head lolling to one side. She was barely breathing. "Oh, God," I said. Shondra was already on the phone to 911. I tried to get ZZ to wake up, but she was completely out of it.

[She just passed out—I don't know why.]

I thought hard about the reading I'd done on carfentanil, then pulled out my own phone and hit the speed-dial number for Caroline. She got it on the first ring. "Hello?"

"Caroline! You have naloxone on hand, right?"

"Yes. Why?"

"Bring it and a syringe to the main house, fast! We're in the lounge!"

ZZ wasn't breathing.

I started mouth-to-mouth. Carfentanil worked by paralyzing muscles, including the ones that made you breathe. All I had to do was keep ZZ breathing until Caroline got here. Sure, no problem.

I blocked out everything but the rhythm of inhaling and then expelling air, making ZZ's chest rise and fall. Just like blowing up a balloon, only I was saving a life instead of decorating for a birthday party.

I wondered if I'd see *her* ghost, too.

CHAPTER THIRTEEN

It seemed to take Caroline forever to get there. When she finally did arrive, I was so deep into what I was doing I didn't even hear her—she had to physically pull me away.

"What happened?" Caroline snapped. ZZ's eyes were wide open, making her look like she was already dead.

"Carfentanil," I said. "I think she was poisoned, but I don't know how—"

"You sure?"

I didn't hesitate. "Yes."

Caroline had a hypodermic and glass vial in one hand, and now she used one to fill the other. "We'll know in a minute," she said grimly, and jabbed the needle into ZZ's thigh.

We watched anxiously as Caroline pumped the drug into ZZ's system. Naloxone is fast-acting and powerful, often countering the effects of an opiate overdose in less than a minute.

ZZ still wasn't breathing.

Caroline immediately started giving her mouth-to-mouth.

"Ambulance is on its way," Shondra said. "Is there anything we can do to help?"

Caroline didn't answer verbally—she was busy. But she waved the offer away.

In an emergency—as opposed to a crisis, which I rank as less urgent and more common—I've found that focusing on the known facts helps calm people down. And by people, I meant me. "It's okay. This is normal. Naloxone hydrochloride can take up to five minutes to work, though it usually kicks in within sixty seconds. Caroline's just making sure ZZ keeps breathing while the drug takes effect."

Shondra gave me a flat, evaluating glance. "How'd you know?"

I looked down at Caroline, then took a few steps away and motioned for Shondra to join me. "I don't know, not for sure," I said under my breath. "But I thought there was a good chance that our killer would try again, so I did a little preemptive research on the 'Net. Naloxone is the antidote for overdoses of powerful animal tranquilizers."

"All of them?" She sounded skeptical.

"Just the ones that are opiate-based. But those are also the ones most likely to kill a human being."

"What if it doesn't work?"

"Naloxone isn't dangerous itself. But if it doesn't work—I don't know." I glanced at the door helplessly. "When is that damn ambulance going to get here?"

"It's working," Caroline announced.

We both hurried back and knelt down. ZZ's eyes were closed now, but she was breathing on her own. "I think you called it," Caroline said. "She's not out of danger, but the fact that she's breathing means the naloxone's working."

"What now?" I asked.

"We get the paramedics to put her on a respirator, make sure she keeps breathing. Then she'll have to be monitored closely and given regular doses of naloxone—it has a short half-life, probably shorter than what she was poisoned with. But there's the possibility she could sink into a coma."

"Brain damage?" I asked.

"Probably not. You got to her fast, right?"

"Not fast enough," I said.

"As long as she wasn't deprived of oxygen for long, she should be fine. Assuming that an opiate was all she was drugged with."

"That's a good point," Shondra said.

[Here's another one.] I jumped a little; I'd almost forgotten Tiny was there. [How was she poisoned—and is the poison still around?]

I hadn't even thought of that. We needed to find the source, fast—what if someone else keeled over?

At that moment I heard the first faint howl of the siren. And I realized I had a decision to make. "Caroline—ZZ needs to be monitored and redosed, right? Can that be done here?"

Caroline looked confused. "Here? I suppose—but she needs to be in a hospital, Foxtrot. She needs blood tests, life support, monitoring—"

"I'll take care of it," I said. I pulled out my phone, started searching for home medical services. "Full-time nurse, oxygen, defibrillator in case of a cardiac event, regular shots of naloxone. We'll set up a hospital bed in her room."

Shondra looked at me like I'd just lost my mind. "No. That's crazy—"

"No, it's *necessary.* We'll get the paramedics to take blood and get it to the hospital, but ZZ stays *here.*"

"I can't allow that," Caroline said.

"You don't have a choice," I countered. "In the event of a medical emergency where ZZ is incapacitated, power of attorney falls on me. That includes a Living Will clause that specifies I get to make any and all decisions regarding life-preserving measures and whether or not to pull the plug."

Caroline had gone from puzzlement to shock. Shondra, though, was starting to get it.

"Someone just tried to kill my boss," I said. "If they can get to her in her own home, they can get to her in a hospital. But here, I can control the situation. I can vet every single person who comes near her. I can hire guards to stand outside her door twenty-four hours a day. Hell, I can rent a tank and park it in the driveway."

I looked from Shondra to Caroline and back again. Shondra was on board, and Caroline was on her way. "Nobody gets to her," I said. "I won't let them. Are we clear?"

They both nodded, and then the paramedics were pounding at the front door.

I was only half kidding about the tank. What I actually had in mind was going to be parked at the foot of ZZ's bed, and was much harder to get past than a mere armored vehicle.

Tanks, after all, didn't have a supernatural sense of smell.

I got to work.

I put Shondra in charge of finding guards; I knew she'd have the connections and would personally vouch for anyone she hired. Medical services were next, and I lit a fire under the guy I talked to—a fire I stoked with fat, thousand-dollar bonuses for speed of delivery and setup. He promised he'd have someone out within the hour. I went to a different outfit for nursing, because I wanted a larger pool to draw from—better chances of getting someone immediately and fewer problems with scheduling afterward. I did all this while convincing the EMTs she couldn't be moved off site, making sure the staff knew what was going on, and reassuring the occasional worried guest who wandered in. Hana Kim was horrified, while Mr. Kwok did his best to remain stoic. Kenny Gant was astounded, while Keene seemed heartbroken. He told me he was going to have a specialist flown in from Geneva, this "Absolutely brilliant guy Keith told me about. Knows his way around a seizure, he says. He'll get her on her feet in no time."

And I never left ZZ's side.

Tiny, I thought at him. *I need you to find out how ZZ was poisoned, but I can't just let you roam all over the house. Can you change into something small and unobtrusive?*

[I can, but I'll need to slip away, first].

Go ahead. I don't think anyone will notice—we're all too busy.

Everyone was still in the atrium. The paramedics were keeping an eye on ZZ, Shondra was talking into her cell phone, Ben Montain was hovering nearby with a worried look on his face, and Kenny Gant was standing in a corner and shaking his head. Sheriff Brower was upstairs, trying to solve the case by stomping around searching through wastebaskets.

Tiny crawled under a nearby chair, out of everyone's line of sight. A moment later, a Yorkshire terrier darted out from beneath the chair. It took me a second to recognize it as such; I've seen bigger guinea pigs. Tiny's new form could have easily fit in the palm of my hand, and when it scampered up the stairs no one else seemed to notice.

All this activity was the easy part. It's what I do, after all, and the more details I had to manage, the less time I had to actually think about what had just happened. But I couldn't submerge myself in work; getting ZZ squared away was important, but catching whoever poisoned her was just as vital.

It took a little under two hours to come together. Finally, I had ZZ in her own room, in a top-of-the-line hospital bed, hooked up to a respirator, with an IV drip in her arm and sensitive equipment monitoring her vital signs. There were two guards at her door, and an experienced nurse was at her side. They'd given her another shot of naloxone about an hour after the first one.

What I hadn't managed to do was find her son. Every call I made to Oscar went straight to voice mail.

I had tracked down ZZ's doctor, though, a man with the improbable name of Sang Singh. He was tall, thin, bald, and extremely angry with me.

"You must have her moved to a hospital immediately!" he demanded once he'd finished examining her. "She is in a coma!"

"I realize that," I said. "But she's in no immediate danger. We can monitor her at home just as easily as at the hospital."

"Easily? Easily? This is not a question of ease. This is a woman's life we are talking about. Whether or not you are inconvenienced is hardly the issue!"

"I misspoke," I said carefully. "Dr. Singh, ZZ's welfare is just as important to me as it is to you. But she left very explicit instructions in her Living Will, and I'm legally obligated to follow them. Now, are you going to help ZZ get through this, or spend all your energy fighting me?"

He glared at me through black, horn-rimmed glasses. "I am familiar with her Living Will. It does not endorse endangering her life through denying her proper medical attention, only that she does not wish to have her life prolonged artificially if there is no hope of her recovering. That is *not* the case here."

"That's not for you to decide. That's for whoever has power of attorney—which is me."

His eyes narrowed. "I don't understand why you are doing this. How did this even happen?"

"Someone tried to kill her." I paused for a second to let that sink in. "Twice. That's why there are guards outside, and why she's not leaving this house. I expect you to come by every day to check on her, and I promise that ZZ will go straight to the hospital once the perpetrator has been caught. Okay?"

He still looked angry, but I didn't think it was at me anymore. "A killer? You are sure?"

"A maid was poisoned two days ago. She didn't survive."

"But—perhaps an accident, something in the house?"

"No. The maid was injected. ZZ, we don't know yet."

Dr. Singh fell silent. "Injected?" he said at last. "How?"

"We don't know that, either. But Sheriff Brower will confirm that there's an ongoing murder investigation, even if he's less than forthcoming with details."

At that very minute, Brower opened the door and marched in. "I'm going to have to confiscate everything in your kitchen. All the food, anyhow."

I nodded. "Understood. I doubt you'll find anything there, though. Ben already told me what he gave ZZ to eat today, and nobody else who ate the same thing has had any symptoms."

"You'll pardon me if I don't take his word for it."

"No, of course not."

[Foxtrot?]

Tiny? Where are you?

[Under the bed.]

There's not a lot of room under most hospital beds, but then Tiny wasn't taking up much space at the moment. *Find anything?*

[I think so. Empty teacup with traces of both ZZ's scent and carfentanil clinging to it. Small table in the lounge, beside the couch.]

"Sheriff? I think ZZ was having tea in the lounge, earlier."

"You're just remembering this now?" he snapped. "Dammit, you better hope a maid hasn't cleaned that up." He stalked out of the room, pulling another pair of blue latex gloves out of his back pocket as he went.

"Sheriff?" said Dr. Singh, hurrying after him. "I would like to speak to you, please."

That left just me and Beatrice, the registered nurse, a formidable-looking woman with a craggy face and white hair. "Could you leave us alone for a minute?" I asked.

Beatrice nodded. "I'll be right outside if you need me." She closed the door behind her.

Tiny scooted out from under the bed. "Good Lord," I whispered. "You're . . . well, *tiny*."

[Two point eight inches tall, to be exact. I'm mimicking the form of a dwarf Yorkshire terrier named Silvia, who died in 1945.] He abruptly ballooned up to golden retriever size. [That's better. Hard to squeeze into something that small.]

"Yeah," I said. "I feel the same way about this dress I bought for New Year's." I walked over to the door and locked it. "Okay. Here's the drill. I'm putting you on guard duty. Anyone comes in here and tries anything, you stop them. I know you don't need to eat—how about sleep?"

[A habit I gave up long ago.]

"Good. But we're going to need a new cover story. You can't do an effective job while hiding under the bed, and if you do have to repel a murder attempt, I don't want to have to explain how a gigantic hellhound materialized out of thin air and saved ZZ's life. It's—it's . . ."

[Inversely Baskerville-ian?]

I stared down at him. "You're very well read for a supernatural canine. I'm starting to think Scooby-Doo is more than just a cartoon."

[Please restrict your comparisons of me to literary ones, please. Television gives me a headache.]

"Okay, Scooby-Don't. Here's the plan. I'm going to take Tiny the golden retriever out, and bring Not-So-Tiny the ferocious watchdog back in. I'll check in with you periodically, using the pretext of bringing you food and walking you. Tango and I will continue to look for the killer."

[Agreed.] That's what he said, but he didn't sound happy.

"Look, I know you'd rather be on the hunt, but I need someone here I can trust. You saved me back at the graveyard—and I *know* you won't let anything happen to ZZ, either."

[It's all right, Foxtrot. Guarding is in my blood as much as hunting is; I have no problem with staying put.]

"Good. Now . . . let's pick out a suitable outfit for your new position."

He modeled a few for me. The Irish wolfhound was impressive, as was the Great Dane, but I didn't want to rely on size alone; I needed his appearance to be scary, something that would make any would-be assassin freeze in his or her tracks. Doberman pinscher was close, but I thought he needed more muscle.

"What about the form you used when you took on Topsy?" I suggested.

[I'd rather not. That's a very particular form, and I like to reserve it as a last resort. It tends to attract attention.]

Fair enough; I had enough to worry about without having to explain where I found such a one-of-a-kind über-dog on short notice.

We finally settled on a rottweiler, a breed—Tiny informed me—that the Romans used as war dogs. To me, it looked like a cross between a pit bull and a Doberman on steroids, which was just about perfect. "Okay. Now shift back into micro-Yorkie mode and I'll smuggle you out of here."

He did, but before I could shove him in a bag there was a knock on the door. Tiny immediately scooted under the bed. "Who's there?"

"It's Cooper," said a familiar voice. "You want to tell your rent-a-thugs I ain't the Antichrist so they'll let me in?"

I unlocked the door. Cooper had his beat-up straw hat in his hands, and looked like someone had just reminded him that John Lennon was still dead. "All right if I come in?" he asked.

"Uh—yes, of course." I hadn't expected Coop to show up—Oscar, yes, but not the caretaker of the graveyard.

He went straight to the foot of ZZ's bed and stared at her, twisting his hat in his hands. "Hey, Zelda," he said softly. "How you doin'?"

"She can't hear you," I said. "She's in a coma."

"Oh, you'd be surprised what people are aware of, even when they're like this. I been fast asleep and woke up knowing all the lyrics to a song playing in the next room. You're just hearing us on another level, aren't you?" He was talking to ZZ, not me.

I didn't contradict him. With all that I'd learned in the past few days, who was I to say he was wrong? Maybe some version of ZZ was hovering over her bed right now, listening to our conversation and trying to figure out what the hell was going on.

"How'd you hear, Coop?" I asked.

"Vic came down and let me know. Said she just collapsed, but there were all kinds of crazy rumors about why. Knew if anyone would have the straight goods it'd be you." He gave me a long, serious look. "So what happened, Foxtrot? What's wrong with her?'

"It looks like someone poisoned her, Coop. And Maria, too."

His eyes widened. "For real?"

"Yeah."

"That's monumentally fucked up."

"It is."

Cooper shook his head. "Who'd do this to her? And why?"

"That's exactly what I'm trying to figure out."

At that moment a commotion broke out in the hall: Oscar, shouting at the guards who wouldn't let him in. "The prodigal son finally puts in an appearance," I muttered. "Excuse me."

I strode over to the door and yanked it open. "It's all right," I said. "He's family."

"*Thank* you!" Oscar glared at both guards, who stared back as impassively as stone lions. "I *live* here, you jackbooted mercenaries. And I don't appreciate being *manhandled*."

I sighed and ushered him inside. From what I could smell as he stepped past me, he'd been spending the last few hours with his good friends Sherry and Brandy.

"Oscar," Cooper said with a nod.

"What's he doing here?" Oscar demanded. "Good Lord, my mother's on her deathbed and she's being attended by a *grave digger*? Is this some sort of sick *joke*?"

"Cooper came to pay his respects, Oscar."

"*Did* he?" Oscar fixed Cooper with a bloodshot eye. He was a bit more sauced than I'd first thought. "Or did he come to *finish the job*?"

"Oscar, that's enough. You're *way* out of line—"

"I am, am I? I think *not.* Lines are the purview of *this* gentlemen, lines and joints and, and . . . and *popping*!"

"Beg pardon?" Coop said, looking bewildered.

"Cocaine! Marijuana! Pills! I know what you get up to, down in that little shack of yours . . . you've practackly got a *phermacy* down there." Oscar swayed a little on his feet.

Okay, not a bit more sauced, a lot more. I rolled my eyes. "Terrific."

"My dear mother was drugged, and *you're* the druggie. Drugger. Drug-using drug person."

Coop shook his head again, sadly. "I just came by to see how she was doing. Guess I better go." He put his hat on and headed for the door.

"Don't think I don't *know* about you and her," Oscar growled at his back.

Cooper stopped.

"Oh, boy," I said. "Coop, I'm sorry. It's just the overpriced booze talking—"

"I can speak for *myself,*" Oscar said. "And I know what I know. My mother has always been indiscreet—except in *your* case, Mr. Cooper. When it came to an actual *custodian,* even she knew well enough to keep it hidden."

Cooper turned around slowly. There was a lot of regret in his eyes, but his back was straight. "I wasn't always a custodian, Oscar. You take care of her, you hear?"

Then he opened the door and slipped away.

"Good riddance," Oscar snarls. "Grave digger, my arse. Gold digger is more like it."

I shouldn't have been surprised, let alone shocked, but I was. ZZ never cared much for social conventions; it wasn't the idea that she had an affair with a groundskeeper that bothered me, it was the fact that she kept it a secret.

"How is she, Foxtrot?" Oscar asked. He hadn't approached the bed yet, as if he was afraid she was contagious. "She looks . . . terrible."

Which, while not exactly tactful, was true. I'd always thought an unconscious person breathing with the aid of a respirator looked ghastly and unnatural, and seeing a parent like that must have been twice as bad. "She's going to be all right, Oscar. She wasn't deprived of oxygen for any length of time, and we've got her on a powerful opiate antagonist. When she wakes up—"

"Which is *when*, exactly?" He still sounded angry, but with Cooper gone I was the only one in the room for him to unload on. The only one who was conscious, anyway.

"I don't know."

"How did this *happen*? Dammit, Foxtrot, you have your pert little nose stuck in every corner of this estate, and yet you stand idly by while someone sneaks into our home and tries to murder my *mother*?"

"I'm sorry."

"Don't be sorry. *Be better.*" He glared at me for a second, and then looked away. "That's what *she* always said to me. When I was a boy." His voice had gotten softer. "It was never an accusation, though. Always an encouragement. She knew I *could* do better, most of the time. I just didn't bother."

"Where were you, Oscar? I've been trying to reach you for hours."

"Can't you tell? I was drinking. As my sorrows have recently learned how to swim, drowning them requires not only complete immersion but holding them under the surface until they quit struggling." He punctuated this statement with a hiccup, which took a little of the sheen off its elegance. "An inny case, my whereabouts are irrelevant. Where were *you*?"

Doing my best to prevent this and failing was the honest answer, but what I said was, "Trying to figure out who poisoned Maria, actually. If I had, ZZ wouldn't be in that bed."

Oscar looked befuddled. "Maria? *She* was poisoned?"

"It looks that way."

"Then . . . good God, Foxtrot. Have we *all* been poisoned?" He put a hand to his chest as if afraid his heart might suddenly decide to abandon ship.

"No, Oscar. That's highly unlikely. But whoever poisoned Maria and ZZ is most likely still here."

He scowled. "The grave digger. I knew it! That grimy, flea-infested Bohemian—"

"I don't think so, Oscar. Even if he and ZZ did have a thing, I can't think of any reason for him to try to kill her—"

"I can. Five million of them, in fact."

"What are you talking about?"

"I've seen Mother's will, Foxtrot. She likes to pull it out from time to time and wave it under my nose to make sure I behave myself. There's a stipulation in it—one I wasn't meant to see, I'm sure—that when she dies one Franklin Cooper is to receive five million dollars from her estate. I'd say that's plenty of motive to put her in an early grave, wouldn't you?"

Chapter Fourteen

Five million dollars.

Oscar was right. That was more than enough incentive to bump someone off—but only if you were aware of that fact in the first place. "Does Cooper know?"

"He must," Oscar replied.

"So you don't know that for sure."

"Perhaps we should ask him. I say, old boy, did my mother happen to mention the contents of her will while you two were reliving the Summer of Love? Oh, you don't recall? What with all the illicit reefer-sex while grooving to Jimi Joplin?"

"I think you mean Janis Hendrix."

"Whomever. He's not going to admit it, is my point." Oscar staggered a little, and put his hand on the bed rail to steady himself.

"You should go, Oscar. I'm looking after ZZ. I won't let anything happen to her."

"Anything *else,* you mean."

Ouch. Still, I kind of deserved it. "Go. She'll be fine."

Oscar nodded. He looked down at his mother, then away. He blinked a few times rapidly, then straightened himself and marched toward the door. His path there was a little crooked, but he managed. He left without having the last word, which was unusual for him.

"All clear," I said.

Tiny squirmed out from underneath the bed. [What do you think? He seemed genuinely distraught.]

"Yes, but why? Is it because his mother nearly died, or because he's overcome with remorse for trying to kill her?"

[You know the man better than I. All I can say for sure is he reeked of alcohol.]

"Which is hardly out of character." I shook my head. "Let's get you re-introduced. I want you back here at your post as quickly as possible."

Smuggling him out of the room was easy. I headed straight for my car, and called Shondra as I walked. I told her I was bringing in some extra canine help, which she didn't sound crazy about. "My guys can handle security, Foxtrot. A guard dog is overkill."

"Maybe, maybe not. But the friend I got Tiny from made the offer, and since I have to take Tiny back today anyway, I said I'd give this new dog a chance."

"Your friend has a lot of dogs."

"He's a miracle worker. You wouldn't believe some of the pooches he works with. Circus dogs, trackers, search-and-rescue . . . they come to him smart, and leave smarter."

"So he's a trainer?"

"Kind of. Like a dog whisperer, but better. A dog babbler."

"If you say so . . ."

It didn't take me long—I just drove into town, stopped at a pet store to buy some supplies, and drove back again. Tiny shifted into his new rottweiler form and rode beside me in the passenger seat.

"So, what do we call you now?"

[Good question. What do you suggest?]

"Zanzibar Buck-Buck McFate."

[That does have a certain ring to it. Bit long, though.]

"It's from a Dr. Seuss story. How about we shorten it to just Zanzibar?"

[Done.]

Zanzibar was a much more serious dog than Tiny. He didn't so much walk as prowl, his eyes alert and wary. I brought him inside, introduced him to the guards, and told them he was highly trained. "He won't let you near ZZ, though, so don't even try."

One of the guards, a muscular guy in his thirties with a mustache from the seventies, said, "What if there's a medical emergency, or a fire?"

"Then he'll stand down."

The other guard, a stocky man with a blond crew cut, said, "Really? He's that smart?"

"You'd be amazed."

I assured them that I'd be back to walk and feed him, then put down a dog dish and water bowl. "I'll be back in a few hours," I told him.

[I'll be here.]

I went downstairs and back outside.

Tango? I thought.

No answer. She must have been out of range. I walked around the grounds, calling her name in my head every few minutes until I got an answer. <*I'm over here, Toots.*>

I found her at the edge of the animal enclosure, right next to the fence. She was staring up at Oswald the ostrich, who was staring right back.

"Tango. I've got news, and it isn't good—"

<*I know. I've been watching all the excitement and eavesdropping. Someone tried to kill ZZ by poisoning her, with the same stuff that was used on the maid.*> Tango yawned. <*'Scuse me. Late night.*>

I frowned. "You seem to be taking this in stride."

<I'm a cat, Toots. You say death and dismemberment, I say Circle of Life. I'm more upset that we screwed up, which is why I've been spending the last few hours hunting down leads instead of wringing my paws.>

Well, there was a certain cold-blooded—and very feline—logic to that. "What have you come up with?"

<I'm not sure. But the giant chicken here has some interesting things to say.>

Oswald cocked his head to the side, as if he knew we were talking about him.

"Him? You're kidding. I don't know how big his brain is, but I'm pretty sure the only things he has room for in it are identifying food and Houdini's biography."

<He's not the brightest bulb on the Christmas tree, I'll admit. But he notices things that don't belong, and that's what he saw last night.>

"Can you be a little more specific?"

<He saw a person enter the menagerie in the middle of the night.>

"Who?"

<Well, he's a little unclear on that.>

"Male or female?"

<Yes. Probably.>

"Short? Tall? Fat? Thin?"

<Let's not get bogged down in details. It walked upright on two legs, that much he'll swear to. And it had a little box that lit up.>

"He can't tell the sex or size, but 'a little box that lights up' he remembers?"

Tango blinked and somehow made it seem like a shrug. *<He likes things that light up. They make him happy.>*

"Okay, so our mysterious two-legged person had a cell phone. So wha—" I stopped. "Wait. Maybe it wasn't a cell phone."

<What else would it be?>

I told her about the GEQ, Estevez's arrest, and why Tiny and I thought he couldn't be guilty. "If someone stole the controller out of Estevez's room, they could have used the GEQ to commit the murder. Maybe that's what Oswald saw."

<Or maybe he just saw someone with a cell phone. Hang on, I'll ask him.>

Tango opened her mouth and emitted a series of short hisses, followed by a snort. Oswald puffed up his throat, then hissed and snorted back.

<He says the person he saw didn't talk to the shiny box. Also, he thinks this season's crop of grasshoppers is nice and crunchy.>

I nodded. "Was the person with the box holding it in two hands or one?"

More snorts, more hissing. *<He's not sure. He only saw the person for a moment when he or she went inside, and another when they left—>*

Oswald interrupted her with more noise. Tango listened intently. *<He says the two-legged one probably ate it.>*

"Why would he think—oh. The person he saw didn't have it when they left."

<That seems to be what he's saying. Also, there's a definite note of envy in there, and not a little bitterness.>

"I'll keep that in mind the next time I make a call within ten feet of him. You know what this means?"

<That our perp has an amazing grasp of that mysterious human invention you call the pocket?>

"Now who's bitter? No, Tango—it means it's possible they got rid of it in the menagerie. *And it could still be there.*"

<Then what are we waiting for? Let's go hunting.>

* * *

The estate menagerie takes up a lot of real estate. It can accommodate animals both small and large, from lizards in terrariums to grazing bovines the size of a truck. I thought we should start with the bigger, nocturnal animals; they were the ones most likely to have seen something.

We walked in through the path that led past Oswald's enclosure. There were habitats on either side, but the animals they held had most likely been fast asleep when their late-night visitor strolled by.

Then we came to an enclosure that held a plain, earthen burrow. I knew what was in it, just as I knew the animal was largely nocturnal. "Hey, Tango. How's your Spotted Hyena?"

<Spotty. But I can give it a shot.> Tango opened her mouth and emitted a series of most un-cat-like noises: groans, whoops, and a sort of giggle.

We waited. After a moment there was an answering whoop from inside the burrow. A few seconds later, a sleepy-looking pair of eyes above a blunt snout poked out.

I made a point of knowing which animals were present in the menagerie at any given time, even if I wasn't all that well-versed on their finer points. I knew, for example, that spotted hyenas mostly slept during the day and made some pretty weird noises at night, but that was about it. I had vague notions about their behavior, but I'd be the first to admit my knowledge was largely drawn from Disney cartoons.

<Okay, you've got his attention. What do you want me to ask him?>

I hesitated. The hyena stalked out of his den, stretching his hind legs one after the other like a cat, then shaking his head like a dog. He stared at me curiously.

"Uh, I guess we should do introductions. Hi, I'm Foxtrot, and this is my translator, Tango."

Tango emitted more whoops, grunts, and a kind of

chattering laugh. The hyena replied in kind, making it sound like two lunatics sharing a private joke.

<He says, good for you. His—whoops, I mean her—name is Bongo. If she talks to you, will you feed her the small cat with the big mouth?>

"No, but I'll come by later with a nice juicy piece of raw meat."

More grunting and giggling. *<For a promise I will give you some lies. Come back with the meat and I'll tell you which ones are true.>* Bongo sat down, splayed her hind legs, and began licking herself just like a cat. When I saw *what* she was licking, I realized that she was a he after all, and any answers I got were going to be unreliable at best.

"Okay, we'll play by your rules. Did you see a human being walk past your pen late last night?"

<I did. He was ten feet tall and covered in termites. Also, he was carrying the moon.>

"I see. What did he do with the moon?"

<She fed it to the crocodile. Then she danced on the back of the hippo and ate some termites. They were delicious.>

Dammit, I couldn't even rely on Bongo using the right pronoun. But there must have been *some* truths buried in there, right? "What did she do then?"

<He turned himself into a flamingo and flew away.>

Terrific.

<I'm going back to sleep. Come back with the meat at a reasonable hour and we'll talk more.> Bongo turned around and padded back into his den.

"This is my own fault," I said. "I should have come prepared with bribes. Informants always want a payoff, right?"

<Sure. But some animals will say anything for a treat.>

"True enough. I could wind up getting a confession

from a greedy giraffe—*Yeah, yeah, I drove over that guy with my pickup. Now hand over the bushel of acacia leaves.*"

<Let's sort this out. What do you figure she actually saw?>

"*He,* Tango. That was definitely a *he*. And I'm guessing he saw someone with a light source—maybe a cell phone, maybe the controller, maybe just a flashlight."

<Hate to disagree with you, Toots, but are you saying she didn't know her own gender? 'Cause that was most definitely the female article she was using.>

I sighed. "No, Tango, I'm saying *he* was screwing with us. You know, telling us a blatant lie right up front? The real question is, how much truth did he add to the mix."

Tango's voice was getting that annoyed tone to it again. *<That doesn't make a whole lot of sense. If you're going to lie to someone, do you advertise the fact with the first thing you say? No.>*

"But that's exactly what Bongo did. He *told* us he was going to lie to us."

<Maybe she was lying.>

"Is this making your brain hurt, too?"

<Little bit.>

"Good. Okay, let's go with your scenario. Our friend Bongo is not only a pathologically honest liar, he's a transsexual opportunist with a keen eye for giant dancing hippo fetishists. That work for you?"

<I think you're getting a little worked up.>

"You think I'm worked up now, wait until I chow down on some grasshoppers and turn myself into a penguin."

<Have fun. I hear they're especially crunchy this year.>

"Can we get back to finding the controller, please?'

<Hey, you're the one having the meltdown. I'm just correcting your grammar.>

I strode down the path, Tango trotting behind me.

The hippos—two of them—were no more than gray bumps sticking out of the water. I didn't know a lot about hippos, either, but I did remember one interesting statistic Caroline tossed at me: Hippos were responsible for more deaths every year in Africa than any other animal. Plus, they were generally aggressive and unpredictable. I didn't know if they were nocturnal or not.

I stopped and stared at the pool. Tango stopped beside me. *<I really hope you don't want to have a conversation with these guys.>*

"You don't speak their lingo?"

<I do, but I hate getting that close to water. Can you believe animals actually live *in that stuff?>*

"Let's keep going. I want to talk to some animals past this point, and see if we can find one that's reasonably reliable."

We got lucky at the very next pen . . . kind of.

I heard a gruff chuffing noise and saw a short, squat animal with a dark underside and a white top. He was a new acquisition for the menagerie, illegally smuggled into the country and then abandoned when his new owners decided they didn't like they way he smelled. So much for the glory and fame of being an Internet meme.

"How's your Honey Badger?" I asked Tango.

<Not that good. I speak a pretty clear Wolverine, though, and the tongues are similar. Want me to give it a try?>

"Sure. Ask him—or her—if they saw a human being here last night."

Tango chuffed and snorted, while the honey badger watched her intently. He replied as soon as she was finished, and went on for quite a while. Tango's reaction was . . . well, have you ever seen cats encounter something that truly unnerves them? Their eyes get wider, their ears go back a little, their tails start to twitch. That's what happened to Tango.

"Well? What did he say?"

<*Um.*>

"He said um?"

<*No, no, he said more than that. A lot more.*>

"You're having trouble translating?"

<*I wish. Actually, the gist of it came through loud and clear—I'm just not sure how I should phrase it. Other than carefully.*>

"Well, do your best."

Tango gave me a quick glance, then looked back at the honey badger. <*Okaayyy . . . I'm just gonna use the word* mumble *if I'm unclear on a meaning, all right?"*

"Fine."

<*He'd really like to mumble your mumble mumble and then rip off your mumble and eat it.*>

I blinked. "That seems a little rude—"

<*Wait, I'm not finished. Then he'd like to mumble all over your mumble, let it sit in the sun until it's good and ripe, and then mumble the rotting parts until they mumble mumble worms mumble skull mumble roll around and wriggle in delight, something something.*>

I stared at the honey badger. It stared back calmly.

"That's not really useful," I said.

<*Not in a practical way, no.*>

The honey badger chuffed and growled a few more times, then waited expectantly.

"Do I even want to know?"

<*Actually, it's not as bad as you might think. This time, he said he didn't see anyone come this way last night. Though he did throw in a few adverbs that weren't exactly necessary.*>

"Think he's telling the truth?"

Tango licked one of her front paws. <*I get the feeling he says pretty much whatever's on his mind. So, yeah.*>

The honey badger coughed, grunted, and whined a few more times. Tango stared at the animal quizzically, as if she couldn't quite believe it was real. <*Wow. That's just—I'm not sure how to take that.*>

"More mumble mumble?"

<*He says men have tried to stab him with spears and shoot him with arrows, but their weapons weren't strong enough to penetrate his skin. Then he talks about his own . . . weapon, and how strong it is, and how he'd like to use it to mumble mumble* my *skin.*>

"Charming."

<*Yeah, he's a regular silver-tongued devil. Can we go before he proposes matrimony, cannibalism, or both?*>

Tango and I went back to the mansion. I needed to know if the controller was at the bottom of the pond, and I couldn't really find that out until the residents were awake. We'd return after dark—and I'd use the time between now and then to prepare.

First, I did some serious research.

Despite being herbivores, hippos were considered to be the most dangerous large animal in Africa—maybe even the world. Statistics varied wildly, but it was generally agreed they killed more people than crocodiles or lions. The average hippo weighed between one and a half and three tons, their teeth were up to twenty inches long, and they could outrun a human being. Weirdly, despite spending most of their time in the water and having webbed feet, they weren't very good swimmers; they hardly ever went into deep water. Mostly they just waded, using the water to help support their weight.

They were only kind of nocturnal; in areas with little

human habitation they liked to bask in the sun, but in more populated regions they stayed in the water during the day and came out at night to feed on vegetation. The two in the pool might have seen something, or they might not have—either way, I couldn't count on them being co-operative.

Then I looked up hyenas. After a few minutes, I glanced down at Tango—who was curled up on my lap, napping—and said, "Okay, you were right."

She didn't bother opening her eyes. *<Of course I was. About what?>*

"Our pal Mr. Chuckles. Or Ms. Chuckles, I should say. I find this hard to believe, but . . . females hyenas have boy parts."

<She sure did.>

"This is amazing. Why aren't you amazed?"

She lifted her head and opened her eyes halfway. *<I'm sleeping. Sleep is important. I'll be amazed later.>*

"They have an actual, functioning, you-know-what."

<Mm-hmm.> Her head sank back down and her eyes closed.

"She gives *birth* through it. I can't even imagine that."

<I'm trying not to. Also, sleeping.>

"Did you know this? Is this why you're all who-cares and let-me-sleep?"

<No, I'm all let-me-sleep because I'M SLEEPING.>

"Oh. Sorry."

A few minutes went by.

"Oh, wow."

No response.

"I know the honey badger is supposed to be fierce and all, but—you're just not going to believe this."

<If I do, can I pretend this is a dream?>

"It's got incredibly thick skin, like flexible armor. When our potty-mouthed little friend said he'd shrugged off arrows and spears, he wasn't exaggerating. Plus, these beasties are rated as the most fearless animals alive—they've been known to drive *lions* away from a kill and eat it themselves. In fact, there are stories about honey badgers biting off a male lion's . . . you know."

<*Pride and joy?*>

"You could say that. Though I'm guessing that afterward his pride didn't stick around and he didn't get much joy. Know what a honey badger's natural enemy is?"

<*Overcaffeinated chatterboxes who can't take a hint?*>

"It doesn't *have* one. It shares the same continent with some of the nastiest predators on the planet, and none of them will go near this oversized weasel. You familiar with the Cape buffalo?"

<*Only in a linguistic sense.*>

"They're aggressive African bovines that weigh up to a ton and have sharp, curving horns. And should a Cape buffalo also be dumb enough to step on a honey badger's burrow, the badger will attack it. The buffalo, not the burrow."

Tango finally gave up, rose to her feet, and stretched. <*I'm starting to understand the impulse.*>

"They'll eat *anything*—animals, plants, insects. And when they do eat other animals, they eat every last piece, from the fur to the bones. They never seem to get tired, they're so strong they rip apart turtles with ease, and they consider cobras to be a tasty snack."

Tango yawned so hugely all I could see was her open mouth, then jumped off my lap. <*That's great. Clearly, the honey badger must be our killer. He poisoned two women by just looking at them cross-eyed, which he can do because he's so badass.*>

"Sorry. I can get a little carried away when I go into research mode."

<No kidding. I've seen kittens on catnip with more restraint.>

"Knowledge is power. I'm charging up."

<With trivia. What we need to know is who tried to kill ZZ.>

"I've got an idea how to find that out, too. But it's sort of dangerous."

<We're going to let the honey badger loose and terrorize the suspects until someone confesses?>

"Not so much. I thought we'd let it slip at dinner that I think I know where the controller is and see if anyone tries to retrieve it."

<Or they could just try to stop you from doing the same. In a permanent sort of way.>

I got up and slipped my shoes back on. "There's always that possibility. But I've got allies the killer doesn't know about, right?"

<Don't get yourself killed, Toots. That would annoy me.>

"Well, we can't have *that*, can we?"

I checked in on ZZ while Tango roamed around the house and did her best to make friends with as many people as possible. Tiny had nothing new to report; ZZ's condition hadn't changed, and nobody but medical personnel had come near her. I told him to keep up the good work, then spent the next little while tracking down each and every guest.

I told all of them the same thing: that ZZ was expected to make a full recovery shortly, and that she would be very disappointed to wake up to an empty house. I insisted that they all put in an appearance at dinner, and that I would be hosting in ZZ's place.

Nobody gave me an argument, though I had to settle for leaving Oscar a voice mail—according to Shondra, he was last seen staggering toward his bungalow and presumably sleeping off his bender.

I had quite the list of suspects, but I hoped that tonight I could at least narrow it down; if my insinuations provoked any sort of response later, I could pretty much guarantee the killer was one of the guests. If not, I was hoping I might actually find the controller itself—though that was going to be tricky, too.

I looked at Tango and sighed. "Okay, so my after-dinner plans including snorkeling with a pair of thousand-pound killer animals in the dark, while a more human murderer may or may not be lurking in the bushes."

<Sounds like a fun evening to me. But hey, I've still got two lives left . . .>

Chapter Fifteen

Normally, ZZ would go over the menu with the chef for the nightly meal and make suggestions or deletions. When she wasn't available, I did it—but before I could, I had to make sure there was actually food to eat. Sheriff Brower had confiscated every edible scrap from the kitchen, even though the carfentanil had clearly been put in ZZ's tea.

Ben Montain, dressed in crisp chef's whites, sat across the dining room table from me. He seemed a little nervous, though this was hardly the first time I'd had to stand in for ZZ. "Thought we'd start with a cold soup course. Got a nice gazpacho I been meaning to try out."

"Sure, that'd be great in this heat." I tapped away at my laptop, ordering supplies from an online grocery store that delivered. "Salad?" Tango, in my lap, purred as I worked. She seemed to have won over the house pretty quickly, though Victor wasn't a fan. Allergies.

"Wild greens with thinly sliced pear and Gorgonzola."

I frowned. "Mmm—that could be a problem. Kenny Gant is lactose-intolerant."

"Really? Huh." He had some handwritten notes in

front of him, which he shuffled through. "Oh, yeah. Uh, sorry—how about goat cheese for his, instead?"

"If you think it'll work, sure." I studied him as he muttered to himself and scribbled on a piece of paper. It wasn't like him to make a mistake like that—he was usually very detail-oriented. "Everything okay, Ben?"

"Sure, yeah, fine."

<Uh-huh. He's twitchy and he won't make eye contact. You see that, right?>

No, I had a lobotomy and my eyes removed while you were out shamelessly seducing the household staff. Sssh. "You seem uncomfortable. Is this about our lunch?" I deliberately avoided using the word *date;* best to keep this professional for now.

He looked up, his eyes wide. "Hmm? No, no, of course not. I'm just a little thrown by the whole murder-and-arrest thing."

That made perfect sense, but his answer seemed a little too quick and a little too glib, as if he was telling me what he thought I wanted to hear rather than the truth. Or maybe I was just in an overly suspicious frame of mind.

Then again, maybe I was just suspicious enough.

"Yeah, it's been crazy, hasn't it? I keep thinking about what I was doing while Maria was killed. I mean, there I was, only a few miles away, watching a movie on cable while someone I knew was being murdered."

Ben shook his head. "I know. We just go about our business, thinking everything's okay, and right at that second everything's changing forever."

"It wasn't even a good movie." I paused, then casually asked, "What were *you* doing?"

He looked at me, and blinked. When he answered, he reached up and rubbed the side of his nose first. Touching your own face is a common sign that you're lying; the theory is that it's an unconscious attempt to cover your mouth, almost as if you're physically trying to hide the truth. Uh-oh.

"I was in the Big Apple, actually. Met some friends for a few drinks, stayed out a little too late."

"Really? I couldn't tell. The next day, I mean; you seemed pretty perky."

He smiled, but it seemed forced. "Well, that's just what us Montains do. Up with the rooster and down with the owl, we used to say. Sleep is for rich people."

He abruptly realized what he'd just said, and flushed. "Oh, damn. I'm sorry, I didn't mean—"

"It's okay. If ZZ were awake to hear that, she would have laughed loud and long. Wouldn't she?"

He nodded, but still looked ashamed. "Yeah. Yeah, she would. Guess I'm just feeling a little . . . bad. About the whole situation. But I promise it won't affect dinner, all right?"

"I'm sure it'll be up to your usual high standards. Okay, let's move on to the main course . . ."

Face touching wasn't definite proof of a lie, of course; sometimes people just touched their faces. But there was something else, something harder to identify. Fortunately for me, Tango figured it out.

<Hey. You notice his hick accent gets thicker when he's trying to convince you of something?>

No, I thought back. *Not until just now . . .*

It was a bit of a crunch, restocking the kitchen in time, but I managed. Only two people didn't show up for dinner that night. One was in a coma; the other was in jail.

Even Oscar was there, which I suppose shouldn't have come as a surprise. The closest he ever came to playing a sport might have been sitting in the bleachers at Wimbledon, but when it came to alcohol he had the constitution of a marine.

Hana Kim still looked downcast, Mr. Kwok solemn. The normally cheerful Kenny Gant was quiet and thoughtful, while Keene seemed to have indulged in more than just alcohol as an appetizer. He didn't say much, but kept staring at the overhead chandelier as if he expected it to burst into monkeys at any moment.

I sat at the head of the table, where ZZ usually did. I stood up and said, "Hello, everyone. Thank you for coming. ZZ believed—*believes*—in the frank and open discussion of ideas, in a convivial environment. That's a direct quote, by the way. That's why you were invited, but not why you're here right now.

"I've known ZZ a number of years now. She's one of the most outspoken women I've ever met, and I have a tremendous amount of respect for that. But she doesn't just have opinions; she believes in putting her money where her mouth is. If someone can prove her wrong, she's more than willing to change her mind. For her, the important thing is to *speak* your mind—to share what you know and what you believe, and to listen to others do the same. She also believes in accountability. 'Anyone can say anything or pretend to be anyone on the Internet,' she tells me, 'but get them to talk to you face-to-face and you'll find out the courage of their convictions.' That's why these salons are held—to give people the chance to talk face-to-face.

"But today, someone did their best to *shut her up*."

I paused, and not just for effect. It was hard to keep the anger out of my voice, and I wasn't sure I should. "Maybe it was because of something she said. Maybe it wasn't. But either way, I *know* she wouldn't allow herself—or anyone else—to be silenced. So we're going to carry on—even though ZZ isn't here—because she would be royally pissed at me if I didn't insist on it."

I sat back down. There was a long, drawn-out moment of silence, which was unfortunately the exact opposite of what I was hoping to inspire.

Then Oscar sighed. "Oh, for God's sake. This may not be Mardi Gras, people, but it's not a wake, either. Mother has faced worse opponents in the chemical arena and defeated them; I wouldn't worry about a little nap." He signaled the drinks trolley with the push of a button.

"Arena? Chemicals?" Keene said. He blinked rapidly and grinned at Oscar. "Gladiatorial combat via pharmaceuticals? I can't have heard that right. Please tell me I heard that right."

Oscar stared at the wineglass being filled on the trolley with the morose fascination of a man in a lifeboat studying a bottle of his own urine. "You assuredly did. Remind her to tell you about the summer of '76 and her trip to Sante Fe. For months afterward she insisted small lizards were living in her hair. I spent a great deal of time trying to find them, but I was five."

Keene nodded sagely. "Well, better lizards than bats, I always say. Those buggers can come out of anywhere."

"Indeed." Oscar picked up his drink and drank off half of it in two swallows. "I'm sure you and Mother could spend hours comparing notes on the taxonomy and migration patterns of hallucinatory fauna. Also, moose flange interspersed with the occasional spigot of Krakatoa."

There was a pause while everyone tried to figure out if Oscar was having a stroke. Then Keene grinned and shouted with laughter. "Ha! Well played, my friend, but I've partied with the weirdest of the weird. Your phrasing was impeccable and your intonation brilliant, but you'll have to go a lot farther to moose flange *my* Krakatoa spigot."

"What are they *talking* about?" Hana Kim asked me. Mr. Kwok looked just as puzzled, and a little disturbed.

Kenny Gant took a sip of his own drink. "Oscar's just having a little fun."

Keene was still chuckling. "Yes, absolutely. But I, on the other lobe, am having a *great deal* of fun. Which can, you know, sometimes lead to being made fun *of.* Totally redundant in my case, of course, because I'm *already* made of fun. You could mix me up with some eggs and flour, pour me in a pan, and make *fun pancakes* out of *me.*"

"You're *stoned,*" Hana said. She sounded more wistful than disapproving. Mr. Kwok decided to compensate by radiating enough disapproval for both of them.

Oscar finished his drink and placed his glass on the trolley for a refill. "Which is, in my opinion, the only rational approach to the current situation."

"I don't think so," said Mr. Kwok. "The situation is quite serious. Two poisonings have occurred—what if there is another?"

Both Keene and Oscar paused with their drinks raised.

Kenny Gant shook his head. He wore his usual floral Hawaiian shirt, and a necklace of white puka shells. "Not unless Juan Estevez breaks out of his cell. Sheriff Brower took him away in handcuffs, remember?"

Kwok glared at Gant. "This does not mitigate the danger. He could have poisoned something else beforehand: food, drinks, even something we only touch. There are ways."

Gant lifted an eyebrow. "I guess you'd know all about such things, what with all the doping scandals in professional sports these days? Seems to me every time an athlete tests positive for a banned substance, it always comes back to the coach."

Every diplomatic instinct I had was screaming at me to interrupt this before it got really ugly—but I forced myself to ignore them. People reveal things when they're upset, and I wanted the pot to simmer a bit before I started adding my own ingredients.

"That's not fair," Hana said. "Mr. Kwok was cleared of all charges."

Keene leaned forward, his elbows on the table, and studied Kwok as if he'd never seen him before. "Charges? Do tell."

"They were groundless," Kwok said stiffly. "A smokescreen, designed to cast doubt on my abilities."

"Ah, doubt," said Oscar, still eyeing his own glass. After a moment he shrugged and took a healthy swallow. "Can't let it run one's life, can one?"

"Never!" Keene declared. "Life can be many things: a board game, a magazine published in the nineteen fifties, possibly a generic brand of health and beauty products. But one thing that it's *not,* is . . . Um. Lost my train of thought."

"Check the last junction," said Oscar. "I believe that's where it jumped the tracks."

I sensed it was time to add my two cents. "Has anyone considered that Brower might have arrested the wrong person?"

Dead silence.

"Hmmm," said Oscar.

"What?" said Hana Kim.

"No way," snorted Kenny Gant.

"Surely not," said Mr. Kwok.

"Whee!" said Keene. "Sorry, couldn't contain myself—this is the most fun I've had since the *last* time I had this much fun. If not Estevez, then who?"

"Good question," I answered. "But think about this: Maria was shot with a poisoned dart fired by Estevez's quadracopter—but who was at the controls? We all saw him demonstrate it, right? It looked pretty simple to me."

Everybody studied everybody else, while trying to look like they weren't. Five pairs of eyes, darting and staring and quickly looking away.

Tango had been under my chair the entire time, listening. *<Well done, Toots. You've put the feline among the avian, to coin a paraphrase.>*

Thanks, but I'm not done yet. "Here's something you may not know. Estevez claimed that not only was he innocent, but the flight log of the controller would clear him."

"And did it?" Oscar asked.

"We don't know. It couldn't be found."

"Well, that doesn't make sense," Kenny Gant pointed out. "Why would he get rid of the thing if it would prove he didn't do it?"

Mr. Kwok grunted. "Because the real killer did so, obviously."

Hana shook her head. "Not necessarily. He could be lying about it to make himself look innocent. If he knew no one would ever find it, no one could prove he was lying, either."

Thank you, Hana; that's exactly where I wanted the conversation to go. "That's easier said than done, though. Footage from security cameras proves that Estevez didn't leave the estate between the first murder and his arrest—so if he hid the controller, he hid it somewhere on the grounds."

"Aha!" Keene exclaimed. "Brilliant! We shall comb the estate within an inch of its finely groomed life, and *find* the thing!"

Oscar gave him a sour look. "Do you have any idea how large this property is? Searching the house alone would take weeks, and that doesn't take into account outbuildings or servants' quarters."

I nodded. "True. But I'll bet we could narrow it down

if we approached it logically. Where would be the best place to hide a small, handheld electronic device?"

"Another dimension," Keene said. "No, wait. That's the first place I'd look."

"You could bury it," Kenny Gant said. "Dig up some sod and put it back. Be almost invisible."

"You'd need a shovel," I said. "Or some sort of digging tool. Then you'd have to get rid of that."

"There are many nooks and crannies in this place," Oscar said, "but the maids are extremely thorough. If it were me, I'd do my best to destroy the evidence."

"How?" asked Mr. Kwok. "Garbage cans can be searched. Fire seems unlikely—burning plastic gives off a terrible stench."

"How about inside something?" Hana suggested. "Techies like Estevez always carry around a multitool—I saw him with one the first day. He could have unscrewed the back of an appliance or vent or something."

"Now you're thinking," I said. "But that's still problematic. If he did that in a public area, he'd risk getting caught. His own room would be too dangerous, too. Outside is more likely."

"Inside the lion cage!" said Keene. "You've *got* lions here, right?"

"Not at the moment. But there are dangerous animals in the menagerie."

"Some of which have pools," mused Oscar. "Shallow, but quite muddy. I daresay you could throw almost anything in there and not have it dredged up for years. I threw a small metal car in the hippo pool when I was six, and remember trying to find it years later when Mother had the pond drained for some reason or other."

"Any luck?" Kenny Gant asked.

"No, but I did discover a number of ancient golf balls—my grandfather enjoyed the game."

"Do the police know about your theory?" asked Mr. Kwok.

"Sheriff Brower doesn't care about the controller," I said. "The fact that he found the poison in Estevez's room is enough for him."

"But not for you," said Gant. "You think he was framed?"

I knew he was, but I couldn't say that. "Let's just say I'm not convinced he's guilty."

"And here's the soup!" Keene announced. "Excellent—solving crimes always make me *famished*."

We ate our soup in silence. *<You think that'll do it?>* Tango asked.

We'll see.

"I think we should look for the controller," Hana said over the salad.

"I'm in!" declared Keene.

"I suppose," Oscar said grudgingly. "If Estevez didn't poison Mother, then we must find the one who did."

"If we're going to do this, we should be organized about it," said Gant.

"Perhaps teams of two would be best," said Mr. Kwok.

"Why?" asked Gant. "There's a lot of ground to cover, and we can do that quicker if we split up. Or are you afraid the poisoner is going to strike again?"

"It is not that," said Kwok. "But it would seem chances are high the poisoner is one of us."

There was another moment of silence.

"We partner up to keep each other honest," said Keene. "Terrific idea. I pick Foxtrot." He grinned at me with such glee it was hard not to grin back.

"Unless it's one of the staff," said Gant. "In which case, the controller has no doubt already been removed from the premises."

"That is a possibility," I admitted. "But I still think a search is worth doing."

We strategized over the main course. I called up a map of the estate on the wall screens and we divided the house and grounds into grids, assigning different teams to each one. Keene and I would take the menagerie and outbuildings, Kenny Gant and Hana Kim would search the grounds, and Mr. Kwok and Oscar would look through the house. We all agreed it made sense for each team to switch assignments once they were done, to provide fresh eyes that might see something the first team missed.

By the time we got to dessert, Hana Kim was taking notes, Oscar's drinking had slowed noticeably, and even Keene started providing intelligent suggestions. We ended dinner by agreeing to meet at nine AM for breakfast and then begin the search.

Nobody pointed out the obvious: If the poisoner was one of us, chances were he or she would try to sneak away during the night to either move or destroy the controller. But I could see from the looks on their faces as we said good night that it was on everybody's mind.

What I didn't tell any of them was that I had my own plans.

After dinner I went upstairs to check on Tiny—or rather, Zanzibar. He lifted his head alertly when I walked in. [Foxtrot. Nothing to report, I'm afraid.]

"Well, I've got something." I told him about how the dinner went, and what I intended to do now. I could tell from the look on his face he wasn't happy with my plan.

[I should be there. You'll be a target.]

"I'll be fine. Even if the killer shows up, he or she won't expect me to be there—I didn't say anything about the menagerie myself."

[It's not just the killer I'm worried about.]

"What, you mean the pit of man-eating vipers I'm going to search? Relax—my research shows they're actually quite timid." I hadn't told Tiny about the hippos; I figured he had enough to worry about without knowing I was going swimming with a couple of enormous, ill-tempered, aquatic warthogs. "Oh, and I brought you a little something." I opened the Tupperware container I'd brought with me and set it down on the floor. "Beef Wellington. Hope you're okay with leftovers."

He sniffed at it and licked his chops. [I sense you're trying to distract me.]

"Is it working?"

[I'll tell you when I'm done.] He tore into the meal and devoured it in less than thirty seconds. Then he sat back, licked his lips again, and said, [No.]

"Well, try not to worry. I need you here, and I'll have Tango with me to stand lookout. Her night vision's as sharp as her claws, and she'll give me a telepathic shout if anyone comes within a hundred feet."

[Mmmm. I suppose. But be careful, all the same.]

I assured him I would, then patted ZZ's hand. "Don't you worry, either, boss. I'm gonna get whoever did this to you, I promise. But first I have to borrow some of your vacation gear."

ZZ's past indulgences have included forays into hang gliding, rock climbing, kayaking, and of course sky- and scuba diving. I had to dig through a storage room to find what I needed, but I managed to uncover a face mask and a waterproof flashlight—I wasn't experienced enough to mess with anything like tanks or a regulator. Besides, the water I was going into was only five or six feet deep.

Tango, though, was looking at me like I was planning a trip to the moon. *<Is this really necessary? Can't we just lie in wait and see if anyone shows up?>*

"We could wait all night and not get any results. This way, at least we'll know if the thing's actually down there."

<*What's wrong with waiting? I'm* good *at waiting. Waiting is highly underrated—and besides, there's no guarantee you'll find it even if it is there.*>

"Well, I have to try."

I had just one more errand: I picked out a big hunk of meat from the walk-in freezer, thawed it out in the microwave, and stuck it in a ziplock bag. That went into my backpack along with the mask, flashlight, and a few more items. Then it was time for a trip to the zoo.

Bongo—which I'd learned was the Banda word for "hyena"—seemed pleased to see us. She yipped and giggled while intently watching me pull out the bag of meat.

<*She says, "What took you so long?"*>

"Tell her I had to go to the moon to get the meat and my flying rhino was out of gas." I'd also learned hyenas practiced deception in the wild, sometimes giving false warning cries to convince other hyenas to run away when there was no threat present. I thought Bongo needed to know I could make stuff up, too—if nothing else, maybe she'd appreciate the joke. Of course, even if she did, how would I ever know?

More whoops, chuckles, and yips. <*She's heard moon-meat can be poisonous, and is offering to taste it for you.*>

I grinned. "Sure. Tell her she can have some now, and the rest after she's answered my questions."

I tossed a chunk of the meat over the fence, where Bongo pounced on it and swallowed it whole. When hyenas gather around a kill, they don't eat in order of dominance the way some packs do–it's strictly first come, first fed. As a result they learn to feed *fast:* A full-grown hyena can down a gazelle fawn in two minutes.

"Okay, then. You want the rest of this, you're going to

have to tell me the truth. What did you see last night, when the two-legged one was here very late?"

Tango translated, listened, then translated the reply. *<He was playing with a small glowing box. When he was done she threw it in the hippo pool. Then she left.>*

"Wait. He or she?"

<Sorry, Toots. Bongo's a little unclear on gender in other species. I don't think she's trying to screw with you, she's just uncertain.>

I sighed. "Well, that'll have to do. Thank her for me, will you?" I dug out the rest of the meat and chucked it over the fence, where it disappeared down her gullet as fast as the previous piece.

I eyed the hippo pool nervously. If I were the killer, I'd pick one of two spots to throw the controller: either in the very center of the pool . . . or fairly close to the bank where the hippos entered and exited, where it stood a good chance of being stepped on by half a ton of herbivore and driven deep into the mud. If that were the case I'd have to go to much greater lengths, probably involving Caroline, a tranquilizer rifle, and a metal detector. I hoped that wouldn't be necessary.

"All right, let's do this," I said. I marched up to the edge of the hippo enclosure, Tango trailing behind me.

At least one of the hippos appeared to be awake; I saw a single brown eye with a horizontal slit peeking at me from just above the waterline. The other hippo was just a grayish bulk beside it. "Um, hello."

Tango emitted a loud, groaning bellow that didn't sound like it could come from a cat's mouth. I stared at her.

<What? That's how they sound.>

There was no reply for a moment; then the hippo that was looking at us snorted water through its nose. It made a few irritated-sounding snuffling noises.

<Terrific start. He said, "What the hell do you want?">

"I'd like to go swimming in your pool."

Grunts, splashing, snorts. *<"No. Go away or I'll bite you in half.">*

Charming. "Let's make a deal. I just want to look for something on the bottom of your pool—it won't take long. Let me do that, and I'll give you some of these." I opened the backpack and pulled out one of half a dozen cantaloupes I'd crammed in there. While hippos generally ate grass, they had prodigious appetites and seemed to like anything in the melon family. I was hoping these two were partial to what I'd chosen, since hauling watermelons around wasn't really practical.

The hippo eyed the cantaloupe, then opened his mouth. And when a hippo opens its mouth, it opens its mouth; I could have dropped an office chair in there. I pitched the cantaloupe in, feeling a little like I was throwing a grape into the Grand Canyon. The hippo's mouth closed. He didn't bother chewing.

"So, we good?"

A long pause, followed by a single snort. *<"More.">*

I had five left, and I threw three of them into that gaping maw. "That's it for now. You get the rest when I've done my swim."

Even though it worked with Bongo, I really wasn't sure if the same would hold true with the Big H. For a creature that liked to chow down on 150 pounds of vegetation at a time, a few cantaloupes might not be worth the trouble. But when he snorted and snuffled his reply, Tango translated it as *<Then hurry up.>*

I glanced around. Nobody in sight. Was I really going to do this?

I was wearing a borrowed swimsuit from ZZ's closet under my clothes. I kicked off my shoes, skinned off my pants and top, then dug the flashlight and diving mask out of the backpack and stuffed my clothes in. "Keep a sharp eye out, okay? Anyone comes anywhere near here—"

<*I'll let you know. Good luck, Toots.*> She gave a visible shudder.

I climbed over the fence and waded in.

The water was warmer than I expected. Warm and muddy, with things floating in it. I tried hard not to think about that; hippos—much like humans—like to poop in water. At least they were herbivores.

I made sure the mask fitted snugly around my eyes and nose, turned on the flashlight, and waded out to the center of the pool. I felt horribly exposed. If Mr. or Mrs. H decided they didn't want me in their home after all, I'd have to thrash my way through this muck all the way back to the fence, a good thirty feet or more. I felt Mr. H's horizontally slitted eyes on me the whole time.

But I was committed now. I took a deep breath and plunged my head under the surface.

Silt swirled in front of my eyes in the flashlight's beam. The water had a green tint to it, like swimming in mouthwash—murky, muddy mouthwash. It was only about five feet deep, so it wasn't hard to reach the bottom. Easy to reach, but not so easy to see; the closer to the bottom I got, the thicker the silt. I wound up groping my way through the muck with my hands, using touch more than sight to try to locate what I was searching for.

When I couldn't hold my breath any longer, I popped up to the surface. Mr. H was still watching me with those eerie eyes; it felt more like being studied by a giant snake than the distant relative of a whale.

I took a deep breath and submerged once more. I was trying to work in a spiral pattern, starting at the center of the pond and working my way outward, but it was hard to stay consistent with no visual markers. I kept expecting to hear a massive splash as Mr. H changed his mind and decided to make good on his threat to chomp me in half. Even though hippos were herbivores, there were documented cases of stressed individuals eating other animals—even engaging in acts of cannibalism.

My fingers brushed against something hard and angular. I grabbed it and surfaced, but it was just the crushed remains of a beer can. Down I went again.

And then I found something else.

This time I held it up to the flashlight's beam and examined it while still submerged. Rectangular, with bits of glass glinting in the light . . .

I'd found it.

<*Foxtrot! Someone's coming!*>

The panic that surged through me fought with my growing need for air. Should I surface and risk detection, or try to stay here and hope whoever it was kept going?

And then I heard—and *felt*—the heavy splash of something big launching itself deeper into the water.

Uh-oh.

CHAPTER SIXTEEN

Decisions, decisions . . .

This one should have been easy to make. Definite threat from half a ton of toothy aquatic animal versus possible threat from an unknown human being equals Foxtrot heading for dry land ASAP.

But.

Said human being might be a cold-blooded killer coming to retrieve the vital piece of evidence I held in my hand. Said toothy animal could just be going for a swim.

So.

My lungs broke the stalemate. They didn't care about the finer details of risk management, they just wanted oxygen. I compromised by surfacing as quietly as I could, trying to keep my head mostly underwater. Since the diving mask covered my nose, this wasn't as successful as I'd hoped.

I found myself face-to-face with Mr. H. He snorted, spraying my mask with water. I stayed very, very still. *Tango?*

<Somebody's coming down the path. Can't tell who, yet, though they're trying to be quiet.>

Uh-huh. Can you handle sentry duty and translate at the same time? I have a hippo here who's trying to tell me something.

<Oh, right. He wants his cantaloupes.>

Can you tell him I'd be very, very happy to give him the cantaloupes? But that I need to get out of the water, first?

I heard some bellowing from Tango's direction. It was amazing, the range of sounds she could produce from that tiny throat.

Mr. H grunted in response. *<He wants to know if you need any help.>*

I had visions of that immense gray snout flicking me out of the water like a seal with a beachball. *Tell him I'm good, thanks.*

More noise from the shore. Mr. H. blinked once, slowly, then sank down out of sight. This failed to reassure me, and I began to move slowly toward where I'd climbed in.

<Hold it, Toots—he's here.>

He? He who?

"Foxtrot?"

Great. Of all the people it had to be . . .

"Didn't know swimming with hippos was a thing," said Keene, peering at me with his hands thrust in the pockets of the long leather coat he wore. "Dolphins, yes. Bloody great river hogs? Had no idea."

The water I stood in was only waist-deep, but it was enough to hide my hands as I stuffed the controller up the leg of my swimsuit and into the small of my back. "Keene. What are you doing out here?"

"Same as you, I suppose—trying to catch the bad guy. Also, is one of the animals loose? Something was making an awful racket in the bushes over there."

"It's just a cat." I waded out and faced him through the wire fence. "This doesn't look good, you know."

He eyed me appreciatively. "Looks all right from here. Except for the odd trace of slime. And the smell. Plus, the swimsuit itself isn't really your style. Other than that, though, you look *brilliant*."

I sighed. "Not me—you. A suspicious person might think you came out here to look for the controller yourself."

He frowned. I noticed, for the first time, that he was wearing the leather coat over a bare chest. "Well, there is that. I take it you were doing the same, though."

"I'm not a suspect, Keene. The search was my idea in the first place, remember?"

"True. Find anything?"

I studied him through the wire. He didn't seem like a killer—and I'd been unable to discover any motive he might have to kill ZZ.

"You think I'm the *killer*, don't you?" he said, grinning. "Oooh. I feel *dangerous*." He raised one bushy eyebrow and gave me what he no doubt thought of as an evil look.

I did my best not to laugh. When they were handing out charm, Keene no doubt conned his way into getting double portions. "No, I don't. Would you mind tossing my clothes over the fence? I'd rather not climb back over barefoot."

"How am I supposed to be the nasty mastermind when I'm doing favors for you? You are seriously buggering up my whole evil vibe, y'know? But all right."

He picked up my backpack and pitched it over the fence. It landed right beside me. "Thanks. Mind turning your back?"

"You're really not getting the whole evil thing at all, are you?"

I gave him a look. He rolled his eyes at me and turned around.

I used the opportunity to stick the controller in the backpack, then slipped off the swimsuit while making sure Keene wasn't sneaking a peek. I got dressed and stashed the mask and flashlight, thinking hard the whole time. If Keene was the killer, what would he do once we were both on the same side of the fence? Attack me, then try to retrieve the controller himself? We were all alone out here. Maybe I should have come armed with something other than a snarky feline.

<Hey! A little respect, if you please!>

Oops. Sorry, didn't realize I was thinking that loud.

<It takes a while to get the hang of it. But I wouldn't worry about him trying to jump you.>

Easy for you to say.

<That it is, and you know why? Couple reasons. First, his body language's all wrong. He's a lover, not a fighter—if he was going to attack you, he'd be all tensed up. Second, you have me watching your back.>

No offense, but he's a little out of your weight class.

The disdain in her mental voice was acute. *<Please. You ever see a five-pound tabby take down a Great Dane? It's all about attitude, sweetie. That, and ten little claws moving at the speed of thought.>*

Okay—guess I don't really have much choice at this point.

I slipped the pack on over my shoulders and started to climb. I was at the top when Tango added, *<But you're a good runner, right?>*

I gritted my teeth and climbed down.

"So, what's the plan?" Keene asked. "Hide in the bushes and wait for the real villain to show up? We might have to keep each other warm."

"You can do what you want. Me, I'm going home—I didn't find anything, which means it isn't here, which means the killer isn't going to show." Unless, of course, he just did . . .

Keene looked disappointed, but not homicidal. "That's it, then? No midnight skinny-dipping for me? No stakeout with the lovely but impatient Your Foxiness?"

"I told you to stop calling me that."

"No, you said I couldn't call you Foxy. *Your Foxiness* is a much more elegant title, only conferred upon royalty. And foxes."

I turned around and walked away, trying to seem casual but on high alert. If he didn't buy it, I'd know any second.

"Foxtrot. Stop."

I froze, then spun around.

Keene wasn't smiling anymore. "Look, I'm sorry if you think I'm making fun of you. I'm quite serious about helping. I promise I won't screw anything up, all right? No more kidding around."

I shook my head. "Thanks, but I really don't think we can accomplish anything else here. We'll tackle things again tomorrow, all right?"

He nodded, and his smile came back. "Cheers. Walk you back to the house?"

"Sure."

<I'm right behind you, Toots.>

Before any of us could take a step, though, there was a tremendous bellow from the hippo pool. I winced, then said, "Hang on a moment. Got something to take care of, first."

I got the last two cantaloupes from the pack and threw them over the fence. Mr. H snarfed both of them down, then snorted derisively and went back to where he'd been when I first arrived. Mrs. H never stirred.

What did he say? I asked Tango as we left.

<Thanks, believe it or not. He may be gruff, but he did help us out.>

That he did. I'll see about getting him some extra fruit tomorrow. Gotta keep our sources happy, right?

<Y'know, I think you're getting the hang of this.>

We went back to the house, where I told Keene good night and got in my car. It had been a long day, and I needed to shower and sleep. But I had one thing left to do, first.

Maybe I should have taken the controller to the police. Maybe the killer had left fingerprints on it or some other trace, but I was pretty sure he or she wasn't that stupid. No, if there were any kind of usable evidence still attached to the thing, it would be electronic—and Sheriff Brower just didn't have the resources or the budget to extract anything useful.

I, on the other hand, had Avery.

Avery Shubert lived in town, only one street over from me. He was my go-to guy for all things computer-related, and I'd known him a long time. He kept fairly late hours, so I wasn't worried that I'd be waking him up.

He answered the door in a tuxedo. Avery was short and chubby, had mousy-brown curly hair, and exuded a kind of Zen-like calm at all times. He looked more like a waiter than James Bond, even in the tux, but he had the attitude to pull it off. "Foxtrot. Is everything all right?"

"Nobody else has died, if that's what you mean. But I need your help, nowish."

He motioned me in. "Please. Details?"

I walked in, closing the door behind me. "I've got some hardware that requires your full attention. It's been immersed in water, and maybe worse."

I looked around. Avery was an upper-class geek, which meant he liked all the same toys that other geeks did but could afford the very best ones. Framed original Syd Mead sketches from *Blade Runner* hung on the wall, signed first editions of the Lord of the Rings Trilogy—the books, not the movies—stood on the designer bookshelves, a projection TV tricked out to look like the screen on the bridge of the *Enterprise* took up most of one wall. "Uh, what's with the tux?"

"Hmm? Chess club meeting. Long story. The device?"

I pulled it out of the backpack and handed it over. It was in pretty bad shape; it had obviously been stepped on as well as submerged. The case was broken, the glass smashed. Avery handled it as delicately as a piece of tissue-paper origami, turning it over in his hands and examining every inch.

"What was it used for?"

"Remote-controlling a quadracopter."

"And the information you're looking for?"

"Flight log, if possible. When it was used, where it went, any video footage it stored."

He nodded. "I'll get right to work. Call me in the morning."

"Nine fifteen okay?"

"Yes."

And that was that. Avery handled all ZZ's tech, from installation to maintenance, and no one was better. If he said he'd have something for me by nine fifteen, he would. I thanked him and headed for the door.

"Foxtrot?" he called after me. I stopped. "How's ZZ doing?"

"No change. She's hanging in there."

"Is this device connected to what happened to her?"

It was hard to keep anything from Avery; he put things together very quickly with little information. "Yeah. In fact, it may be a murder weapon. I guess I should have told you that first."

He shook his head. "It doesn't matter. I'd do it anyway. I'll be sure to document every step thoroughly."

"Thank you. I'll talk to you tomorrow."

Home. Shower. Bed. Exhausted.

Alone.

I tossed and turned, unable to get to sleep. Too many things to obsess over, too many things to worry about: What if the killer set the mansion on fire? What if someone tailed me to Avery's place, broke in, and attacked him? What if Keene really was the killer, knew I'd found the controller, and was right this moment sneaking into my house to get it back?

That last one bothered me a lot. Keene shouldn't have been there. No matter how charming and roguish he was, him showing up at the hippo pool made him look guilty as hell. Maybe Tango was wrong about him being a lover and not a fighter.

I kind of wondered what sort of lover he'd be. Selfish, probably. Lots of one-night stands, used to getting what he wanted. Pretty package, with not much inside.

But still, that was a pretty cute package . . .

No. Don't think about that. Focus on the facts. Like the fact that Keene was seen in the graveyard with something suspiciously like the controller when Maria was killed. Wandering around a graveyard, reading headstones . . . was that romantic, or creepy? Funny how often those two things blurred together. A guy did one thing and it was sweet and surprising. He did another and suddenly you were being stalked.

Keene flirted with me, but he'd never made me feel unsafe. Not until now, anyway.

I rolled over, punched my pillow a few times, and pretended it was now much more comfortable. Sure.

I'm never going to get to sleep.

Nope. Not ever. I'm just going to lie here and mummify. Archaeologists will discover my pajama-clad body a thousand years from now and murmur, "Look! Her alarm never went off!" Then they'll shake their heads sadly and put me on display in the Insomnia Wing of the Horrible Fates Museum.

And what's going on with Ben? What is he trying to hide from me? I couldn't think of any reason Ben would want to hurt ZZ, but maybe he needed to be on the list of suspects, too.

I groaned out loud. Who *wasn't* a suspect, at this point? Me, Tango, and Tiny.

I was still fretting when I finally fell asleep, and had troubled, murky dreams that involved being chased by hippos and toy helicopters. I couldn't get away because I was wearing these huge shoes made from cast iron that weighed a thousand pounds each, and they were on the wrong feet, and the shoelaces were in a million knots that turned into snakes when I tried to untie them . . .

I didn't so much wake up as escape. I sat straight up, stared around me blearily, and mumbled, "Never wearing boots again." Then I got up, went downstairs, made myself an extra-strong mug of Irish breakfast tea, and drank it in the bathroom.

I called Shondra before I left for work. Nothing to report, no one tried to do anything to ZZ in the night. No change in ZZ.

I arrived at the house early—it was only eight thirty, and the guests weren't meeting to conduct the search until nine. I called for Tango. and got an immediate response.

<Hey, Toots. How'd you sleep?>

Terrible. Let's hit the graveyard again, all right? I need to ask some follow-up questions.

<You sure?>

No. Let's do it anyway.

The sun had been up for some time, but the grass still glittered with dew. Tango met me at the gate to the graveyard. <*What's the plan?*>

"I took some pictures of the controller before I gave it to my friend. I want to see if any of the animal spirits who saw Keene in the graveyard can identify it as what he was holding."

<*Good thinking—but I don't know how reliable your witnesses will be. Most pets don't know the difference between a cordless phone and a TV remote.*>

"I beg to differ. Every cat I've ever met could recognize a can opener from a block away."

She licked her paw and considered. <*Okay, I'll give you that one.*>

I squared my shoulders. I could do this. Sure, it had been a steep learning curve, but now I understood the rules. I had made contacts, established myself as a presence. I wasn't a clueless newbie fumbling around; I was a trained professional on a specific mission. Go in, talk to the locals, collect some data. No problem.

Don't think about the elephant. Don't think about the elephant . . .

<*You're thinking about the elephant, aren't you?*>

"Well, I am *now*."

<*Sorry.*>

I opened the gate and we walked through.

This time, I didn't gawk at all the spirits bounding, flying, and scurrying around me. I just marched straight into the thick of it, keeping my eyes out for a particular individual: the white crow, Eli. He'd pointed me in the right direction last time, and I thought he might do so again.

Unfortunately, he didn't seem to be around and I didn't have time to look for him. I could go searching for Two-Notch myself—but that meant going out to the border again, and risking another encounter with Topsy. I wasn't ready for that.

Then I spotted another bird that I recognized: Fish Jumping, the parrot. He was perched on a headstone, preening one brilliant green-and-blue wing with his beak. I approached him and said, "Hi. Remember me?"

He regarded me quizzically, then said, "Awk! Girl on a date! Girl on a date!" *Greetings and salutations, Miss Foxtrot. I do indeed remember you, and hope your endeavors are proceeding apace.*

"My endeavors . . . well, they're endeavoring, I guess. But I could use a little help."

Certainly, dear lady. Whatever you wish I shall provide, be it in my power.

"There was someone here in the graveyard, two nights ago. The same guy that came along and interrupted my date. Did you see him?"

Fish Jumping cocked his head to one side. *I believe I did, actually. Spent a great deal of time looking at the headstones and reading the inscriptions out loud. They seemed to affect him profoundly.* "Awk! Crying and laughing! Crying and laughing!"

So Keene had been telling the truth about that. "Did he have one of these?" I held up my own cell phone. "Or did it look more like this?" I called up the picture of the drone controller on the screen.

Fish Jumping leaned in and peered intently at the screen, then back to consider the phone itself. *He did have one of these small devices with him. He fiddled with it using primarily his thumbs, or pointed it at a headstone and flashed a light. It looked a great deal like the one you're holding, not the little picture upon it.* "Awk! Not the same! Not the same!"

"You're sure?"

Fish Jumping drew himself up proudly. *Madam. Representatives of my particular species are renowned for the acuity of both their eyesight and their memory—and I can assure you, death has not diminished either of those abilities in myself.* "Awk! Damn right! Damn right!"

"Sorry if I sound doubtful—I just need to be certain."

<*Looks like Keene is in the clear,*> Tango said. <*If you trust the word of a parrot.*>

"Tango!"

<*Just sayin'.*>

Fish Jumping eyed Tango curiously. *How rude. You do understand that I'm dead, don't you?* "Awk! Bad kitty! Bad kitty!"

<*Yeah, yeah. You understand that we're not exactly helpless, right? Just because I can't touch you doesn't mean I don't have friends who can. Did you know there's a leopard buried here?*>

There's no need for threats. I have no reason to lie. "Awk! Don't kill me again! Don't kill me again!"

I sighed. "Thank you for your help, Fish Jumping. Tango, let's go."

I walked away, Tango behind me. "What was that all about?"

<*Setting a tone. You play nice, I play not-so-nice. Makes you look better by comparison.*>

"Oh. We call that 'Good Cop, Bad Cop.' It's kind of a cliché, actually."

<*Among humans, maybe. But animals don't do clichés–and anyway, it's better than beating a dead horse.*>

"Say what?"

<*You know, if we run into a big animal we need to interrogate. If a dead horse is already intimidated by us, we don't have to threaten to beat it.*>

I took a second to digest that, trying to figure out if Tango was yanking my leg. I gave her a look, but she looked back at me with typical cat inscrutability—well, maybe just a touch too much innocence. "Okay . . . aren't you worried what this behavior is going to do to *your* reputation?"

She yawned. *<As I said before—I'm a cat. I don't much care what anyone thinks about me.>*

Which was when we saw Topsy.

You wouldn't think an elephant was capable of sneaking up on someone, but that's what this one did. I guess she'd maybe gone outside the graveyard, onto the estate itself, and approached the gate from the same side I had; the hedge had kept her out of my sight.

And now she was blocking the exit.

It was clearly something she'd thought out. The hedge was at least nine feet high, so I couldn't leap it the way I had the fence. I couldn't go through the gate, and if I turned around and ran she'd catch me. Tiny might have been able to slow it down, but I didn't think Tango could do the same.

<Uh-oh.>

"No kidding," I muttered. "Let me handle this."

<It's all yours, Toots.>

I'd faced down bullies before. Sometimes it was all about what Keene would call "front": how expensive their clothes were, how cool their car was, how up-to-the-second their technology appeared to be. Or, if you were an electrocuted ghost elephant from the turn of the century, how big and bright the lightning bolts arcing between your tusks were.

Pretty big. Pretty bright.

Okay, so I didn't have much in the way of front. Sometimes it was all about attitude—unflappable calm in the face of imminent danger, mild amusement at being threatened, an unspoken implication that you could wreak havoc with a single phone call. Considering that the last time I'd met Topsy I'd run like a cockroach fleeing a flashlight, I thought the unfazable option was closed, too.

But that was okay. Neither one of those was really my style. I preferred good old-fashioned negotiation. It was a martial art in its own right, with holds, strikes, and throws designed to play to your strengths and capitalize on your opponent's weaknesses. I had a black belt in this particular skill, and a really killer pair of shoes to go with it—not to mention my secret weapon.

"Hello, Topsy," I said. I couldn't see her eyes, which was disturbing; they were just two more patches of darkness in the shadowy bulk of her skull. I could see the harness of chains she wore on her head, though, and the little crackle of sparks that leapt from link to link. "I think it's time you and I talked."

My secret weapon gave a little mental cough. *<Uh, prowlers don't always understand human speech.>*

I paused. "Then this would be a really bad time to tell me you don't speak Elephant."

<No, I can manage a passable Pachyderm. I'm just a little worried about what you're going to say.>

"Leave that up to me, okay? Just translate."

<Okay, okay.>

"What do you want?" I asked Topsy.

The sounds that emanated from Tango's mouth were almost as eerie as when she spoke Hyena. I've read that some of elephant communication is in ultra-low frequencies that humans can't even hear, which probably explained the long pauses in between sounds.

Tango listened to Topsy's reply, then relayed it: *<"I want you to go.">*

"Out of the graveyard?"

<*"Yes."*>

"What do you offer me if I do this?" Even though leaving the graveyard was exactly what I wanted to do, I had to ask for something in return; any demand had to be met with a response to keep the negotiation on an equal footing.

<*"I will not crush your spirit when you die."*>

Well, that was comforting. It showed an alarming awareness of the situation, though—Topsy knew what she was and where we were.

"I will go," I said.

Topsy shuffled to one side, unblocking the path. <*Careful, Toots. That was too easy.*>

I should have listened to her. But I made a classic negotiating mistake: I was so eager to close the deal I took the first offer on the table, and didn't look at it closely enough. I substituted bravado for due diligence, and strode past Topsy with my head high.

Or tried to, anyway.

She let me get directly opposite her before she grabbed me with her trunk, snaking it around my waist like an anaconda pouncing on a rabbit. Cold, heavy darkness squeezed my ribs together . . .

Chapter Seventeen

Topsy lifted me off the ground—not far, just a few inches, but enough to let me know how completely helpless I was. She turned me so I was facing her, and bellowed at me.

"What—what's she saying?" I managed. I could hardly breathe; it felt like I was being bear-hugged by a glacier.

<She says she'll let your spirit alone, but maybe she should crush your body first—just to make sure you have one.>

"That . . . won't be necessary," I gasped. "But thank you . . . for offering."

Tango looked at me like I was crazy, but she repeated the message. Topsy considered me for a few seconds afterward, then dropped me to the ground. It was less than a foot, but it felt as if I'd fallen a mile. My knees gave out and I crumpled to the ground.

<Foxtrot! Are you all right?> Tango was right there beside me, anxiously rubbing up against me.

"I'm fine," I said shakily, and got to my feet. Topsy produced another bellow, then abruptly turned and shambled away.

"What—what did she say?" I asked.

<That you should never come back. Or else.>

Wonderful.

By the time we got back to the house, I'd managed to pull myself together enough to appear like a competent professional rather than a terrified survivor of a supernatural shakedown. Everyone was already gathered at the breakfast table. Hana Kim gave me a cheerful hello, while Keene looked like getting up this early was the equivalent of running a marathon. He nodded blearily and downed a shot of espresso.

Kenny Gant was halfway through an omelet, while Mr. Kwok was sipping a cup of tea. Oscar was nursing a Bloody Mary and some buttered toast. I went straight to the head of the table and said, "Good morning, everybody. I have some news."

I told them about finding the controller, though I didn't mention Keene was there. I was now pretty sure he had an alibi for the night of the murder, and there was no point in making him look suspicious to everyone else.

"Good Lord," Oscar said. "You went into the hippo pool? By yourself? Are you *mad*?"

"And why didn't you wait until this morning?" Hana Kim said accusingly.

"Because she wanted to see if one of us would do the same thing," said Kenny Gant. "Smart move. I take it nobody else showed?"

I carefully didn't look at Keene. "No. Whoever the killer is, either they didn't know about our search plans, or I beat them to the punch. Either way, I'm having it analyzed by an expert right now. If he can pull any relevant data from it, we have a good chance of nailing the murderer."

Now I risked a glance at Keene. He seemed a lot more

awake than he had a minute ago, but not concerned; if anything, he appeared hurt.

"When will you know anything?" Oscar asked.

I glanced at a clock on the wall. "My guy is going to call any minute. I'll have news then."

Right on cue, my phone chimed.

I met everyone's eyes, one by one, before I answered; if a killer was looking back, he or she disguised it well. "Hello?"

"Foxtrot. No good news. Unit's been thoroughly trashed, on every level. Nothing retrievable in any form."

I kept my disappointment from my face. "I see. Very good. I'll arrange for the police to pick it up—everything's documented?"

"Of course."

"Thank you. I'll talk to you later."

I hung up, but didn't say anything for a moment. Neither did anyone else. I could try to bluff, maybe draw the killer out—but I'd tried that tactic once already and only snagged Keene in my net. No, the killer hadn't shown because he or she wasn't worried, and they weren't worried now. "I'm afraid the controller was a dead end," I said. "My expert couldn't find anything."

"Maybe your expert wasn't good enough," Kenny Gant said. "You should have turned the controller over to the police."

"They're welcome to take a stab at it now," I replied. "But believe me—if my guy says he can't get anything, then there's nothing to be had. This isn't TV—Sheriff Brower doesn't have a high-tech lab in a back room that can extract DNA from the sweat of someone's fingertips. And even if he did, I think our killer's too smart to leave any obvious traces behind."

"So what are we to do now?" asked Mr. Kwok.

"I don't know," I admitted.

"I do," Oscar said. "I'm going back to bed." He got up, nodded at everyone, and left. I could almost see his hangover trailing along behind him.

"Think I'll pay a visit to Caroline," announced Kenny Gant. "She was going to show me some footage of a Liger—amazing animals. Cross between a lion and a tiger, believe it or not."

Hana Kim muttered something about training. Mr. Kwok frowned and sipped his tea. Keene yawned and said, "Well, I suppose I'll do what every musician does with a disaster."

"What's that?" I asked.

He gave me a sleepy grin. "Write a song, of course. In fact, I've been working on a little something I'd like you to give a listen to. After brekkie?"

"Uh, sure."

I retreated to my office. Tango joined me, trotting along at my heels. It was amazing how fast everyone had accepted her, but cats are like that: They just move in and declare ownership. "I don't suppose you detected any suspicious reactions from the group when I broke the news," I asked her as I shut the office door.

<*Sorry, afraid not. What are you going to do next?*>

"Me? I'm going to call Sheriff Brower. Then I'm going to gargle with broken glass and drink some salted lemon juice."

<*Why would you do that?*> She sounded puzzled.

"Because it'll be such a pleasant experience compared with the previous one."

Tango shook her head. <*Humans are weird. You know that, right?*>

"Seven lives and you're just figuring that out now?"

I sat down and prepared myself mentally. There's a particular frame of mind you have to get into when you know people are about to yell at you, and a subset you need to apply when you know you've screwed up. You can't get too defensive, but you can't just meekly let them browbeat you, either. Accept consequences, not judgment; you've made a mistake, but that doesn't mean you're incompetent. Let them get angry, answer their questions as honestly and politely as you can, try to figure out how to fix the problem when they've blown off enough steam to be reasonable again, and whatever you do don't lose your own cool.

I talked to Shondra first, bringing her up to speed. She was upset, of course—leaving her out of the loop on a covert operation was tantamount to blasphemy in her books—but I downplayed the danger of the situation as best I could. "I needed you focused on ZZ's safety," I told her. "This was a simple search, over in a few minutes. You would have turned it into a huge production with scuba gear and searchlights and whatnot."

"Whatnot is my *job,* Foxtrot. I'm very good at whatnot. My whatnot expertise is what you pay me for and might just save your life."

"I know. I'm sorry. Please stop saying whatnot."

"Promise me you won't do something that stupid again."

"*That* stupid? I promise."

She sighed. "You're already quantifying other gradations of stupidity, aren't you?"

"You know me so well. Gotta go, I have further stupidity piling up on my desk."

Then I called Brower.

It wasn't pretty. It wasn't pleasant. There was yelling, though not on my part. I was threatened with incarceration, three times. When he finally calmed down I assured him that Avery had documented everything and had many impressive credentials to back up his observations. Then

I gave Brower Avery's address, apologized one final time, listened to him swear at me, and then hang up.

"Well, that went just *swell*," I said. "I wonder if I can still catch the killer when I'm in a jail cell."

<*Don't worry about it. Brower's all hiss and no slash.*>

"Don't you mean . . ."

<*What?*>

"Never mind."

My phone rang, showing an unlisted number. I answered. "Yes?"

It was Keene. "Hello, love. You available yet? I need your pretty pink ears."

"Why didn't my phone show me your number? I have it programmed in."

He chuckled. "I'm a rock god, Foxtrot. I go through more mobiles than Ozzy does bats. Now, are you coming downstairs to hear my latest creation or do I have to sing it over the phone?"

I bowed to the inevitable—humoring the guests' requests, no matter how odd, was part of my job. "I'll be right down. Where are you, the theater?"

"Good Lord, no. This wee tot is barely out the chute—he's hardly ready to stagger out in front of the footlights just yet. No, I'm down in the library."

Well, at least I wouldn't have to deal with full amplification and a drum set. "I'll be down in a minute."

"Ta."

I slipped my phone in my pocket and stood up. <*You're not actually going to go, are you?*>

"I have to. It's part of what I do."

<*Foxtrot. You can't. Don't you know that every time a string made of catgut is plucked, the tormented soul of a feline yowls throughout the underworld?*>

"Really?"

<*Well, no. But it makes my whiskers twitch.*>

I headed for the door. "First of all, catgut hasn't been used for musical instruments in decades. Second, if you really don't like music, you don't have to go."

<I didn't say I don't like music. I just have a very narrow definition of the word.>

"Uh-huh. I'll leave the door open a crack so you can come and go as you please. I shouldn't be long."

On my way there, I passed Hana's room. I paused, listening, and heard a rapid-fire tapping of computer keys coming from within. Huh. Didn't sound like she was training for the next Olympics to me.

An idea came to me. It wasn't a completely ethical idea, and normally I would have told it to take a hike—but I was investigating one murder while trying to prevent another, so maybe my conscience could stand bending the rules this once.

I pulled out my phone and called Avery. "Hey. Have you been descended upon by the forces of law enforcement yet?"

"Not yet." He didn't sound worried, but he never did. "Anything I need to know?"

"Just that I'm a terrible person. I need you to do something else for me, when you have a minute."

"Which is?"

"I have a guest spending a lot of time on the 'Net but keeping it secret. I'd really like to know—in general terms—what she's doing."

"Sure. I have remote access to your server—I'll take a look and pass along the information." He paused. "As soon as I've finished talking to the police, who just showed up."

"Thanks a million. Bye."

Since Avery was the one who set up all our Internet access and troubleshoots our system, I knew it wouldn't take him long. You know, unless they arrested him—and that would have been a huge mistake on Brower's part.

The only things scarier than Avery's skill with computers were the lawyers that owed him favors.

Keene was waiting for me in the library, barefoot, dressed in torn jeans and a loose-fitting silk shirt in a brilliant shade of orange. On anyone else the outfit would have screamed *homeless pirate;* Keene somehow managed to cram the phrase *but lovable* between the two words. He was sprawled out on the couch with an acoustic guitar in his hands.

"Ah, my audience arrives at last," he said. "I was starting to worry you wouldn't show."

"No, you weren't."

"No, I wasn't," he admitted cheerfully. "Pass up a private performance by yours truly? I don't mean to sound vain, but there are fans out there who would sell a kidney for this."

I took a seat on a large, overstuffed chair. "Vain? Not at all. Are you planning on going for a jog later, maybe a little run on top of the lake?"

"Depends on my mood. Might just turn the whole thing into a nice Cabernet and go for a swim instead."

"That sounds a lot more enjoyable than paddling through hippo dung."

"Yeah. So you really had the thing the whole time?" He was watching me intently, but didn't seem angry. If he were, I wouldn't blame him.

I shrugged. "Sorry about that. But you showing up when I was expecting the killer . . . well, you can see my point, right?"

He nodded. "Oh, absolutely. A bit dim of me, I admit—in my defense, I plead an overabundance of enthusiasm and wine. But *you* should have known better."

"What, now *you're* the voice of reason?"

"I agree, it's *very* odd. Let's stop and go back to me

being the irresponsible one and you being all clearheaded and bright-eyed, shall we?"

"Done. Can I hear the song now, or do you need one of my kidneys?"

He strummed the guitar softly, once. "All right, you asked for it. It's not done, but—well, here we go."

His fingers found the frets he was looking for, and he started to play. It was a gentle, simple melody, not what I had expected at all; Keene's hits were mostly post-punk, fast-paced rockers with catchy riffs you could dance to.

He sang:

Everybody loves you but not like I do,
Everybody loves you but you don't get a song
They say that you're cute but you can't go out with them
They say that they love you but you can't come along

One day you're gonna leave me, you're really gonna break my heart
I know that day is coming but all that I can do
Is to love you right now, love you this very moment,
I'll love you forever
That's my love for you.

He let the final notes hover in the air. "Well? What do you think?"

I blinked. "That's really nice. Does it refer to what I think it does?"

"It's about animals, yeah. Companions. The animals that people love, pets or otherwise. Most of them don't get as long a life as we do, do they? But we fall in love with them anyway. Sad . . . but inspiring, too."

I studied him, and saw someone different than I had a few minutes ago. Underneath the foppish hair and the boyish smile and the party-like-there's-no-tomorrow facade, there was something else—something deeper and wiser. Something that understood pain.

"Yes," I said. "Sad but inspiring. I don't know if anyone's ever written a love song about pets before."

He laughed. "*Every* song's been written before, Foxtrot, just like every story's been told. The secret to success is to write it or sing it or tell it in your own way. That's why cover versions of songs become hits."

"Or remakes of movies."

"Yeah, exactly. Everything's unique but nothing's original, as someone said once."

"Who?"

"No idea—but he was probably quoting someone else."

"Well, even if it wasn't original, I thought it was great."

"Well, thank you."

I looked at him. He looked at me.

"Okay—I'll see you later—bye," I said, and then I was in another room wondering what the hell just happened and why was the damn air-conditioning suddenly not working?

And thinking about what might happen next.

I went back upstairs and hid in my office. Tango wasn't there, so I used the time to catch up on some paperwork. Funny how my obsessive-compulsive side tends to show up when there's something I don't want to think about.

When Avery called I was hip-deep in invoices, trying to figure out if we should get another quote on resurfacing the driveway. "Using me for your one phone call? I'm flattered."

"Police are gone. I'm still here."

"They give you much grief?"

"Nothing I couldn't handle."

Which, for Avery, meant they tried to chew him out

and discovered their jaws just weren't strong enough. Avery's skin wasn't just thick, it was impenetrable. "Good to hear. You have something for me on my other problem?"

"Yes. Your guest has been spending all of her time on a South Korean MMORPG."

"M and M what now?"

"M-M-O-R-P-G. Massively multiple online role-playing game. A shared-universe video game on the net."

"Oh. Like World of Warcraft? Even I've heard of that one."

"Like that, yes. But your guest—who goes by the online handle of Starhammer—is more into science fiction than fantasy. She seems to exclusively play a game called Galactic Lance Battalion, which has a dedicated following of professional gamers."

"Wait. Did you say professional gamers?"

Now he sounded amused. "Yes. It's a huge industry, complete with corporate sponsorship and international tournaments. Big names, big prizes. In South Korea they fill stadiums with fans who watch important battles on Jumbotrons."

"I think I'm getting the picture. It's the Olympics of video games."

"That's one way to put it."

"So how good is she?"

"I'd put her in the semi-pros. Plenty of potential, good eye for strategy, but she takes a lot of criticism online for her lack of dedication. She only manages a few hours every day—sometimes she even takes a day off."

I thought about all the hours Hana Kim put into gymnastics training; I was amazed she found any time to go online at all. "Sounds pretty dedicated to me."

"Not to this community. Gamers on this level practically live online; there's been more than one recorded fatality."

I frowned. "Fatalities? How do you die from playing a video game?"

"You really have to work at it. In 2005 a South Korean man died of organ failure after playing for fifty hours straight. In another case a guy in Taiwan died of cardiac arrest after playing for forty hours in a row."

I shook my head, even though he couldn't see it. Sometimes the need to deny something required more than just words. "That's crazy."

"So is putting on a helmet and shoulder pads before letting a bunch of three-hundred-pound linebackers slam into you. But people do that for a living, too."

He had a point. Becoming an Olympic athlete probably required just as many hours as it did to become a professional gamer, and wasn't exactly without physical hazards of its own. "I don't think my guest is in any danger of organ failure—she's got this whole other career thing that sort of eats up her time. But obviously, she's looking to branch out."

"Anything else?"

"Yes. Can you tell me if she was playing between the hours of ten PM and five AM two nights ago?"

"Give me a second." No more than three went by before he said, "Yes. Definitely active that whole time."

"Could it have been faked?"

"If someone logged on as her and played as her, sure. But they'd need to be as good as her, too—which greatly narrows the field."

Another suspect down. Hana Kim might yearn to be a video game champion instead of a world-famous gymnast, but she wasn't my killer. I was starting to feel better; the day hadn't begun that well, but things were definitely looking up.

Where had the morning gone? Both my stomach and the clock were telling me it was time for lunch. I wanted something hearty, stew or pasta or maybe a side of beef. My hunter-gatherer genes were talking to me, and they wanted something they could sink their chromosomal teeth into.

Or, you know, maybe a nice salad.

It was only eleven thirty or so, but I knew Ben would be in the kitchen preparing lunch—I could breeze in there, grab something, and be back at my desk before my monitor got cold.

That was the plan. It was a good plan—simple, straightforward, with a clear, obtainable objective. It should have worked. But I didn't have all the facts . . .

The breezing part went reasonably well. I was through the door and saying, "Hey, Ben, what's—" when the breeze abruptly died.

Ben Montain looked a little like an opossum frozen in the beam of a flashlight. An opossum with his arms wrapped around a tall, gorgeous blonde in a very short skirt and very high heels.

"—cooking?" I finished.

She didn't look happy to see me, either.

Chapter Eighteen

Blonde? Did I say blonde? More like snow white, if Snow White was trying to pick up a few extra dwarfs. The look on her face was about the same temperature, and she had the kind of cheekbones that were made for disdain. That, and maybe cutting diamonds—like the ones that glinted in her ears.

"Hi," I said. "Foxtrot. Nice to meet you." This was a blatant lie, but I have an automatic routine I drop into when I'm shocked and it always starts with me introducing myself. If an ax-wielding maniac ever jumps out at me in a dark alley, I'm sure my last words will be, "Hi! My name is *AAAAAHHH!*" followed by the bleeding and the screaming and the dying.

The look on Ben's face was a combination of surprise, guilt, and fear. He dropped his arms and took a quick step away from her, an act that didn't seem to bother her at all.

"Hello," she said. "I'm Anna. Are you an employee, as well?" She said *employee* as if it were a breed of small, unpleasant dog.

"Foxtrot is Ms. Zoransky's executive assistant," Ben said quickly. "She more or less runs this place."

"I see." I could practically see her file me away as inconsequential. "Well, I was just on my way out. I'll talk to you later, Benjamin." And with that she strode past me and out the door I'd just come in.

Ben smiled at me. "She's . . . an old friend of mine."

"I *see*," I said, though I really didn't. "Well, you know what they say—you can't make new old friends." It was an absurd comment to make, but I didn't know quite what to say.

"Yeah." There was an uncomfortable silence.

"She came to tell me some news," Ben finally blurted. "About my family."

I cocked an eyebrow. "Oh? Nothing bad, I hope."

"No, just weird. She's been digging through genealogy websites, and found out we—my family, that is—are connected to an American Indian tribe. It's a whole branch of relatives I never knew existed."

I studied his face. I could definitely see Amerindian traces there: not the color of his hair, of course, but it was present in his bone structure, the tone of his skin, and his dark eyes. "That's interesting. Which tribe?"

"The Cowichan. They're from Vancouver Island, in Canada. Famous for their totem poles and sweaters."

"What's the connection, exactly?"

"That's the weird part. An ancestor of mine married a Cowichan woman sometime back in the 1800s, but the local tribal records don't seem to list her. She's something of a mystery, but she had a bunch of children and they scattered to the four winds."

"And here you are."

Now he looked a little more at ease. "Yeah. A few generations later and in another country entirely. Funny how things turn out."

"Yes. You never know what's going to pop up when you don't expect it, do you?"

Okay, that was a little mean—but I knew he wasn't telling me the whole truth about Anna. Nobody looked that guilty unless they had something to hide, and I was starting to get a little sick of being surrounded by deception. "Anyway, I just came in to see how lunch was progressing. What are you serving?" I kept my voice brisk, and both of us shifted into our professional roles. Neither of us actually sighed in relief, but some of the tension went away.

Unfortunately, so did my appetite. I got a quick rundown on the lunch menu, told him it sounded fine, and left. Time to check on ZZ.

Nothing appreciable had changed, other than the fact that the hallway had suddenly turned into a flower garden: Bouquets of every size and color lined the corridor, some of them with balloons.

The security guard, a beefy, bald man, said, "They've been coming all morning. Didn't want to put them in the room until I got your okay."

I nodded. "Good thinking. I'll get Shondra to check them out and then I'll have a maid move them inside."

The guard let me into the room. Tiny, in his new rottweiler form, lifted his head from his front paws. [Foxtrot. Any news?]

"Let's see. I've eliminated Keene and Hana Kim from the suspect pool. The controller for the drone turned out to be useless. Oh, and I think an old girlfriend of Ben's just showed up."

[Is that relevant?]

I shook my head. "To the case? Probably not. It's just a little upsetting, is all."

[I'm sorry to hear that. Do you want to talk about it?]

I frowned. Did I want to discuss the trials of my mostly theoretical love life with a shape-shifting ghost dog? Oddly enough, the answer was yes. "I just caught him in the kitchen with his arms wrapped around a blonde. An extremely attractive blonde wearing diamond earrings. Who wears diamond earrings before noon? Either she's got way too much money or she's trying to impress someone. And I think I know who."

[I've never found earrings to be terribly impressive myself. Or diamonds.]

I laughed. "I think Ben was probably focusing more on her legs. High heels and a very short skirt."

[That's something I've never understood. How does balancing on two tiny little sticks make a woman more attractive?]

"By changing her posture. Chest goes out, butt goes up, muscles in the legs bunch to make them more defined. Strong legs and prominent breasts are desirable from an evolutionary point of view; they mean she can provide lots of milk for her offspring and escape from predators."

Tiny considered this for a moment. [And the butt?]

"Beats me. Women like a nice firm tush, too, and I still don't know why. Something to hang on to, I guess."

[That was a cogent and well-thought-out explanation, Foxtrot. Thank you.]

"Yeah, yeah. I'm a real whiz at explaining the birds and the bees to the dogs. Too bad I can't apply that knowledge to my own life."

I sank into a beanbag chair upholstered in deep purple velour. Tiny got up, walked over, and sat beside me on the floor. [Don't be discouraged, Foxtrot. Sometimes it feels like you'll never find a mate, but life will surprise you. Romance can blossom under the strangest circumstances.]

"Oh? Give me an example, Mr. Love Expert."

[I'm no expert—but I do have an example. Would you care to hear it?]

I leaned my head back and closed my eyes. "Sure. Go ahead."

[Forty or so years ago, a dog-food company decided to hold a contest. They advertised in newspapers and magazines all over the country, as well as on radio and TV. They were looking for dogs; extraordinary dogs, of every kind. The biggest, the smallest, the fastest, the smartest. They organized regional contests at state fairs, and planned to pit the winners against one another in a nationally promoted event held in New York City.

[The results were not always what they expected—or, for that matter, desired. One of the initial winners in the Largest Dog category was a brute named Atlas. He weighed close to three hundred pounds, stood three and a half feet tall at the shoulder, and reached nearly seven feet in height when he stood on his hind legs. He was covered in shaggy gray fur, with floppy ears and a jowly muzzle.

[Atlas's owner was a rural hermit named Jimmy Joe Burl. Born and raised in the Appalachian Mountains, Mr. Burl had spent the last thirty years crossbreeding Alaskan timber wolves with the largest domesticated breeds he could find: Irish wolfhounds, Great Danes, English mastiffs. Nobody knows exactly what Atlas's lineage was, but there was no denying the result.

[Mr. Burl wanted the prize money, but the environs of New York proved somewhat overpowering to someone who had never used a flush toilet. The noise, the people, the skyscrapers all intimidated him. Once he'd delivered Atlas to the arena hosting the contest, Jimmy Joe headed straight for the nearest bar for some solitude and the comfort of whiskey.

[Another contestant, this time in the IQ category, was a Border collie named Daisy. Daisy understood eight hundred words and could do a variety of tasks on command, including sorting objects by size or name. Atlas was a giant; Daisy was a genius.

[The executives of the advertising agency congratulated themselves on a successful campaign. But while their expertise in marketing and promotion was considerable, the logistics of housing, feeding, and controlling a building full of animals proved to be their undoing. The pens they had arranged to use as kennels were all of a standard size and strength; they weren't designed for a behemoth like Atlas. A custom-built unit was hastily cobbled together by the arena's staff, without any input from Atlas's owner. Not that it mattered—by that time, Jimmy Joe Burl was unable to form coherent sentences, let alone give practical advice.

[The improvised kennel was placed next to Daisy's.

[Daisy was in heat.

[Saying that Atlas escaped his enclosure doesn't really capture the essence of the act. A romantic would say that once he became aware of her, Atlas would let no physical barrier stand between them; that he simply ignored the constraints of the physical world and instead followed the urgings of his heart.

[A pragmatist would put it differently: Atlas methodically destroyed his own cage, and then Daisy's. It took some time, and was rather loud. Staff gathered to watch, but no one tried to stop him. The ad agency was called, and a junior executive showed up and attempted to drive Atlas away with a hose. This proved to be an unwise decision, for both the executive and the hose.

[Daisy, by all accounts, watched this entire endeavor with rapt eyes. When her suitor had finally ripped enough planks from her pen to allow him entry, she proved more than willing to reward him.

[It was at this point that Jimmy Joe Burl arrived, his anxieties replaced by an alcohol-fueled confidence that turned his stagger into a swagger. He took one befuddled look at what Atlas and Daisy were doing—there was quite the crowd gathered around them by this time—and said, "If'n there's pups, I get half." Then he threw up on the ad executive, who had just regained consciousness.]

I grinned. "I'm guessing there were pups."

[Indeed there were—two of them. I was one. Daisy's owner raised me, but quickly saw that I would outgrow her abilities and household. After extensive research, she gave me to an organization that trained me.]

"What about your sibling? What happened to him or her?"

He didn't reply right away, and when he did his voice was sad but firm. [I'd prefer not to discuss that.]

I changed the subject. "So who named you Tiny?"

[My mother's owner. She was a wonderful woman, but I wish she'd chosen more carefully. As I said, most dogs just don't understand irony.]

"Well, most humans don't understand a lot of things. But I think there's one that I *do* understand, now. That huge, ferocious form you used in the graveyard—that was how you looked when you were alive, right?"

[Yes. Ergo the irony.] He paused. [So what about your name?]

"My nickname, you mean? My dad gave it to me. He started calling me that when I was really little. Then when we got a cat, my dad said we should call it Tango. I loved to dance, so I thought that was great. I used to dance around with Tango in my arms when she was a kitten."

[I'm sure she recalls those times fondly.]

"I hope so. I'm kind of afraid to ask her. I mean, sure, I thought it was great, but when you're a kid, your understanding of how things work and what's going on isn't always reliable. For instance, the reason my dad called me Foxtrot was because he didn't want to swear in front of me; so instead of using one F word, he used another. I didn't know what it meant, just that he would sometimes blurt it out if he stubbed his toe or something. To me, it was just a funny word I liked to repeat. To him, it was a private joke—though I did eventually figure it out."

[How?]

"My mom sort of gave it away. *If she's Foxtrot and the cat's Tango, you get to be Whiskey,* she'd say, and then laugh. It confused me for the longest time, because my dad didn't drink—not even beer. Then one day I put it together."

Tiny looked thoughtful. Some breeds of dog can pull that off better than others, and apparently a rottweiler is one of them. [Whiskey, Tango, Foxtrot. That's the NATO phonetic alphabet used for radio messages. It stands for the letters *W, T,* and *F.*]

"Right. And *WTF* is now Internet slang."

[For?]

"Let's just say it's an expression of surprise and leave it at that, okay?"

[And you weren't bothered by the deception?]

I shook my head. "No, it wasn't like that. You had to know my father, I guess. He had a pretty raunchy sense of humor, but his heart was as big as a house. He was always there for me—I never felt safer than when he was around. I still miss him."

[How long has he been gone?]

"He died three years ago. Heart attack."

Tiny came over and rested his big head on my knee. [I'm sure he misses you, too.]

I blinked back an unexpected surge of tears. "Thank you." I put my hand on Tiny's head, which felt solid, muscular, and warm—not like a ghost's at all. "I guess you would know, wouldn't you?"

I looked over at ZZ, at the steady rise and fall of her chest. I wondered if being in a coma was sort of halfway between life and death, and what she was experiencing right now if that were true. Was she talking to her own parents, both of them now dead? And if she was, would she remember any of it when she woke up?

If she woke up.

I got to my feet. "I have to get back to work," I told Tiny. "Oscar and Kenny Gant are my two main suspects now, and only one of them has a clear motive. I need to find out if the other one does, too."

[Good luck. I'll be here.]

I slipped out of the room, nodded at the guard, and went downstairs. Kenny Gant had said he was going to talk to Caroline, and it was possible he was still there. If I hurried, I could catch him before lunch.

I found them in the menagerie, feeding the animals. When I walked up to them Caroline was laughing at something Kenny had said, and Kenny himself was illustrating his point with one hand while using the other to lean against a railing. His arm was almost, but not quite, touching Caroline's back.

"Hey, you two," I said as I approached. "Once again, I show up too late to catch the punch line."

Caroline gasped, then got herself under control. "Oh, Kenny was just telling me a story about a commercial he shot using an alpaca. Seems he didn't know about the spit problem."

"Spit problem?"

"Yeah," Kenny said. "I knew that llamas—and even camels—spit at people when they get really upset, but its handler told me that didn't happen with alpacas. Boy, was he wrong."

"Well, it is rare," Caroline said. "Generally they only spit at each other, as a display of dominance. But it can happen if they're really upset."

"Then somebody must have crapped in his alpaca chow

that morning, because he sure did unload on me." Kenny shook his head, smiling. "You know that scene in *The Exorcist,* with Linda Blair spewing pea soup? It was like that, only right in my face. I kept expecting the thing's head to spin around."

"And on that note," I said, "lunch is almost ready. Pretty sure we're not having pea soup."

"I'm so hungry I might eat it anyway," Kenny said. "Guess I better get a move on. Nice talking to you, Caroline."

"You too," Caroline said.

"I'll catch up with you in a minute," I told him. "Just have a few details to discuss with Caroline."

Kenny nodded and strolled off in the direction of the house. I waited until he was gone before saying, "You two seem to have hit it off."

Caroline shrugged, but she was still smiling. "We have a lot in common. And he's funny."

"Funny is good. Funny is nice."

"Yeah, it is. So . . . what did you want to talk to me about?"

"Um." *Well, I was wondering if you were aware your new romantic interest might be a murderer.* "I was wondering if . . . the night Gant's monkey was tranquilized. Did he come by to check on him?"

She looked a little embarrassed, and a little pleased. "Uh, yeah. As a matter of fact, he did."

I knew that look. "Oh. I'm guessing he stayed for a while?"

Now she looked flustered. She thought she was about to get in trouble for becoming involved with a guest. I quickly added, "That's absolutely fine. In fact, that's what I wanted to talk to you about."

"About me and Kenny?"

"Yes. I recently realized that our policy on how staff

are supposed to interact with guests is unclear, and I thought I should clarify things. If you and Kenny want to date, that's perfectly all right. Really. Sooo . . . did he spend the night?"

It was an awkward segue—and not very professional—but I needed to know if Gant had an alibi.

Caroline hesitated, then gave me a shy smile. "He did. Said he was just there to make sure Amos was okay, but other things happened." She paused. "Several times."

I raised my eyebrows. "Uh-huh. Um, congratulations. So he was with you *all* night?"

"Yes. He got there at eleven and left a little before six."

"I see. Well, I hope things keep . . . uh, happening." No, that wasn't lame or awkward at all.

I covered up with a professional smile and then excused myself, citing work. She nodded good-bye, but I could see that she was still a little puzzled. Hey, if my supervisor had shown up just to tell me it was okay to boff my new boyfriend, I'd look puzzled, too.

I trusted Caroline. If she said Gant was with her all night, then that eliminated him as a suspect. Which left only one person.

ZZ's son, Oscar.

I went to lunch. Kenny Gant was in a good mood; Hana Kim seemed depressed; Mr. Kwok was impassive. Keene was his usual cheerful, irreverent self, and Oscar didn't show. We mostly ate in silence.

Afterward, I went to check on ZZ and brought Tiny some food. No change in ZZ's condition. Tango checked in with me and had nothing to report. Neither did Shondra.

Then it began to rain.

It was light at first, the kind of drizzle you sometimes got in late autumn. That increased to a steady rainfall, then to an actual downpour. It was as if Mother Nature were turning on a faucet at a very deliberate, measured rate. When it reached its peak, it immediately began to decrease at exactly the same speed. I might not have noticed this if I hadn't been sitting at my desk and staring out the window, trying to figure out how to approach Oscar. I wondered idly if the rain was going to go all the way back down to zero and start over.

That didn't happen. Instead, things got crazy.

The precipitation abruptly jumped back up the dial to torrential. The intensity of it was a little unnerving, but at least it was back to behaving the way weather usually did: unpredictably.

Then it got worse.

Water poured from the sky like a hole in God's bucket. The hammering of the rain on the roof was deafening, and the visibility outside the windows was close to zero. This must what it was like when it rained in the desert and the sheer volume of liquid turned gullies into rivers within minutes. I'd never seen anything like it.

A brilliant flash lit up the sheets of rain outside my window, though I didn't see the bolt of lightning that caused it—and at the very same second, a tremendous *CRACK!* split my ears and made me jump to my feet.

That was close, I thought, my heart pounding. Had it hit the house? It couldn't have—the power was still on. I quickly unplugged my computer in case the next one did strike us.

It happened again—the blinding flash and simultaneous *BOOM!* And again, I didn't see a bolt, just a bright light outside the window as if someone had turned on a thousand-watt lightbulb on the roof.

Which was when Eli showed up.

The white crow flew out of the storm and through the window without breaking the glass, then swooped down to land on the edge of my screen.

"Um," I said to the spirit. "This isn't good, is it?"

Strangely, he seemed to be wet. I didn't have time to remark on it, though, because Eli immediately blurted out, "You gotta get him to calm down!"

"What? Who?"

"The Thunderbird!"

"Slow down. I don't know what you're talking about."

He bobbed up and down in agitation. "And I don't have time to explain! Just go up on the roof and talk to him!"

There was another ear-splitting strike and flash. This time, the lights flickered.

"He's gonna completely lose control, and soon," Eli rasped. "Just go! I'll talk you through it!"

And suddenly I knew who he was talking about.

I ran for the door, then down the hall and toward the broom closet at the end of it. There was a ladder inside the closet, bolted to the wall, that led up to a hatch in the roof. Going up there during an electrical storm was complete idiocy, of course—but at least I wouldn't be alone. I'd have Eli with me.

And the person causing the storm.

I yanked the closet door open, nearly stumbled over a bucket, and started to climb. I knew who I'd find on the roof; he told me once he liked to come up here to look at the stars and think.

I threw open the hatch and stuck my head out, getting completely drenched in the process. There he was, just like I thought.

Ben.

He stood on the peak of the roof, one foot to either side. He wore only jeans, his feet and chest bare. He was holding on to the lightning rod that jutted from the roof with one hand, and seemed oblivious to my arrival.

"Ben!" I called over the rain. *"Ben!"*

He turned his head toward me slowly. The look on his

face was dreamy, unfocused. He had a slight smile on his lips.

And lightning dancing in his eyes.

Or more accurately, between them—a tiny jagged bolt crackled from one iris to the other, as if he had a Taser implanted in his brain and his eyes were the electrodes. "Foxtrot?" he said. He sounded more asleep than awake.

Then the next bolt hit. It smashed down on top of his head like the blue-white hammer of a furious god, and I screamed. I was sure that the next thing I saw would be his blackened, smoking body pitching off the roof.

But that didn't happen. His hair stood on end, and sparks skittered around the lightning rod like nervous fireflies, but it didn't even change the expression on his face.

Eli swooped out of the rain and landed on the roof. "Talk to him. He needs to hear a human voice."

"Talk to him? What am I supposed to say?"

"Tell him the truth about what he is."

"I don't *know* what he is!"

Eli's voice was now as calm as Ben's face. "I do. Just listen to me . . ."

So I did. Oddly enough, I think it was my experience as a professional assistant that let me deal with the situation without panicking. When things really hit the fan, it was people like me who often wound up saving the day—not because we had the solution, but because we could efficiently convey the pertinent information from the person in charge to the people on the ground. And in this particular situation, Eli was definitely the person in charge.

"Ben," I called out in a firm voice. His gaze had wandered back toward the sky, but now he blinked slowly and focused on me again. "Listen to me. You created this storm. And now you have to stop it."

"Foxtrot," he said again. "No, that's . . . I can't do that. How could I do that?"

"Because you're a Thunderbird. You aren't just descended from the Cowichan Indians, you're descended from a supernatural tribe of beings that could take on human form. They assimilated into human society a long time ago, but their powers and abilities live on in their bloodline."

The slight smile on his face had turned into a frown of consternation. "I'm not . . . human?"

"You're still *you,* Ben. You're not going to sprout feathers and a beak. Thunderbirds were ancient and powerful spirits that could cause and control storms, but when they transformed they were indistinguishable from mortals—so much so that they interbred with us. You're still a member of the human race, Ben. Think of this as just getting an inheritance from a distant relative."

I sounded like I knew what I was talking about, right? So did every newscaster with a tiny speaker plugged into his ear and an expert on the other end. The trick was to project confidence and sincerity, think on your feet, and try not to let your pauses get too obvious.

"How do you know all this?" Ben asked. He sounded a little more alert, but still not fully there. "I don't. I don't know anything. I just know what Anna told me, and that didn't make any sense."

Anna? How was she involved? "What did she tell you, Ben?"

"That it was time to . . . wake up. She told me to look at the sky. That was all—just to look at the sky. So I did. I've looked at the sky before, you know." He sounded faintly resentful. "Nothing like *this* ever happened. But this time, it felt different . . . it felt like something inside me was coming to life. I think . . . I think Anna did this to me, somehow."

Great. Not only had an ex-flame entered Ben's life, apparently she was some kind of sorceress, too. "That's not important right now, Ben. Right now, you have to concentrate on the storm. On shutting it down."

The smile came back. "That's not so easy. Calling it up, that felt natural. Felt right. But now that it's here . . . it's kinda like giving birth, I guess. One way only."

Terrific.

Chapter Nineteen

"He's just nervous," Eli said. "It's his first time. Just talk him through it."

Oh, yeah, fine. Reassure a newly minted Thunder God that this was natural, nothing to worry about. *You can do it, honey. You just need to practice your self-control; why, you should have seen what happened the first time Thor whipped up a storm. I know it's embarrassing, but it's just because you're so excited. Try thinking about baseball.*

"Ben," I said. "You have to trust me, okay? I trusted you when you tied that blindfold on me, and now it's your turn. All right?"

He gave me a slow, dreamy nod.

"Remember who you are. What you do. When you're cooking, who's in control?"

"I am." His voice was slow, hesitant.

"You sure? Pretend you're cooking right now. Who's the boss in your kitchen?"

"Me." Better, but not perfect.

"The *sky* is your kitchen, Ben. All that wind, all that rain and thunder and lightning, those are your ingredients. Can you *feel* that?"

"I . . . I can. I *can*."

"The storm isn't an infant, Ben—it's an entrée. And it's *done*. Time to switch off the oven. Time to let everything cool down."

"Yeah. I think . . . I think I can do that." He frowned, and turned his attention from me to the storm itself. He reached up with one hand, his fingers spread, and the rain began to slow. "Turn it down," Ben muttered. "Turn it down."

The downpour gradually eased off. Lightning stopped flickering above us. I held my breath.

"Damn storm," Ben growled. "You listen to *me*. *I'm* in charge here. My kitchen, my *rules*. And *you* . . . are . . . *done*!" He clenched his outstretched hand into a fist, and the rain came to a stop. The clouds swirled, then parted. I could see blue sky again.

"Thank God for control-freak chefs," I whispered.

Ben looked back at me. Both of us were dripping wet, and I was starting to shiver.

"Okay," he said. "I have clearly lost my mind. Thank you for humoring me. Now, could you kindly call the nice men in the white coats to take me away?"

"How about we go downstairs, dry off, and talk over a cup of something hot, instead?"

"How about hot and alcoholic?"

"I think I can arrange that."

Eli chuckled. "Nicely handled, kid. I think I'm starting to like you." And then he hopped off the edge of the roof and swooped away.

Ben carefully climbed down to the hatch, and I went down the ladder to make room for him. He closed the hatch behind him.

I took him to an unoccupied room and let him inside. "Towels and a robe are in the bathroom," I said. "Get yourself dry and comfortable. I'm going to change my clothes, then grab us some coffee and something to spike it with. Don't whip up a tornado or anything while I'm gone, all right?"

"I—can I do that?"

"I don't know. Just stay put."

My cell phone was trying to get my attention, so I answered it while striding briskly down the hall. By the time I'd gotten back to my office I'd reassured two guests, given Carl Jeffrey the okay to rent a pump, and been told that lightning had destroyed two trees. I changed quickly—I always kept two changes of clothes at the office—and went downstairs, grabbing two mugs of coffee from the carafe in the kitchen and a decanter of something amber from the sitting room.

I returned, knocked on the door with the side of my foot, and heard him say, "Come on in, unless you're a blizzard."

"Can you get the door? My hands are kind of full."

He opened it. ZZ liked her guests to feel stylish as well as comfortable, so the robe he was wearing was not only warm and fluffy, it was styled like a mandarin's coat: Golden dragons chased themselves against a deep purple background, and intricately embroidered vines climbed his lapels. Considering what I'd just seen him do, the overall impression he gave was that of a wizard who had lost his hat. And shoes.

I came in, shut the door with my foot, and set down the mugs of coffee. I poured a generous shot into each, then handed one to him. "Here."

We sat on the edge of the bed, him near the head, me near the foot. We drank some coffee, discovered the amber liquid was brandy, and glanced at each other nervously.

"I'm not crazy, am I?" he said at last.

"Afraid not."

"I'm a Thunderbird."

"Afraid so."

He nodded, looking grave. "And how in the hell do you know all this, exactly?"

I opened my mouth, and then closed it. "Um. I . . . can't exactly tell you."

He frowned. "Why not?"

"Oh, boy. This is going to be tricky . . . let's just say that you're not the only supernatural being around, okay?"

His eyes widened. "You mean you—"

"What? No, no, no. I'm not a—a witch, or anything like that. I'm just me. But I might be in contact with . . . beings . . . who are definitely not ordinary. And said beings have sworn me to secrecy. But then you cooked up a hurricane and one of them told me to calm you down and I didn't know what to do so he told me what you were and where you came from and that's about all I know. Okay?"

He looked at me steadily for a few seconds. "No."

I sighed. "I just—dammit, this isn't up to me. I want to tell you exactly what's going on, but I made a promise and what's going on is kind of important and I just *can't*. I know how frustrated you are because *my* whole worldview got turned upside down a few days ago and I've been dealing with it all alone, but people are depending on me and *I just can't*."

I found, to my complete and utter surprise, that I was close to tears. It wasn't fair; to find out that maybe I wasn't in all this craziness alone, that there was another human being—okay, mostly human being—that I could maybe talk to, and then realize I *couldn't*? That was just too much.

"Hey," Ben said. "Hey, I'm sorry." He reached out a hand, put it on my shoulder. "I shouldn't be surprised that you know what's going on—you always do. And you're awfully good at making sure everything *keeps* going on, or stops, or does whatever it's supposed to. That's *why* people depend on you."

"Thank you," I said, trying not to sniffle.

"Look, I trust you, okay? If you say you can't fill me in, then I have to believe you've got a good reason for that. And I already know more than I did when I climbed up on the damn roof. So all in all, I'm ahead, and you haven't broken any promises. Right?"

I did my best to smile. "Yeah. I guess that's true."

"So. Tell you what. There's something I've been meaning to bring up, but I just didn't know how. Seeing as how you now know more about me than I do, maybe this won't come as any surprise—but I feel I have to tell you, anyway."

Uh-oh. I didn't know if I could handle that at this precise moment. Was he going to say what I thought he was? "Stop," I said. "Now is *not* the time, okay? I just told you I *can't* spill the beans, so now you're going to? That is totally unfair. No bean spillage."

He took his hand off my shoulder and looked down. Took another long swallow of his brandied coffee. "I'm not who you think I am, Foxtrot," he said quietly.

That wasn't what I expected, but I had the sinking feeling I knew what was coming next. When a man you're interested in makes that kind of statement, it usually means one of two things—and I was pretty sure he wasn't gay.

"You're married," I said. "Is that who Anna is? Your wife?"

He gave me a confused frown. "What? No! No, Anna's my *sister*."

"Your—wait. Your *sister*?" That was the last thing I expected to hear. "But she was . . . she looked . . ."

"Upper class? Sophisticated? Well off?" He shook his head. "Yeah, well—that's because she is. And no, she didn't marry money. She was born with it—just like I was."

It was my turn to frown. "That's your shameful confession? You're *rich*?"

He shrugged. "Not me, my family. Grew up in a house almost as big as this one, but a lot less fun. My father owns a chain of restaurants, but he's also a classically trained French chef. So am I."

"But—ZZ found you in a diner!"

"That she did. But six months before that, I was running my own restaurant. At least, I *thought* it was mine—but my dad was the one who really owned it. And when I told him I wanted to make a few changes, he wouldn't let me. We had a massive fight, which ended in him saying I wasn't as good as I thought I was and me telling him I was and I was going to prove it. *Without* his help."

I was beginning to get the picture. "So you hit the road and got a job in a little greasy spoon. Was that supposed to impress him, or piss him off?"

Ben laughed. "A little of both, I guess. At first, anyway—but once I realized how hard it actually was, it stopped being about him and more about proving something to myself."

"And did you?"

He grinned. "I did, yeah. In fact, I was thinking about moving on when ZZ came in and made me that offer. From fast-order cook to private chef, all on my own? Seemed to me that would settle any argument as to how good I was. So I took the job—and here I am."

"Until your sister tracked you down."

"Anna's pretty damn sharp. We don't always see eye-to-eye, but she's always looked out for me. But now—this whole Thunderbird business . . ." He shook his head. "I have to talk to her. I mean, if I'm one, then she must be, too. Why didn't she explain? How long has she known about this?"

"You said she was doing genealogy research. Maybe this is so recent she hasn't figured everything out yet."

"Maybe. But telling me to look at the sky and wake up . . . that sounds deliberate, doesn't it?"

I had to admit it did. But I also knew what it was like to have information you weren't allowed to share. "Maybe she told you all she could."

He looked troubled. "Maybe. In any case, I need to ask her in person."

And now my head chef was to about to leave. *Good job, Foxtrot.* "I understand. Can you at least do dinner tonight? That'll give me time to find a replacement."

"I'm not quitting, Foxtrot. She's staying at a hotel nearby—I'll talk to her tonight."

Well, that was one crisis averted, at least for the moment. I better make sure I had someone lined up as a replacement, though—I found it hard to imagine a person who could call up a thunderstorm keeping his day job grilling steaks and mashing potatoes. "Good. Well, I'll see about getting you some dry clothes, and we'll talk later. All right?"

"Sure. And Foxtrot—thank you." His stare was intense enough to make me uncomfortable. "I don't know what would have happened if you hadn't talked me down. That storm was . . . well, it was *eager.* Does that make any sense?"

I got to my feet. "It sort of does. Try not to make it hail in the dining room, okay?"

I left him there, found some sweatpants and a T-shirt a famous athlete left behind, and dropped them off. Then I went looking for my cat.

I found her in a second-floor bay window, looking out

over the extremely wet lawn. *<Hey, Toots. Some storm, huh? Glad I was inside.>*

"Some storm, indeed. Tango, do you know what a Thunderbird is?"

<Sure. One of my former humans drove one. Always complained about the gas mileage.>

"That's not what I'm talking about." Then I told her what I *was* talking about.

When I was finished explaining what had happened and what our resident chef now was, Tango seemed unconcerned. *<Hmm. And Eli was the one who filled you in?>*

"Yes. But he took off before I could ask him any questions."

<Yeah, his type are like that. They prefer asking the questions to answering them. But if he doesn't have a problem with it, neither do we. Everything's fine.>

"He didn't sound fine when he first showed up. He sounded—" I stopped. Actually, when I thought back, Eli hadn't really sounded panicked—just urgent. Like when upper management wants you to think something has to be done *right now,* but they don't want to give the impression of losing control. That's exactly what Eli had sounded like. And when the impending crisis had passed, he'd sounded less relieved than . . . *satisfied.*

Maybe I should have been angry, but I wasn't. This hadn't been a deliberate test, like me talking to Two-Notch; it had been an actual situation that needed dealing with, and I'd dealt with it. My immediate superior had put his faith in me, and I'd delivered. I felt proud, and I deserved to.

But that didn't mean Eli and I weren't going to talk about this—oh, no. Every win came with a payoff, and I intended to collect mine. Graciously, of course, and without bragging—when you accepted an award, you kept your speech short and made sure you thanked everyone who helped you along the way.

But you didn't forget to take the trophy home.

Now I had to deal with Oscar. I still found it hard to believe that Oscar would have his own mother killed; he could be greedy, shortsighted, and irresponsible, but I always thought that beneath it all he genuinely loved ZZ. Were my instincts that wrong?

I needed to know more. Oscar obviously wasn't going to tell me anything—but maybe his friend Francis the jockey, would. Of course, first I had to find him.

As it turned out, that wasn't difficult. The Jockeys' Guild had a Facebook page with a search function, and the name Francis generated a number of hits. The guild had provided photos, too, so it wasn't hard to identify the Francis in question. A little more digging on the Internet gave me a local address and contact number.

Time to pay Mr. Francisco Alvarado a visit.

Francis lived in Hartville, just like I did, but apparently his job didn't pay as well as mine; he had a dingy apartment on the third floor, and the elevator was out of service. The front door to the complex should have been locked, but someone had blocked it open with a stack of supermarket flyers. The same person, I suspected, whom I passed in the lobby carrying a box marked CLOTHES. She didn't look happy about the elevator situation; I hoped she didn't live on the top floor.

The directory downstairs had told me which apartment Francis lived in. When I knocked, there was an immediate reply from behind the door: "Hang on! I'll be right there!"

He was already talking when he opened the door. "Decided you needed a hand after all, huh—" He stopped in mid-sentence, clearly expecting someone else.

"Hi!" I said brightly. "As a matter of fact, I do need a hand. Mind helping me out?"

He looked blank for a second, and then he remembered who I was. "Oh. Right. Sorry, I thought you were Janey. I offered to haul some boxes for her, but she wasn't interested. I mean, she said she was fine by herself."

"Her loss," I said. It might be a cliché, but soothing a man's wounded pride with a little flattery never hurt. Francis grinned and said, "What can I do for you, Foxtrot?"

"Invite me in so we can talk?"

"Sure, sure. Come on in."

He opened the door wider and ushered me inside. The apartment was small, but neat and clean. Racetrack posters adorned the walls, and there was a glassed-in cabinet displaying a number of trophies. The furniture was worn and mismatched, the bookshelf made from boards and bricks. A man proud of what he did for a living, but he hadn't gotten rich from it.

"Can I get you something? Glass of wine, maybe?"

I sat down on the couch. "A cup of tea would be nice."

While he puttered around in the kitchen—which was just a tiny nook on the other side of a counter—I glanced around, trying to get a clearer picture of who he was. Paperback thrillers on the bookshelves, mostly Tom Clancy and Michael Crichton; a few potted plants; and a large, wall-mounted plasma TV. Less than a year old, too, which I knew because I'd been researching plasma screens for ZZ a few weeks ago. Looked like Francis had gotten an influx of cash recently.

"So, you're a jockey," I said as he came back with two mugs of tea.

"It was either that or become a garden gnome," he said as he put the mugs down on the coffee table and joined me on the couch. It had the feel of a joke he'd told a few hundred times before. "And being a jockey pays better. When I'm working, anyway."

I'd done a little research before I set out. "Especially when your horse wins, right?"

"This is true," he said. "But I've ridden a few winners, as you can see." He casually gestured toward the trophy case.

"So you have. Ridden any lately?"

The smile on his face shrank noticeably. "I've been sidelined with an injury. The jockey business is high-risk."

"That it is. You can wind up in the hospital, or worse. And really—other than a few standout stars—most jockeys don't make a lot of money. Thirty or forty thousand a year on average? For a job that requires you to travel a lot and put your life on the line in every race? I feel for you, I really do."

The smile was creeping back. If he couldn't get admiration, he'd settle for pity. "I won't lie to you—it's hard. People think it's glamorous, but—"

GRAAAAARRR!

He stopped in mid-sentence. The noise we'd both heard came from out in the hall, and from the volume and intensity you'd swear King Kong had just stepped on Godzilla's tail while wearing steel-toed boots. I did my best to match the amazement on Francis's face. "What was *that*?" I blurted.

"I don't know. It sounded like—I don't know *what* it sounded like."

"Think we should look?"

"It's probably nothing."

GRAAAAAAAAARRRRRR!

I raised my eyebrows. "*That* was nothing?"

"No, that was definitely something. I just don't know if we should—"

I gave him a slight smile and an understanding nod. "Oh. Never mind, I'll go check it out."

I started getting to my feet, but he sprang off the couch like he was spring-loaded. "No, no. I'll go." He headed to the door, while I stayed by the couch.

"Be careful!" I called after him.

He opened the door cautiously and peered out. "I don't see anything."

GRAARRRR!

"It's coming from down the hall," Francis said over his shoulder. "Around the corner, I think."

"But what *is* it?"

"I'll go see. Stay here."

Perfect.

I didn't have time for much of a search, but there was only one place I needed to check—the fridge. Luckily, Francis wasn't much of a cook, and his refrigerator didn't hold a lot in the way of groceries; what I was looking for stood out quite plainly. I pocketed a sample, closed the door, and was back in place seconds before Francis returned.

"Nothing," he reported with a puzzled look on his face. "One of the other tenants came out to look, too, but all she saw was a cat. No way a cat made a sound like *that*—not unless it was a lion passing a kidney stone."

Or one that spoke the same language. "That's really weird. It makes me feel sort of . . . unsafe."

Now was his chance to play the strong male protector. "Hey. It's okay. I'll fight off any stray lions that happen to wander by." He grinned in a way that was supposed to be charming, but only made it to smug.

"I'm sorry," I said. "I really have to go." I brushed past him, shrugged off his increasingly desperate attempts to reassure me everything was fine, and fled out of the apartment and down the stairs.

I met Tango in the lobby. "Great job. What *was* that?"

<Howler monkey, mostly. With a little alligator thrown in for bellow.>

"Alligators bellow?"

<Oh, yeah. You'd be surprised.>

Chapter Twenty

I knocked on Oscar's door. This time when he answered he was alone. "Hello, Foxtrot. I suppose you'd like to come in and berate me for a while, since it's been hours since you last had the pleasure."

"I seem to recall that you did most of the berating during our last private chat, Oscar. Which means it's my turn."

He gestured me in sardonically, and I accepted with a cheery smile. Once inside I made myself comfortable on a chair that probably cost what I make in a month. Okay, actually a month and three days—I ordered the thing for him, so I knew to the penny. "Now. Do you want to offer me a drink to go with the one you're about to pour yourself, or shall we skip the formalities and get right to the berating?"

He was already at the bar. "The formalities, as you call them, are all that keep me from sticking my head in the oven and turning on the gas. We can't let our standards slide over a little tongue-lashing." He came over and handed me a drink—gin and tonic, heavy on the gin. Once Oscar learned your favorite drink, he never forgot it.

He sat across from me, his own glass in hand, and regarded me levelly. "Well? Have you come to tell me Mother's cut me out of her will entirely, and I should start listing the furniture on eBay? Or are you simply going to exercise your power of attorney and begin charging me rent?"

"Neither one, unfortunately. No, I'm here because of five little letters and two little numbers. Care to guess what they are?"

"Not in the slightest."

"Then I'll just tell you. CYP3A4-X. Sound familiar?"

"It sounds like a license plate."

I reached into my pocket and pulled out the plastic vial I'd taken from Francis's fridge. "Maybe this will refresh your memory." I put it down on the glass top of the coffee table between us.

He stared down at it, then back at me. "And what, may I ask, is that?"

"That, Oscar, is a chemical called an isoenzyme. It's found in many animals, and it's very important. What it does is help metabolize chemicals in the bloodstream, so toxic levels don't build up."

"Fascinating. Is this your roundabout way of suggesting I enter a rehabilitation facility? Because if so, your sales pitch needs work."

"No, Oscar. This is what you and Francis planned to administer to the horses you were going to dope in order to win races. CYP3A4-X causes drugs to break down more quickly than normal, so that by the time the horses were tested they'd be clean. It's a clever scam; did you come up with it, or did Francis?"

He regarded me over the rim of his glass as he took a careful sip, then lowered it. "Really, Foxtrot. What an outlandish idea."

"I suppose it depends on what you use to dope the horse. I was surprised at how many methods there were; I thought the basic idea was to give them the equine equivalent of espresso, so they'd run faster. Turns out there are several different strategies, including giving them painkillers so they can push themselves past their own limits. Or tranquilizers, to calm them down so they perform better. Francis didn't seem to have anything like that in his fridge—but I suppose it would be better to have someone else hold on to the actual illegal drug. You know, like a partner that was bankrolling the scheme."

"I see. Would you care to peek inside my refrigerator, Foxtrot? All you have to do is ask."

I shook my head. "No, Oscar. You're too smart to leave anything like that out in the open. In fact, you may have already disposed of the drug in question—by leaving it under Juan Estevez's mattress."

The ironic disdain on his face vanished. Genuine anger smoldered in his eyes, and he set his drink down with a sharp *clack!* "You believe I poisoned Mother. With a *horse tranquilizer*."

I met his eyes calmly. "Did you?"

He got to his feet. "Come with me."

I stood up. He led me into the kitchen, where he opened the fridge. He reached inside and took out a small jar of cold cream—the all-natural kind with no preservatives. I have something similar, and I keep it in the fridge, too.

Oscar handed it to me. "Disregard the label. This is dermorphin—or, as it is more commonly known, frog juice."

"Frog juice?"

"Yes. It's derived from the skin of *Phyllomedusa sauvagei,* a species of South American frog. It's both a painkiller and stimulant—ideal for horses. Until recently, there wasn't even an accurate test for it, and it's thirty to forty percent stronger than morphine. It would make an excellent murder weapon, don't you think?"

I eyed the jar skeptically. “And why are you telling me this?”

“Because I very much doubt Mother was poisoned with anything so esoteric. If I were the killer, I would have used this—but I certainly wouldn’t reveal that to you. What does that tell you?”

He had a point. ZZ and Maria were both poisoned with carfentanil, not dermorphin. *If* what I was holding contained what Oscar claimed, he was unlikely to be the killer.

“How do I know this isn’t what it says on the label? It’s not like I have a chemical assay kit in my back pocket.”

He sighed and closed the refrigerator door. “Send it out to be tested, of course. I’m intimately familiar with your competence, Foxtrot, and have no doubt you’ll pull whatever strings are necessary for some hapless, lonely laboratory technician to get you the results within hours. But in the meantime you’ll have Shondra place me under the equivalent of house arrest, and I do not appreciate the curtailing of my freedom that will cause. Therefore, I will provide further proof of my innocence, in the forlorn hope that you will go away and never speak of this again.”

After this speech, he returned to the living room, drained his drink, and prepared another.

“Okay, I’m listening,” I said. “Prove away.”

“I wasn’t home the night Maria was killed. I was, in fact, out obtaining the dermorphin in question.”

I frowned. “No, you weren’t. You didn’t leave the estate.”

“Which you know how?”

“Security cameras.”

Oscar raised one eyebrow. “Please. I’m a grown man, Foxtrot—do you really think I’d allow Mother’s overpriced watchdog to dictate my comings and goings? Ms. Destry is reasonably good at what she does, but I grew up on this land. There are ways to exit without being caught, and I've been taking advantage of them since I was a teen."

A hole in Shondra's perimeter? She wouldn't be happy about that, but that was a problem for another time. "Who else knows about your secret escape route?"

"No one I've seen in years. And I very much doubt the girlfriend I had when I was seventeen would be prowling around the estate looking to assassinate people with a flying drone."

"Can you prove any of this?"

"Sadly, I can. Francis's contact for the dermorphin was to meet us in a run-down little all-night diner off the interstate. We had gone into town together after dinner, and then he pretended to drop me off at the house just before ten. I left via my hidden route, and he picked me up outside on the road. We arrived at the diner just before eleven. I'm sure the waitress there—a woman with the unlikely name of Jerrileen—remembers us, because we were there for hours. Francis's associate arrived at around four thirty AM.

"I hope you realize," he continued as he reached down and opened a drawer, "that were I the villain you believe me to be, right about now is when I would pull out a handgun and announce you would never live to tell anyone your theory."

He pulled out a notepad and a pen, instead. "As I am not, I am simply going to write down the name of the diner and directions to get there. I presume you will follow up with all due diligence and thus my name and reputation will be restored to their former tarnished glory."

I took the paper from him. "I will, thanks. Though I'm a bit surprised you're being so cooperative."

He gave me a withering look. "Don't be. Believe it or not, I want my mother's attacker brought to justice as much as you do. And once you deduced the nature of my relationship with Francis, any thought of profiting from the endeavor promptly died. You're not stupid, Foxtrot, and neither am I. Do me the courtesy of at least regarding me as a worthy opponent, will you?"

I couldn't help but grin. "I do, Oscar. And for the record—I never believed you were actually behind the murder attempt. But I had to investigate every possibility."

He nodded graciously. "I understand. Now go catch the bastard, will you?"

I let myself out.

I did follow up, of course. I called the waitress at the diner, who did remember Francis and Oscar and the third guy who met them. I overnighted the cold cream jar and its supposed dermorphin to a lab I know in New York that would get me an answer fast—don't ask how I knew about them or why they owed me a favor—but by then I was pretty sure Oscar was telling the truth.

So who was left?

Cooper definitely had a motive, but I didn't see how he could have gotten into Estevez's room to steal the controller and plant the poison. No, it made far more sense that the killer was on the inside—someone who knew when Estevez's room was empty.

There was only one person I hadn't talked to since the attempt on ZZ's life: Juan Estevez, the accused. I doubted very much that Sheriff Brower would let me anywhere near him in person, but there were other ways. I got on the phone to ZZ's lawyer, and she called another lawyer, and they called someone else.

Networking. I loved it.

And when all was said and done, the next voice I heard on the phone was Juan Estevez himself. He may have been locked up, but that didn't mean he was in solitary confinement.

"Foxtrot?" he said. He sounded puzzled. "My lawyer said I should talk to you. Look, I didn't try to kill your boss."

"I know that. And I'm now doing my best to prove it—so any information you can give me would be a big help to both of us."

"But—you're the one who got me arrested in the first place!"

"And I'm really, really sorry about that. But we both know you were set up, so let's just let bygones be bygones and work on getting you out of there, okay?"

There was a pause, but it wasn't a long one. "Right. Yeah. Okay, what do you want to know?"

"Who would want to frame you?"

"I—I can't say. I mean, I don't know." Now he sounded nervous. And his choice of words seemed to indicate he was afraid of telling me what he knew.

"Juan. You're already in jail and charged with murder. I don't see how telling me *anything* could possibly make your situation worse."

"At least I'm alive."

What? He was behind bars, and likely to stay there. Who could he possibly be afraid of—

And then I got it.

"The government," I said. "You were developing this for the government, and now you think some CIA assassin is going to slip into your cell and inject you with cyanide in your sleep if you open your mouth. Right?"

Silence.

"Okay. I understand why you don't want to talk, so just listen. The government isn't after you. For one thing, they wouldn't have gone to all this trouble; it would have been much easier to just plant drugs on you or something. For another, why would they want Maria or ZZ dead?"

"Maria was just collateral damage." His voice was tight. "ZZ was the real target. She was going to out me on the Internet, raise a public outcry. This project was supposed to be under the radar; any kind of backlash would have killed it. That's what they told me."

"Who? Who told you that, exactly?"

"My . . . handler."

That stopped me dead. "Oh, good God," I breathed. I was starting to see the shape of the thing. "Juan, R and D geeks don't have *handlers*. They have supervisors, or managers, or maybe liaisons, but they don't have handlers."

"Well, I did." He sounded sulky.

"Did you ever meet this handler in person?"

"Of course not. Encrypted emails only. And dead drops."

I knew what that was—a fancy way of saying someone would leave you a package at a remote but publicly accessible location, and you'd come by later and pick it up. "Dead drops of what?"

"Cash. Lots and lots of cash. That's how I knew he was the real thing."

I shook my head, even though he couldn't see it. "You've been reading too many spy novels, Juan. You're a US citizen on US soil, not a revolutionary in a South American jungle—though the South American angle is getting stronger and stronger."

"What do you mean?"

"Lots of cash to develop a remote-control assassination device. Who do you think would love to get their hands on a few of those?"

"Drug lords, you mean? No way. When those guys off someone, they want everyone to know—they don't use poison, they use bombs and automatic weapons. The

GEQ is a weapon of *subtlety,* not mass destruction." There was a note of wounded pride in his voice.

But he had a point. So, if Estevez's mysterious financial backer wasn't the CIA or narcoterrorists, who did that leave?

I asked Juan a few more questions, but he didn't have any other useful information. I thanked him, told him to hang in there, and hung up.

Somebody wanted to kill ZZ, and pin the crime on Juan. Somebody with a bunch of money to spend, and a reason to spend it.

But who?

Follow the money is always good advice. Whoever the killer was, they'd invested a lot in this project. That suggested they had a lot to gain.

What else had they bought?

The graveyard itself was worth a lot of money, but it wasn't for sale—so maybe the killer had bought other land, nearby.

I spent a lot of time paying for ZZ's indulgences, so I was intimately familiar with the kind of paper trail large purchases generated. Finding out who owned the land adjacent to the graveyard wasn't hard, but getting the name of the majority shareholder in the shell company who'd bought it eighteen months before took a little more digging. *That* gave me the name I'd been after all this time—but it still didn't prove they were the killer, just that they had motive.

But it did start me thinking, And even though the answer I came up with seemed ludicrous at first, it did hold together. There was one simple way to prove it, too.

I headed upstairs, checked in with the security guard at the door, and went inside. Tiny looked up when I entered and told me, [Nothing to report, Foxtrot.]

I looked down at ZZ. At least she was breathing on her own, now; the doctor had given the okay to remove the respirator a few hours ago. "Hey, boss. You'll be up and around in no time, I guarantee. And when you are, you won't have to worry about the person who did this to you, either. I'm about to put them behind bars."

Tiny's ears perked up. [You know who the killer is?]

"I think I do, Tiny. But I'm going to need you to help prove it."

[What do you need me to do?]

"Leave your post, I'm afraid. But it'll be worth it."

When we left, the guard—a muscular black man with steel-rimmed glasses—looked down at Tiny curiously. "I gotta ask," he said. "Where's he do his business? I been on shift six hours, the guy before me eight, and neither one of us seen him get walked."

"Oh, there's an en suite bathroom," I said with a straight face. "He knows how to use it." Then I walked away, Tiny right beside me.

We were in the foyer when I heard Ben call out, "Foxtrot! Talk to you for a minute?" He stood in the hall in his cook's whites, looking anxious.

I glanced down at Tiny. "Stay here, okay? I'll be right back."

Tiny rolled his eyes, but lay down on the floor of the foyer.

I walked over to Ben. "What is it?"

He looked around. "Not here. In my office, okay?"

"All right." I followed him to the kitchen, then the small room he used for his office. There was space for a tiny desk and two chairs; I pulled up one while he leaned against the desk with his arms crossed and looked nervous.

"Okay," I said. "What's going on? Is it about your . . . heritage?"

"Not exactly," he said. "More about my future."

"That sounds a little ominous."

"Does it? Isn't supposed to. The last thing I want right now is ominous." He ran a hand through his shaggy blond hair. "These last few days—they've been crazy, haven't they? Maria getting killed, ZZ in a coma, me and you all mixed up in some kind of supernatural weirdness that I would have laughed at a week ago."

I couldn't disagree with that. "It's been crazy, all right. I wouldn't blame you for wanting to leave it all behind."

He stared at the floor, a pensive look on his face. "Yeah. That'd be the smart thing to do, wouldn't it? Hit the road. Maybe go to Vancouver Island, try to find a few more of my kind. But that would just lead to more weirdness, wouldn't it? For all I know, Thunderbirds don't get along with one another. I might get into a scrap that would level the eastern seaboard."

Now, there was a frightening thought, and one that was too big to wrap my head around at the moment. I was about to catch a murderer—that was about all my poor overstressed noggin had room for right now. "I don't know what to tell you, Ben. I don't have any easy answers. This—whatever this is—is as new to me as it is to you. I'm keeping my head above water, but I haven't figured out how to swim yet."

"I kind of figured that. You usually seem to have all the answers, but—well, it doesn't matter. That's not what I wanted to talk to you about." He uncrossed his arms and let them hang down at his sides, where they twitched like they needed something to do.

"Oh, good. So this is about something *really* earth-shattering, like tonight's appetizer?"

He smiled ruefully. "I wish. I called my sister this afternoon."

"And?"

"And I didn't get to talk to her. Her voice mail told me she's out of the country. 'Gone to Europe to bolster their failing economy,' as she put it. No other details. She must have been on the way to the airport when she stopped in here."

"Sounds like she doesn't want to talk to you."

"And I don't feel like chasing her around the globe. Now here's the weird thing: When I realized that, I actually felt relieved."

He was resting his seat and hands on the desk, his palms flat and his fingers gripping the edge, his weight on his arms. It was making the muscles in them bulge out, and I was trying not to stare. "Relieved? Why?"

"Because I *like* it here, Foxtrot. It's like I belong. And it's not just the job, or the people—it's something else."

He cut his eyes to the side, avoiding mine. Even though he hadn't asked a question, it felt like he had.

"I'm . . . not sure what you mean," I said. Which wasn't true; I knew perfectly well what he meant. What I didn't know was how I felt about it.

"I guess what I'm asking," he said, bringing those dark eyes up to look into mine, "is if you feel it, too. Because if you do . . ."

I didn't know what to say. So I stood up and kissed him, instead.

This was not as romantic as it sounds. It was, in fact, more out of panic than passion. See, I *always* knew what to say, even when I didn't. I even had a whole list of things to say when I didn't know what to say, and I was very good at saying them—so good that only the people who knew me really well could even tell I was at a loss.

But right at that moment, I couldn't remember a damn one.

He smelled good. He *tasted* good, like chocolate with a hint of mint—he must have been snacking in the kitchen.

I wish I could say he was a good kisser, too, but the truth was I couldn't tell; I'd caught him completely off guard. Ever kiss someone—I mean *really* kiss someone—when they weren't expecting it? It's like going upstairs in the dark and miscalculating how many steps there are. Your foot comes down on something that isn't there, your whole body lurchs, and there's this terrible moment of vertigo, shock, and embarrassment. You just screwed up something you thought was a piece of cake.

I pulled back immediately. From the look of consternation on his face, you'd think I just told him a rutabaga had been elected pope.

"Whoa," he said. "That's—I didn't mean—"

"No, it's okay—I didn't—I mean you didn't—"

"I was talking about—"

"No, no, it's fine—"

"Stop." He took me gently by the arms, which was about the only thing preventing me from bolting so fast I would have left a Foxtrot-shaped hole in the wall. "Listen to me. That was—well, it was awkward, but it wasn't *wrong*. You just caught me off guard, is all."

I stopped trying to swallow my own tongue and met his eyes. They were just as gorgeous, but very serious. "Really?"

"Really. When I asked you if you felt the same, I meant about this place. About feeling . . . like we belong here. Like this place is special, somehow."

"Your office?"

He grinned, which just made me want to kiss him again. I managed to stifle the urge. "No, not my office. Not even the estate. I think it's the graveyard."

I blinked. I opened my mouth, but nothing came out.

"That's it, isn't it?" he said. "When you talked about being in contact with other supernatural beings. It has something to do with the graveyard. I can *feel* it."

"Yes," I blurted. Maybe this would get me in trouble, but I had to give him *something*. "Yes, the graveyard is important. I can't say why, but it is. And guess what? I'm supposed to protect it."

"You are?"

"Yeah." I'd thought telling someone else my secret—well, a tiny bit of my secret—would be a relief, but it just made me feel anxious and guilty.

"From what?"

"Someone who wants to destroy it and turn a fast buck. But I think I know who, and I'm working on proving it."

"Can I help?"

There was that damn urge again. I took a step back and said, "Thank you—but no. You've got enough on your plate, and I'm not supposed to involve anybody else. But don't worry about me—I can do this."

He nodded. "I have absolutely no doubt that you can. And since I'm sticking around, maybe you can even tell me about it, someday."

"I will if I can," I said. Then, before one of those awkward pauses could set in, I said, "Well."

There was that pause. Dammit.

"I better get back to making dinner," he said.

"Right. I better get back to—that thing I was doing," I said.

And then I turned around and left.

I found Tiny sitting patiently in the foyer. [At last. Everything all right?]

"Fine," I muttered. "Come on. Let's go catch us a killer."

CHAPTER TWENTY-ONE

I led Tiny out to the parking lot, and then to one particular vehicle. It was locked, of course, but I knew that wouldn't stop Tiny. Human beings have five million olfactory receptors spread out over an inch and a half of epithelial tissue; bloodhounds have four *billion* spread over fifty-nine square inches. Yes, I looked it up—like I said, I'm a research geek by nature.

Anyway, a car isn't a hermetically sealed environment. And even with the heavy rain washing away any traces on the outside of the vehicle, there were still scent particles inside. A bloodhound could identify a scent with as little as a single cell—and all I needed were two.

I told Tiny what we were looking for. He stared at me thoughtfully for a moment. [I see. That would explain a great deal. I can't say that I'm all that surprised, though. I did warn you.]

"That you did. Now, make with the sniffing, please."

He shifted from muscular rottweiler to sad-eyed, droopy-eared bloodhound, and began to sniff around the car. He concentrated on the cracks around the doors and where the windows met the frame, then crouched down and crawled under the chassis. He came out wearing a satisfied, doggy smile.

[It appears both of us were right, Foxtrot. What tipped you off?]

"The money trail. He's been buying up land around the graveyard, presumably for some kind of big real estate development. With ZZ out of the way, all he had to do was convince Oscar to let him purchase the land. Knowing how greedy Oscar is, I don't think it would have been a hard sell."

And that was when Kenny Gant, the owner of the vehicle in question, strolled up.

He had a suitcase in one hand, and was clearly planning on leaving. As soon as he realized I was standing next to his car with a bloodhound next to me, he stopped dead. The easygoing smile never left his face, though; Kenny Gant was a born salesman, and he didn't spook that quickly.

But then again, he'd probably never faced down a real spook.

"Hello, Foxtrot," he said, ambling toward me casually. "Here to see me off?"

"I didn't know you were leaving, Kenny. Urgent business elsewhere?"

"Yes, as a matter of fact. There's a deal I've had cooking that appears about to boil over. Pleasure, alas, must make way for commerce." He glanced down at Tiny curiously. "Yet another dog? You're going to give Caroline a run for her money in the animal department."

"Oh, this one's just a loaner. I needed him to confirm a theory, which he just has."

Kenny's eyes were clear and guiltless. He was good, I'd grant him that.

But I was better.

"I really think you ought to go back in the house, maybe

help yourself to one last glass of cognac," I said. "Once Sheriff Brower gets here, you won't get another chance for a while. A very *long* while."

The puzzled look on his face was letter-perfect. "Sheriff Brower? What are you talking about?"

"I'm talking about a murder plot so ridiculous I can barely believe it myself. You might actually have a shot at avoiding conviction, just because the DA will have a hard time convincing a jury to take this story seriously."

"Okay. Before you have me locked up, how about letting me in on the joke?"

I met his eyes squarely. "You used a monkey to frame a robot."

The grin that broke out on his face was a masterpiece of disbelief and astonishment. Really, I wished had a picture of that grin; it deserved to be framed in some museum dedicated to the great deceivers and con men throughout history. "I *did*?" he laughed.

I laughed right back. "Yes, Kenny, you did."

"And not just any monkey," he chortled. "A *drunk* monkey, right?"

I stopped laughing, but not grinning. "No, Kenny. Amos was a decoy. You knew what would happen if you fed him booze, and you came prepared with the tranquilizer pistol. The monkey that killed Maria by plunging a spring-loaded syringe into her belly—the one you spent months training to do just that—wasn't drunk at all. He was a little confused, because ZZ was supposed to be in the room and not a maid, but he did what he was supposed to. Then he climbed back down and got into his cage in your car, and you took him away in the morning."

Kenny wasn't laughing anymore. He still seemed merry, but there was a certain calculating look in his eyes. The look of a salesman who'd just realized his pitch wasn't working and it was time to switch tactics. "Oh, sure. And the GEQ prints on the window and the poison in Estevez's room?"

"Both planted—the tracks by the monkey, the poison by you. You slipped a little something into Estevez's drink at dinner that night—it was easy, when everyone's eyes were on the monkey. He slept so deeply you had no problem sneaking into his room and getting the GEQ feet and remote, and it was just as easy to go back in the morning and replace the feet. The remote you threw in the hippo pool on the way to see Caroline. You—and your monkey—were with Caroline all night, giving you the perfect alibi. Only you killed the wrong woman, didn't you? So you had to try again."

"I suppose you have a crazy theory about how I did that, too, huh?"

I shrugged. "No, there you just waited for your opportunity and brought ZZ a cup of tea. You figured she'd never wake up, so it didn't matter how blatant you were—all you had to do was make sure you didn't leave fingerprints on the saucer, and stash the remaining carfentanil outside wherever you'd hidden it the first time. But she did wake up, Kenny; about fifteen minutes ago. And once she was strong enough to talk, she told me who gave her the tea."

That was a lie, of course. But I had to bluff; I couldn't really prove what I was saying, and if he got in his car and left he could be out of the country before I could find a way to stop him.

He stared at me, his smile seeming a little forced, now. "Two monkeys, huh. And how did you arrive at this frankly hard-to-believe revelation?"

I nodded at Tiny. "You know animals, Kenny. You know how good at tracking a bloodhound is. This particular dog belongs to a friend of mine; he's a federal investigator who specializes in illegal animal trafficking. People coming in with exotic birds drugged to the tailfeathers and stuffed into luggage, that sort of thing. When this dog indicates that he's found the scent of two different capuchin monkeys in your car, I tend to believe him. So do the authorities."

Kenny snorted. "So? That doesn't—"

"It doesn't matter, Kenny," I interrupted. I had to keep him on the ropes. "I know you've been buying up land around the graveyard, and ZZ knows who drugged her. You're going to prison."

We locked eyes. Moment-of-truth time—I could see him weighing his options. Everything I had was circumstantial—he could just walk away.

But he didn't know that.

The emotion I felt when he pulled the pistol out of his pocket was an odd combination of terror and triumph. On the one hand, I'd done it; I'd unmasked the killer, proved that I was smarter than he was.

On the other, he might just kill me.

"Yes, this is a tranquilizer pistol, Foxtrot. But it's loaded with a massive dose of carfentanil. If I shoot you with this, you won't fall into a coma—you'll fall into a grave." His smile had returned to full force. He thought he could still win.

Tiny growled. [I'm sorry, Foxtrot—he's downwind, so I didn't detect the chemical.]

"It's all right," I said to Tiny. "He's not going to shoot me."

"Aren't I? I also have a hypodermic with me, Trot. I shoot you, take the dart, and leave the hypo with a few traces of carfentanil inside it beside your body. After your failed attempt to kill your boss, you decided to kill yourself. Tragic, but eminently believable. And I can explain to ZZ that you gave me the tea to give to her—I can be very persuasive when I want to be. Haven't you noticed? Caroline sure did."

I glared at him, but I couldn't think of an epithet strong enough to call him. Then I did. "Gant, you stink worse than hippo dung. A whole pool of it."

And that's when Tiny sprang.

Gant shot him in the chest, which is exactly what Tiny was hoping for. Carfentanil, despite its powerful anesthetic properties, didn't have much effect on ectoplasm.

And tranquilizer pistols were only good for one shot.

Bloodhounds, though, aren't the most agile of creatures. Gant dodged backward, and Tiny's lunge fell short. Gant turned and ran, back toward the house. Tiny and I chased him.

<Foxtrot! This the bad guy?> Tango's voice in my head, loud and urgent.

Yes! Where are you?

<Right behind you!>

I didn't bother looking. Gant darted to the left, heading toward the side of the house, with us in hot pursuit. Exactly what we were going to do when we caught him, I wasn't sure.

Around the side of the house. Down to the pool and past it.

Through the gate, and into the graveyard.

I halted at the threshold, Tiny skidding to a stop behind me. Tango shot past both of us, a black-and-white blur, calling out *<What are you waiting for? Let's go!>*

"Um," I said.

Now Tango had stopped, too, about twenty feet away. She looked back at us impatiently, and then she got it. *<What, are you worried about Topsy? There are three of us! We can take him!>*

A scaredy-cat, Tango definitely wasn't. But whether she was right or not, I couldn't let Gant get away. I took a deep breath, and sprinted into the graveyard.

Gant was already out of sight, but I had a bloodhound

with me. I just followed Tiny, who led me straight to the stand of oak trees around Davy's Grave. I couldn't see Gant—but then he stepped out from behind one of the trees. He was breathing hard, but he had the pistol out and aimed at me.

"Thank you for giving me time to reload," he panted. "That dog of yours is going to be dead in about a minute, you know. I can't believe it's still on its feet."

"He's tougher than he looks."

"Then I won't waste another dart on him. Next one goes straight into you."

I couldn't see Tango, but I could hear her in my head. *<Stall him, Toots. He's right under a tree, and I'm halfway up it already.>*

No! Tiny can take a dart full of carfentanil, but you can't. And if you leap on him, the gun might fire and hit me anyway.

"You know," said Gant, his breathing slowing, "This is actually better. Less chance we'll be disturbed. I'll leave the gun, too, right beside the body of the dog."

Tiny, I think now would be a good time for the real you to make an appearance, don't you?

I can't, Foxtrot. I'm not allowed to let anyone but you see me transform.

Oh, crap. That made sense, actually.

But Gant was ready now; if Tiny tried another lunge in his bloodhound form, Gant would shoot—and this time he'd hit me.

But he wasn't going to do anything right this minute. Gant's grin was back, because he thought he was in control again. He couldn't see what I could: the circle of ghost animals that was starting to form around us. Dogs, cats, birds, even shimmering goldfish swimming through the air; they all gathered around the Protector of the Graveyard to see what was going to happen.

"You know, I really thought I'd planned this thing right to the hilt," Gant said. "Using a drone to kill someone is hardly news—the army does it all the time—but training a monkey to do the job? That was such an unlikely scenario I thought no one would ever even consider it. But you did. Bravo." He kept the gun trained on me and fished in his pocket with his other hand.

"Thanks, but I had help."

"Is that supposed to scare me? Am I supposed to believe the cavalry is going to come riding in to save you?" He took out a small, plastic-wrapped pack, shook a cigarette halfway out, and put it up to his mouth.

"No, not really." I had brief visions of Ben appearing on the crest of the hill, striking a manly pose, then calling up a tornado to throw Gant into another time zone. Oh, and he had his shirt off—Ben, not Kenny.

"No? I'm disappointed in you, Foxtrot." He replaced the cigarette pack in his pocket and dug out a lighter. "You don't have a lot of cards left to play. I figured you'd try to run a bluff, at the very least. It's not like you have anything to lose."

"A bluff? On an old wheeler-dealer like you? You'd see right through it, Kenny. No, I thought I'd try something else."

He smiled around his cigarette, then lit it casually and pocketed the lighter. "Screaming for help, maybe? You could give it a try, but it's guaranteed to get you shot."

"That's true. Unless I'm screaming for help right now, and you can't hear it."

He looked thoughtful. "Cell phone?"

I shook my head. "No. Maybe I should have called someone before running after you like a damn fool, but I didn't. I *did* yell—in fact, I'm yelling right now—but it's not so much a scream for help as a cry for attention."

"You're not making a lot of sense, Foxtrot."

I smiled. "That's probably because I'm doing something a little crazy. I mean, deliberately trying to attract the ghost of a homicidal elephant by using the spiritual acoustics of a mystical nexus via a telepathic cat? That's not exactly a rational solution."

Gant's expression was getting more and more puzzled. Either I was trying to distract him with nonsense, or I was having some sort of breakdown. He kept the gun trained on me but began glancing around nervously.

He didn't see the hulking black form rise slowly on the crest of the hill behind him. He didn't see the animal spirits part to let the giant, shadowy shape lumber through their midst. He didn't see the electricity silently arcing and flashing from her chains as she shambled toward us. But I did, and I let it show on my face.

"I'm not falling for that," Gant said. "There's nothing behind me, and I'm not taking my eyes off you."

"That's fine," I said softly. "Do me a favor, would you? You're standing upwind, and I really don't want to die with your smoke in my eyes."

He made a magnanimous gesture, and stepped to the side. As he did so, a breeze caught the red ember of his cigarette and made it burn just a little bit brighter.

Topsy was already angry. When she saw Gant's cigarette, her anger flared into rage.

I didn't know what I was expecting. I didn't even know for sure if Topsy could hurt anyone except me. But I did remember that detail about what set off her final rampage: when her drunken handler tried to feed her a lit cigarette.

I gambled. Kenny lost.

With a deafening bellow I think even Kenny heard, Topsy lowered her head and charged. She rammed one of her midnight-black tusks right through Gant's chest, and tried to lift him off the ground with it.

Gant's eyes flew wide open. He rose a foot or so into the air, and then lightning exploded through his body. Sparks crackled from his eyes, his mouth, the ends of his fingers, while bolts of blue-white leapt in jagged arcs around his torso. I could smell burning hair and leather.

Then Topsy lowered her head, and Gant slid off the tusk and onto the ground with a boneless thump. Wisps of smoke curled up from his body, but the tusk had left no visible wound.

<Well done.> said Tango. *<Or medium rare, at the very least.>*

Quiet. This is the tricky part . . .

What had just happened to Gant was horrifying, but I couldn't afford to show weakness right now. Topsy and I stared at each other. This was our third face-to-face meeting, and the previous two hadn't gone well. But this time, I wasn't running away and I wasn't backing down.

I took one step forward. Very carefully, I put my foot on the still-burning cigarette that lay where Gant had dropped it, and crushed it out.

Tango—translate this. "We don't have to be enemies. I'm not like him." I pointed at Gant's smoldering corpse. "You hate the little fire that people hold. I know. It burned you, and then later it burned down your home."

Topsy pawed the ground and trumpeted. *<This is my home now. You will not take it away.>*

"I'm not going to, Topsy. I'm going to keep it safe. You were drawn here, and so was I, because this place is special. The man you just killed—he wanted to destroy this place. I was trying to stop him."

<You did not. I did!>

"Yes, you did. That's why I called you here. I wanted you to stop him, because he was my enemy as well as yours. *And I'm the reason you could.*" I put as much emphasis on the last sentence as I could, and hoped Tango managed to convey that.

After listening to Tango's translation, Topsy paused before replying. <*You did nothing—it was my tusk that ended him.*>

"Was it? Have you ever been able to affect someone still living before, Topsy? Have you?"

This time, the pause was much longer, and her answer shorter. <*No.*>

"I gave you that power. That's what I do; I'm a facilitator. I help others to do what they do best, and . . . *stomp out* whatever problems arise. As long as I'm here, protecting the graveyard, no one will harm it—because I have *many* friends, and they all want to help me as much as I've helped them. You've met two of them already. I would like you to be another."

I did my best to keep my breathing slow and steady as Tango translated. Either Topsy went for it, or she didn't. This was the moment in negotiations when you laid your cards on the table and hoped the other party offered to shake your hand.

<*You want me to be . . . of your family?*>

"Yes, Topsy. That's what I want. I want you to take your rightful place." Elephants were matriarchal, with the females forming groups. Those groups often intermingled, without hostility—they left the dominance displays to the males. The males were solitary, while the females preferred groups; and a female had just invited Topsy to join her group. And even though Topsy had learned to hate and mistrust human beings, she'd also been alone a long, long time.

<*I will join your herd.*> She raised her trunk and trumpeted once, then turned and shambled away. I made my way on shaky legs over to the nearest bench and sank into it.

[That was expertly handled.] Tiny came over and licked my hand. It was the first time he'd ever done that, and it was oddly reassuring.

Tango clambered down from the tree and joined us, jumping into my lap. <*What he said, only more so. You showed her who's boss.*>

"That I did, but not how you think. See, elephant families are usually ruled by the oldest female in the group. When I told Topsy I wanted her to take her rightful place, I was offering her the top spot. She's the boss, not me."

<*Wait. So that wasn't a facedown, it was a . . . job interview?*>

"Kind of. She's my social superior, but she's also responsible for keeping the herd safe. In the wild, that means choosing ranging territory and protecting calves. Here—well, I guess she'll protect us."

<*Or insist we relocate to the nearest amusement park, where the foraging for candy apples and peanuts will be better.*>

[I doubt that will be a problem. The graveyard tends to attract, not repel. In fact, I foresee other visitors in our future.]

"One crisis at a time, okay? Let's just sit here for a second and breathe."

[Those of us who can, you mean.]

<*Oh, relax—you got a working nose, don'tcha? Just inhale and enjoy the nice, fresh—*>

[Smell of burning flesh?]

"Aaaaand I'm done. Let's go alert the authorities, shall we? Brower's going to love this . . ."

Chapter Twenty-Two

Sheriff Brower wasn't happy.

But it wasn't as if he could arrest me for anything. The fact that Kenny Gant had been struck by a bolt of lightning in the graveyard, while unusual, was hardly impossible; people had died in similar circumstances before, and no doubt would again. The freak thunderstorm we'd had shortly beforehand seemed to offer a convenient, if not entirely satisfactory, explanation.

My theory as to Gant's guilt was met by skepticism, but I insisted that Gant himself had confessed to me before running off to his own accidental electrocution. Further proof could be obtained by checking Gant's records and premises; I was sure they would turn up proof of both a second monkey and the purchase of carfentanil. That, plus the real estate Gant had bought up, would provide both motive, opportunity, and the murder weapon. And if not—well, Gant was dead. That was justice, of its own sort.

I wish I could say that was the end of the whole affair, but it wasn't. ZZ wasn't in danger from Gant anymore, but she remained in a coma. And that, it appeared, was something neither a reincarnated cat nor an ectoplasmic dog could do much about.

The salon had come to a close, and my boss—the one without tusks—was still comatose. I did all the necessary things I always did to keep the household running, which included seeing the guests off. Well, the ones who weren't dead or in jail, anyway—and Juan Estevez was apparently being released soon. I gave Avery the task of proving Gant was the one sending the encrypted emails to the inventor, and he seemed to think it was doable. Coming from Avery, that meant it was practically already done.

Hana Kim and Mr. Kwok had just left. Keene, as usual, was the last one out the door. His driver had already loaded his bags into the limo, and was waiting patiently behind the wheel. I went upstairs to see what was keeping him.

The door to his room was open. "Hello?" I said, poking my head in.

Keene sat at the writing desk, staring at the screen of a small tablet with a folding keyboard. "Just a sec," he murmured, and tapped a few keys.

I stepped inside. "Checking your fan mail?"

He glanced over at me and grinned. "Just finishing up a song, actually—well, the lyrics, anyway. Tune still needs a bit of mucking about."

"Nice to know you find the environment so inspiring."

"Not going to demand a percentage, are you? 'Cause I've got nasty Tasmanian Devil Attack Lawyers to deal with that sort of thing." He paused. "I think. Or maybe those are my accountants. I can't tell the difference between the two, most of the time. They all dress the same."

"I don't think ZZ invites you here to make a profit."

"Yeah. How's she doing? Any change?"

I shook my head. "Doctors say everything looks good—heart, respiration, reflexes. She just needs to wake up."

Keene nodded, then closed his tablet and got up. "Well, I'm off to the studio. But here, take this." He pulled a card out of his pocket and gave it to me. There was no writing on it, just a printed phone number. "It's my private mobile, the one I never change. Well, not unless the paparazzi steal it from my mum's purse when she's out shopping—then I have to start all over again. Call me if there's any word, good or bad, will you? ZZ means a lot to me."

I took the card and pocketed it. "I'll do that."

He picked up the tablet and walked over. For some reason, I was a little slow getting out of the way, and we both wound up facing each other sideways in the doorway for a second. I thought he was going to make a typical Keene remark, but he surprised me. "Take care of her, Foxtrot. I plan on coming back, and I don't want it to be for a funeral."

I met his eyes. "I will, I promise."

Then he was past me, moving down the hall, and I was alone again.

Well, not really, of course. I was in a house filled with staff, all of whom were doing their best to pretend everything was back to normal. It wasn't though; not only was their employer upstairs in a coma, but they'd had murder, weird weather, and death by lightning bolt to contend with in the last week. And those were just the things they knew about.

I—as usual—was the only one who knew everything that was going on. Animal apparitions, Native American storm spirits, and murderous monkey assassins: Yep, all in a day's work for Foxtrot Lancaster, Administrative Assistant of the Highly Unusual.

I needed a drink. And a bed. And complete and utter silence. And my brain removed and placed in a jar of chamomile tea. Okay, that last part was supposed to be soothing but just came out weird. Which seemed much too appropriate for my liking.

I sighed, and went to find Ben Montain.

Ben and I hadn't really talked since Kenny Gant had his fatal run-in with Topsy. I knew he must be dying to question me—especially about the lightning—but I'd had a million details to take care of. Plus, I had to figure out exactly what I could or couldn't tell him.

I found him in the pantry, doing inventory. "Hey," I said.

"Foxtrot! I've been waiting—I mean, I want to—what *happened* out there?"

"It wasn't lightning," I told him.

"I *know,*" he said. He sounded excited. "I could tell. I mean, I could *feel* that it wasn't lightning. It's hard to explain, but—well, it's like I have these new senses. I can tell you exactly how windy it is outside right now. I can tell you *humid* it is. I can feel it when the temperature changes. Isn't that *wild*?"

"Yes. Yes, that's great. You're obviously connecting with your heritage. Just take it easy, okay? No more torrential downpours out of nowhere, please."

"Don't worry, that's not going to happen. I'm going to start small. Maybe a whirlwind in the dining room, or a snowstorm in the library." He grinned at the look on my face. "Hey, come on. When something this crazy happens to you, you've got to keep your sense of humor."

"True. Hold on to that thought, will you? Because, really, this is funny."

"What is?"

I took a deep breath. "What happened with Gant? It had to do with . . ."

"Yeah?"

An electric elephant. Who died over a hundred years ago, killed by Thomas Edison. Who wandered over from

Coney Island because the mystic graveyard next door—which contains ghost parrots, hamsters, goldfish, ferrets, snakes, and the occasional shark—called to her. And I know all this because of my new friends, the used-to-be-dead linguistic expert cat and the shape-shifting ectoplasmic dog.

". . . something I can't talk about," I said miserably. "It's really complicated, and sort of ludicrous, and mostly unbelievable. But I can tell you it didn't involve another Thunderbird."

"Oh." He looked nonplussed for a moment, and then his manic grin came back. "Well, I'm not worried. I mean, I feel like this is the *beginning* of something, you know? Something *amazing*."

The beginning? To me, it felt more like an ending. The killer had been caught, the elephantom was no longer a threat, and all the guests were leaving. I should have felt happy, but I didn't. I told myself I was just worried about ZZ, but I knew that wasn't it.

"Well, I'm going to check on ZZ," I said. "I'll see you later, okay. Try not to whip up any dust devils in the kitchen."

"Not even small ones? Could be handy for mixing ingredients." His grin seemed to hold all the elation I was missing. I did my best to imitate it, and when I failed dismally he didn't seem to notice.

I left him in the kitchen and went upstairs to check on ZZ. The guards had been dismissed, but both Tango and Tiny were waiting for me, Tiny at the foot of the bed and Tango curled up on the divan.

"Hey," I said. I sank onto the divan next to Tango. She gave Tiny a knowing look, stretched, then made herself comfortable on my lap.

<Hey, Toots. You seem a little down.>

"It's nothing. Post-crisis adrenaline crash, that's all."

<You did good, kid. Time to break out the catnip and celebrate.>

"I'm not really much of a catnip person, Tango. All that chasing of imaginary mice just looks exhausting."

<Then I suggest sleep. A nice daylong nap is always refreshing.>

"Normally I'd agree with you. But right now?" I glanced over at ZZ's still form. "Sleep doesn't seem that appealing, either."

[Perhaps not,] said Tiny. [But you should rest, anyway; you'll need to be at your best.]

Suddenly I was a lot more awake.

"What's that mean? I'll need to be at my best for what?"

[For the discussion.]

"The discussion? What discussion?"

Which was when the ghost crow swooped through the wall and landed on the bedpost.

Eli regarded me with a bright eye, his head cocked to the side. "Foxtrot. Congratulations."

"Thank you," I said automatically.

"Tiny? Tango? Could you two give us a moment?"

Both of them got up without a word and headed for the door. I thought I'd closed it behind me, but it was ajar now. Tiny nudged it open a little more with his nose, and turned to give me a look I couldn't quite decipher. Then both of them were gone.

"So," Eli said. "You did it. Mostly."

"You're welcome. Mostly." That was a little snarkier than I'd intended, but I was weary and in no mood to play games. I deserved some recognition, and not the kind that came with qualifiers.

"Hey, take it easy. You figured it out on your own, which is exactly what you were supposed to do. What happened to your boss, that wasn't your fault. Mr. Gant was responsible for that, and you kept him from finishing the job. And that whole 'I'm a facilitator' thing? Nice work."

I'd always taken praise from my superiors with a grain of salt—it was manipulative as often as it was sincere, and an inflated ego generally led to disaster—but for some reason, getting kudos from a phantom bird I'd met a few days before gave me a warm glow inside. "I was right, wasn't I? The reason Topsy could affect others was because of me?"

"Pretty much, yeah."

"Nice of you to let me know. Before it became a matter of life or death or anything."

He gave me a raspy crow chuckle. "Part of the reason you *could* do that was because you figured it out. That's just how it works."

"Uh-huh. Just like you knowing about everything that goes on in the Crossroads—that's part of how things work, too, isn't it? Including knowing about the presence of a certain elephant that's been dead for a hundred years."

"People do better when they learn things for themselves. And you did good."

"I know," I said. "But did I do good *enough*?"

Eli cocked an eye at ZZ, then back at me. "Well, that's what I wanted to talk to you about. I can pretty much say *yeah, you did.* Not perfect, but nobody expects that. You're only human, after all."

He abruptly spread his wings and flapped his way up onto the top of the IV pole. "And a competent, capable human is exactly what is needed in this position. You've made your qualifications eminently clear."

"Position?"

"Yes. Guardian of the Crossroads is the official title. You'd keep on doing pretty much exactly what you've done so far—protecting the nexus from threats. Sort of a local Sheriff of Spirits."

I shook my head. "Hold on. I thought the threat was taken care of."

"This one, yeah. But as you've already figured out, the Crossroads tends to attract wandering spirits and other supernatural beings. You've already got Topsy and a Thunderbird; who knows what else will show up?"

I thought about that. The last thing I wanted was to put my friends in harm's way—but that's exactly where they were, living right next door to a giant magical weirdness magnet. ZZ had almost been killed twice already; what would happen if I couldn't protect her? "Sheriff, huh? I don't suppose it pays well."

"Not a dime."

"Does it come with any benefits?"

"Every job comes with benefits. This one offers danger, the unknown, lots of hard work, danger, and the possibility of an early demise. And did I mention the danger?"

"Tempting. Do I at least get a gun?"

Eli clambered from one end of the IV stand to the other. He peered down at the saline bag as if it were a shiny rock. "No. But you do get deputies—two of them. I thought you'd probably like to stick with the pair you've already got."

"Tiny and Tango? How do they feel about this?"

The crow chuckled. "They'll be fine with it. They like their jobs and they like you. You're the one with a decision to make."

I sighed. "Can I think about it?"

"Go ahead. I'll wait."

Terrific.

Negotiation was something I was good at. Even exhausted, stressed out, and coming off an adrenaline high, I could spot an opportunity to make a deal. Eli clearly wanted me on board, and forcing me to choose now was a classic way to pressure me into signing a contract without reading the fine print. It also meant I could ask for something extra and probably get it.

I thought about ZZ. She was important to the continued existence of the Crossroads, but Eli didn't seem terribly worried about her health. Which meant either he knew she was going to wake up—or he could make that happen whenever he wanted.

And then there was Ben, and his Thunderbird status. Eli clearly knew quite a bit about that, and I'd never get a better time to ask for answers.

I could ask for one, and probably get it. I could try for both, and maybe get one.

But neither of those options *felt* right.

Negotiation is essentially a selfish act. You're trying to get the most out of a deal, and give away the least. It's competitive, because that's what works in the business world.

But this *wasn't* the business world. This was a world of ghosts and afterlives, where the strongest binding force wasn't a contract but an emotion; where love was powerful enough to defeat death.

"I accept," I said. "I'll do my best, I promise."

Eli bobbed his head once, the bird equivalent of a nod. "Thank you, Foxtrot. I'll provide you with whatever support I can, but don't expect too much; you wouldn't believe how much red tape I have to deal with."

"I understand," I said. "Working in a hierarchy, right? Everybody's got to answer to somebody else."

I didn't think crows could smile, but Eli managed it. "If that's the analogy that works for you . . . but it's not really accurate."

"Why not?"

"Because a hierarchy tends to stifle innovation, become predictable. Doesn't leave much room for surprises."

And with that, Eli took off and swooped through the wall.

"I hate to tell you this," I said to the wall, "but I *knew* you were going to do that."

"Foxtrot?"

I spun around.

ZZ blinked at me groggily. "Why . . . are you talking . . . to the wall?"

Then she got all blurry as tears practically spouted from my eyes, and I was hugging her and laughing and yelling, "Yes! I *knew* it! *I knew it!*"

Love is a powerful force.

But sometimes a little faith helps, too.

Tango took the news of ZZ's awakening with typical cat indifference, while Tiny actually let out a bark of joy. Then I put them both outside before I broke the news to everyone else—I didn't want them trampled in the stampede of people into ZZ's bedroom.

Which was more or less what happened. I stayed right beside the bed for most of it; it might have been selfish of me, but I thought I'd earned the right to see all those hugs and smiles and tears of joy. Tough Shondra was all quivering lips and sniffles, while even stern Victor kept wiping his eyes. Cooper showed up with balloons and a grin a mile wide.

When Oscar arrived, though, I left the two of them alone. Some moments—like those between a mother and son—should be private.

The doctors gave ZZ a clean bill of health. No brain damage, just a little residual dizziness that should pass after a few days' bed rest. She already had me running around, letting everyone know that she was all right and planning a party to celebrate. First, of course, I had to tell her the whole story while she ate one of Ben's omelets—she waved off a suggestion she start with tea and lightly buttered toast, insisted she was ravenous.

". . . And that's when Gant was struck by lightning," I finished.

ZZ frowned at me, her mouth full of egg, cheese, and mushrooms. She chewed, swallowed, then announced, "That is the most preposterous story I have ever heard. Is this some sort of test to see if my mind's still working?"

I assured her it wasn't. She still looked skeptical, but told me I'd done my usual expert job. Then she asked for more orange juice, her laptop, all the windows opened, and some uptempo jazz music on the stereo.

"Oh, and Foxtrot?"

"Yes, ZZ?"

"While some people might say that rewarding an employee for saving your life sets a bad precedent, I'm fairly sure you won't try to take advantage of my generosity. Give yourself a raise—five thousand dollars a year. And thank you."

"You're very welcome," I said with a smile. "Did I ever tell you about the time I fought off a swarm of ninjas coming over the back wall?"

"I have no doubt that you could, dear. Could you bring some strong coffee along with the orange juice? I'm off tea."

When I was done running errands for her, I went outside to check on Tango and Tiny; I hadn't had a chance to sit down and talk to them since ZZ woke up. I found them in the gardens, Tango sunning herself on a bench, Tiny sprawled out beneath her. He was in his rottweiler form, because that was the one the staff had gotten used to.

I sat down next to Tango. "Well, guys—it looks like we're going to be hanging out together for a while."

<We are? Why? Is there another threat?>

[No, Tango. Eli asked Foxtrot if she wished to continue in her duties.]

Tango got to her feet, looking indignant. *<What? How would you know? I thought it was your nose that was sharp, not your ears.>*

[I didn't overhear it, I deduced it. The Crossroads obviously needs to be guarded, and we've demonstrated we can do so ably. It simply makes sense that Eli would ask her if she'd like to stay on.]

Tango stared at Tiny suspiciously. *<Somebody tipped you off, didn't they? You dogs always stick together.>*

[Whereas you cats never do. Maybe you should talk to one of your superiors.]

<Maybe I will. When I get around to it.>

Cats are agile in both body and temperament; Tango demonstrated both as she suddenly sprang into my lap and started purring loudly. *<Great news, Toots. I was hoping we'd get to stay. Well, that* I'd *get to stay, anyway.>*

"I'm glad, too. I guess we should figure out some formal living arrangements—"

<I hear there are some fine kennels in the area.>

"I'm not putting Tiny in a kennel. There's plenty of room for both you at my place."

Tango wasn't purring anymore. *<What? You want me to* live *with this canine? I hardly know him!>*

"But—I mean, you two work together—"

She got off my lap and marched to the end of the bench, looking back at me over her shoulder. *<Work is one thing, sharing living space is another. You know how long it took me to train the last dog I had to live with?>*

[About the same length of time it took for him to learn how to avoid you?]

"Hey, come on. We can work this out—"

<Already have. Scooby-Doofus can stay with you. I'll live here; lots of space, and the food is good. One of us should be on site at all times, anyway.>

"I . . . I guess that'll work."

<Of course it will. Now, if you'll excuse me, I think Ben and I need a little bonding time.> She jumped down off the bench and strutted away, her tail high.

When she was gone, Tiny said, [She loves you a lot, you know.]

"Yeah? Then why did she just ditch me?"

[Because she's too proud to share you, and too stubborn to admit it. You have to need her, but she can't acknowledge that she needs you. This way, she keeps her independence and still gets to spend most of her time with you. Plus, with me in the house, you're better protected while you sleep. She'll never admit that, either.]

I reached down and scratched him behind the ears. "You got it all figured, huh?"

[Well, I did have some help. Tango was right: I knew we were going to be stationed here for an extended period of time. Dogs are good at networking.]

"And cats are good at being independent. Or at least looking that way."

[Even cats have to answer to someone. Tango is most likely on her way to receive her marching orders right now.]

"Marching orders?"

[Perhaps that's not quite accurate. Stalking orders? Marching suggestions?]

"Maybe we should just leave military comparisons out of it."

[Agreed.]

We sat in companionable silence for a moment. It'd be nice to have someone else around the house—someone to talk to, or just curl up beside me on the sofa while I read.

[So. We should set some guidelines—house rules, as it were.]

I blinked. "Um. Sure, I guess. What did you have in mind?"

[While I don't need to physically relieve myself, I do like to keep abreast of neighborhood news and enjoy a little exercise. Minimum twenty-minute walk, every morning.]

"Ten."

[Fifteen.]

"Fifteen, with a twice-weekly option to cancel in bad weather."

[Done.]

"Do you shed?"

[It depends on the breed. But being ectoplasmic in nature, it tends to fade away on its own after a few minutes.]

"That's handy. Okay, you're allowed on the furniture."

[How generous of you.] He paused, looking serious. Rottweilers, it turned out, were good at looking serious. [There's one other thing. My identity.]

"What do you mean?"

[Your colleagues know me in two forms: a golden retriever, and this one. If I'm to remain here, I should choose a default I occupy the majority of the time.]

"Good point. Something all-purpose, I guess. Not too big to be awkward, not too small to be laughed at. And smart, too—I don't want people freaking out when you do something intelligent."

[How about this?]

His outline shifted, becoming less bulky but a little furrier. His colors changed from the black and tan of the rottweiler to an odd configuration that looked as if the lower half of one dog had been merged with the upper of another: His back, tail, and head were speckled black and white, while his legs, chest, throat, and lower muzzle were tan. To add to the effect, one of his eyes was brown and the other an icy blue-white.

[What do you think?] he asked.

I studied him. "Distinctive," I admitted. "Is this an actual breed, or some rare hybrid?"

[It's called a blue heeler, or Australian cattle dog. The breed was established by crossing Northumberland drovers dogs with wild dingoes; they're highly intelligent and hardworking, respond well to training, and prefer constant companionship. They bond strongly with their owner and are quite protective. They make excellent guard dogs.]

"I like it. It suits you."

He panted at me happily. [I'm glad you think so. I'll also need a new name.]

"I guess you will. Too bad—I really liked Zanzibar Buck-Buck McFate."

[I have one in mind. If it meets with your approval.]

"Which is?"

[I'd be honored if you'd call me Whiskey.]

I stared down at him. He stopped panting and looked back at me, his eyes hopeful.

"I think that's a perfect name for you," I said softly, and leaned down and put my arms around him.

Whiskey. Tango. Foxtrot.

Sounded like a nice family to me.

Read on for an excerpt from Dixie Lyle's next book

Coming soon from St. Martin's Paperbacks

"Whiskey!" I said. "Leave the man alone, will you?"

In my head, though, I said, *Smell anything interesting?*

[Mmm. Yes. A species of herb indigenous to southern Africa. An industrial cleaner used by many airlines. And quite a wide array of spices, oils, and chemicals common in starchy, deep-fried snacks such as potato or corn chips, which I surmise is from crumbs caught in the cuffs of his pants.]

I wonder sometimes about the olfactory library Whiskey can access. How is it organized? What does it look like? Is it ranked from most stinky to least, or by some other factor? I always wind up picturing a huge room with floor-to-ceiling shelves and rolling ladders that go right up to the top, filled with slender volumes that emit wavy smell lines when you open them. And down below, dogs sit in overstuffed chairs with their legs crossed, books propped open in front of them, tiny smell-spectacles—smellacles?—positioned over their nostrils—

[Foxtrot. Focus, please.]

What? Oh, right. Sorry. "Follow me, please, Mr. Chukwukadibia."

"I shall."

"I'll have your things put in your room," said ZZ. Abazu nodded and smiled, but he was already moving.

Whiskey kept pace with me, as he usually did. "Did you have a pleasant flight?"

"Oh, my, yes. To see the sunlight on the tops of clouds is both humbling and amazing. I could watch it for hours."

"I know what you mean."

[I don't. Birds are fundamentally insane.]

"How is Augustus?" Abazu asked. "Did the journey upset him? Is he eating well?"

"He seemed very calm when I saw him. Our vet, Caroline, was about to feed him when I left—we can see how it's going for ourselves."

It wasn't a long walk from the house to the liger enclosure, but Abazu peppered me with half a dozen questions before we got there: How long was Augustus on the road? What was he fed while traveling? Had he had a bowel movement since he arrived? I did my best to answer the ones I could and told him Caroline could probably give him information on the rest.

Then we arrived, and Abazu stopped talking.

Augustus's appetite hadn't suffered from the journey; he was tearing into a haunch of beef in one corner of the enclosure, trapping it between his paws and ripping great chunks of it out with his mouth. He glanced over at us casually, then went back to his meal.

Abazu had come to a dead stop, about ten feet away from the enclosure. The look on his face was one of wonder. "Oh, my," he whispered. "He is . . . *magnificent*."

"He is that," I agreed.

[Hmmph.]

Oscar was nowhere in sight, but Caroline was still there. She walked up to us and said, "He's settling in well. Hasn't gone for a swim yet, but he checked out the pool."

"Caroline, this is Abazu Chukwukadibia. He's one of our guests."

Abazu tore his gaze away from Augustus. "A pleasure, madam. You are in charge of his well-being?"

"That's right," Caroline said.

"He is healthy? Free of parasites, not injured?"

"I haven't had a chance to give him a full physical, but he appears to be perfectly healthy."

"Very good. Very good. A tremendous responsibility. You know this, yes?"

Caroline nodded. "I do, Mr. Chukwukadibia. I take it very, very seriously."

He studied her for a second, then broke into a wide grin. "Yes, I can see that you do. That is most fine. I shall return later, yes?"

"You're most welcome to do so."

"But first, I have a few things I would like to ask."

As Abazu questioned Caroline, I caught Whiskey's eye. *He seems a little starstruck, don't you think?*

[That's one way to put it.]

You sound less than impressed.

[Cats in general don't impress me. The more cat there is, the more there is to be unimpressed by. I am currently confronted by a great deal of cat.]

That's one way to put it.

When Abazu finished his interrogation, he thanked Caroline profusely and indicated he'd like to return to the house to freshen up. He was very quiet on the way back, apparently lost in his own thoughts, and didn't even glance around his room when we got there. He told me he'd see me at dinner and closed the door.

The last guest to arrive was Luis Navarro.

He pulled up in a very new, very black Mercedes. ZZ had gone back inside by then, and I was the only one around. I walked forward, Whiskey at my side, to greet him.

He took two hardshell suitcases out of the trunk as I approached. He was tall, broad in the shoulders, with an immaculately tailored dark suit that managed to look casual and dressy at the same time. His hair was shiny and black and cut short. He had that boyish look to him some Latin men have, his lashes just a little too long and his cheeks just a little too round, but he balanced that with a strong jaw and piercing eyes. He gave me an easy smile when he spotted me. "You must be Foxtrot," he said. His voice was warm and deep. "Hello."

"Hello. You must be Mr. Navarro."

"Luis, please."

"All right, Luis. Everyone else is already here; if you'll follow me, I'll show you to your room."

"Thank you."

And that was all he said as he followed me into the house and up the stairs. I kept talking, of course, but he kept his replies to nods and polite murmurs and offered no comments of his own. I got the hint and didn't push; some people are uncomfortable with small talk and trying to engage them is the wrong approach.

"Dinner is at six, drinks at five thirty," I said, opening the door to his room.

"Thank you very much, Foxtrot," he answered. He looked around his room with a careful, considering eye as he placed his bags on the floor; it seemed to meet with his approval, because he nodded before turning back to face me.

"You have wireless Internet, of course?" he asked.

"Yes. The password is on a card on the nightstand. You have my number; call me if you need anything else."

He frowned, ever so slightly. "Really? I would have

thought you'd have staff to take care of such mundane tasks."

"We do. But I'm something of a control freak; everything gets routed through me. You want more towels, I have to okay the color and weave before the maid brings them up."

His frown turned into a smile. It was a nice smile, one that reached all the way up to his eyes. "That's very diligent of you. I'll try not to take up too much of your time."

"Not a problem. Just doing my job." I smiled back, gave him the professional I'm-leaving-now nod, and took a step backward.

He took the same step forward, as gracefully as if we were dancing, and stopped at the precise second I did. His smile stayed the same, but his eyes locked with mine. "And what if I require something a little more . . . esoteric?" he asked gently.

I blinked. Neither his voice nor the expression on his face had changed, but his body language was subtly different in a way that was hard to explain; poised, somehow, while appearing relaxed. Like some internal gear had shifted, but he hadn't stomped on the gas yet.

"That depends on what you have in mind," I said carefully.

He gazed at me for a second before answering. "Tequila," he said at last. "I have a fondness for it, but only particular varieties. Purely as a sipping drink, you understand; I value a well-made tequila the way some value a good scotch."

"Give me a name and I'll do my best."

"Casa Dragones is my favorite, though a bottle of Milagro Unico will do. One hundred percent blue agave, both of them. The Milagro is flavorful and smooth, yet somewhat playful."

"It sounds . . . intriguing."

"Mmm. The Dragones is delicately sweet, with an underlying fire. And most satisfying—even more so if you have someone to share it with."

Somehow, I didn't think he was talking about tequila any more. "I'll see what I can do . . . but you may have to wait. These things can take a while."

Oddly, he didn't seem disappointed. "Yes, I understand. Hopefully, you will be successful before I leave." He nodded once more, more formally, and closed his door.

"Huh," I said to Whiskey as I walked away. "Well, I've been hit on aggressively before, but that was a weird combination. Full steam one second, then back down to zero without taking offense. Almost like he was just going through the motions."

[It could be he had other things on his mind.]

"You mean like Augustus?"

[I mean like the firearms he was carrying.]

It was my turn to stop dead.